# THE FINE ART OF LYING

A NOVEL

ALEXANDRA ANDREWS

HARPER
*An Imprint of* HarperCollins*Publishers*

HarperCollins books may be purchased for educational, business, or sales promotional use. For information, please email the Special Markets Department at SPsales@harpercollins.com.

hc.com

FIRST EDITION

Designed by Bonni Leon-Berman

Library of Congress Cataloging-in-Publication Data has been applied for.

ISBN 978-0-06-347207-5

26 27 28 29 30 LBC 6 5 4 3 2

# THE FINE ART OF LYING

**Also by Alexandra Andrews**

*Who Is Maud Dixon?*

For my mother

# THE FINE ART OF LYING

# PROLOGUE

VENETIAN RED.

That was what sprang to mind first: the crimson-hued pigment favored by Renaissance artists like Titian and Tintoretto. The blood pooling at Clare's feet was the same rich and rusty shade, as if an old master were about to dip in a brush.

She admired the way its smooth surfaces reflected the light. El Greco, too, she remembered, had used Venetian red to stunning effect.

For a few moments, Clare's mind took refuge in the dry, academic minutiae of art history she knew so well. But the relief was short-lived. A car alarm blared shrilly from the street outside, and she stood up, her heart pounding. As the horror and panic she'd just barely kept at bay flooded in, she reached out a hand to the wall to steady herself.

*What was she doing?* Marveling over the luminous beauty of bodily fluids?

Over the past few weeks, she had made a series of bad decisions, one after the other. Worse, she'd done it with her eyes wide open. She'd known what she was doing was wrong, but she'd done it anyway. Even so, she'd never in a million years have guessed that those choices would lead her here, where she was right now: standing stark naked over a dead body.

Clare looked down at her hands. A few of her fingers were smeared with blood. So was her wedding ring.

*What had she done?*

She took a long, slow breath through her nose. She needed to focus. There would be time to ask herself those things later. But first, only one question mattered: What should she do now?

The right answer was obvious: find her phone and call 911. Of course that's what she should do.

Still, Clare stayed where she was, staring down at her pale fingers.

From somewhere just beyond the realm of rational thought, another option beckoned. What if she just . . . walked away?

She looked around. She could wipe down the doorknobs and the sink faucets. She could gather up everything that belonged to her and walk out the front door. With any luck, she'd be home in thirty minutes.

At the thought of home, another wave of horror rose up like nausea. Home—where her husband and daughter lay snug in their beds, oblivious to everything that had happened tonight.

The panic washed over her, tsunami-like, and Clare's mind retreated once again to the safety of art.

*Interior in Venetian Red* by Matisse—that was another one. Oh, and of course: his masterpiece from 1911, *The Red Studio.* Venetian red coated its entire surface. Paintings upon paintings hiding within the real painting, like nesting dolls.

Clare swallowed down another wave of panic.

Sadie loved nesting dolls.

*Two Months Earlier*

## CHAPTER 1

"SHHH," SADIE WHISPERED, EYES WIDE with fear. "We have to be quiet, or they'll get us."

"Who will get us?" Clare murmured back.

They were hiding in a little-used closet filled with moth-eaten towels, broken tennis rackets, and a host of other castoffs she had yet to identify: The light bulb had been blown out for years.

"The monsters," Sadie said. "They're right outside."

"Are they nice monsters?" Clare asked hopefully.

Sadie shook her head solemnly. "No, Mama. They have lava blasters."

Clare snapped her fingers. "But wait! What a coincidence. I packed us lava-proof suits this weekend."

Sadie closed her eyes, as if unable to bear her mother's naivety.

"The monsters already stole them."

"Even the supersecret, backup set I packed?"

"Yes. Even those."

Why did her daughter's imagination always bend toward worst-case scenarios? It must have come from her side. Jed was too much of an optimist.

"I'll make new ones," Clare pronounced, bundling her hot, pink-cheeked child into her lap. "I'll keep us safe. I promise."

Suddenly a rustling noise emerged from somewhere nearby.

"What was that?" Sadie yelped, the fear in her voice no longer part of the game.

"It's just a creaky, old house," Clare assured her.

But then it happened again, louder this time, and punctuated by what sounded like scraping claws. Sadie shrieked. Clare, unsettled now, too, fumbled at the doorknob. Sadie shot out of the closet like a bullet, and Clare was close behind her.

"Sadie?" She could hear Jed racing down the hallway. "Clare?"

He rounded the corner.

"What's wrong? What happened?"

"Something's in there," Clare said, pointing at the open door.

His voice fell. "Oh."

"It's a feral animal or something."

Jed knelt and addressed Sadie in a cheerful voice: "Honey, will you go downstairs and find Grammy? She's setting up for the party, and I think she needs some help from the birthday girl."

Sadie eyed him skeptically.

"There's also a bowl of frosting in the fridge," he said. "You can have one lick."

That did the trick. When their daughter had disappeared around the corner, Jed turned back to Clare.

"He's not feral," he said in a patient tone.

"Who's not feral?"

Jed glanced behind him to make sure Sadie had really gone.

"I bought Sadie a rabbit for her birthday," he whispered. He smiled impishly, like he expected her to tousle his hair.

Clare was confused. Jed deferred to her on almost everything to do with household management. The one time she'd asked him to pick up milk on his way home, he'd called from the supermarket to ask what kind. Whole? Two percent? Skim? A minute later he called back to ask which brand. Then a third time: quart or gallon? And now he had brought home a living creature without mentioning it to her?

"He looks *just* like Arthur."

Jed had talked about his childhood pet many times, but Clare hadn't realized he wanted another. She squinted into the closet. She still couldn't see anything, but there was that rustling again.

"Sadie's going to love him," he added.

"Don't rabbits eat their own poop?"

She wasn't sure where she'd picked up that information, but it was the only thing that came to mind.

"Not if you care for them properly."

"Right."

"I'll do all the work," he assured her. "Don't worry about a thing."

Experience suggested otherwise to Clare. Jed liked big gestures—he'd proposed on one knee in the middle of Central Park—but he did not like the minutiae of domesticity. Milk procurement, for instance.

"How did you get him out here?"

They'd driven to East Hampton from Manhattan the day before, and she was pretty sure she would have noticed a spare mammal in the car.

"Mom brought him. She loves rabbits. Speaking of, it's almost five."

Cocktail hour was sacrosanct in the Bast household: At five p.m. sharp, Dorothy Bast held court over Triscuits and sharp cheddar. Back in the city, the fare was more elevated, but out here, standards were allowed to slip.

"Can we just leave him in there?" she asked.

"Rabbits are burrowers—they feel safest in small, dark places. Besides, it's only for another half hour or so."

As they walked back down the hallway, Jed put his arm around her shoulders. "You'll love him, I promise." Then he frowned. "What were you two doing in that closet anyway?"

"It's our monster hideout."

"You have this whole beautiful house to explore"—he gestured around his parents' sprawling summer home—"and you hang out in a creepy old closet filled with mouse droppings?"

Clare shrugged. "Sadie likes it."

"Well, I don't think it's particularly hygienic. Could you please find a new monster hideout?"

"I'll see what I can do."

TWENTY MINUTES LATER, Clare found Sadie on the back porch with her grandparents. She was now wearing a pink smocked dress and matching hairbow instead of the blue pinafore Clare had put her in. She wasn't surprised: Jed's mother had a history of surreptitiously redressing Sadie in clothes she'd bought herself. Clare sat down on the wicker couch and pulled her daughter onto her lap.

"Hi munchkin," she whispered.

"Hi, Mama. Is it time for presents yet?"

"Soon."

The Basts' neat green lawn stretched toward a granite pool where a watermelon pool float bumped quietly against the edge. Six lounge chairs lined the pool, each topped with a blue-and-white-striped cushion. Behind them, the boundaries of the property were marked by long hedges, kept at pristine right angles by an army of landscapers.

Jed and his sister had spent long, sun-soaked summers out here as children, playing tennis at the Maidstone club and biking to town for ice cream. It sometimes shocked Clare that her daughter would grow up in the same rarified air. It was a far cry from the icy public pool in Binghamton where Clare had spent her own summers.

Dorothy's voice suddenly pierced the air: "Oh, *shoo*!"

The porch was lined with blue hydrangea bushes, and the flowers attracted fat bees that careened into the sitting area like off-kilter drunks. Dorothy swung at one wildly with a pink plastic fly swatter. She kept several close at hand for just this purpose.

"Grammy, bees are good," Sadie told her. "Bees make honey."

"I prefer sugar, dear."

Jed's father leaned forward to sandwich a slice of cheese between two crackers and only narrowly avoided being swatted by his wife. Clare could hardly blame Dorothy; it was easy to forget that Abe was there. He'd worked ninety-hour weeks at his law firm for five decades. Now he stumbled around his retirement years like a blind man who'd lost his way. He had never learned to play golf or bridge. He didn't seem to know what to do with himself, other than get in his wife's way.

Jed appeared in the doorway. "Mom, can I get you a drink? Wine? Champagne?"

"Grant is making me some sort of grapefruit concoction," she responded, referring to Jed's sister's husband.

"What would you like?" Jed asked Clare.

"I'm fine for now."

"You're sure?"

Clare nodded.

"And Sadie? A martini for you, I presume?"

Sadie never tired of this bit. "Daddy!" she shrieked in delight. "That's for grown-ups!"

Jed turned back into the house and nearly collided with his sister. Lauren had just showered, and her wet hair was combed into neat ridges and tucked behind her diamond-studded ears. She was four years younger than Jed and pretty in a very blond, WASPy way. She wore a white dress that showed off her long legs and tennis-toned arms. She and Jed were the same height—five feet eight—but standing next to each other he came off as short and maybe even a little squat while she seemed impossibly willowy.

Jed stepped aside to let her out, and her daughters, Chloe and Scarlett, ages seven and nine, tumbled after her. They ran down to the lawn like sylphs, their long, brown legs flying beneath them. Sadie wriggled off her mother's lap to follow them.

"I can't believe we'll be in our own house next summer," Lauren said, watching the three girls chase one another around the grass. "I'm kind of sad about it."

She and Grant had recently bought a house a few streets away. They planned to renovate it over the winter before moving in. Jed would never admit to feeling jealous, but Clare knew it rankled him that his much younger brother-in-law—who still called people "dude"—was able to buy a second home before him. They were hardly struggling—Jed was general counsel at a midsized hedge fund—but they definitely did not have a spare six million dollars lying around. Grant, who worked in venture capital, apparently did.

During the year, Grant and Lauren lived in a duplex on Eightieth and Park, and Chloe and Scarlett went to Harwick, the same all-girls school that Lauren had attended a generation before. It seemed to be a foregone conclusion that Sadie would end up there, too. Jed had gone white the one time Clare had brought up the idea of sending her to a Montessori school.

Lauren sat down, took a sip of her mojito, and turned to Clare. "I forgot to tell you—I was chatting with someone the other day who knew you. Cassandra something. Yee maybe? Ying? You went to Columbia together?"

"Oh, Cassandra Yang. She's great. We went on a disastrous road trip to Marfa together once. Where did you run into her?"

"At the New Museum. A friend invited me to join her on an after-hours tour, and Cassandra was the curator who showed us around. I guess you must have been a few years behind her?"

"Well, we started out the same year," Clare said with a laugh.

"Oh, right. I always forget how long you've been doing it."

Clare had been most of the way through her PhD in art history when she got pregnant. She'd planned to take a couple months of maternity leave before returning to finish her dissertation, but Sadie had spent the first five weeks of her life in the NICU. When Clare finally brought her home, she hadn't been able to stomach the idea of handing her over to a nanny, as they'd once planned, and her dissertation had been gathering dust ever since. She still requested formal extensions from Columbia periodically—a requirement if your degree takes more than five years—but all of her friends from the program, including Cassandra, had long since moved on with their lives.

"Will you start working on your dissertation again once Sadie's back in school?" Lauren asked.

"That's the plan," Clare said, though in truth she had tried and failed to return to it several times the year before. The prospect of actually finishing it seemed remote.

Jed reemerged from the house and handed a glass of white wine to Clare. She couldn't remember whether she'd asked for it, but she took it gratefully.

"Thank you, love."

"Didn't I train him well?" Dorothy piped in.

THIS WAS THE first year that Sadie actually understood the concept of presents, and she attacked them with relish. Every time she unwrapped something, even the six-pack of socks from the Basts' housekeeper, she exclaimed, "Oh, wow!" with total, unadulterated amazement. Clare adored her daughter's unbridled enthusiasm. She had bought her a little red tricycle with a wicker basket up front. Inside was a stuffed teddy bear wearing its own tiny helmet. As Sadie rang the shiny silver bell over and over, Grant asked, "Is that it? Should I put the burgers on?"

Jed stood up and said with a sly little smile, "Actually, I think there might be one more. . . ."

He disappeared into the house and emerged a minute later with a huge metal cage clattering against his leg. Cowering in one corner, as promised, was a tiny white rabbit with blazing red eyes.

Lauren gasped and stretched out her hand toward it. "Arthur!"

"Can you believe it?" Jed said. "I found a breeder in Connecticut."

He placed the cage on the ground and gestured for Sadie to come closer. She didn't move.

"What is it?" she whispered to Clare.

"It's a bunny," Clare said, gazing into the animal's nightmarish eyes.

"A *rabbit*," Dorothy corrected her.

"Do you want to hold him?" Jed asked Sadie.

She glanced again at Clare, who tried to look encouraging.

Jed cupped his hands in front of him. "Hold out your hands, like this." Sadie copied him, and he placed the quivering animal in her hands. Sadie stared at it, transfixed. The rabbit kicked out one of its hind legs, and Sadie dropped him with a yelp. The poor creature scrabbled at the worn wood planks.

Jed laughed. He scooped up the rabbit and held it against his chest in one hand, stroking its shiny fur with the other. Clare couldn't help thinking that there was something wrong with a grown man petting a bunny, but she couldn't say what.

Over dinner, both Jed and Dorothy tried to steer Sadie toward a more distinguished name than the one she had chosen: Noodle.

Sadie, however, would not be swayed. And when her husband and mother-in-law weren't looking, Clare leaned in to whisper in her daughter's ear: "Good for you."

## CHAPTER 2

ON THE FOLLOWING WEDNESDAY, CLARE left their apartment to go meet Jed at a party at his boss's home. They were back in New York City, and Sadie had started school again. Clare was feeling unusually buoyant.

She knew Dorothy would say it was too late in the season to be wearing the dress she had on—sleeveless ivory silk, with a cowl neck and raw edges—but she didn't care. It was still warm enough. She wore her long hair loose around her shoulders, where it refused to sit flat. It had grown coarser and wavier since she'd had Sadie, and the color had burnished to a darker, deeper auburn. Her pale skin was set off by wine-red lipstick. On nights like these, when she made an effort, she could almost convince herself that Jed was right and she did have a Julianne Moore thing going on.

Clare rode the elevator up to the Wolfes' apartment alone, a small crystal chandelier clattering above her head. She hoped she wouldn't be the first to arrive. She doubted that Jed had even left the office yet.

To her relief, the elevator doors slid open onto a noisy din. Emil, the Wolfes' live-in bodyguard, stood at attention in the foyer. He usually wore fitted black athleticwear, but tonight he had dressed up in a shiny dark suit. Clare found Emil's presence a bit melodramatic—especially the bulge in his jacket where she could just make out the outline of a gun—but Jed claimed that the Wolfes' wealth required it. Clare nodded at him and continued into the apartment.

A waiter in black tie stood in front of a wide staircase sweeping up toward the second floor. Clare helped herself to a champagne flute off his tray and turned into the large living room on the left. It was painted a deep, glossy aubergine and had five windows overlooking Park Avenue. On the opposite wall, a massive red, yellow, and orange Rothko commanded attention. The last time Clare was there, Jed's boss had given her a detailed play-by-play of the bidding war he'd won for it. He and his wife, Tasha, were prolific—though, in Clare's view, somewhat unimaginative—

art collectors. Tasha was also on the board of New York's Museum of Contemporary Art. Clare knew almost down to the dollar how much money they would have had to donate to the museum to finagle that seat, and it was more than most people earned in a lifetime.

Alec Wolfe was the founder of a hedge fund called Gatepost that managed close to a billion dollars in assets. Six months earlier, he'd recruited Jed from his father's old law firm to replace Gatepost's longtime general counsel, who had died suddenly from a heart attack. Jed had been friends with Alec's younger brother in grade school, and Alec said he wanted someone he knew he could trust.

Clare had been surprised when Jed told her he wanted to take the job; he'd always disparaged colleagues who sold out for the financial sector, and he'd originally told her way back when they first met that he'd wanted to work in legal aid. But he said he'd do a short stint at Gatepost as a favor to Alec, who was offering enough money to set them up comfortably in just a few years. He suggested he might even want to go into public service afterward. Clare had argued that they were already comfortable, but to Jed, comfortable meant a four-bedroom apartment *and* a second home in the Hamptons. To sway her, he'd promised to work shorter hours at Gatepost. Clare had gone along with it, but in fact, Jed soon started working most nights and weekends again. Even when he wasn't working, he seemed constantly preoccupied, which was new. He said he was still on the steepest part of the learning curve and things would settle down soon. Secretly, Clare worried he was too straight-edged to succeed in the cutthroat world of finance. Jed had a rigid, almost-childlike concept of right and wrong.

Alec Wolfe, on the other hand, fit the mold of the brash financier well. He cared nothing for social niceties or, as he liked to call it, "PC bullshit." He believed most people were still just cavemen at heart, ready to clobber the next guy for his buffalo meat if necessary.

CLARE SPOTTED HER hosts installed near the grand piano, greeting guests with their usual volubility. Alec looked heavier than she remembered, his wife even thinner. Tasha, in an emerald-green sequined dress, caught Clare's eye over the crowd and gestured for her to come over.

"You look fabulous," she trilled, kissing Clare on both cheeks and giving her dress a once-over. "Prada?"

"On sale at Theory," Clare laughed.

"Oh, darling, just lie."

"To you?"

"To everyone!"

"Except me," Alec interjected, pointing a stubby finger at her. "You're the only one who gives me honest advice."

Alec sometimes liked to consult Clare on pieces he was considering buying. He claimed her opinions had a "purity" that his dealers' perspective lacked.

"But you never take it," Clare said.

"That's because I get bullied by my art consultants."

"You don't get bullied by anyone."

He glanced pointedly at Tasha.

"Well, with one exception," Clare said. "Speaking of, happy anniversary."

Every year, Alec and Tasha threw an over-the-top anniversary party at their triplex apartment on Park Avenue. With her high cheekbones, faux eyelashes, and couture-laden wardrobe, Tasha was obviously a woman comfortable commanding attention. She'd grown up in Moscow then Switzerland and had one of those unplaceable European accents that faded in and out depending on the context. A few years earlier, after Russia invaded Ukraine, she'd stopped emphasizing her Moscow roots. A wife of one of Jed's colleagues had once told Clare that Tasha had relatives who were friendly with Putin, but Clare doubted the truth of that. Tasha herself had admitted that her father grew up in a seedy neighborhood on the eastern fringes of Moscow. He'd died when Tasha was five, and she'd moved to Zurich two years later when her mother remarried.

Clare had sent flowers that morning, but the arrangement she'd picked out was half the size of the smallest one in the room. She and Jed had become friendly with the Wolfes over the past few months, but there was no pretending that the two couples occupied the same echelon. They went out for dinner every now and then, and Clare and Jed had spent Memorial Day weekend at their Southampton house, but it was hard to get close to people who thought that flying first class—rather than private—was a genuine hardship.

"You look as ravishing as ever," Alec said. "Where's your husband?"

"You tell me. He never leaves the office anymore."

"He's a damn boy scout; that's the problem. Too fastidious—even for a lawyer. But I made him promise not to work late tonight." Alec caught someone's eye behind Clare and bellowed out, "Lucas! Get over here!"

Clare excused herself. She had learned that the Wolfes were best experienced in small doses. She took another sip of champagne and scanned the crowd for Jed. She noticed a few people she knew from other Wolfe gatherings, but her husband's familiar mop of sandy hair was nowhere to be found.

She moved through the far doorway, which took her into the dining room, where the table was laid with various cheeses, pâté, oysters, shrimp, lobster tails, and roast beef. It looked like a PSA for gout.

She slurped a single oyster and surveyed the opposite wall, where a Richard Diebenkorn had recently been replaced by a large frame of Hirst's ubiquitous rainbow dots that collectors never seemed to tire of. Clare couldn't stand them and audibly scoffed. Embarrassed, she tried to cover it up with a cough and glanced around to see if anyone had noticed.

A man with dark, wavy hair shot through with gray was standing at the other end of the table, watching her. His eyes were green and bright, his narrow nose slightly crooked. He was dressed more casually than the other guests, in an unstructured linen jacket and a white button-down. He looked to be a bit older than Jed: early fifties, maybe.

"I take it you're anti-dot?" he asked in an amused voice. He had a slight accent, but Clare couldn't quite place it.

"Oh, I can get behind a good dot," she said. "As long as it's a dot with a point of view. Give me Kusama. Give me Baldessari. Give me Howardena Pindell. These are just . . . wallpaper."

"Expensive wallpaper."

"I think that's the point," she replied in a stage whisper.

He laughed and moved closer.

"I'm surprised to hear someone at this party reference Howardena Pindell. Not many people know her work."

"Well, they should." Howardena Pindell was an artist in her eighties who had made beautiful mixed-media works out of hole-punched dots.

"I agree." The accent was French, she decided.

A waiter appeared next to them, and each plucked a fresh glass of champagne off his tray.

"How do you know Alec and Tasha?" the Frenchman asked. "Or did you just sneak in to insult their collection?"

Clare smiled. "I like their Rothko."

"Everybody likes a Rothko," he countered.

"True."

"Have you seen their new Ruscha?"

Clare shook her head.

"Come. I'll show you."

She glanced around again for Jed but didn't see him, so she agreed. She followed the man up the carpeted staircase. He passed the second floor and kept on climbing. He moved in a peculiar, loose-limbed gait, almost as if he were dancing.

"Are we supposed to be up here?" she asked.

There were, in fact, a handful of guests on the third floor, along with a bar draped in white fabric. The doors to the broad terrace were open. Next to them, two tall sculpted topiaries twinkled with lights.

"This way," the man said, and she followed him into a dimly lit room with a pool table. On one wall was a large painting with the words "God Knows Where" overlayed on an image of snow-capped mountains. They stood in front of it for a moment.

"I'm waiting for your scathing take," Gabriel said.

"Sorry to disappoint," she said. "It's nice. I mean, of course it's nice. It's a Ruscha: It's cool. It's pretty. It's expensive. And it's exactly what I'd expect Alec to have on his walls. I mean, it's not like he's going to showcase a Catherine Opie portrait, right?"

The man laughed and clapped his hands. "There it is. I knew you had it in you."

Clare covered her face with her hands. "I'm such a gracious guest."

"Well, as long as we're being impolite—come have a cigarette with me on the terrace."

"I don't smoke."

"Of course you don't. No one does anymore. That's why you have to keep me company."

She hesitated and glanced at the doorway leading back to the stairs. If she was being honest with herself, there was no one down there she particularly wanted to talk to. And in addition to actually getting her references to contemporary artists, this man had a brightness to him that tugged on her. She followed him out through two large French doors onto a broad terrace. In between the boxwoods and dogwood trees—full-grown trees—heat lamps glowed brightly. There was no one else outside.

They walked to the edge of the balcony and looked down. Below them, cars inched slowly up and down Park Avenue. The sun had set, and a sharp wind had picked up. Clare shivered.

The man lit a cigarette, and as soon as she smelled the smoke, she was transported back to her early twenties. She had just moved to the city. She lived in Bushwick with her best friend, Maggie, and a creepy guy named Garth who'd answered their ad on Craigslist. She didn't smoke often—only when she was drunk, huddled outside dark bars on the Lower East Side—but she'd always loved having her cigarette lit for her. Two heads inclined toward each other. The sudden flare of light and burst of camaraderie. That first delicious taste and the long exhale. God, those years felt far away now.

She glanced behind her. "One drag," she said, holding out her hand.

He smiled, and their fingers brushed when she took the cigarette from him. She barely inhaled but was still overcome by lightheadedness. It had been years since she'd taken even one puff. She gripped the sandy stone of the balustrade to brace herself.

They stood looking out at the darkening city for a few moments in silence. Then he turned and finally asked the obvious question: "Who are you?"

"Clare Bast. Who are you?"

"Gabriel Prévost."

"Ah," she said in recognition. He was a well-known art dealer. She took one more drag of the cigarette and handed it back to him. "I know your gallery," she said, exhaling.

"You've been?"

"Not for years."

"Oh, that's a good sign. We must be doing something right."

She laughed. "It's me. I've been . . . distracted. I've actually been meaning to go see your new show. Eduardo Salas, right?"

"Tell me when you're coming." He pulled a card from inside his jacket and handed it to her. "I'll show you around."

She took the card but said, "Please don't be offended if I don't make it. I rarely do most of the things I'm meaning to these days."

"Why is that?"

"I don't know. I seem to be lacking in momentum."

"Come," he said. He leaned in closer and added, after a beat: "I'd like you to."

Their arms were now touching on the railing, and Clare could feel the heat through his jacket. She held his gaze. His eyes were fringed with thick, dark lashes. Neither spoke for several seconds. Clare felt an unaccustomed surge of heat rise up her body. At first she thought it was just embarrassment at her lack of reserve.

Then she realized it was desire. It had become such an unfamiliar sensation that she hardly recognized it.

She cleared her throat.

"I should go find my husband now. Thanks for the cigarette."

The intensity in his expression immediately receded and was replaced by a wry smile. "Of course. It was nice to meet you, Clare."

She walked directly to the powder room and swilled water in her mouth. She washed her hands with a bar of black soap. She looked at her reflection in the mirror. Her cheeks were pink.

BACK ON THE first floor, Clare was scanning the room for Jed when a hand clutched her elbow. She turned to find Tasha directly behind her.

"Did I see you talking to Gabriel Prévost?" she asked, leaning in so close that Clare was enveloped in an overpowering cloud of Fracas.

The color in Clare's cheeks deepened. "Yes, why?"

"I'm so glad you found each other. I was hoping to introduce you. He's doing some work for Alec, and I told him he had to talk to you—you know more about art than anyone we know."

"I doubt that."

Tasha rolled her eyes. "Take the fucking compliment, Clare."

Clare smiled. "Thank you."

"He'd be a great resource for you. And vice versa."

"I appreciate all your help, Tasha. I hope you know that."

Once, after too many glasses of wine, Clare had confided in Tasha how stalled she was on her dissertation; how worried she was that she'd never pick it up again. A few days later, with no warning, Tasha had called to tell Clare that she had made an appointment for her with Clement Rosier, MoCA's chief curator of painting and sculpture, one of the most powerful people in the art world.

Clare hadn't been sure what to expect from the meeting. Not a job offer certainly; no one gets a curator's position at the country's top modern art museum with half a PhD. Clement had been exceedingly gracious, but he seemed as baffled as she was over the purpose of their introduction. Despite Tasha's good intentions, the interaction had left Clare feeling more defeated than before.

"I don't do favors," Tasha told Clare. "You know that. It's up to you to figure out what Clement can do for you. I only set up that meeting to guilt you into that conversation with my godfather. Which he still talks about incessantly, by the way."

Tasha's godfather, Viktor, was a collector of early abstractionists, and Tasha had asked Clare to speak to him about her work on Blake Webley, a successful but enigmatic midcentury painter who was the subject of Clare's dissertation.

"I'm glad he found it useful," Clare said. "He turned out to be very knowledgeable." This, she felt, was a diplomatic way to describe a man who had been much more interested in explaining to her his own theories on early abstract expressionism than in seeking her perspective. When Viktor referred to Kandinsky—"my compatriot"—as the inventor of abstraction, he hadn't taken kindly to her suggestion that Francis Picabia or František Kupka might have beaten him to the punch.

"You're kind," Tasha replied. "I have no doubt that he was insufferable, but now he gets to say he has an eminent Webley scholar on speed dial, so—mission accomplished."

Clare was about to take issue with the word "eminent," but she knew that Tasha would chide her for it. Clare hated to act (and feel) like a self-effacing twit—what kind of example was she setting for her daughter?—but the accolades she'd once accepted as rightly hers now felt too glaringly exaggerated to let stand.

The truth was, Clare was deeply embarrassed to have as much money as she did without working, like a budding Dorothy Bast. So why did she find herself envying Tasha, who didn't have a job either and was much wealthier than any Bast?

The main reason, she supposed, was that Tasha had made her own money as opposed to inheriting it. She'd started her career at the investment bank Roth Briggs, which is where she'd met her future husband. Alec had once recounted his courtship to Clare as if it had been a hunting trip. "You should have seen her," he said about Tasha. "She was twenty-two, drop-dead gorgeous, and sharp as a razor blade. She had men running in circles around her. But I worked fast. I snapped her up her first week there."

"Not true," Tasha cut in. "It *was* my first week, but *I* chose *him*. I heard someone screaming obscenities into his phone a few desks away from mine. The guy next to me—Brian something—goes, 'They call that guy Vlad the Impaler. He destroys anyone who gets in his way.'" She paused and smiled. "Any guesses?"

"Alec?" Clare supplied.

"Within two weeks, we were dating," Tasha said. "Brian never spoke to me again."

"For the record," Alec said, "I have never impaled anyone."

Tasha put her hand on top of Alec's. "No, Alec is never cruel. He's driven. When he sees something he wants, he goes after it, like a bull."

"If I'm a bull, you're a shark!" Alec exclaimed.

"Hardly."

"You're right," he said. "Not a shark. A fox. You'd never stoop to brute force."

Tasha laughed, finally conceding the point. "Maybe. But that's only because no matter how hard I pushed or how loudly I yelled, nobody was ever going to feel threatened by *me*. I have to use more roundabout methods."

Tasha turned to Clare. "You know, Alec and I both made managing director the same year. Nobody was surprised about his promotion, but I know they were by mine. '*Her?*' I could hear people whispering when I walked down the halls. I looked like I was supposed to marry money, not make it. But that's what happens when your methods are subtle. You keep on winning, and people assume it's by accident."

"What are your methods?" Clare asked.

"Simple, darling. I make it my business to know what every person in the room wants. If you know that, then—*poof!*—you become the most powerful person there. Desire is what makes the world go 'round, and if you don't know how to exploit it, you'll never get anywhere. I'm not talking about sex—or not just sex. It's everything: business, politics, relationships. You find out what someone wants, and then you either become that thing or you become the person who gets them that thing." She took out a tube of crimson lipstick and applied another coat. "Luckily, I have always been exceptionally talented at sating other people's desires."

Jed had blushed openly at that pronouncement.

Clare had been taken aback, and frankly envious, of this brazen attitude. Tasha was co-owner of Gatepost, but she'd never actually worked there. She'd left Roth Briggs when they had children—two, teenagers now—and never gone back to work, but she didn't seem to suffer from any of Clare's anxiety over her aborted career. She sat on a dozen different boards and collected art and houses as if they were tchotchkes. Being that rich was a full-time job. She spent her money liberally and with a flagrancy that Clare almost admired. Tasha seemed impervious to shame, and Clare longed to be so free and unencumbered.

And, of course, to live a life surrounded by art. To not just admire it from afar, but to *acquire* it. To be allowed to touch it, hold it, even lick it if she wanted. All without any self-recrimination or guilt. No, when Clare thought about it, it didn't sound like a bad life at all.

Clare suddenly spotted Jed across the room, chatting with an old friend from law school. Clare extracted herself from Tasha's grip and wended her way to her husband. When she put her hand on his back, he turned and smiled broadly.

"Hello, beautiful," he said and pecked her on the lips. "Are you all right? You look flushed."

Clare instinctively brought the back of her hand to her cheek. "It's hot in here."

"I'll see if they can open a window."

"No, no, I'm fine." Clare turned to kiss Vishal and his wife, Lena, who had gone to Harvard with Tasha. "How are you two? It's been a while."

"We're good," Lena said. "Jed was just telling us about the rabbit."

Clare shook her head. "Don't get me started."

"I'd file for divorce. I really would."

"Hey!" Vishal said with mock affront.

"I'm not kidding," Lena retorted.

"I can't say I haven't considered it," Clare said, "but these guys are the only lawyers I know." She turned to Vishal. "Are you taking new clients?"

Jed laughed and pulled her close. "Don't answer that, buddy."

## CHAPTER 3

THE NEXT MORNING, CLARE WOKE a little before five and eased out of bed so she wouldn't wake Jed. She'd gotten good at this since developing insomnia during her pregnancy. She crept into the hallway and immediately stepped in a pile of rabbit poop.

"Fantastic," she whispered to no one. *Just fantastic.*

She hobbled into the kitchen for a paper towel, and when she flicked on the lights, she found the culprit's long, pale form stretched out on the granite floor.

Clare sighed. Noodle was making it a habit to escape from his cage.

"Come on," she said, picking him up. "Back to bed." He flopped in half like a wet rag and one red eye opened and peered at her accusingly. She placed him back in his cage in the corner of the room and closed the latch. He settled back into a fitful sleep, one ear twitching.

The day before, Clare had told Jed that she thought Noodle was depressed.

Jed had laughed. "He's not depressed. He's a rabbit. They sleep a lot."

Clare turned the coffee maker on and looked at her own reflection in the darkened windows. Her skin looked ghostly pale.

Jed, who fell asleep thirty seconds after his head hit the pillow, was constantly urging her to get a prescription for Ambien. She didn't know how to tell him that she actually looked forward to those hours of wakefulness in the inky darkness. It was the only reliable time when Sadie—or, in fact, Jed himself—wasn't pulling on her attention. Her mind was free to wander where it wanted; it wasn't on someone else's leash. Besides, she hated the idea of being trapped in some groggy stupor if Sadie ever needed her in the middle of the night.

Clare drank her coffee in the still-dark living room. Every so often, a light in the building across the street would flicker on and illuminate a stranger cinching the sash of her robe or turning on a kettle. Clare loved watching these other lives unfold like a silent movie. She attached stories to the characters, like the woman on the seventh floor who must be having an affair because she whispered fervently on the phone while her husband slept. Or the man two floors above her who had lost his job but couldn't bring himself to tell his wife; he always stared dolefully into the mirror after knotting his tie.

The sky slowly pinkened and grew pale, and the details of the room she was sitting in emerged from the shadows. Jed's mother, who had worked on and off as an interior designer over the years, had decorated the apartment herself. Clare would have preferred clean lines and modern furniture, but she'd been trying to make herself amenable to her mother-in-law, so she'd ended up with chintz and tchotchkes—and she was still pretty sure Dorothy didn't like her.

Clare picked up her phone, checked her email, and then found herself googling Gabriel Prévost. As soon as his face appeared on the screen, she turned it off and put it back down on the coffee table. A few minutes later, she picked it up again and started scrolling.

Sadie appeared at six-thirty with her blond curls matted at the back of her head and her cheeks flushed from sleep. Even now, three years in, Clare's heart still heaved when she saw her each morning.

"Hi, sweet pea," she said with a smile. "How'd you sleep?"

Sadie pulled down one leg of her ducky pajamas. "Good. I dreamed about Noodle."

"I hope it was a nice dream."

"We put spaghetti sauce on him and ate him."

"Yikes. Let's not do that."

Sadie nodded thoughtfully. "Okay."

"Do you want pancakes?"

Sadie's eyes widened in excitement. "I'll get the aprons!" she shouted, dashing out of the room before Clare could respond.

Jed had given them matching aprons the previous Christmas, and Sadie now insisted they wear them for any kitchen-related task.

She returned a moment later, apron strings flapping, and spun around for her mother to tie them. "Don't forget boots!" she said, wiggling a little.

A few months earlier, they'd been making cookies while listening to music on Clare's phone and "These Boots Are Made for Walkin'" had come on. Sadie had frozen stock-still, as if possessed. "What *is* this song?" she'd whispered.

"Do you like it?" Clare asked.

"Oh, Mama, *I love it.*"

It had been one of Clare's proudest parenting moments. Now, whenever they cooked together, matching aprons and Nancy Sinatra were nonnegotiable.

Clare put the music on softly. Even at a barely audible volume, those twangy opening beats cascading in on top of one another filled her with delight.

"Are you ready, Boots?" she asked over her shoulder.

"Start walkin'!" Sadie hollered back.

"Shhh," Clare said, laughing. "Daddy's still sleeping."

"In fact," Jed said from the doorway, "Daddy is *not* still sleeping."

Sadie yelped in surprise.

"I'm sorry," Clare said, covering her mouth. "Were we too loud?"

Jed shook his head. "Far be it from me to stop those boots from walking."

Clare and Sadie started crooning to each other along with the music: "You keep lyin' when you oughta be truthin'. And you keep losing when you oughta not bet."

"That was so good!" Clare cried. "You got it this time!" Sadie usually garbled the lyrics into one long indecipherable nonsense word.

Sadie looked down at the ground and smiled, her face turning beet-red. Clare knew her inability to take a compliment came from her.

"Come here, Boots," Clare said, pulling her daughter into a squeeze.

AN HOUR LATER, Clare was trying to usher Sadie out the door to school, but her daughter was too busy buckling her baby doll into its stroller. The doll, stripped naked and covered in streaks of Sharpie, seemed to be sending Clare a silent plea for help with her one open eye.

"Sadie, if you want to press the elevator button, you have to do it. We're going to be late."

Sadie ignored her.

"I'm pressing it . . ." Clare warned.

"Don't!"

"Then come do it."

Sadie stomped over and stood on her tiptoes to reach it.

They lived on the top floor of a large, brick building on the corner of Park Avenue and Eighty-Second Street. When they'd been looking to buy, Jed had insisted on only seeing penthouses because they were "far above the hubbub." Clare had gone along with it, but what she hadn't factored in was the very obvious fact that Sadie's school would be down there in the hubbub, the grocery store was down there in the hubbub, everything was down there in the hubbub. All they'd done was create an extra-long commute *to* the hubbub.

And it was long. The elevator was slow and creaky because the building was old. ("Prewar! As long as it's prewar!" his mother had shrieked when they told her they'd found a place; she and Abe had helped with the down payment, so who were they to argue?) Most mornings they ended up waiting almost ten minutes.

"Where's the alligator?" Sadie asked. She was definitely old enough to know that the word was elevator, but Clare couldn't bring herself to correct her. It was too cute.

"I don't know, lovebug."

"Why is it taking so long?"

"I don't know. We just have to be patient."

"Why?"

"Because we can't control how long it takes."

"Why?"

"Because we are not elevator technicians."

"Why?"

"Because we didn't go to school for that."

"Why?"

Clare sighed. "I don't know."

"Where is it?"

"It's probably a few floors below us."

"When is it coming?"

Clare didn't answer.

"Mama, where's the alligator?"

Finally, the godforsaken alligator arrived, and they clambered on. After a slow, jerky descent, they were ejected into the lobby.

Clare greeted Gino, the doorman on duty.

"Good morning, Mrs. Bast," he replied. "Good morning, Sadie!"

"Happy birthday!" Sadie bellowed. She had recently adopted this as her all-purpose greeting.

"Thank you," he said sincerely.

The first chill of fall was in the air—early this year—and the leaves on the trees rustled like cheerleaders' pom-poms. The streets, as always, were teeming with kids on scooters and parents pushing strollers. Clare put on a small frozen smile and a faraway look in her eyes, in case she saw anyone she knew but didn't know she knew. This happened fairly frequently. Acquaintances seemed to appear out of nowhere like pop-up targets in police-training simulations. ("Clare? It's me, Gretchen! Jed's friend from Penn!" or "Clare? It's Francesca! From Music Babies!") But on that particular day they made it the three blocks to Sadie's school without any run-ins.

Sadie attended the same nursery school—Saint Mary's—that Jed and Lauren had gone to. It even had the same headmistress, a sturdy woman in orthopedic shoes named Mrs. Dwyer. Little about the school or Mrs. Dwyer had changed in the past thirty years: Girls still wore smocked dresses every day, and it was still harder to get into than Harvard.

When they arrived at school, one of Sadie's classmates, Lisbet, was already in line outside the building with her mother.

"Hi, Mina," Clare called out.

Among a bounty of acquaintances, Mina had become her closest—maybe only—friend on the Upper East Side, in part because she was one of the few other mothers at Saint Mary's who didn't use a nanny, and she also had an only child. They often ended up taking the girls to the park together after school.

Clare had been surprised by how isolated she'd felt after moving in with Jed uptown. Most of her friends from her PhD program had scattered to various curatorial or academic jobs across the country; and the ones who'd stayed in the city, along with a few old coworkers and college friends, lived downtown or in Brooklyn. Maggie, her best friend, had moved to Denver three years earlier. The two had met in college and moved to the city together afterward. Clare had been devastated when she left.

Clare had worked hard to build a friendship with Mina, and she was grateful for it, but she often wished that it replicated some of the closeness she had with Maggie. For whatever reason, it didn't. Clare's attempts at self-deprecating jokes or candor always fell flat with Mina. Most of the time their conversations evolved into an endless exchange of escalating compliments. Clare had realized over the past couple of years that that was the easiest way for women to communicate their goodwill toward one another. For now, it would have to be enough.

"Morning, Clare. Morning, Sadie," Mina said. "Ooh, love that jacket." She rubbed a hand up and down Clare's sleeve.

"Oh, thanks. Great boots."

They were saved from the flattery arms race by the opening of the big wooden doors and the appearance of Mrs. Dwyer in her long wool skirt. "Good morning, families," she called out, indicating that school was officially open.

AFTER CLARE HAD deposited Sadie in her classroom, Mina reappeared at her shoulder.

"Want to grab a cup of coffee?" she asked.

Clare nodded. "I could use several."

They walked over to Fifth Avenue. Traffic was stalled, and they could barely hear each other over the din of car horns and some unseen jackhammer. The Metropolitan Museum of Art stood still and stolid across the street. Clare stopped for a moment to look at it.

"You used to work there, right?" Mina asked.

"In the development office. It was my first job out of college."

"Remind me where you went to school? Bennington?"

"Not quite." Clare smiled. "SUNY Binghamton. I grew up there."

Clare's mother, Nessa Regan, had worked in the university's financial aid office for almost thirty years. A single mother, she used to bring Clare to work with her on school holidays and set her loose in the university art museum. The place had always bored Clare on field trips, but when she was allowed to explore it on her own, she felt like she'd stumbled upon a hidden world, a world that felt in some ways more real than her own. She could remember coming across a self-portrait by a German artist named Käthe Kollwitz when she was around fourteen. It was a woodcut from 1923, and the expression on the artist's face was arrestingly haunting. Clare just stood there, transfixed. The accompanying text said that her youngest son had died just a few days after joining World War I, and she never recovered from the grief. For weeks afterward, Clare couldn't get that face out of her mind.

Something happened to her when she looked at certain works of art, she realized: a slight internal shifting or rearrangement. It was like there was a tuning fork inside of her that she would otherwise never have known existed, and then all of a sudden, something hit it just the right way, and it started to hum.

There wasn't much of an organizing principle to the things that affected her, even now. It could be a Brancusi sculpture: The sweep of slick brass, the veined wood, the cold marble—the combination could make her sick with longing. Walking into a James Turrell installation had once drawn a thick, involuntary sob from her body. Carsten Höller had done the opposite: infused her with such a sudden influx of joy that it had felt like an invasion. The way the light hit the folds of a gown in a Jan van Eyck—she could *feel* that color somewhere in her chest. She really could.

She wondered: If you gathered everyone who'd had a reaction to, say, a particular Rembrandt painting into one room, would they have anything else in common? What did this one guy who had lived hundreds of years ago know about her—Clare Regan's—inner workings? Something. It was uncanny.

Nothing in her life until then had prepared her for these feelings. She and her mother didn't go to church; she didn't do hard drugs; the music on offer was Kelly Clarkson and Justin Timberlake—she hadn't had a lot of opportunities for transcendence. Once she experienced it, though, she realized it was the exact thing she'd been craving all along.

She was a good kid: She studied hard; she helped cook dinner; she rarely complained. The prospect of disappointing her mother terrified her. But every so often she'd be overcome by the feeling that if she didn't get a reprieve from the sheer *everydayness* of her life, she would combust.

Her high school boyfriend had once tried to show off by going ninety mph on the highway, and Clare had surprised them both by urging him to go faster and faster, even after they'd passed a hundred and five. She'd loved the feeling of being pressed back into her seat, hurtling toward the unknown.

Art, she found, scratched a similar itch. It granted her a brief, blurred view of something beyond the ordinary. It hinted at another way of living, one that valued mystery over certainty and freedom over security. It encouraged her to fix her gaze on the horizon; to imagine the possibility of escaping not only Binghamton, but everything familiar to her.

But she'd had no sense of what to *do* with these reactions. She couldn't paint or draw: She had no talent for making it and got no enjoyment out of it, only frustration tinged with boredom. Still, something in her was pulled forcefully to art. Back then, like most kids, she thought everything had a reason. She thought *she* had a reason—that there must be a slot for her somewhere in the world; she just needed to find that Clare-shaped void. Art seemed to offer a signpost. She never felt as fully *herself* as when that inner part of her started to hum.

During her senior year in college, she sent her résumé to every museum, auction house, and gallery in New York. Getting an interview for a job at the Met had felt like winning the lottery. She still remembered what she wore to the meeting: a pilly black dress from H&M and a pin of her mother's that reminded her of a Calder brooch Simone de Beauvoir had worn on the back of one of her books. Clare thought it lent her a whiff of the Left Bank, though it had probably come from the glamourless jewelry counter at Boscov's, Binghamton's fading department store.

Clare was astonished when she got the job, though ultimately it ended up having very little to do with art. Mostly what she did was ask rich people for money.

And then she accidentally became one of them.

CLARE AND MINA turned into the Church of the Heavenly Rest on Ninetieth Street, which had rented out its beautiful vaulted side chapel to a soulless Australian coffee chain. Clare always found the place depressing: a literal shrine to capitalism.

Mina tapped on the counter with her perfectly manicured fingers as she pondered her options.

"Do you have single-source milk?" she asked.

The barista recited a practiced spiel: "Whole, skim, oat, almond, soy."

"Right, but is the whole milk single-source—like from just one cow?"

"It's from a carton."

"Never mind. I'll have an iced decaf latte with oat milk."

They settled at a high-top table near the window. "What's single-source milk?" Clare asked as she shrugged off her jacket.

"It's one of Tim's new investments. It's from small farms that don't mix milk from different cows. I mean, think about it: Babies don't drink milk from all different mothers. It's totally unnatural."

"So is drinking milk meant for baby cows, if you follow that line of logic."

Mina gave her a look like she was being difficult.

When their order was called, Clare retrieved Mina's oat latte and her own iced coffee. Mina grimaced after her first sip.

"What's wrong?"

"I don't think she shook the carton before pouring it." She wriggled off her stool to go negotiate with the staff.

When Clare had first started spending time in Jed's world—a self-contained little bubble bounded by Central Park and Lexington

Avenue—she'd been surprised by how disgruntled everyone in it always seemed. They treated complaining like a competitive sport, and they were all very, very good at it—even Mina, who was, for the most part, warm and considerate. Clare probably shouldn't have been so surprised; most people wanted more than they were allotted. But here it just struck her as inefficient. These people had so much yet it seemed to give them no satisfaction.

Now, five years in, she understood better how wealth could breed desire instead of sate it. When you're able to arrange almost every aspect of your life exactly how you want it, the few inconveniences that remain will drive you crazy, in the same way that a single crooked picture frame is often more vexing than a room in total disarray. A few weeks earlier, Clare had called a sushi restaurant to complain about her delivery taking too long to arrive, and she'd stopped in the middle of her sentence, shocked to hear the words coming out of her mouth. She'd waitressed for years and remembered being dressed down by customers for problems she had absolutely no control over. Now, here she was, doing the same thing: assuming she had an inalienable right to convenience. She'd become one of *them*.

Mina returned—with an iced tea—and smiled at Clare. "So . . . I have some news," she said. "We're having another baby in February. A boy."

"Oh, that's fantastic! Congratulations."

"What about you?" Mina asked with a coy smile. "Do you think you'll have another?"

"I don't know," Clare answered honestly. Jed had made it clear that he wanted another child soon, and several after that, but she was still hesitating. "I'm not sure I'm ready yet."

"Well, get on it, Mama. Take it from me: It can take longer than you think, so you should start trying before you're ready."

"But then what happens when you find yourself nine months pregnant and you're still not ready?" Clare asked with a laugh.

Mina waved a hand in the hair. "Oh, the hormones take over. Didn't you read that book by Belinda Bettleman?"

"Which one?"

"*Hormones as Heroines.*"

"No. I think I read her other book. About mindful parenting."

"Oh, I loved that one."

"Yeah, it was pretty good," Clare conceded. "But do you ever find those parenting books sort of depressing?"

"How so?"

"They go on and on about how important it is to always be calm and positive and consistent. But honestly, who can be like that all the time? It's like they're setting you up to fail. Or, if you do succeed, it's because you've become some serene, smiling zombie. It doesn't seem possible, or particularly wise, to erase who you actually are, and how you actually feel, and put on this ridiculous mother mask that's just like everyone else's."

Mina cocked her head. "Mother mask?"

"That calm, cheerful facade you're supposed to wear all the time, to hide whatever else you might be feeling: boredom, irritation, rage, anxiety, any immoderate emotion of any kind. Maybe some vestige of past desires, misgivings, regrets . . ."

Mina looked taken aback. "I've never regretted having Lisbet."

"I've never regretted having Sadie either. I adore her—more than I ever thought possible. It's *me*. I've turned into this person I don't even recognize. I mean, a grown woman can only say 'whoopsie-daisies' so many times before she becomes a stranger to herself, you know?"

Mina just looked her. She did not know, it seemed. Clare told herself to stop talking, but instead she just forged on ahead. "And you know how the books are all so obsessed with routine? Rigid nap time, bedtime, mealtime. *Structure.*"

Mina nodded slowly.

"Then we're beholden to that schedule, too, which makes every day just more of the same. Day in, day out, nothing new. We're deliberately shielding our children *and* ourselves from the unknown. Sometimes it feels like we're just counting out the days until we die—a life measured out in goldfish snack packs."

Mina studied her for a moment. "Are you okay, Clare?"

Clare took a breath and laughed a little.

"I'm just tired. I haven't been sleeping that well."

"You should. It's life-changing."

"So I hear."

There was a moment of awkward silence, but Mina broke it almost immediately: "What's that lip color you're wearing? *So* chic."

## CHAPTER 4

AS CLARE LEFT THE COFFEE shop, the day took a turn: Tasha Wolfe called.

"Where are you?" she demanded.

"Eighty-Ninth and Fifth, why?"

"Stay there. I'll pick you up in five minutes."

"For what?" Clare asked, but Tasha had already hung up.

At another time in her life, she might have been put out by Tasha's presumptuousness, but now she welcomed the distraction. All she'd do at home was stare blankly at her dissertation without writing a word before finally giving up to fold laundry. She leaned against the side of the building to wait, turning up the collar of her trench coat to block the breeze.

Ten minutes later, Tasha's chauffeured Mercedes pulled up to the curb, and the driver scurried out to open the door for Clare. She slid into the backseat next to Tasha, who was wearing four-inch Louboutin heels and a black leather skirt. Clare had never seen Tasha in jeans or sneakers. In the Hamptons, she'd once caught sight of Tasha in leggings on the way to work out, and it had been as discomfiting as seeing one's teacher in a negligee.

"Am I being kidnapped?" Clare asked.

"You're accompanying me to the Eduardo Salas show at Gabriel Prévost's gallery."

"What? I can't. I have to pick up Sadie at twelve-thirty."

"I'll get you back by then."

"Tasha, I really can't."

"Clare, you really can. It'll do you good to get your head back in the game. Go see some art at least—and while you're at it, spend time with someone who can be helpful to your career."

"You gave up your career, and you seem happy."

"I'm better at leisure than you are," Tasha said matter-of-factly.

"Great, I can't even hack it as a lady of leisure." Clare laughed. "My mother would be so proud."

She was joking, but she did often wonder what her mother would think of the life she was leading. Nessa had worked right up until the day she died. She was always telling Clare how important it was for a woman to be able to take care of herself. Clare got her first babysitting job when she was twelve and waitressed all through high school and college. Now she found herself living on Park Avenue, unemployed and supported entirely by her husband. It sometimes gave her an odd sense of vertigo, though not necessarily in a bad way. She'd certainly achieved her goal of escaping Binghamton.

TEN MINUTES LATER, they pulled up outside the Prévost-Kline gallery on West Twenty-Sixth Street. The building looked like a modern fortress, angular and intimidating. A plate-glass window was tucked into the intersecting concrete planes, through which a yellowish light glowed. White letters on the glass announced the current show: BRAVE NEW WORLD | EDUARDO SALAS.

"How long have you known Gabriel?" Clare asked as they climbed out of the car.

"A few years. We were introduced at some MoCA thing, and Alec took a shine to him. He knows his stuff, and he's not as precious or humorless as some of the other dealers we've worked with."

Clare had been to the gallery once or twice, but she'd learned its backstory only the day before, when she'd called an old friend from Columbia to ask. According to Lev, who knew everyone in the art world, Gabriel had started it with his partner, Michael Kline, in the late nineties. Back then, the gallery had been one room on Broome Street, no staff, and a roster of artists no one had ever heard of. They grew slowly—taking on a few estates and inching into the secondary market to make ends meet—until they finally had their big break three or four years in: Rand Ashland, a young painter from South Carolina whose fun-house-mirror portraiture started earning Prévost-Kline six-figure commissions. Soon after that, they followed the exodus from Soho to Chelsea, where their streak of talent-spotting continued with Tony Fang and Kingston Wells.

Gabriel and Michael gained a reputation for their over-the-top opening-night parties. They had once filled the gallery with a two-foot-deep layer of rustling autumn leaves; another time, at an opening for an overlooked member of the Light and Space movement, guests had sipped drinks and conversed in pitch darkness until late in the evening, when all the works lit up in unison. Gabriel and Michael understood the power of spectacle, and they knew how to leverage what were clearly vast stores of personal charm to build relationships with deep-pocketed collectors. Gabriel mostly handled the Europeans while Michael took on the West Coast clientele. They split the New Yorkers. Prévost-Kline didn't occupy the rarified air that the big global galleries did, but they'd been more successful than most of their early SoHo brethren.

Clare pulled open the heavy wooden door and held it for Tasha. Following her in, Clare found herself enveloped in a warm, bright space. The building's harsh exterior felt protective once you were inside.

A beautiful twentysomething woman in seventies-style eyeglasses looked up from behind a glass desk.

"Morning," she said. "Let me know if I can help."

"We're here to see Gabriel," Tasha announced. "Tasha Wolfe and Clare Bast."

Clare suddenly felt self-conscious. She edged toward the perimeter of the room, studying the walls. The paintings depicted smudged, not-quite-real landscapes. There was something dreamlike about them. The painter was Chilean and had been showing for years, but she'd only heard about him the year before when a work of his had sold for four times the estimate at a Phillips contemporary auction.

Clare liked the pieces, but she was having trouble focusing on them. She kept glancing at the double doors at the back of the room and then forcing herself to look away. She didn't want Gabriel to find her craning for a glimpse of him. Then it suddenly occurred to her that he might have no idea who she was. The name Clare Bast could mean nothing to him. Their conversation had lasted all of ten minutes.

The front door heaved open again, and two other women entered, chatting cheerfully. Clare listened in on their conversation, which fluttered lightly between the paintings and their shared disdain for a mutual coworker who ate hot stew at her desk every day.

After another minute, Gabriel entered from the back of the room, apologizing for the delay. He was wearing dark jeans, a white button-down, and a smile that seemed to be hiding a secret. At the sight of him, something in Clare shifted. She had a physical response to his presence; it was as simple as that, almost as if *he* were a Brancusi or a van Eyck.

"Tasha," he said, going to her first and kissing her on the cheek. "I'm so glad you could make it." He turned to Clare. "And Clare—you found your momentum."

"Tasha lent me some of hers," she said, inordinately pleased that he remembered the details of their conversation. She gestured around the room. "The paintings are beautiful."

Gabriel looked at her silently for a moment. "But?"

"No 'but.'"

Gabriel kept looking at her with a wry smile. After a moment, Clare continued, "Well, if I had to say something, I might say they were a bit derivative of Peter Doig."

Gabriel laughed. "Well, if I didn't represent him, I might agree with you." He stepped closer to her and brushed his cheek against hers. "Lovely to see you again," he said in a quieter voice. Clare stepped back and turned away to hide the color rising in her cheeks.

Gabriel showed them around the exhibition and told them a bit about the artist, who was still only twenty-six. "It'll be interesting to see where he goes next. He's still finding his own style. He's done a few paintings recently that are quite a departure from this work."

"Can we see them?" Tasha asked.

"They're not here. They're still in Santiago. I went down there a month or two ago."

"Well, if they're any good, I expect you to give me first refusal."

"Tasha, you know you're at the top of my list."

"I better be."

Tasha's phone rang loudly in her purse, and she pulled it out to answer it. "Hi, honey, what's up?"

Clare and Gabriel turned away to allow her some privacy, but she didn't seem to need or want it, because she continued her conversation at top volume.

"Remind me where you work?" Gabriel asked Clare.

"Oh, I don't," Clare said with an awkward laugh.

"Really? You sound very much like someone in the business."

"You mean opinionated?"

"Well, yes, but they're interesting opinions, which isn't always the case."

"I guess you can credit that to half a doctorate in art history."

"Half?"

"I never finished my dissertation." Clare had never stated that fact so baldly in the past tense. She usually took refuge in gerunds: She was working on it or she was taking a break from it for a little while.

"Why not?"

"I don't know. A few different reasons, I suppose. I lost faith in academic criticism. I lost faith in myself. I had a child. It was no longer imperative for me to earn a living." She shrugged, mildly surprised by her own frankness. For some reason it seemed pointless or unnecessary to dissemble with him.

"Well, all the better: Now you get to simply enjoy the work unfettered by academic or professional preoccupations."

"It would be nice if it worked like that. But no, I find myself estranged from it more than ever."

"That's terrible."

He looked genuinely aggrieved, and she laughed a little at the intensity of his reaction.

"It's not so bad, in the grand scheme of things."

"But who lives in the grand scheme of things? We each live in our own lives."

Tasha sighed loudly and dramatically. Clare and Gabriel turned back to her.

"Is everything okay?" Clare asked.

"It's Nina. She's having an absolute fit over her Yale application. I have to go back uptown before she chucks it out the window and follows through on her threat to apply early to Bard. I'm so sorry."

"Don't be sorry," Clare said. "It's no problem. Let's head back."

"Clare, don't be ridiculous—we just got here. Stay. I'll send the car back for you."

"No, no, that's such an imposition. I'll go with you."

"That's absurd. If you're worried about the car, then I'll keep it. But *stay*."

Tasha blew them both a kiss and bustled out of the gallery before Clare could continue the argument.

One of the women behind Clare laughed loudly at something the other one had said. "Stop!" she cried, squeezing her friend's arm. "Stop it right now!"

"So what was your dissertation about?" Gabriel asked.

"Blake Webley."

He looked at her oddly.

"Is that surprising?" she asked.

His frown abruptly smoothed out. "No, not at all. I'm sorry, continue."

"I first got interested in Webley because we grew up in the same place," Clare said. "He left Binghamton for Manhattan when he was sixteen, to try to make it as a poet. He fell in with Frank O'Hara, who introduced him to the de Koonings, and that's when Webley started painting. He never really fit in with the Abstract Expressionists—their drunken escapades sort of terrified him—and he eventually joined a quieter bunch down at Coenties Slip: artists like Agnes Martin, Ellsworth Kelly, and Robert Indiana. I'm sure you know all this. Stop me if I'm boring you."

"Not at all. Go on."

"So Webley is usually classified as an Abstract Expressionist, but I put forth the argument that he was the one who really kicked off the Minimalist movement, even though guys like Frank Stella and Donald Judd get most of the credit. Do you know that it was Webley who first got Agnes Martin interested in the grid?"

"I didn't know that. That's interesting. It's too bad you never finished."

"Maybe not. You know, I think I sort of ended up drinking the Kool-

Aid. Webley was a really interesting guy—very well read, very cerebral. He said he only fell into painting because no one would publish his poems. But at the same time, he hated any high-minded attempts to intellectualize the visual arts. He thought the work should speak for itself. Just look at it. That's all you can do. You can't pin down a feeling that's ineffable, whose whole point is its ineffability. He wouldn't let museums or galleries put up any explanatory text on the walls. And then there I was, with my grad school reading list, citing Walter Benjamin, trying to explain what made his work so powerful, but in the end, I discovered that Webley was right. There's no point trying to dissect the experience of standing in front of a work of art. It can't be examined or interpolated or explained. It can only be experienced.

"And actually, that's what I love about art: the mystery of it. No one—in the thousands of years that it's existed—has ever given a satisfactory explanation of what it actually *does*. Why does it affect us? How does it affect us? Why do certain works of art affect some people and not others? Millions upon millions of words have been written about art—I've read a lot of them—and not a single sentence has come close to capturing that visceral response I have when I actually look at a painting by someone like Blake Webley. It's like attraction. It's not logical. It's chemical."

Gabriel studied her with a quizzical look on his face.

"I'm sorry," Clare said, flushing. "I'm rambling. It's been a long time since I've talked about any of this."

"Please don't apologize. I was just wondering whether you'd like to get a coffee with me. I have some time before my next meeting."

"Oh." She checked her watch. She still had more than an hour before she had to pick up Sadie. "Sure, that sounds nice."

Gabriel excused himself for a moment, then reappeared with an umbrella and a navy jacket. They walked out into the gray morning and a light drizzle. Clare buttoned up her coat.

"This is Paris weather," Gabriel said, turning up his collar.

"Is that where you're from?"

"I'm from the South. Toulouse. But I went to university in Paris, and I worked there for several years before moving here."

"What prompted the move?"

"It's a cliché, but there really is an energy here that you can't find anywhere else. You know one of the first things I noticed? When New Yorkers wait for the subway, they lean over and peer down the track to spot the train coming. In Paris, everyone just stares ahead, waiting patiently. That's when I knew that I was a New Yorker at heart. I'm always peering down the tracks, searching for what's coming, what's next."

"Well, I guess you've succeeded with that. Didn't you discover Rand Ashland and Tony Fang?"

"We did, yes. In the first decade, I really did feel like we were introducing important art and artists into the conversation. I'm proud of that. But over the years, we moved more and more into the secondary market. It makes more sense from a financial perspective. I still have a few artists I manage, but I've lost some of that sense that I'm helping steer anyone's career. I think it's natural, as you get older, that you want more security. You make certain compromises."

"Yes, I suppose, though security is also static. There's something, I don't know, energizing in the striving, the expectation, the uncertainty." Clare suddenly regretted her choice of words. "That sounded callous; I realize that poverty is not invigorating for anyone. That's not what I meant."

"I know what you meant. We all spend so much time trying to get to the place where the uncertainty and anxiety will end and then, when you get there, you find that living without uncertainty or anxiety is a kind of living death. Or, more likely, you find you still have it, but it's about things that are harder to fix."

They reached the coffee shop, and Gabriel held the door open for her. She stepped into a small, intimate space with windows fogged over from the humidity. They ordered their drinks—a double espresso for him, a cappuccino for her—and settled at a small, marble-topped table in the back corner.

"So why were you so taken aback when I mentioned Webley?" Clare asked, untucking her long hair from her scarf.

"It seemed like an odd coincidence, that's all. I actually have a small Webley painting in my possession right now."

Clare was surprised. Most were in museums. The others went for several million dollars. "Which one?"

"*Longfin*. From 1958."

"That can't be right. *Longfin* is at MoCA."

Gabriel smiled and raised his eyebrows. "Is it?"

"I saw it there earlier this year."

He didn't reply; he just kept looking at her with an amused expression.

"MoCA wouldn't sell it, would they?"

He tipped his head slightly.

"They deaccessioned a Blake Webley?"

Deaccessioning—a museum selling works from its collection—was a controversial practice. Invariably critics accused the institution of raiding its coffers for shortsighted profit. The works involved had often been donated by people who thought they were doing a public service—democratizing access to great art—and it wasn't a good look to put the work back into private hands to raise some extra cash.

The practice had become more widespread during the pandemic, when museums were struggling to stay afloat and the national governing body of museums had loosened the rules around what they could do with that money. Deaccessioning was usually done publicly, through the big auction houses, but Clare hadn't heard of any Webley coming to market, let alone *Longfin*. She mentioned this to Gabriel.

"It was a private sale, done quickly and quietly. I was given the impression that I should not share the details of it too widely."

"And how's that going?"

"Until this morning, it was going just fine. You're not going to call up the *Post*, are you?"

She smiled. "Did you buy it for yourself?"

"That would be nice, but no. For a client."

"The Wolfes?"

"Of course not. Tasha's on the MoCA board. There are rules about that."

Clare shook her head. "I can't believe they sold *Longfin*. What a shame."

"Do you think so? I don't agree. MoCA needs to diversify its holdings. They need more work by people of color and women and contemporary artists. It has to be a living, breathing institution, not a monument to the heyday of Abstract Expressionism or, if you prefer, Minimalism, which it's threatening to become. They still own several other Webleys."

"I'm with you on all of that. It just breaks my heart that only a handful of people will ever see that painting again. It will wind up on some billionaire's yacht, or worse, sequestered in some free port." Free ports were large, secure storage spaces that existed outside all tax jurisdictions, like boats in international waters. Wealthy people used them to avoid paying taxes, which, on something like a Webley, could run into the hundreds of thousands of dollars. At any moment in time, countless works of art were locked up in free ports, where nobody could see them.

The coffee shop had grown more crowded. They had begun to lean in toward each other to make themselves heard. When Clare took another sip of her coffee, she found it had grown cold.

"Would you like to see it?" Gabriel asked.

"*Longfin*?"

He nodded.

"It's at the gallery?"

"At my house. It's close by."

His face maintained an open, neutral expression, and Clare wasn't sure what exactly was happening—was there another question lurking behind the one he'd asked out loud?

"I'm sorry," she said. "I can't. I have to get back uptown."

Gabriel smiled sadly.

"Another time perhaps."

"Maybe," Clare said noncommittally, standing up to gather her belongings.

OUTSIDE, THE RAIN was coming down harder, and Gabriel insisted she take his umbrella.

"Are you sure?" she asked. "You'll get soaked."

"There are worse fates," he replied with a small, droll smile.

Clare thanked him and abruptly turned to go. She suddenly found it necessary to put some distance between herself and Gabriel. She worried about what would happen if she didn't. But when she reached the corner, she couldn't help but look back. He was still standing in the same spot, rain pouring down his face, watching her. She quickly turned away and stepped into the street, prompting an oncoming truck to blare its horn and veer violently around her.

Unnerved, Clare hailed a passing taxi instead of walking to the subway as planned. She felt a strong desire to sweep up her daughter in her arms and take her straight home to safety.

## CHAPTER 5

"SWEETHEART, CAN YOU BRING ME the ladle, please?" Clare asked Sadie.

It was the next morning, and they were making pancakes yet again. Repetition, however, seemed to have drained the project of some of the joy that had infused it the day before. Worst of all, Clare had forgotten to wash the dirty aprons—an unforgivable sin, according to her daughter.

Sadie opened the utensil drawer and held up a spatula. She looked at Clare questioningly.

"That's a spatula. The ladle, please. The big spoon."

According to the top-selling parenting book on Amazon, written by an early-childhood-development specialist and "mama of three," small jobs gave kids self-confidence.

Sadie held up the measuring spoons and jingled them lightly on the rusted ring that bound them together.

"Bigger. The really big spoon."

Clare looked into the drawer. The ladle was sitting right on top, but she bit her tongue. She didn't want to accidentally rob Sadie of self-esteem for the rest of her life.

Sadie continued staring into the drawer until Jed swept in and picked up the ladle. "Here you go, m'lady," he said, presenting it to Clare on one knee like an engagement ring.

Sadie, unsurprisingly, began to wail with unrestrained fury. Jed looked baffled, unaware of his transgression. While he tried to appease her with a variety of other large utensils, Clare turned around and started spooning batter onto the hot pan, eliciting a satisfying sizzle. She felt Jed's eyes seeking hers out, pleading for assistance. Instead, she watched the pancakes bubble and flipped them methodically one by one. As she reached for a plate to pile them on, she could think of only one thing: She still had Gabriel's umbrella.

TWO HOURS LATER, she was standing on the sidewalk outside the Prévost-Kline gallery, her fingers resting lightly on the door handle. She hesitated before pulling it open.

What was she doing?

Was this a terrible idea?

She hardly knew how she'd gotten there. It seemed like she'd dropped Sadie at school a minute ago and then materialized in Chelsea. She was simply returning Gabriel's umbrella, she reminded herself. That was all.

She pulled open the door and stepped inside.

"Morning," the woman at the front desk said in the same distracted tone as yesterday. She showed no hint of recognition.

"Morning," Clare replied, beginning a slow circuit around the room. She'd do a lap and then leave the umbrella with the receptionist. She leaned in to examine the paintings she'd seen just the day before, perceiving a different, more sinister quality to them this time.

Suddenly, Gabriel's voice echoed around the small room: "Back for more?"

Clare spun around. She hadn't heard him come in.

"I couldn't get them out of my mind," she said.

"I have the same problem."

"And I brought your umbrella back," she blurted out, holding it up as evidence.

"Thank you. I didn't expect you to do that. Though I'll admit I'm happy to see you again."

She felt herself grow warm and took a small step backward. "I thought of another dot painting I'd take over a Hirst, by the way. *Dot (#4)* by your man Ruscha."

Gabriel nodded appreciatively. "That's a good one. I thought you might say a Lichtenstein."

Clare shrugged a shoulder. "Sure, I'd take one of those, too."

She heard herself keep talking, almost as if she were overhearing a stranger: "To be honest," she said, "I couldn't get *Longfin* out of my mind either. It occurred to me that I'd be a fool to turn down the chance to see it one last time, if it's going to disappear into private hands any day now.

"I'd love to show it to you."

"Is now a bad time?"

"Not at all. Let me just tell my assistant."

He disappeared into the back room, leaving Clare alone in the gallery. For once, her mind offered up no thoughts or worries. The silence was a supreme relief. It was all background, no foreground.

Gabriel emerged a few moments later in the same peacoat he'd had on the day before.

They walked mostly in silence. The clouds were low and gray, threatening more rain. Clare felt pulled along by an unseen force, as if the future were already waiting for her, as unchangeable as the past. But what *was* the future awaiting her at his house? She didn't know what understanding, if any, existed between them. They'd made no agreements, no commitments. The attraction between them felt as physical and tangible as a table or a chair to her, but she had no evidence that it was even perceptible to him.

She glanced over at him. He moved his body with that casual nonchalance she remembered from the Wolfes' party. He seemed so relaxed that suddenly she felt embarrassed for imagining there might be something else going on. Of course he didn't want to sleep with her. It would take a radical kind of creativity to reenvision a body that had spent the morning tying ribbons around pigtails as something sexual. Even Jed didn't see her that way anymore. It would almost be a type of perversion.

But then Clare thought about Caravaggio's Madonnas. Before him, painters had always depicted Mary as generically maternal and ethereal. But Caravaggio painted her as a specific, sensual, bodily woman. The model for at least one version was supposedly his mistress, Lena, a courtesan. He took the ultimate emblem of maternal love and turned her into a real woman with a real body and real desires. It was possible. Never mind that Caravaggio was a violent man who was ultimately convicted of murder.

Besides, did Gabriel even know she was a mother? She couldn't remember whether she'd mentioned it or not. It shocked her to realize that, in their two charged interactions, the fact of Sadie's existence had been entirely peripheral.

They turned onto West Twentieth Street, a long, quiet row of town houses. When they got a quarter way down the block, he put his hand lightly on her back to turn her toward a glossy black door.

She hadn't expected him to live in a brownstone. She thought only families lived in houses, and she knew from googling that he didn't have a family. He was divorced from a Brazilian artist known for her video installations. No children. She wondered if he'd googled her. He wouldn't have found much of interest. A few pictures with Jed from the society pages. An out-of-date bio on the Columbia website.

As he punched in the code to unlock the door, Clare felt a brief stab of panic. What if there was no Webley? What woman goes willingly into the home of a man she hardly knows, without anyone knowing where she is? But she didn't turn around. She followed him in, as if she were under a spell.

The house was beautiful. Many of the historical details—the wide crown molding, the old plank floors—had been preserved, but everything else was modern. The entire rear wall had been ripped out and replaced with windows. Through them, Clare could see an outdoor garden with a stone fountain at the center. As she looked, the rain started up again.

His living room was large and furnished in muted tones. Between the entrance and the sitting area was a long wooden dining table that looked like it could seat eighteen. And there was art everywhere. Sculpture, paintings, even a small light installation in one corner. She looked at it all in wonder as Gabriel took the coat from her shoulders and hung it in the hall closet.

"Your house is beautiful."

"Thank you. The architect is an old friend of mine."

She spotted *Longfin* on the wall near the back windows and walked toward it.

"I thought it might be in a safe."

"I only have it for a short while; I want to enjoy it."

She stepped closer. The painting was small and square—two feet by two feet. Webley had first built up a whitish impasto, then drawn in a grid of red lines with small incisions, like a jailhouse tattoo. The lines weren't perfect; they wavered and wobbled. There was life to them.

It was different seeing it here. There were no crowds, no bright lights and sharp sounds ricocheting around the large rooms, as there were at MoCA. There weren't hundreds of other works pulling on her attention. It was just her and the painting. She even lost awareness of Gabriel standing behind her.

Without realizing what she was doing, she reached out a hand toward the painting. She stopped within an inch of the surface, her fingers trembling in the air.

"Go ahead," he said quietly from behind.

"Are you sure?" she asked, but already her fingertips were skimming the surface.

The texture was rough and almost sandy. She drew back quickly, charged by her transgression. As an art historian, she was supposed to guard against such infractions; the oils in skin can discolor or degrade a painting. They had studied cases where a single dark fingerprint had showed up years after the offending finger actually touched the paint: The damage bided its time.

"It's got this incredible energy to it," she said, "almost as if it were alive."

"John Ashbery once called Webley's work 'indescribably brutal,'" Gabriel said. "I love that phrase."

Ashbery had actually called it "*exquisitely* brutal," but Clare didn't feel the need to correct him.

"Can't you tell me who the buyer is?" she asked, turning back to Gabriel. Now that she'd seen it up close, she was already calculating, like an addict, how to see it again.

He smiled and shook his head.

"How much longer do you have it?"

"A couple more months."

"Isn't that sort of unorthodox—for you to hold on to a painting for so long before passing it on to the owner?"

"In the art world, nothing is unorthodox. But in this case, it's for a very boring reason. My client wanted to make the purchase next year, for tax reasons, but he would have lost it if we'd waited. He arrived at this solution, and I agreed because this is a client I very much want to keep. Besides, who turns down the chance to own a Webley, even if only for a couple of months?"

She faced the painting again.

"Since you're the expert," Gabriel said, taking a step closer, "maybe you can tell me what the story with the title is. I've never gotten a good explanation for it."

"Webley never explained his titles. It's some type of fish I think. Many of the artists who moved down to Coenties Slip in the fifties were inspired by its history as a landing spot for wooden sailing ships in the late nineteenth century. You can find a lot of nautical imagery—boats, sails, rigging, fish—in their works."

"It doesn't look like a fish to me."

"By this point he'd stopped being representational."

Gabriel stepped forward and stood next to her. She could tell he wasn't looking at the painting; he was looking at her. She kept her eyes on the wall, but every inch of her thrummed with the consciousness of his body next to hers.

Finally, she turned toward him and met his gaze. Neither of them changed their expression. There was no more talk of art, no more polite smiles. They stood looking at each other in silence. They were both aware that they had already crossed a threshold. Then he brought his hand up slowly and placed it on her chest.

"Your heart is beating very fast."

She nodded.

He moved his hand slowly around her body, toward the small of her back, keeping his eyes locked on hers, studying her for some sign of hesitation. He found none. He pulled her toward him, and he kissed her.

She didn't resist. Not even a little. She opened herself to him entirely. Her whole body felt charged with some foreign force; it wasn't so different from how she'd felt when she touched the surface of *Longfin*:

possessed. Every one of her molecules buzzed with life. She pressed herself into him. She wanted to feel the weight and solidity of his body against every part of hers. They stumbled a little, and she put a hand against the wall to brace herself.

"Come upstairs with me," he murmured into her neck.

"No," she said. He took a step backward, but he'd misunderstood. She didn't want to go so far because she knew she'd lose her nerve on the way.

"Here," she said, nodding at the couch.

He pulled her on top of him so she was straddling him, facing the painting. They sat there for half a moment and looked at each other. She should have been shocked at what was happening. She should have stopped it. She should have stood up and walked away. But she didn't. It all felt so natural, almost preordained. Something had started, and she was going to see it through. There was no getting off the train.

She leaned forward to kiss him again, and he pulled off her shirt. He unclipped her bra and held her breasts in his hands reverently. He leaned forward to put one in his mouth.

The desire rising up in Clare felt overpowering. She was overtaken by a yearning for recklessness and abandon. She was sick of being careful. She was sick of being good. She was sick of locking herself up in a tidy little container. In that moment she would have done anything he'd asked of her.

They stopped to take off the rest of their clothes. Gabriel's body was brown and lean, and when he pulled her toward him, his skin seemed to have been permanently warmed by the sun. He pulled her on top of him again and entered her. She gasped hoarsely. She felt, ridiculously, as if she might start to cry. Her body was humming with pleasure, yet it kept demanding more and more and more of it. She felt almost frantically ravenous. She was gasping for air, like she was drowning. She couldn't get enough of this, of him.

Gabriel put his hand on her hips to slow her down, but she couldn't. Something was building inside of her, pulling her forward. It was too strong. There was nothing she could do. Gabriel closed his eyes and dropped his head on the back of the couch, breathing heavily. His fingers dug into her skin.

When it was over, she collapsed onto his chest. She could feel his heart pounding violently against hers. He ran his hands up and down her back slowly, releasing small, shivering aftershocks of pleasure. She turned her head and watched the rain stream down the window. She didn't regret a thing.

Not yet.

## CHAPTER 6

IT WAS STILL RAINING WHEN Clare hurried out of Gabriel's house two hours later. She walked over to Tenth Avenue to hail a yellow cab going uptown. She didn't want Gabriel's address in her Uber history.

It was nearly one in the afternoon. She'd called Mina before she and Gabriel had started up for the second time to ask her to bring Sadie home from school with her. They had done this a few times before, when one or the other of them had gotten caught up with something. Clare suspected Mina had never been unable to pick up Lisbet because she was fucking an art dealer in Chelsea, but you never know.

The air in the taxi was warm and fetid. Four battered Black Ice air fresheners dangled from the rearview mirror and smelled worse than any odor the driver could possibly be covering up. Clare cracked the window and watched the blurred city stream past until, as they passed Forty-Second Street, she felt the guilt slam into her with annihilating force. She thought for a moment she might throw up. She loosened the scarf around her neck and took several deep breaths.

What had she done?

She knew some people probably thought she'd married Jed for his money, but she hadn't. She'd loved him. She loved him still.

They had met when she was twenty-four, and she'd had no inkling, on their first date, of how radically the evening would change her life. It was raining then, too. They'd been set up by one of her coworkers at the Met, who was dating Jed's college roommate. He'd strolled into Bemelmans Bar at the Carlyle Hotel wearing a green Barbour jacket over his suit and tapping a long, steel-tipped umbrella on the ground. She couldn't get over the elegance of that umbrella, with its curved wooden handle polished to a sheen. Her own was a cheap black fold-up she'd bought in the subway station that morning. She'd woken up hungover and missing her credit card after a night out at Brooklyn Steel; someone had offered her a free ticket to the Neko Case concert there, and she'd had a policy then of always saying yes to new experiences. Sitting at Bemelmans Bar the next evening with Jed—another consequence of saying yes—his manifest *adulthood* had struck her as an interesting novelty in itself.

Jed was a decade older than she was, but with his round face, ruddy cheeks, and mop of boyish blond curls, he looked younger. He was an associate at Fisk & Baum, the firm where his father was managing partner. He told her that he'd wanted to go into legal aid after law school, but his parents had insisted that he follow in the family footsteps. It turned out to be the right decision, he claimed: He made enough money to be able to support a family one day, and he still did a lot of pro bono work at the firm.

Clare knew from her work in the development office that Dorothy and Abe Bast had given consistent sums to the Met for years, but she didn't realize quite how wealthy the family was until a couple of dates in, when he confessed that most of their money had come from his mother's side; Dorothy's grandfather had started a successful brokerage firm. Clare didn't think Jed's wealth mattered to her at the time, but she later realized that many of the qualities she found attractive in him—his confidence, his optimism, his comfort and ease at navigating the world—stemmed directly from his privileged upbringing.

Perhaps she should have been intimidated by his background, but he made her feel like *she* was the special one. He'd often look at her with wonder in his eyes and say, "I've never met anyone like you before."

"You mean someone who went to state school?" she once joked.

"No," he insisted. "Beautiful and elegant and cultured, but without any of the arrogance or entitlement that usually go along with that. You really have no idea how spectacular you are."

Clare started to like the version of herself that she saw through his eyes. She had never been an object of devotion before. Her other boyfriends had not treated her like this, nor had her childhood prepared her for Jed's onslaught of affection. She knew her mother loved her, but all evidence of it had been doled out frugally. Nessa Regan was not a warm or effusive woman. She was sensible and stoic. She drove below the speed limit. She reused tea bags. She never set the thermostat above sixty-six degrees. And whenever Clare broke the house's habitual silence, Nessa always looked startled, as if she'd forgotten she had a child.

Clare's parents had divorced when she was six, and her father had retreated from them like someone trying to back slowly out of a room without anyone noticing. He was remarried with two young sons by the time Clare was ten. She occasionally spent weekends with them growing up but barely saw them after college. As adults, they were locked in an uncomfortable pattern of overformality: stilted phone calls on birthdays; talking over each other, unable to find comfortable footing. "I'm sorry, you go." "No, you were saying?" "Nothing. It doesn't matter."

So when Jed showed up, bubbling over with affection, she received it with amazed gratitude.

"You're the best thing that ever happened to me," he told her over and over.

They started dating in late 2019. Three months later, the pandemic hit, and Jed suggested that Clare come stay with him at his apartment in the East Seventies. She readily agreed: It had seemed like a safe harbor in the storm. She'd been ridiculously happy—guiltily so—during those months of isolation. They used to put on Sam Cooke and waltz around the living room. Jed loved to show off the dips and spins he'd learned at Knickerbocker dancing school as a kid. He'd come home from CVS or the grocery store—the only places that were open—with silly gifts for her: a ring pop once, a box of peroxide-blond hair dye another time. (She took the ring, but refused the dye.) They took bubble baths together and played endless rounds of gin rummy. She bought her first cookbook and made elaborate, usually disastrous, meals for him. Jed sang goofy off-the-cuff songs for her: "Clare, with the hair beyond compare. How I love to stare at your derriere." She loved his sweetness and earnestness. He wasn't trying to be cool. He wasn't trying to be anyone other than himself.

Since Jed was worried about his parents' susceptibility to Covid, Clare didn't meet them until almost nine months into their relationship.

During their first, awkward dinner together, she got the distinct impression that Dorothy did not think she was good enough for her son. She asked—twice—when Clare's "people" had come over from Ireland and expressed dismay—"Oh dear, what a shame"—that she didn't play tennis. (Jed's introduction to her own mother went better, but when Clare asked for her opinion, Nessa said only, "If you love him, it shouldn't matter what I think.")

Over the following months and then years, Clare had tried hard to win Dorothy over. She invited her to private viewings at the Met. She washed all the dishes when they stayed at the East Hampton house. She let Dorothy curate their entire wedding registry and decorate their apartment. She started using "summer" and "lunch" as verbs. She even took tennis lessons.

Nothing seemed to work. Dorothy's snide comments—always delivered with an unnerving smile—continued. Worse, Clare realized that Jed almost always took his mother's side. The kind and chivalrous man Clare remembered from their months of pandemic lockdown now seemed almost childlike, overly eager to conform to his family's expectations, with the assumption that she, too, would fall in line. Was that why he'd chosen someone so much younger—because he thought she'd be pliable? She tried to explain her concerns to Jed, but he always assured her that he loved her for *her.*

Jed's friends did little to dispel the feeling that she was a bumbling expat in a foreign country. They were never outright rude, but they showed little interest in getting to know her. Their conversations revolved around acquaintances she hadn't met or memories she wasn't a part of. They all seemed to know the same people from the same handful of elite colleges and prep schools or from summers on Long Island. She figured that with time, she'd start to belong to some of the memories, but their conversations oddly remained stalled in the past—the apparently golden years of their teens and twenties. As an outsider, she had nothing to bring to the table.

Her own friends were more welcoming toward Jed—and clearly thrilled that she'd found someone who treated her so well—but it was obvious that he did not really fit into their scene. The dinners Clare arranged always felt forced and awkward. If he'd come straight from the office, Jed would be the only one in a suit and tie, and his stories about disastrous depositions or last-minute settlements always fell flat. A sense of disappointment would often pervade the taxi on the way home, but by the time they were curled up in bed together, Clare would feel only gratitude. He was her refuge. Soon she got into the habit of seeing her friends on her own.

IT WAS JED who'd encouraged Clare to apply to graduate programs. She used to complain regularly to him about how impossible it was to shift to another department at the Met. And she couldn't get a curatorial job anywhere without a PhD.

"So go get a PhD," he said with a shrug, as if he were suggesting she go pick up a ham sandwich.

The thought had occurred to her before, but she'd never seriously considered it. The application process was too onerous, the program too long, the requisite debt too daunting. The schools didn't charge tuition, but the stipend they offered was hardly enough to live on. And, in truth, the job prospects afterward were still pretty dismal.

But Jed's optimism—and, after he proposed, the tantalizing promise of financial security—wore away at her, and she sent out applications while wedding planning. She was shocked when she got into Columbia. She had only half committed to the idea of going back to school when the acceptance arrived, but who turns down an Ivy League education?

They ended up getting into their first big fight right after she started the program, when Jed suggested that Clare write a thank-you note to his mother. He explained that Dorothy had asked an old friend on the board to put in a good word with the admissions committee.

Clare was aghast. "You didn't tell me she was doing that."

"I didn't want you to get your hopes up in case it didn't work out."

Clare felt humiliated; she thought she'd been accepted on her own merits. She told Jed that she wished Dorothy hadn't meddled. She didn't want special favors; now she'd always have a lingering doubt about whether she actually deserved to be there. Jed accused her of being ungrateful. After a twenty-four-hour standoff, Clare had capitulated and written the note.

They got married in East Hampton and moved to a beautiful three-bedroom apartment on Park Avenue. Jed started pushing for a baby almost immediately. Most of his friends—along with his younger sister—already had children. Clare admitted that she hadn't even decided whether she wanted them at all. The question had always seemed abstract to her—practically hypothetical; she'd thought she had years to decide. Jed, however, was persistent.

"You'll love being a mother," he assured her.

"But there's no going back if you're wrong," she'd pointed out.

Ultimately, she'd agreed to leave the decision up to fate and found out she was pregnant a month after going off birth control.

Jed, it turned out, had been right. From the moment Sadie was born, Clare had been shocked at the annihilating force of love she felt for this tiny, four-pound creature. Her body had never processed so much emotion before. At times she felt nauseated and off balance from it, like someone who'd been rescued half starved from a desert island and immediately fed a twelve-course tasting menu. Wasn't there supposed to be an acclimation regimen of nutritious gruel first?

Clare sat with her in the NICU day after day, her hands resting inside the incubator so her daughter would know she was there.

"Don't worry, Mama's here," she'd whisper over and over, slowly getting used to the sound of that word in her mouth. Eventually, she was allowed to hold Sadie outside the incubator, but there were so many wires attached to her that it felt like she was being handed an undefused bomb. Her child's stark, terrifying vulnerability churned up a surge of newfound protectiveness in Clare. When a doctor ripped off a piece of medical tape on her too roughly, Clare wanted to gouge his eyes out.

During those weeks in the NICU, Clare felt every past ambition for her life reorient itself. She couldn't have cared less about Blake Webley or Abstract Expressionism or publishing in the right journals. All she wanted was for her baby to be okay. She ached for ordinary everydayness with the same vigor that she'd once derided it.

Her plea was granted: Sadie came home tiny but healthy. Still, Clare couldn't stop thinking about how easily it could have gone the other way. Under the harsh fluorescent lights of the hospital, she'd seen through to another future, one where Sadie was taken from them, and it haunted her. She never thought she'd miss the wires and constant beeping, but at home, she was terrified knowing that there were no fail-safes. There was only her. She used to sneak into Sadie's room four or five times a night to make sure she was still breathing. She canceled all the interviews they'd set up for night nurses and nannies because she didn't trust anyone else to maintain the same vigilance she did. She told herself she'd go back to her dissertation when Sadie was older and stronger.

Nothing in her life had prepared Clare for becoming a stay-at-home mother, especially to a baby with a fragile immune system. Clare was terrified of catching Covid—or any infection—and passing it on to Sadie. She stopped seeing most of her friends because she knew few of them wore masks anymore. Plus, she was always so tired. Maggie had moved to Colorado by then, lured by a job at the *Denver Post* and the promise of fresh air—New York City had lost its luster for a lot of people who spent the pandemic holed up in a tiny apartment. They still spoke on the phone regularly, but it was clear to both of them how much their lives had diverged. Maggie still went out to bars and concerts, not to mention an actual office; Clare barely left her apartment. Her whole world had contracted.

And then the unimaginable happened: Clare's mother died.

Nessa Regan—hearty, resilient, uncomplaining Nessa Regan—had a heart attack at work and didn't even make it to the hospital. By the time Clare got the call, her mother was already gone.

The shock was inexpressible. How could her mother just disappear? They were never close in the same way that, say, Maggie was close to her mother—Nessa and Clare didn't giggle together or confide in each other—but she was still her *mother*. She'd met Sadie only once. Clare had a single photo of her mother and daughter together: Nessa's face obscured by an N95 mask so that Clare couldn't even tell if she was smiling or not.

When Sadie was around six months old, Clare forced herself to visit the Met to look at some of her favorite paintings. As her footsteps echoed on the marble floors, she had a sinking realization: She felt nothing. Absolutely nothing. She moved from one room to the next searching for that glorious hum that, when she'd first felt it, had altered the entire course of her life. But not a single work of art had elicited anything close to a visceral response. The hum was gone.

That was the day she realized that she'd become someone she barely recognized: vague where she had once been sharp, apprehensive where she had once been assured, cautious where she'd once been daring. Jed still doted on her as much as he ever had—maybe even more—but they rarely had sex anymore, and all their conversations revolved around Sadie.

Sadie.

She was the compensation for all of this. Clare adored her daughter. She could stare at a single dimpled elbow for hours. She couldn't stop sniffing her; the scent was like a drug. She spent nap time scrolling through photos of her, waiting for her to wake up.

She threw herself into motherhood with the same determination and discipline she'd once reserved for academics. She studied parenting books as if there would be exams. She pored over Amazon reviews before buying so much as a sippy cup. As Sadie got older, Clare learned to react to tantrums with equanimity, and to tame her own temper into submission. She answered a stream of nonstop questions patiently. She stopped cursing. She set boundaries and explained the rules evenly and logically. She started calling the toilet "the potty," even in her own head. She played make-believe and invented silly songs. She smiled all the time.

Was she happy? It was hard to say. There were periods of both delirious joy and mind-numbing boredom. She knew how lucky she was to have the things Jed had given her: a loving husband, a comfortable house, financial security, a healthy child. But gratitude, she was starting to suspect, was not quite the same thing as happiness.

One afternoon, while searching for one of Sadie's missing sneakers, a phrase popped unbidden into her mind: *Things can't go on like this.* She didn't know where the thought had come from. But in the days and weeks that followed, it kept returning again and again, like a ticker tape running across the bottom of her consciousness: *Things can't go on like this.*

But they did, of course. Things just kept going on. She continued to search for lost shoes and play Candy Land and slice hot dogs. Until finally, one rainy September morning, something changed. She walked into a stranger's home to look at a painting and fucked him on a couch.

A thread that had been fraying for years just . . . snapped.

SADIE WAILED AS Clare buckled her into the stroller. She didn't want the playdate to end.

"It's okay, Boots, we'll come back soon," Clare murmured over and over like an incantation. "We'll come back."

At the door, she thanked Mina again.

"Anytime," Mina responded with a smile. "I hope you had a nice morning."

"Oh, just work," Clare said breezily, surprised at how easily the lie rolled off her tongue.

She hoped it would be that easy to lie to Jed. She'd decided in the car uptown that she would take this secret to her grave. She told herself this was a kindness; she would do it for Jed. She doubted his ability to withstand the truth.

At her baby shower years before, Clare remembered watching her mother's reactions to the presents she received: a visor for the baby to wear in the bath to keep water out of its eyes; a box that kept diaper wipes warm at all times. Nessa was obviously mystified by them, and as she was leaving, she said to Clare, "You know, you can't shield a baby from every discomfort. They need practice dealing with frustration and disappointment. Otherwise, they'll be unprepared for real trouble, which comes for all of us in the end."

Clare had found them grim words for a baby shower, but now she couldn't escape the suspicion that they were probably true. Jed had never been calloused by experience, and look where it had gotten him. The truth would destroy him.

CLARE WAS GRANTED a slight reprieve when he called and said he had to work late again. She ordered Chinese food and opened a beer. She tried to distract herself from flashbacks of her morning with Gabriel, but she couldn't concentrate on a TV show or a book. She ended up scrubbing the oven inside and out, her go-to remedy for anxiety.

Finally, she called Maggie. She'd been the one who'd come up with their "say yes to everything" policy, so in a way, she had been responsible for Clare agreeing to a first date with Jed. Maggie had an insatiable curiosity about the world—it was why she'd become a journalist—and in those early years, they got swept up in countless enthusiasms and escapades together.

Every Saturday they'd embark on a new activity in a neighborhood they'd never been to before: surf lessons in Far Rockaway, karaoke in Koreatown, bird-watching in Jamaica Bay. Clare once dragged Maggie to Rego Park for an underground art show she'd heard about. The "show" ended up being a seventy-year-old woman touring them around the home she'd lived in for half a century, every nook and cranny of which was filled with dolls she'd made out of castoff materials. They left three hours later, blinking in the sunlight, staring at each other in horror.

"I'm going to have nightmares for weeks," Maggie said.

"Don't you sort of wish you had a passion like that, though?" Clare asked.

"You can make trash dolls if you want to," Maggie had replied with such sincere kindness that Clare had burst out laughing.

It had become their catchphrase, a way of showing support to each other. When Maggie told her she was moving to Denver, Clare had said it with tears streaming down her face: "You can make trash dolls if you want to."

Maggie picked up on the first ring: "Hey, Chachi."

Clare smiled. She couldn't even remember where that nickname had come from. "Hey. You busy?"

"Just watching Dave watch football." She'd recently moved in with her boyfriend, another reporter.

"Fun."

"So fun."

"Jed's lack of interest in sports is basically half the reason I married him."

"God, what does he do with his time? I think Dave would have a nervous breakdown if he couldn't watch men chasing each other around on TV."

"I mean, he just works. All the time."

"I thought that's why he took the new job, to spend more time at home."

"So did I."

"That sucks, I'm sorry."

"It's okay. It gives me the opportunity to shovel chicken lo mein into my mouth and talk to you."

"So what's new? Any progress on the dissertation?"

"Of course not."

When Sadie started school, Clare had tried to pick up where she'd left off. Instead, she'd found that she could only stare at the words blankly. They were impenetrable to her. She couldn't decipher what she herself had written only a couple of years earlier. Even worse, she detected a sheen of glibness clinging to the whole thing. She caught herself wondering, *What's the point?*

When she was teaching undergrad courses at Columbia, her students sometimes asked her that question. They weren't apathetic; they were deeply interested in social justice or politics or medicine, and they saw art as a distraction from that more pressing work. She dutifully trotted out platitudes about how culture could change society, too. But she didn't like her answer any more than their questions. There was something off-putting to her about describing art as a tool. It was too reductive.

Sometimes she quoted a Camille Paglia line: "Civilization is defined by law and art. Laws govern our external behavior, while art expresses our soul." But maybe she'd liked it only because it seemed to somehow bless her union with Jed: law and art.

The truth was, she had started to doubt the importance of studying art, too, even before she'd had Sadie. The critical texts she read tended to sap all the beauty and the mystery from the art she loved. Now she found she could barely understand them; they sounded like nonsense to her.

She didn't know whether the whole thing was one great big con—that really, there was nothing to understand, and having Sadie had pulled the wool from her eyes—or whether she had simply been kicked out of that beautiful world where bright, clever people talked about ideas and beauty for their own sake. It didn't matter. The fact was, she couldn't get back in. She had been languishing as ABD—"all but dissertation"—for years.

"Come on," Maggie said, "just finish it. Who cares if it's not as good as you want it to be? Just churn something out and move on with your life."

"Believe me, I would if I could. I would *kill* to be able to churn something out."

"Maybe you need a life coach."

"You're my life coach."

"You should definitely fire me then."

"Never."

"And sue for damages."

Clare laughed.

"Remember when I tried to convince you that you should pierce your tongue?" Maggie asked.

"Okay, you really are an awful life coach."

"In my defense, we'd been awake for like thirty hours. I wasn't at my best."

"Oh yeah, that was after that weird party in Astoria, right?"

"Where you hooked up with that performance artist. Damien? Darren?"

"Darius."

They both started laughing.

"Oh, it's nice to hear you laugh, Chach."

"At least Darius was good for one thing."

They fell silent after a moment. Clare knew this was her opening to confess that she had cheated on Jed. She wanted to. She never kept secrets from Maggie. But she couldn't do it. She just couldn't do it.

Maggie wouldn't judge her, but she also wouldn't laugh naughtily and ask how the sex was. She'd be taken aback and concerned, because Clare had so obviously done a terrible thing, a terrible thing that was entirely out of character. This was not a trash doll. But right now she didn't want to feel remorse, because underneath all the guilt and the shame was something else: She felt alive—truly alive—for the first time in ages.

She said nothing.

WHEN JED FINALLY came home, Clare found it easier to face him than she'd expected. He was distracted, as he so often was these days, and gave her an absentminded peck on the lips.

"How was work?" she asked.

"Fine. How was everything here? How's Sadiekins?"

"She's zonked from her playdate with Lisbet."

"Which one is she again?"

"Mina and Tim Gellman's daughter."

"Oh right."

And that was it. Twenty minutes later, he was asleep.

## CHAPTER 7

CLARE LAY AWAKE ALL NIGHT, her thoughts pulled in one direction by desire—the memory of Gabriel's lips on her skin, the hunger in his eyes—then whipsawed back in the other direction by an equally powerful feeling of shame. The following morning, when Gabriel called, she knew the moment she heard his voice which force had won out. She agreed to see him again just a few hours later.

As soon as he opened the door, he had his hands on her. He was different from most of the other men she had slept with in her life, maybe because he was older, or French, or just because he was who he was. He grew quiet, almost solemn, when he brought her up to his bedroom. There were no smiles, no laughter, no words at all. He undressed her slowly, and held her wrists when she tried to hurry him along. He laid her down on the bed and investigated every inch of her body, hungrily, with eyes, hands, tongue. He moved slowly and leisurely, as if they had all the time in the world. She writhed beneath him, trying to pull him into her, trying to satisfy the need that had welled up in her again to an almost unbearable degree. But he kept up his slow tour, pausing at her shoulders, her knees, her Achilles tendon. She started to grow angry. Was he toying with her? Did he want her to beg for it? Fine, she would. She would beg for it. Until finally, with just the smallest hint of a smile, he submitted to her.

He entered her, and she gasped loudly. He stayed there, still, as she struggled to catch her breath. She pushed herself against him, trying to urge him into a faster rhythm, but again, he stopped her. He moved slowly, methodically, patiently, as her fingers gripped the sheets. Finally, his eyes took on a wild sheen, and he pushed himself into her more and more urgently until they both came in a rush of gasps and clawed flesh. Afterward, they lay on the bed, staring above them, panting. To her deep mortification, Clare felt suddenly as if she might start heaving great, body-racking sobs at any moment. She covered her eyes with her forearm and willed herself to calm down. Her fingers were trembling.

Gabriel propped himself up on his elbow and looked at her. He pulled her arm off her face. She squeezed her eyes shut and a few errant tears rolled down the sides of her head. She laughed, embarrassed. He didn't react. His fingers continued to trace lazy circles around her navel. "Do you want coffee?"

She nodded.

Gabriel got out of bed and pulled on a pair of black boxer briefs. Clare sat up and looked around. Not a single blanket and pillow was left on the bed. She leaned over the side of the bed in search of her clothes.

"Take your time," Gabriel said, leaving the room.

DOWNSTAIRS, IN THE kitchen, Clare settled on a high stool at the counter while he spooned espresso into a Bialetti pot.

"How long have you lived here?" she asked, looking around the room. It had marble countertops and sleek, sparkling-clean appliances.

"Eight years, but I bought it a few years before that. The renovation ended up being the nail in the coffin of my marriage."

"How so?"

"My wife thought I had become too bourgeois, with my constant talk of light fixtures and doorknobs. When we met, I was young and brash. We were going to revolutionize the art world together. And then, well . . ." He gestured around him at his elegant surroundings.

"What—you sold out?"

"Maybe, in a way. But I think we just wanted to lead different kinds of lives."

"I once heard a story about Elaine and Bill de Kooning—they were walking up Park Avenue during the forties, when they were dirt poor, and Bill pointed at one of the fancy doorman buildings and said, 'It could be worse, we could live there.'"

Gabriel laughed. "Yes. That's Beatriz."

"Are you still close?"

"We are. Our friends think we're lunatics. But we work better like this. We're not lovers anymore, but we're still family."

Clare felt an unwelcome pang of jealousy. She'd googled Beatriz Barros and found herself looking at images of a strikingly beautiful woman with long black hair and a sharply defined gray streak. Her face was large and angular. Her eyes were huge. She looked like a Francesco Clemente portrait. For all Clare knew Francesco Clemente *had* painted her.

"What's she like?"

"Smart. Opinionated." He shrugged. "I don't know. How do you sum up a person?" He handed her a minuscule cup of steaming espresso. "Milk?"

She nodded. As he poured it, he said, "So, will you come back tomorrow?"

"Tomorrow's Saturday. I can't."

"Monday?"

"I don't want to ask my friend to pick up Sadie again."

"I have a meeting at eleven. You'll be back uptown with plenty of time."

Clare shook her head. "I can't sneak down here every morning while Sadie's at school."

"How about I give you a part-time job? Then you'd have a good excuse."

"I'm sure that would go over well with your partner: a cover job for your current fling."

"It doesn't have to be a cover job. Seriously. I do some consulting work outside the gallery; you could help. You obviously have a great eye. And the market for Abstract Expressionists is huge right now—your specialty."

"Of course it is. Everyone wants a big, colorful canvas that won't clash with the drapes or make anyone uncomfortable."

"I see. You're a cynic."

"About the art market? Yes."

"So what does that make me? Vermin?"

"Of course not."

"A necessary evil?"

She cocked her head. "Closer." He certainly seemed necessary all of a sudden.

He laughed and finished his espresso in a single gulp. "So, will you come back?"

She sat back in her chair and took him in—his tousled hair, the irreverent gleam in his eye, the cockiness of his posture. She bit her cheek to force back a smile.

"Yes—but not to work."

## CHAPTER 8

CLARE STARTED LIVING TWO LIVES.

Uptown with her family, she was determined to remain cheerful and engaged. She cut the crusts off PB&Js and played Barbies and fed Noodle just as she always had. But downtown, with Gabriel, she was an entirely different woman. For the first time in her life, sex was unshackled from both the self-consciousness of her youth and the claustrophobia of her marriage. She felt free to ask for what she wanted—things that would have horrified her husband, who tended to treat her body like a fragile figurine he didn't want to break.

The fact that Gabriel *didn't* love her felt like a profound relief: It freed her from the obligation to be lovable. She felt like she'd broken out of a hard, calcified crust that had grown around her. She felt like herself—her real self—for the first time in years, even though this libidinous, adulterous woman was a complete stranger to her. It didn't entirely make sense.

She loved Jed. She wanted to be married to him. But she had become a ghost. Gabriel was putting flesh back on her bones. He was showing her a world where beauty and engagement and excitement still existed. He was reminding her that it was all still there; it hadn't disappeared—she had. She wanted to visit that world a few more times so she could figure out how to bring some of it back home with her. She could be happy again. Her marriage might even benefit from it.

She knew that most people would scoff at that idea as nothing more than a sorry justification for bad behavior. She didn't care. She believed it. It all just hinged on Jed never finding out. That was the key.

And so she vowed to herself, over and over, that she would be obsessively careful. She would leave no trace. She would tell no one. And soon—once she was sated on enchantment and exhilaration—she would end it. Gabriel would understand.

In and out, nice and clean.

FOR A WHILE, it worked. She went down to Gabriel's two, sometimes three, mornings a week. She was late to pick up Sadie once, and she'd assuaged her guilt by buying her an ice cream covered in gummy bears, which plopped off onto the pavement one by one like tiny kamikaze.

She got to know Gabriel better. He told her about growing up in Toulouse, the youngest of three boys. His father had been a lawyer, and his oldest brother followed in those footsteps. Bernard, the middle one, went into engineering. Gabriel had gone to art school.

He realized fairly quickly that he had insufficient talent and opened a tiny gallery next to a noodle shop to show the work of friends who had much more of it. It was the size of a closet and smelled like garlic all the time, but it was always crammed with people.

One of the first artists he showed was a friend named Agnès Lavirotte, who constructed beautiful, intricate works of lace—she'd learned the craft from her Belgian grandmother—depicting rape and other acts of barbarism. She was the first of his artists to really take off. Now her work sold well into the six figures.

"At first," he said, "I was sort of embarrassed by my new profession, as if being a dealer was the consolation prize for failing as an artist. But then I realized that it's an art form all in itself. And I did have a talent for it. In many ways, I was built for it.

"When I was younger, my father would always tell me, 'Life isn't always fun.' That was what he would say when I didn't want to do my homework or my chores or go to church. But every time, I would think to myself, Why not? Why can't it be? Maybe *your* life isn't fun, but mine will be.

"And it has been. Everything in the art world is magnified: the personalities, the money, the glamour, the risks. It's life at a high pitch. Artists see the world with fresh eyes, with wonder, and if you devote yourself to their work, you will, too. It's a beautiful way to spend your time."

"I know what you mean," Clare agreed. "My life growing up felt so drab. Gray and drab. Looking at art was the first time I felt the possibility of life being wondrous. I suppose some people get that from nature or religion, but for me it was always art. It made the world feel so large."

"*Le ravissement*," Gabriel said.

"What does that mean?"

"What's the English word? It's like . . . a beautiful delirium. Rapture."

"Rapture, yes, exactly. Isn't it funny that the language for sex and art and religion is all the same? But I suppose they do share certain qualities. They take you beyond yourself, out of the world of logic and thought into a place beyond words."

"My father never understood that. He just thought the art business was a racket, nothing more, nothing less. Of course, I never deny this. It *is* a racket. We're making up prices on things that have no useful function whatsoever. We decide how much they're worth, and other people believe us and pay it. It's absurd in a way. Totally absurd. But it's also beautiful. All these billionaires who made money in oil and metals and fiber-optic cables—they're spending millions on works of art that don't *do* anything. Yes, fine, they're investments or status symbols, or whatever you want to call them, but I think it goes beyond that. Great art is phenomenally rare and incredibly powerful. Call me naive, but I think most collectors are moved by the art they buy. Or at least, I would have said that twenty years ago. So yes, it's a racket, but it's an honest racket. We're all in on it."

He told Clare about growing bored with the Paris art scene: It was too closed, too conservative for his tastes. He left his gallery in the hands of a woman he had trained and went to New York for what he thought would be just the summer. He met Michael Kline through a friend of a friend, and they found that their visions were almost perfectly aligned—they admired the same artists and despised much of the work that was being celebrated at the moment. Gabriel closed his gallery in Paris, and they set to work building Prévost-Kline.

Twenty-five years later, Gabriel was, by any measure, a success, but he admitted that his old, familiar restlessness had found him once again. Recently, the business of art had begun to feel more and more like any other business—they might as well be selling TVs or time-shares. What had once struck him as gritty and exciting about the New York art world now seemed crude and joyless. The most exciting artists were immediately scooped up by the biggest three or four players in the game. It didn't even make sense to call them galleries; they were massive, international conglomerations, with dozens of outposts across the world. Plus, he and his partner had started to want to move in different directions. Gabriel had taken on more consulting jobs on his own, and that had rankled Michael.

"Why don't you split up the business, or just close the gallery?" Clare asked. "It looks like you've done more than well enough."

"I suppose I worry that I'd just fade into oblivion. If I wasn't in the game, I'd die of boredom."

"That's a bit melodramatic."

"Come work with me. That would keep things interesting."

Clare shook her head. "Not going to happen."

IT WASN'T GOING to happen, but it did become a useful fiction.

One morning Clare showed up at Gabriel's house to find him already on the way out the door. He looked surprised to see her.

"I thought we were meeting on Wednesday," he said.

"It is Wednesday," Clare replied. She took out the calendar on her phone to show him.

It was Tuesday.

"I'm sorry," she said. "I'm an idiot. Do you have plans?"

"I have a breakfast meeting. I'd cancel it, but this client is only in town for a couple days." Gabriel checked his watch. "It's at Pastis. Will you walk me there?"

Clare had not been out in public with Gabriel since she'd started sleeping with him. The idea made her nervous; she'd be so exposed. But the alternative was getting right back on the subway, having just made the forty-five-minute trip downtown. He sensed her hesitation.

"I'm not suggesting we make love on Tenth Avenue," he said with a smile. "It's just a walk."

"Keep your hands to yourself," she replied.

He suggested they stroll along the High Line since the sun was out for the first time in days. They strolled amidst the greenery in silence until, from around a curve, they came upon one of several public art installations along the path: a massive Yayoi Kusama pumpkin covered in red polka dots.

"Do you remember our first conversation?" Clare asked.

"Of course. The dots."

Clare told Gabriel to go stand behind the sculpture, so that he was entirely hidden from view. He went unquestioningly, and she pulled out her phone and took a picture.

When he reemerged, she showed it to him. "There, now I have a photo of you that I can look at whenever I like. Only I'll know you're there."

He looked at it for a moment in silence. Then he leaned in close and whispered in her ear, "Leave your husband."

It had become a joke between them. Sometimes she'd get a text in the middle of the day: "Did you leave him yet?"

She knew Gabriel didn't have any illusions about building an actual life together—he wasn't interested in becoming a stepfather to a three-year-old. He took things lightly; there was always a glimmer of amusement in his eye. He didn't say things straight on, so this entreaty struck her as his way of telling her that he cared. That he liked spending time with her; that he wished they could see more of each other.

Or maybe he actually did think she should leave Jed. She didn't know. She always deleted the messages as soon as she got them, then cleared her trash. When they were gone, she refused to let herself think about them.

"Clare?"

The voice seemed to emerge from nowhere.

Clare looked up. Jed's sister Lauren was standing two feet away on the High Line, staring at her in surprise. A well-dressed woman in her fifties stood next to her.

"What are you doing here?" Clare asked, trying to understand why a woman who rarely left the Upper East Side would be in Chelsea at nine o'clock on a Tuesday morning. She felt a brief stab of panic: Had she been followed?

"The Conservancy Garden is planning a redesign, so we came down here to get some inspiration. This is Briony Lund; she sits on the board with me."

"Hi," Clare said. The woman nodded politely.

"What are *you* doing down here?" Lauren asked, her eyes flickering briefly to Gabriel.

Clare had no idea what to say. She froze.

Gabriel immediately stepped forward and stuck his hand out with a warm smile. "Gabriel Prévost," he said. "I own a gallery a few blocks away. I'm trying to convince Clare to do some work for me."

"Sorry," Clare said, shaking her head. "Gabriel, this is my sister-in-law, Lauren Paulson."

"I had no idea you were considering going back to work," Lauren said.

"I probably won't. As I was just telling Gabriel, I don't really have the time."

"You would if you hired a nanny," Lauren said.

Jed had suggested the same thing last year, but she'd resisted. If she wasn't capable of working on her dissertation, she'd told him, it seemed ridiculous and indulgent to hire someone to care for their daughter.

"We'll see," Clare said with a smile.

Lauren and Briony soon went on their way, but Clare refused to walk Gabriel the rest of the way to Pastis. Instead, she bounded down the steps from the High Line as quickly as she could and hailed a taxi to take her straight home. It took a full ten blocks for her panic to subside and her breathing to steady.

WHEN JED GOT home that night, Clare brought up the run-in before he could. "Did Lauren tell you we bumped into each other today?"

He didn't look up from his phone. "No. Whereabouts?"

"Downtown."

She forced herself to go on: "I actually took a meeting with that art dealer I met at the Wolfes' anniversary party," she said, as if he already knew all about Gabriel. "He wants me to do some work for him."

Jed put down his phone. "Really? What kind of work?"

"Consulting, basically. I'm not making progress on my dissertation, so I started thinking that I might as well do something productive."

"Are you sure you want to take that on? Don't you have your hands full with Sadie?"

"It would be part-time, just while she's at school. I think I'd enjoy it. And maybe it will help me get going on my dissertation again."

"Well, if it's what you really want, then of course I'll support you. As you know, my mother worked part-time, and she was still very present in my life."

Clare frowned. What was he implying? That he would allow her to work only if it didn't adversely affect Sadie, or that she ought to be modeling herself on Dorothy? Either way, it wasn't like she was in a position to argue; there wasn't going to be a job. It was her cover for sleeping with another man.

"What about you?" Clare asked to change the subject. "How's your work going? You seem stretched so thin."

He sighed. "Alec has me wearing a lot of hats right now."

"What do you mean?"

"Almost three-quarters of the capital invested in Gatepost comes from a single client. I made the mistake of telling Alec that I'd be more comfortable if all our eggs weren't in one basket, and now he has me leading a massive marketing push to try to attract new clients. I tried to tell him that I was not the right man for that job, but you know how he is. Once he sets his mind on something . . ."

"Don't they have a marketing department to handle stuff like that?"

"They've never had to prioritize it. They've got one guy, and he's out on family leave."

"That's not what you signed up for."

"It's fine. It'll just take some getting used to."

"You can always go back to the firm if you don't like it."

"How about I just retire early when you become a big-time art dealer?"

"Sounds good. You can be the stay-at-home parent."

"Honestly?" Jed said with heartfelt emphasis. "I'd love that."

Clare believed he meant this; he adored Sadie. But if he couldn't—or wouldn't—even buy milk on his own, she wondered how, exactly, that would work.

Oh right, she realized. His mother would do it for him.

## CHAPTER 9

THE WHITNEY MUSEUM'S DECADE-OLD BUILDING looked blocky and inelegant from the outside, but as soon as you were inside, all the architect's choices began to make sense. The space was both capacious and warm, interesting but not distracting. Sunlight glinted off the Hudson River and streamed in generously through massive west-facing windows.

Looking out one of them on the fifth floor, Clare remarked to Gabriel that it felt like standing at the prow of a boat. Her entire being seemed to billow outward like a sail filled with wind. Life felt imbued with a sense of possibility.

They'd come to see the new Edward Hopper exhibit together, emboldened by their new cover story—that she was working for him. Turning away from the view, they wandered around the exhibit slowly.

Clare had never paid much heed to Hopper, but his work now stunned her. Each image pulsed with loneliness and humanity. The shadows spoke volumes. The paint was applied so luxuriously she wanted to lick it.

And that's when she realized: Her tuning fork was going wild. The hum had returned. It had come back to her.

She looked at Gabriel in amazement.

"What?" he asked.

She shook her head. "Nothing. They're just beautiful."

She stopped in front of a painting called *City Roofs*. There was nothing immediately noteworthy about it, but Clare was transfixed. The colors, so rich and warm. The way the sunlight bounced off the chimneys and windows. All of those windows, each one hiding a different life behind it. That sense of largeness and possibility she'd felt looking out at the Hudson River moments earlier returned.

Her mother-in-law was always cataloging the various right and wrong ways to do things. Clare couldn't even count the number of rules she'd absorbed over the years: no white after Labor Day; no bikinis after age thirty-five; no money talk at the table. But Dorothy was wrong.

There was no one way to live. There were billions. *Trillions.* Every window she passed, every face on the subway, was an example of a singular set of decisions.

Her life was hers to create. She could make any choice she wanted to, as long as she was willing to accept the consequences. Everything was a trade-off. She just had to decide what she wanted. She wasn't trapped. She was free.

She wanted to tell all of this to Gabriel. She wanted to throw herself into his arms and inhale his clean, almost-salty scent. She wanted to melt into his warmth. But she did not. She let her hand graze his gently, then moved on to another room.

WHEN THEY LEFT the museum, Clare checked her watch, and all the elation she'd experienced inside evaporated in an instant. It was twelve fifteen p.m. She had fifteen minutes to get up to Saint Mary's, eighty blocks away, to pick up Sadie.

She jumped into the street to hail a passing taxi while shouting an abbreviated explanation to Gabriel. As she yanked open the car door, she didn't even glance back at his face to see his reaction.

"CAN'T YOU GO any faster?" Clare implored her taxi driver. Their progress had abruptly stalled somewhere in the East Sixties.

In response, he just gestured with a hand out the windshield, where traffic was at a standstill.

"I'll walk," she said, passing a twenty through the plastic partition. "Thanks."

Clare sprinted up Madison Avenue, dodging shoppers milling in and out of Hermès and Chanel.

"Excuse me, sorry," she said, as she pushed past one designer shopping bag after another. Eventually, she just gave up and saved her breath for the fifteen-block sprint ahead of her.

She was already twenty minutes late for pickup. She knew Sadie was safe, but she couldn't stop picturing her daughter's worried face staring hopefully at the doorway. She was probably sitting alone and frightened with some frustrated teacher who had been forced to stay and wait with her.

Clare picked up her pace. Her back was already slicked with sweat.

By the time she reached the school and heaved open the wooden doors, her breaths were coming ragged and short. She sprinted up two flights of stairs to Sadie's classroom then paused for half a second to compose herself.

"I'm so sorry," she said, swinging open the door, "I got stuck in traffic."

Nobody answered. The room was empty. The lights were dimmed, and the blocks were stacked up neatly in a corner.

"Hello?" she called uselessly.

She turned around and ran back down the stairs, nearly colliding with Mrs. Dwyer in the main hall.

"Oh, Mrs. Bast," the headmistress exclaimed. "There you are."

"Where's Sadie?" Clare panted.

"We tried calling you."

"Where's my daughter?"

"Mrs. Bast was kind enough to come and get her."

"Who?"

"Her grandmother. When we couldn't reach either you or your husband, we tried Mrs. Bast. Luckily, she was able to drop everything and come right away."

"What?"

"Sadie was so excited to see her."

"Is that allowed?" Clare asked. Given how many children of billionaires went to Saint Mary's, it had stringent security protocols. She had to sign Sadie in and out herself every day, showing her official badge.

"I've known Mrs. Bast for forty years," Mrs. Dwyer said, before realizing that was not the right answer. "She's at the top of your list of approved caregivers."

Of course she was. Clare had filled out the form herself.

"As I said, we *tried* calling you. It's one o'clock in the afternoon."

Clare took out her phone. It was twelve-fifty-eight, and she had three missed calls from Saint Mary's. They must have come through while she was running up Madison.

"I'm so sorry," Clare said. "It won't happen again.

OUTSIDE, CLARE LEANED against the building, still breathing heavily. She called Dorothy's cell phone. There was no answer.

Clare was racked by a sob. She brought her hands up and covered her face. She hated crying. But now the tears were coming hard and fast, and she couldn't stop them. She turned toward the wall so no one could see her face.

It felt wrong to leave this place without her daughter. It reminded her of when she was discharged from the hospital after giving birth, and she and Jed had left the building alone, without their baby. She'd gone home to shower and change before returning to the NICU. During those few hours in the apartment, she'd been overcome by a sickening sense of disorientation. Almost as if she'd never given birth at all. As if she'd imagined the whole thing, and there was no baby.

What was wrong with her? How had she missed pickup? What kind of mother was she?

She felt out of control. This was not the relief she'd felt when she'd slept with Gabriel for the first time—that delicious abandonment of caution. This was something else. It was terror. Terror at what she might let slip through her fingers.

Clare called Dorothy again.

No answer.

Dorothy would never deliberately keep Sadie away from her, Clare told herself. She wasn't a monster. But from somewhere deep within, a small worry arose: Had she just lost a battle in some long-running war with Dorothy over Sadie—one she hadn't even realized she was fighting? Why else would she feel so frightened?

Clare wiped her eyes and turned toward Fifth Avenue. She could be at the Basts' apartment in five minutes if she hurried.

THE BASTS' LONGTIME housekeeper opened the door for Clare and led her silently into the dining room, where Sadie was swinging her legs on an oversized chair and sipping from a cup of cocoa.

"Mama!" she cried when she saw her. She had a dab of whipped cream on her nose.

"Oh, Boots," Clare said, rushing to her daughter and kissing the top of her head. "I'm so sorry."

"It's okay," Sadie said. "At first I was scared, but then Grammy came. She said you probably just forgot."

"What? No, my love. I didn't forget about you. I could never do that. I got stuck in traffic." Clare looked around the room. "Where is Grammy?"

Dorothy swept into the room from the swinging door that led to the kitchen.

"Oh!" she exclaimed when she saw Clare. "The case of the missing mother is solved," she said with a tinkling laugh. "Would you like some cocoa?"

"Thank you for getting Sadie, Dorothy. I really appreciate it."

"It's lucky my lunch was canceled. What would have happened to this poor, sweet girl if I hadn't gotten Mrs. Dwyer's call?"

"Well, I guess she would have waited ten more minutes for me to arrive. But again, I'm very grateful."

"Sadie is family. As you know, I'd do anything for my family."

"I know you would, Dorothy. As would I."

"Why weren't you at Saint Mary's then?"

"I was doing some research. I got stuck in traffic on the way back."

"Oh dear. Poor Clare. You're juggling so much."

"I'm fine, thank you." Clare rested her hands on Sadie's shoulders and gave them a little squeeze. "Come on, Boots. It's time to go."

"But Grammy said I could try on her fancy jewelry after this," Sadie whined. "She has *real* diamonds," she added in a conspiratorial whisper.

"Sorry, sweetheart. Not today."

"But she *said*," Sadie claimed with rising indignation.

"Not today," Clare repeated.

"We'll do it another time," Dorothy said. "My diamonds aren't going anywhere."

Sadie reluctantly stood up and trudged to the front door. In the foyer, she looked up at her mother. "When I grow up, I'm going to wear diamonds *every day*."

"Uh-huh," Clare said. "Get your coat on."

"Like a princess," Sadie added. "Like Grammy."

Clare jabbed the elevator button urgently. "That's great, sweetheart."

## CHAPTER 10

THAT NIGHT, CLARE AND JED were expected to attend MoCA's annual fundraising gala as guests of the Wolfes. It was one of the art world's biggest parties of the year; every October, collectors, dealers, and artists mingled together in the museum's beautiful Brutalist building in Midtown.

Clare had wanted to cancel—she'd felt too guilty leaving Sadie with a babysitter after her lapse that afternoon—but Jed had told her they couldn't bail at the last minute. Alec would read something into it. He assured her that being late to pick up Sadie once in two years was not the moral failing she thought it was. Clare hadn't been able to look him in the face after he said that.

THEIR CAB LURCHED to a stop outside the museum. The setting sun had anointed its pale travertine walls with a rich, golden glow. Jed stepped out of the car first and held out his hand to help her. He was in black tie, and she was wearing a long, gray silk dress she'd gotten at the Barneys closing sale. Her auburn hair was pulled up off her neck, showing off a black pearl necklace Dorothy had given her as a wedding present. Clare's pale, willowy frame was even thinner than usual, a side effect of her constant anxiety. As she stepped from the car, Jed kissed her hand, and a few passersby turned. It occurred to Clare that they must look enviable: a rich, attractive couple seemingly in love. She fidgeted under their gaze. This was never who she'd dreamed of being. She remembered when she worked at the Met, she had complained to Maggie: "I love art; I just don't like the people who *support* art." And now here she was, one of them. She literally had a check in her purse. Usually, Jed handled the donations after events like this, but this time, Clare had wanted to express her appreciation to Tasha herself. She'd nearly depleted her personal account to write the thousand-dollar check—Clare hadn't made any money since her Columbia stipend ended—but it didn't really matter; Clare rarely used it to pay for anything other than Jed's birthday presents.

The din inside the museum was deafening, echoing off the floors and walls. The main atrium was filled with hundreds of white calla lilies and flickering candles. A jazz trio played in a corner.

Jed held his hand on Clare's lower back and steered her toward the bar. She didn't like being maneuvered, but to object to his hand would have signaled something she wasn't prepared to address. He ordered two martinis; gin for him, vodka for her. That first sip—icy cold and salty—eased some of the tension she was feeling. She glanced around the room nervously and was relieved not to see Gabriel. He'd told her earlier that he couldn't skip the party; it was too important professionally.

She smiled at her husband. He smiled back. She racked her brain for something to say to him but couldn't think of a thing. She'd already asked him about work in the car.

"Do you think Tasha and Alec are already here?" he asked her.

"I'm not sure. Shall we do a lap?"

They walked into the sculpture garden. A large reflecting pool glinted in the dusk, a dark rectangle set into the white limestone pavement. The trees, their leaves already turning yellow and orange, were strung with twinkling lights.

Clare spotted Gabriel standing next to the spindly bronze leg of a massive Louise Bourgeois spider sculpture. He was chatting with Clement Rosier, the curator she had met with the previous summer at Tasha's urging. Clare gripped her glass tighter and took another sip. Gabriel caught her eye and smiled, just barely. She smiled back. She wished more than anything that she could go over to him, lean into his body, talk with him, go home with him.

"Who's that?" Jed asked.

"What?"

"That guy. It looked like you recognized each other."

"Oh, that's Gabriel Prévost. The dealer I'm working with."

"Should we go say hi?"

Clare hesitated for just a moment. "Sure."

As they wove through the crowd, Clare felt like she was heading to the gallows. The idea of her husband meeting her lover sent a bolt of panic coursing through her body. She'd thought about feigning illness and staying home but decided it was better to be present for any potential interaction between them. At least that way, she could try to exert some control over it—and end it quickly.

Gabriel continued talking to Clement, but Clare noticed that his eyes kept darting over to them, measuring their progress. As they got closer, Clare heard that he was speaking French. When they were about a foot away, he stopped talking and turned toward her.

"Clare, what a lovely surprise." He leaned in and kissed her on the cheek.

"Hi, Gabriel. It's nice to see you. I'm not sure if you've met my husband, Jed."

"Nice to meet you," Jed said, holding out his hand. He smiled warmly, and his face was so open and trusting that Clare had to look away. "I hear you and Clare are doing some work together."

"Your wife is very talented."

Jed put his arm around Clare and squeezed hard. "You don't have to tell me."

"This is Clement Rosier," Gabriel said, gesturing to the man next to him. "MoCA's chief curator of painting and sculpture and an old friend of mine."

Clement was dressed in a gray Thom Browne suit—recognizable by its ankle-length cuffs—and round tortoiseshell glasses. He was bald, with gray stubble around the sides of his head and on his cheeks.

"Of course," Clare said. "Nice to see you again."

"What brings you here tonight?" Gabriel asked Jed.

"Alec and Tasha Wolfe invited us."

"Speak of the devil," Gabriel said, looking over Jed's shoulder to where Tasha was sashaying toward them.

"Oh, I'm not the devil," she replied with a wink. "I just sold my soul to him."

She gave everyone double kisses then gave Clare's arm a little extra squeeze. "How are you, darling?"

"I'm good. You?"

"Fantastic." She pronounced the word with relish.

She turned to Gabriel and Clement. "Okay, tell me, boys—who's the next big thing? I want names."

"Well—" Gabriel started, but she cut him off.

"No—don't tell me Eduardo Salas. He's too sentimental."

"It's not sentiment. It's depth of feeling. If you'd held on to your soul, you might know the difference." Gabriel was probably one of only a few people willing to argue with Tasha Wolfe. Maybe that was why Alec liked him so much.

"Oh, that ratty old thing?" Tasha laughed. "Who needs it when I got all this in return?" She gestured around her—the party, the museum with her name on the wall, the pieces she'd donated, the staff fawning over her. She had a point.

"No, give me someone else." She pointed at Clement and said, "Quick. Or I'll have you fired."

Everyone laughed, but Clement seemed to take the threat seriously.

"Frank Obermeyer," he said, naming a sculptor who worked mainly with found materials.

Tasha looked disgusted.

"Do you see the problem here? This is the Museum of *Contemporary* Art, yet it's totally stuck in the past. We need to find the next generation of rabble-rousers, not keep fawning over dinosaurs like Obermeyer. Who's going to find them, if not you?" She directed this last comment to Clement. "I'll get you the money. But find me someone better than Frank Obermeyer—he's been rattling around for nearly thirty years now."

Clare noticed that Tasha used the first person to refer to the museum, as if it belonged to her. That was what most troubled Clare about these events. Museums belonged to the public, but tonight, the public was pointedly kept out—there was heavy security at the door to ensure that—and people like Tasha Wolfe, who were accustomed to being able to buy anything they wanted, could put themselves in charge. Tasha was an enormously powerful voice on the board—she was intelligent, opinionated, and loud, not to mention one of the museum's biggest donors. To her credit, she took her position seriously and was well informed, but she really could have had Clement fired if she'd wanted to.

Clare's head was swimming. Jed's hand—which had returned to its resting place on her lower back—felt like a hot coal burning through her dress. She excused herself and made her way downstairs to a restroom that was rarely used; most visitors didn't even know it was there. Tonight, the whole lower floor seemed empty.

As she turned into the narrow hallway, she realized she had barely taken a breath since parting from the group. She leaned against the wall and forced herself to breathe. All of the guilt and regret she'd been squeezing into a small, locked box for the past six weeks hit her in one go. The whole thing had seemed to work only because her two lives were so separate. When she was with Gabriel, she entered another world where Jed didn't exist. But seeing them next to each other, chatting politely, had toppled that illusion. She pulled at the black pearl necklace around her throat.

She heard footsteps tapping on the floor. She turned just as Gabriel rounded the corner into the hallway. They looked at each other for a moment in silence.

"Are you all right?" he asked.

Clare shook her head.

He moved closer and wrapped his arms around her. Almost against her will, Clare responded by pressing the length of her body against him. And then he was kissing her, there in the hallway, and pushing her against the wall. She could hear her breath coming heavy and fast now. She worried she might lift her dress right there; her actions felt out of her control. Heat was rising up in her, the blood was pounding in her ears.

Then someone somewhere above them dropped a glass, and the sound of it shattering resounded like an alarm. She pushed him away.

Gabriel retreated to the opposite hall and leaned against it. "I'm sorry," he said, breathing heavily.

"It's not your fault." She was already moving away from him. "It's mine. I'm sorry." She ran down the hallway, back toward the party, back toward her husband.

WHEN CLARE AND Jed found their places at dinner, Clare noted with dismay that Gabriel was seated at their table. She smiled politely at him. He nodded back. They'd avoided each other for the rest of the cocktail hour. Gabriel had been engaged in an intense conversation with Alec, while Clare had caught up with Britt Grisholm, an old acquaintance from Columbia who now worked as an assistant curator in the museum's photography department. Tasha had commandeered Jed by the bar.

There were two other couples at the table—friends of the Wolfes whom Clare had met once or twice before—along with a woman with a bleached-blond pixie cut who was introduced as an editor at *Artforum*. She was seated next to Gabriel, and Clare wondered—with more than a little envy—if they were being set up.

Alec raised a glass and proposed a toast: "To great art and even better company."

"Hear, hear," they echoed.

Talk quickly turned to a trip that the Wolfes were taking to Japan for the holidays. Clare zoned out of the conversation and picked at her salad. She was trying not to look at Gabriel, but her eyes seemed to seek him out on their own. She made eye contact with him and abruptly looked away. Suddenly, she heard someone say her name. She looked up. "Pardon?"

It was Alec. "I said, I hear that you and Gabriel are doing some work together."

"Oh. Yes. Sorry, I was a million miles away."

"I hope I'll get a commission, since you met at my house. I'd like to be on the other side of that ten percent for once."

"Sure." She gestured to Jed. "Just talk to my lawyer."

"I always told you to stop wasting your time on that degree," Alec said. "I'm glad you finally listened."

"I haven't given it up entirely. But I'll probably be eighty by the time I actually finish it."

"Why bother? Degrees are useless. I never hire MBAs. They're all coddled pains in the neck who overthink everything."

"Overthinking things is basically an art historian's job description."

"Go out and get your hands dirty, like Gabriel over here."

Gabriel smiled and held up his hands. "Spotless," he said, flipping them back and forth like a glove model.

"Oh, I'm sure we could find some skeletons in your closet," Alec said. "I wouldn't work with you otherwise."

"You think that Ruscha fell off the back of a truck?" Gabriel asked.

"How would I know? You won't tell me who the seller was."

Gabriel smiled but said nothing.

"Is that true?" one of the other men at the table asked. "You don't know who owned it before you?"

"No clue. It just says private collector in the provenance."

"Is that normal?" Jed asked. "For a collector not to know whom they're buying from?"

Gabriel nodded. "Quite. Much of my work involves matching sellers with buyers. If I introduced them, who's to say they wouldn't simply cut me out of the deal the next time."

"So Clare," Alec interjected, "what will you be doing for Gabriel?"

"Looking for Ruschas that have fallen off trucks, I imagine."

"Ah, that's why Gabriel's hands are so clean. He's getting you to do the dirty work."

Clare kept her smile plastered on her face, but she could feel her cheeks getting hot.

"Actually, Clare's been enormously helpful already," Gabriel cut in. "She's been putting together a list of overlooked abstract impressionists for me. So many women and artists of color were ignored during that period. It's great that they're starting to come to light now. And there's a growing market for them."

"Go on, name names," Tasha said.

"Clare?" Gabriel said with a smile. They rarely discussed art when they were together—their exchanges were usually limited to "touch me there" and "slow down"—and he seemed to be getting a kick out of this turn in the conversation.

"Let's see," Clare said. "I think we discussed Lynne Drexler. Who else? Sam Gilliam. Judith Godwin."

"That's right," said Gabriel. He turned to Jed. "What do you think of them, Jed?"

"What?" Jed asked, startled.

"Do you admire Drexler and Godwin as much as Clare?"

Gabriel was provoking him. Trying, perhaps, to show Clare what an ill-suited match they were.

"I agree with Clare on all of it," Jed said with a smile. "That's what the husband's supposed to say, right?"

"Exactly," agreed Tasha.

IN THE CAB home, Jed took Clare's hand in the backseat and held on to it tightly.

"What's the deal with this Gabriel guy?"

Clare was glad the car was too dark for him to see her face. "What do you mean?"

"Didn't that seem kind of odd, the way he does business, keeping all the information to himself?"

"No, that really is the way dealers operate. Most collectors actually appreciate the anonymity, too."

"You're sure he's aboveboard?"

"I don't know him that well yet, but he's very successful and very reputable. Don't let Alec get in your head."

Jed said nothing. Clare could feel her heart thumping in her chest. She wondered if Jed could hear it. Did he know? Could he have seen them by the bathroom?

"What's wrong?" she asked.

"Nothing. I just thought you were focusing on getting back to your dissertation. This seems like a distraction."

"You said you'd support me in this."

"I do. I just want to make sure it's what you really want to be doing. I thought you wanted to be a museum curator."

"I don't know *what* I want to do. I'm trying something new because I'm at loose ends."

Jed put his arm around her and pulled her close to him. "You'll figure it out. Don't worry. I just think that it makes sense to finish your doctorate first. You're so close. It would be such a shame to throw it all away."

Clare didn't say anything.

"Honey?" Jed said.

She smiled at him. "I'll think about it. I promise."

## CHAPTER 11

THE NEXT NIGHT, CLARE AND Jed were due at his parents' apartment to celebrate Dorothy's seventy-fourth birthday. She and Abe still lived in the home they'd raised their children in, on the top floor of a brick building on Eighty-Eighth and Fifth.

The door was opened by Mimi, the Basts' housekeeper, who threw her arms around Jed ecstatically. She'd been Lauren and Jed's nanny, and they were all quick to claim that she was "one of the family." Clare hadn't failed to notice that she was the only family member without health insurance.

"Oh, my beautiful boy!" Mimi cried. She rocked him back and forth slowly while murmuring, "Oh, my beautiful, beautiful boy."

"Hi, Mimi," Clare said, "it's good to see you again."

Mimi nodded at her formally. "Good evening, Mrs. Bast."

"Please, call me Clare." She'd asked Mimi this a hundred times, to no avail. Mimi had never warmed to Clare, maybe because Clare had stolen away her beautiful boy. (With his blond curls and ready smile, Jed really had been cherublike, and Dorothy had the framed photos—dozens of them—to prove it.)

Mimi led them to the living room, where Dorothy and Abe were sitting on opposite ends of the sofa in silence. Nothing in the room had changed since her first visit. It had light blue walls, yellow taffeta curtains, and an overwhelming number of black and white porcelain Staffordshire dogs. On the coffee table were an assortment of hors d'oeuvres, including a horrifyingly gelatinous mess that everyone in the family referred to casually as "shrimp mold" and smeared liberally on Carr's crackers.

Dorothy jumped up when they walked in, smoothing out the wrinkles in her lavender dress. Her mouth, puckered with age, was shellacked in pink lipstick.

"Jed, honey, how are you?" She kissed him on the cheek then moved on to Clare. "Clare, darling, you look lovely." Clare didn't attach too much significance to Dorothy's terms of endearment; she had a unique talent for wielding them without a modicum of warmth.

"Thank you. So do you. Happy birthday."

Dorothy waved her hand. "Oh pish." Dorothy claimed she didn't like a lot of birthday fanfare, but it was clear that she adored being the focus of her family's attention.

Abe nodded at them stiffly without standing up.

These dinners were rigidly formulaic, right down to the opening lines. Soon Mimi would reappear with their drinks—Sancerre for Clare, a martini for Jed—and they would settle into their habitual spots. Conversation rarely strayed far from gossip or the same recapped *New York Times* headlines that everyone else had read. The children were never invited. "It wouldn't be any fun for them," Dorothy insisted. On that point Clare had to agree.

Whenever they came here, Clare remembered the night, two years earlier, that Dorothy had pulled Clare aside at one of these dinners to have a tête-à-tête. "Jed tells me you've got the baby blues," she said, making an approximation of a sad face.

"Is that his term or yours?" Clare asked with a forced laugh, trying and probably failing to hide her irritation.

She'd waved off the question. "I'm a mother, too, dear. I know what it's like. But Sadie's almost a year old. You've got to snap out of it. Jed works so hard. It's not fair that he should have to come home and take care of you, too."

Clare did not remind Dorothy that her mother had just died. Instead, she gritted her teeth and assured her that she was fine.

"I hope so. Because you never want to see your child unhappy, whether he's three or forty-three."

GRANT AND LAUREN arrived a few minutes after they'd sat down. Jed, Dorothy, and Clare popped back up to go through another round of greetings. Abe lifted a trembling, age-spotted hand to take another sip of whatever brown liquor he was drinking.

When everyone had settled down again, Jed took out his present for his mother from his jacket pocket: a large stack of lotto tickets. "Well, Mom, I hope you're feeling lucky this year . . ."

Dorothy adored playing the lottery. When her children were young, she used to have them do the scratch-offs for her, so she wouldn't get the silver scrapings all over her clothes. Now that they'd grown up and moved out, she had Mimi do it for her.

"And a little something else, just to hedge your bets," Clare said, handing over the silk scarf she'd bought at the Met Store.

"Oh, this is too much," chirped Dorothy happily. "I don't need anything other than the company of my beautiful children."

She unwrapped Lauren and Grant's gift next. As soon as she saw the orange box, she brought a hand to her chest. "Oh my *word*."

It was a huge cashmere scarf from Hermès, in all different shades of blue and purple. Clare knew that it must have cost well over a thousand dollars. "Oh, it's *beautiful*," Dorothy enthused. "You shouldn't have."

"Of course we should have," Lauren said. "You deserve it."

Dorothy set the silk scarf aside and draped the Hermès one around her shoulders. "It's stunning. How does it look?"

As Dorothy was showered in compliments, Clare glanced over at Jed, who was smiling tightly. She wished she'd spent more on Dorothy's present, or at least gotten her something other than a scarf, which only highlighted the disparity between the two gifts.

Grant seemed to sense the awkwardness and said, "How's the new job going, Jed? Have we converted you to the dark side yet?"

"It's fine. They have me doing more fundraising than I'd like, but I guess that's what I signed up for."

"That's the name of the game at a hedge fund."

"Not exactly the Supreme Court," Abe barked. Everyone looked startled. He'd given no indication he was even following the conversation.

"I don't think I was ever heading for the Supreme Court, Dad."

"You could have stayed at the firm for a few more years. *My* firm. No need to be so impatient."

"*Dad*." Jed said it like a warning.

"So you got passed over for partner. It happens. That doesn't mean you cut and run. You wait another year. Try again."

"Abe, that's enough," Dorothy said.

"What are you talking about, Abe?" Clare intervened. "Jed left because Alec Wolfe *begged* him to join his fund. He made him an offer impossible to say no to."

Nobody said anything. Dorothy and Abe both stared at the ground. Jed's face was twisted into a pained grimace.

The bell rang to signal that dinner was ready. Even after seven years as a Bast, Clare had never quite gotten use to this particular anachronism. Everyone else stood to move to the dining room, but Clare put a hand on Jed's arm.

"Is that true?" she asked him when the room had cleared out. "You got passed over for partner?"

Jed stared obstinately at a spot on the carpet.

"Why didn't you tell me?"

He looked up at her. "Why do you think?"

"I have no idea."

"Because it's *embarrassing*, Clare. To not make partner at my father's firm? It's humiliating."

"I know you were focused more on pro bono work than on bringing in big corporate clients. That's honorable. Besides, I'm your wife. You don't hide something like that from me." She heard her own hypocrisy as soon as the words were out of her mouth.

"Can we just let this go?" Jed asked miserably.

"Did you lie about Alec, too? Was it really his idea to bring you over to Gatepost?"

"Clare, please."

Dorothy stuck her head in the room.

"Dinner's ready, you two. We're all waiting."

"Coming, Mom," Jed said and walked away from Clare with obvious relief.

Clare stood where she was, looking after him. Were they just going to leave it there? She scoffed lightly and started to follow him out.

"Will you hang back for a little tête-à-tête, Clare?" Dorothy said.

Clare braced herself. This was just the way that the "baby blues" conversation had begun.

"Sure," she said. She followed Dorothy over to the sofa and sat in the spot her mother-in-law was patting lightly.

"I want to ask you to go a little easier on Jed," Dorothy said. "He's under a lot of pressure."

"Dorothy, he lied to me. And no offense, but I really don't think it's your place to intervene here."

"Believe me, I'd rather not, but *now*"—she looked at Clare pointedly—"I think I have to. Lauren mentioned that she ran into you and some art dealer downtown a few weeks ago."

Clare was taken aback by the sudden swerve.

"Yes. We're working together."

"That's all it is? Work?"

"*Excuse me?*"

"Oh, I forgot. Your generation likes it all out in the open. God forbid someone tries to use a little tact or nuance. What I want to know, dear, is whether you're sleeping with him."

"How could you even ask me that?"

"Well, I tried not to."

Having a conversation with Dorothy Bast was like trying to salsa dance on a floor slicked with Vaseline.

"I don't see how it's any of your business, but *no*, I'm not." Clare knew her cheeks were flaming red.

Dorothy sighed. "Everything that happens in this family is my business, Clare."

She leaned forward to smear shrimp mold onto a cracker. "I don't know if you've heard me mention our good friends the Banhoffs? Linda and Don Banhoff?"

Clare tried to keep up with the conversational pivot. "I think so . . ."

"We play bridge together? Linda is the supervising judge for the family court of Manhattan?"

"Okay . . ."

"That's the court that makes custody decisions. Well, I thought if anyone should know, it would be her, so I asked her how adultery affected custody arrangements in the case of divorce."

"You *what*?"

"As it turns out, adultery doesn't really have much of an effect."

The two women stared at each other. Dorothy took a bite of her cracker and dabbed her mouth with a napkin. Clare tried to control her breathing. She had the sense that Dorothy wanted her to unclench herself so that the next hit would find only soft, vulnerable tissue.

"*Unless*—" Dorothy continued, "unless, of course, the affair has adversely affected the child. We both know what happened the other day, when Sadie was left at school. Mrs. Dwyer mentioned that you'd been late to pickup a few other times as well. Now, I'm not sure if you'd call that neglect or *what* the term is, but your extramarital activities do certainly seem to be having an adverse effect on Sadie. She was *terrified* when I had to go collect her. I wouldn't be surprised if she needs therapy." Dorothy pressed her thin lips together as if to say how she regretted that they now found themselves in such unfortunate circumstances. "And then we can't discount your baby blues. Not your fault *at all*, of course, but something to consider nonetheless."

"Dorothy, are you threatening me?"

"Threatening you?" Dorothy put a hand to her heart. "Oh my goodness, no. I just thought you should be aware of the law so that you can make informed decisions. That is something the Basts always have going for us: a keen understanding of the law. And many, *many* friends to help advise us on such matters."

"I can't believe this. Who *are* you?"

"I'm a *mother*, and I want what's best for my child." She paused. "Don't you?"

"Of course I do."

"Then end the affair. Immediately. Before Jed gets any inkling of it. And while you're at it, try to treat him with a little more care and respect. He may have glossed over the details of his new job, but who's really lying to whom in your relationship?"

Clare stared at Dorothy, feeling some combination of hatred and awe. "This is not your place, Dorothy."

"*My* place? I'm the head of this family, and if I ever hear another word about you and this dealer, you will be out of it so fast it will make your head spin. Being a Bast is a privilege, one that you clearly no longer deserve."

"You think you can take my child? Are you serious?"

"Sadie is a Bast," Dorothy said. "*By blood.*"

Dorothy's face abruptly smoothed out and she patted Clare's knee with a hand weighed down by a heavy aquamarine ring. "Well," she said, rising, "I'm glad we had this little chat. I don't see any reason for involving the men in these matters. Some things are best handled among us girls, don't you think?"

She winked at Clare. Then she swept out of the room, leading with her wineglass. "Mimi, that lamb smells *divine*!"

Clare sat stunned on the sofa. She'd never exactly liked her mother-in-law, but she'd had no idea Dorothy had such viciousness in her. When Jed came in a few minutes later to check on her, Clare desperately wanted to tell him exactly what his mother had done—threatened to take away Sadie. But she didn't think she could lie to Jed as easily as she had to Dorothy about Gabriel. And she wasn't so sure he would take her side regardless.

WHEN THEY GOT home, Clare tiptoed into Sadie's room and perched on the edge of her bed. Sadie always looked like she was working so hard at sleeping: cheeks red, brow furrowed. She let out a long, troubled sigh. Clare put her hand on her daughter's back.

Was it possible to be a bad person and a good mother? She knew she was a bad wife; that was a given. But could she still be a good mother?

The books told her that children modeled themselves on their parents, but they didn't say what to do if you didn't *want* them to. Clare didn't like herself all that much right now. That was a cost of an affair that she hadn't foreseen—the way it would make her turn on herself. She'd lost all self-respect. She wanted Sadie to be *better* than her—much better. And she certainly hoped Sadie would never end up in the position she had gotten herself into.

She wanted so badly to protect her sweet girl. She did all she could to guard against drowning, choking, illness, strangers, but now she realized that the real threat was *her.* She was jeopardizing Sadie's fundamental security and well-being. She had convinced herself that what she was doing had nothing to do with Sadie—that if she wasn't found out, there would be no consequences for her daughter. But she knew then that she was wrong. She had introduced a crack in the foundation of Sadie's world that would just continue to grow and grow. She had to close it up before everything came tumbling down.

But as much as she hated to admit it, even knowing what it would cost, she didn't want to end things with Gabriel simply because Dorothy had ordered her to. It was petty, but this was *her* life. No one—and especially not her mother-in-law—should be able to dictate her choices.

Jed had once told her about a term in elder law called "the right to folly." It basically meant that elderly people were allowed to make bad decisions, too. Just because they changed their will and left everything to their new thirty-year-old girlfriend didn't automatically mean that they had dementia. They were allowed to be foolish. (This topic had come up when Abe had invested more than four hundred thousand dollars in a startup aiming to make croquet the new pickleball.)

Clare knew her recent decisions hadn't been great. In fact, they'd been terrible. But they were hers—and *for* her. It had been a long time since she'd made a choice that wasn't dictated first and foremost by what was best for her daughter or her husband.

She was at a crossroads, but she didn't want to take a single step in either direction. She wanted to sit down at the crossroads for a while. She wanted to lie down and take a nap there.

She crept out of Sadie's room and sent a text to Gabriel telling him she was coming over Monday morning. She would force herself to make a decision about what to say to him at some point over the weekend.

# CHAPTER 12

FROM THE MOMENT GABRIEL OPENED the door to her, there was an awkwardness between them that had never existed before, almost as if Clare's decision had raced ahead and beaten her there.

"Hi," she said stiffly.

"Hi," he replied. There was tension in his voice, too. Had he been unsettled by his interaction with Jed as well? Presumably not: He'd followed her to the bathroom and pressed her up against the wall just minutes after meeting him.

"Can I get you something to drink?"

He had never asked that before. They'd always reached for each other as soon as she was in the door. "Sure. A Pellegrino?"

She took off her coat and draped it over her arm rather than discarding it on the floor on her way upstairs, as she usually did. She perched on the sofa and waited for him to join her. He handed her a tall, sweating glass of water and she took a long sip, as much to buy time as anything else.

Gabriel sat on the couch next to her. "Clare," he said. He expelled a long breath.

That was all he had to say. She knew what was coming next. They'd never spoken to each other like this before. She waited to see if she was right.

"I think perhaps the time has come to end things."

She almost laughed. *Had* her decision arrived before her?

"Why?" she asked. She should have just let him do the dirty work of ending things for her, but now she had to know.

"Someone is going to get hurt. And given our respective situations, it's much more likely to be you than me."

"Because I care for you more than you care for me?"

"I *do* care about you. But you have a family. *You* have something to lose."

"So you're making this decision for me?"

"If you want to continue this relationship, then I will. Happily. That's the truth. But I'm telling you right now that I think it's best—for you—to put a stop to it. Now is the time to end things cleanly, without regrets. From here, it will only get more difficult to do so."

Clare took another sip of water and placed the glass back precisely in the circle of condensation it had left behind. She considered telling him that she had come there to end things with *him*, but it would sound so petty. ("You can't fire me—I quit!")

She started nodding before she spoke, as if her body were committing her to a decision before her mind could get in the way.

"Okay," she said. "Let's stop."

"We're on the same page?"

"Yes."

"I'm sorry, Clare, I—"

"It's fine. There's no need to apologize. Really. We both agree." She stood up. "I'm going to go."

"Right now? You don't have to rush off."

"I think I do."

He stood up too and followed her to the front door. With her hand on the doorknob, she turned back to him. She didn't know what to say, but she didn't want to let it end like this: stilted and uncomfortable and cold. That was everything their relationship had stood against.

"I'll miss you," she said with a small, sad smile.

"I'll miss you, too. In another world . . ." He didn't continue.

"I know," she said. "I feel the same way."

When she shut the door behind her, the street in front of her was blurred by tears. She wiped her eyes roughly and started walking back toward the subway. At least she wouldn't be late to pick up Sadie.

## CHAPTER 13

TWO WEEKS LATER, CLARE STEPPED out of the shower to find Jed lying on their bed, scrolling through her phone.

She froze.

"What are you doing?"

He turned the phone around to show her the screen: a picture of Sadie on her birthday, her smile lit by the candles on her cake. "It should be illegal to be this cute," he said.

"Uh-huh," Clare said, willing him to put down her phone. She was almost positive that she didn't have anything incriminating on it—she'd always been careful to delete all of Gabriel's texts—but seeing her phone in his hands still made her nervous.

"Where is she?" she asked. Jed was supposed to be giving her a bath.

"She's watching TV." He continued scrolling through her photos. "What's this?" he asked, holding up the photo she'd taken on the High Line—the Yayoi Kusama pumpkin that she'd asked Gabriel to hide behind.

"It's a Kusama. Don't you like it?"

Jed studied it. "Yeah. It's nice."

"I'm done in the bathroom, by the way, if you're waiting to get in there."

Jed stood up and tossed her phone onto her side of the bed.

When he'd shut the door behind him, Clare sat down on the bed and picked up her phone. She looked at the photo Jed had found, and zoomed in until all she could see were pixels. Gabriel was invisible, but he'd been there. There but not there. Close, but out of reach.

She felt tears welling up, and she shut her eyes tightly to stop them. "Get ahold of yourself," she whispered forcefully.

"What's that?" Jed called from the bathroom.

God, he had the hearing of a jackrabbit. "Nothing!" she yelled back, then stood up to get changed. Speaking of which, where was Noodle?

Ever since Gabriel had ended things, Clare had been trying to recommit herself to the life she shared with her husband and daughter, but it had been harder than she thought. It was like her relationship with Gabriel had opened up a Pandora's box of emotions, and no matter how much she tried, she couldn't quite shove them all back in. Long-dormant desires now buzzed around inside of her, and without Gabriel as an outlet, they had no place to go.

She'd tried to keep herself busy. She'd gone out to dinner with Mina a few nights earlier, and then called two old friends from grad school, Cassandra and Lev, to see if they were free for drinks.

Over the years, as she'd waded deeper into the muck of motherhood, these get-togethers with art-world colleagues had become less frequent. Clare felt like she had nothing to add: She didn't know any of the gossip; she hadn't heard of the really new artists. She had unwittingly proved the naysayers in her program right: When some of the other students had found out whom Clare was married to and where she lived, they had dismissed her as a dilettante.

But Cassandra and Lev had never done that, and she genuinely missed them. Besides, her newfound restlessness demanded that she do *something.*

THEY MET AT the bar at the Hotel Chelsea because it was between the New Museum, where Cassandra worked, and Hudson Yards, where Lev had a meeting. Clare never expected anyone to make the trek uptown.

Cassandra was telling them about an artist with an upcoming exhibition at the museum, and Clare found herself laughing for the first time in weeks.

"He's a nightmare," Cassandra said. "He asked in all seriousness whether he could slam a wrecking ball into the museum's facade because it would 'raise a lot of important questions about institutional patronage.' This from a guy who's been in, like, a single group show at PS1. It's not like he's Maurizio Cattelan. He's just . . ." She shook her head. "I don't know."

"A man?" Clare supplied.

"Yes," Cassandra said, pointing a finger at Clare. "Exactly."

"That's not fair," Lev said. "I'm a man. But then again, I despise myself."

Clare laughed and took another sip of her martini.

"By the way, are you going to that Prévost-Kline party tonight?" Lev asked.

"What Prévost-Kline party?" Clare asked.

"Some opening."

"Why would I be going?" Clare replied. "I go nowhere."

"Weren't you asking about Gabriel Prévost recently?"

It had been Lev whom Clare had called to get the backstory on Gabriel after meeting him at the Wolfes' party.

"So?"

"All right, never mind. Just asking."

"Is he the guy who hosts that crazy party after the Venice Biennale?" Cassandra asked.

"That's him." Lev said. "My friend Griffin went once. He said it was nuts. They stayed up all night roasting lamb on spits outside and foraging for liberty caps."

"What are liberty caps?" Clare asked.

Cassandra snorted.

"What?"

"They're psychedelic mushrooms, *Mom*," said Lev.

Clare groaned. "God, I'm so old."

"You're a lot younger than Gabriel Prévost."

"Okay, fine. I'm just boring."

"Aw, we still love you," Cassandra said, patting her hand.

"So should we go?" Lev asked.

"Where?" Clare asked. "To the Biennale?"

"No, to the opening. It's like five blocks from here."

Cassandra looked at her watch.

"Sure, I'd stop by for a bit."

They looked at Clare expectantly.

It was a terrible idea. Beyond terrible. Not to mention pathetic; he'd dumped her. But Clare had had two martinis. While she didn't believe in fate, she did believe in the right to folly. Why should Abe be the only one who got a free pass?

She tossed back the dregs of her drink. "I'm game."

## CHAPTER 14

THE MUSIC COULD BE HEARD halfway down the block, and the street was packed. There were a handful of other high-profile galleries on the same stretch, and it was a Thursday, which meant one thing in Chelsea: opening night.

Clare had forgotten nights like these. Most Thursday nights now she was in bed by nine thirty, or else at some staid dinner party with Jed. It was incredible to suddenly think about all of this unfolding, night after night, just fifty blocks away. How myopic she had gotten: She'd confused her own little life for just . . . *life*.

As they made their way through the knots of people crowding the sidewalk, Clare spotted a man in a gold lamé jumpsuit and a woman in full Kabuki makeup. The desire to shape how one is seen happens everywhere, from church socials to high school cafeterias, but to Clare it had always seemed more pronounced in the art world, where looks and image making took on an almost religious bent. There was a reverence for spectacle.

The door to the gallery was propped open and Clare could practically see the hot, heavy air bulging out of it. Inside, all three of them immediately took off their coats. They pushed their way toward the bar set up on the side of the room and grabbed glasses of wine, before staking out a small territory in the corner.

"Is it always this crowded?!" Clare yelled over the din.

"I think it's their twentieth anniversary," Lev replied.

Clare remembered Gabriel mentioning something about that. She hadn't realized they were throwing a party. She'd known that he had an entire existence that didn't involve her, of course, but here, at his gallery, in a crush of bodies, she felt it with visceral force. She had been just a bit player in his life.

As she looked around, she caught a glimpse of Gabriel across the room. He was laughing at something and pushing his hair back with his palm. His face was shiny with perspiration, and his sleeves were rolled up to the elbows. As though sensing her gaze, he turned to look over at her. He widened his eyes in surprise. Then he smiled. She smiled back. He started pushing his way through the crowd toward her. Clare excused herself from her friends and went to meet him halfway.

When they were close enough, Gabriel pulled her to him and kissed her on the cheek. She could feel the heat emanating from his body in waves.

"What are you doing here?"

"I was having drinks with friends in the neighborhood. They insisted we stop by."

"I'm happy you came." His hands were resting on her waist, his fingers roving around as if to confirm that she was really there, in the flesh. He pulled her closer, from her hips. She didn't resist. She was feeling reckless, Dorothy's warning forgotten. The heat had limbered up her body; she moved laconically, pliably. Months of being careful, and now this. The crowd seemed to offer them cover. They could have been pushed together by the crush. It offered anonymity, too. Nobody was watching them. Gabriel leaned in close to her ear, brushing his lips against her neck.

"Let's go somewhere else."

"You can't leave your own party."

"I can do whatever I want to my own party."

Clare looked back at Lev and Cassandra, who were engrossed in a conversation with someone she didn't know. She realized that this was precisely the reason she'd come to the party—in the hope that Gabriel would react this way when he saw her.

"Meet me outside in five minutes," she said.

She wended her way back to Lev and Cassandra to say goodbye, claiming fatigue, blaming Sadie. When she got outside, the cool air on her hot skin made her shiver. She glanced around for Gabriel. She saw him across the street, smoking a cigarette, watching her. He nodded his head toward the corner. They walked toward Tenth Avenue, following parallel paths across the street from each other.

At the next corner, Gabriel crossed the street and gripped her hungrily.

"Wait," she said laughing. "Wait."

They were only two blocks from his house. They walked there quickly, practically running. Inside, they went straight upstairs and undressed frantically. Clare fell back into Gabriel's bed, feeling like she had come home. He climbed on top of her, and over his shoulder, she could just make out *Longfin* in the darkness. They'd moved it upstairs early in their relationship, since they spent all their time in the bedroom, and they both liked being near it. Its familiar red lines had become inescapably intertwined with pleasure for her now. Gabriel drew back to look at her.

"I'm so glad you're here," he whispered.

"You're the one who sent me away."

"I was trying to protect you."

His condescension rankled her, but she said nothing. It didn't matter. She was back. They were together. They could talk later.

As if reading her mind, Gabriel began to move down the length of her body. His lips grazed her skin, and she softened under his touch. She had forgotten what this was like: to be entirely in the moment, to be consumed by pleasure.

A muffled thud resounded from below. They both instinctively froze and locked eyes. Then there was another thud, unmistakable this time: Someone was inside the house. All pleasure drained from their expressions. Gabriel put a finger to his lips and eased himself off of her. He pulled on his underwear, and walked silently over to the mantel, where he kept one of his favorite works from his collection: a Jean Arp statue from 1962. It was heavy, bronze, and about the size of a large mallet. He picked it up and padded out of the room.

Clare pulled her knees up to her chest. She strained her ears to hear some clue to what was happening on the floor below, but all she heard was her heart thudding in her chest.

Then there was a louder scuffling sound, and a dull *thwack*. Clare brought her hand up to her throat. She felt unbearably naked. She eased one foot onto the ground, and then the other. She lay down on her stomach and pushed herself quietly under the bed. She stayed there, trying to quiet her breathing. She was sure her heartbeat could be heard a block away. She told herself that Gabriel would be up in a moment and that he would laugh when he found her cowering under the bed like a child.

As if on cue, she heard footsteps on the stairs. But they weren't Gabriel's: They gave off the distinct squeak of rubber on wood. Gabriel had been barefoot.

The footsteps entered the room and stopped. The blanket hanging off the bed obstructed most of her view of whoever was at the door. She held her breath. Two seconds turned into four, into ten. She understood then how time could stretch out and expand itself, how each moment could contain an infinite eternity. The air felt heavy and taut. She thought that if she so much as moved her pinky toe, the person in the doorframe would feel it like a shock wave. Then she heard the sound of rubber on wood again. A pair of sneakers, nondescript black Reeboks, appeared at the foot of the bed, facing away from her. They took a step closer to the wall, and a soft scraping noise followed. Thirty seconds later, the shoes disappeared, and she heard the footsteps echo down the hallway, then on the steps. Eventually, she heard the front door close downstairs.

She still didn't move. She couldn't have said how much longer she stayed flattened under the bed. It could have been two minutes or it could have been two hours; her sense of time had abandoned her. Finally, she eased herself out and stood up. She paused, listening, like a deer in the forest. All she heard was quiet.

That's when she saw it. Or rather, didn't see it . . . her brain registered an absence before anything else. A glaringly empty space on the wall right where *Longfin* had once hung.

It was gone.

She took a step closer and saw a small hole in the wall where the nail used to hang. You'd barely notice it if you weren't looking for it. Clare ran her hand over it and a bit of drywall crumbled under her touch.

*Longfin* was gone.

CLARE CREPT DOWNSTAIRS in the dark, feeling her way along the wall. As she made the final turn onto the ground floor, she stopped suddenly in her tracks. Gabriel lay slumped at the foot of the stairs. She'd almost tripped over him. The Jean Arp statue was on the ground next to him. She held out one hand to steady herself and quickly glanced around the darkened room. It was empty. She squatted down and put a hand on Gabriel's back.

"Gabriel?" she whispered. He didn't respond.

"*Gabriel*," she said more loudly.

Nothing.

Clare put her hands under him and rolled him over. Her eyes were immediately drawn downward. His entire torso was slicked in dark, viscous-looking blood. Clare instinctively recoiled and fell backward onto her heels.

She looked at Gabriel's face. His eyes were open but blank. His beautiful golden skin was pale and sallow. Clare suddenly heard a deep, guttural moan echo through the room, and relief spread through her like a shot of strong liquor. He was alive.

She leaned down closer to hear him better, but he was completely still and silent.

That was when she realized that the sound had come from her own lips. It was still eking out at a low, keening pitch. She slapped a palm over her mouth, and the room went quiet.

"Gabriel," she said again, through her fingers.

His eyes continued to stare unseeing at the ceiling.

She started making strange, gasping sounds she'd never heard herself make before. She felt hot bile rising in her throat. She abandoned Gabriel to dash into the bathroom. She retched over the toilet loudly but nothing came out. After a minute, the nausea began to recede.

She went back to where Gabriel lay and put a hand on his wrist to feel for a pulse: nothing. She put her hand in front of his mouth and nose: nothing.

He was dead. Gabriel was dead.

Clare stayed crouched there, naked, feeling as if she were in a dream. A thought sprang to her mind: *Venetian red.*

Even Gabriel's blood was beautiful.

AFTER COMING BACK to herself, Clare had tried to do the right thing.

She'd found her purse where she'd dropped it by the door and taken out her phone to call 911. But she was stopped by her background photo: Sadie, two years old, wearing Mickey Mouse ears and a tutu.

Clare stared at the screen for a long time.

She couldn't do it. She couldn't dial 911 from her phone. They'd know who she was. She'd have to stay for questioning. Jed would find out. Everything would be ruined—Dorothy would make sure of it. She couldn't let that happen. She had to keep a wall between this life and that life. Between that corpse and her lovely girl.

She slipped the phone back into her bag. I'll find a pay phone, she told herself. I'll find a pay phone and I'll call it in anonymously.

Once she had a plan, she moved quickly. She washed her hands and got dressed. She wiped down any surfaces she might have touched with a paper towel and balled it into her pocket to throw away later. She gathered up her belongings, slipped on her shoes, and put on her coat. As she reached for the front door, she remembered to take the paper towel out of her pocket and use it to turn the doorknob.

She took one final look back at Gabriel. He was exactly as she'd left him.

She quickly stepped out of the house. She shivered violently in the night air and started walking down the block as quickly as she could without drawing attention to herself. She kept herself from looking backward. She muttered, "Pay phone, pay phone, pay phone" to herself under her breath as she retraced the path she'd taken from the gallery just—she finally checked the time—forty minutes earlier.

When she arrived back at Prévost-Kline, the party was still in full swing and she was still whispering the words like a prayer—"pay phone, pay phone, pay phone." She continued to whisper them as she hailed a taxi and got in. But as she rode uptown, the incantation faded.

As she crossed Fifty-Ninth Street, Clare abandoned any notion of finding a pay phone or calling the police or telling anyone anything about what had happened.

She would say nothing. She'd lie if she had to. That's what she had been doing for weeks, and that's what she would continue to do. It was the only way to protect Sadie, to insulate her from the consequences of her own bad decisions.

Fifteen minutes later, she opened the door to her warm, quiet apartment and slipped inside.

## CHAPTER 15

CLARE WENT STRAIGHT INTO THE bathroom and sat on the closed toilet lid. She needed to be somewhere small and enclosed. She put her head in her hands, but she didn't cry. She didn't feel sad. She felt horrified.

She looked in the mirror. Her makeup looked garish and incriminatory. She grabbed a rough washcloth and scrubbed her face with steaming hot water as hard as she could. She felt her skin begin to burn. When she looked up, her face was shiny and red like raw meat.

Then she had a sickening thought: That's what Gabriel was now. Raw meat.

"Stop being hysterical," she whispered. It was something her mother used to say to her. She stood up and brushed her teeth, avoiding eye contact with herself.

When she slipped into bed, Jed rolled over. "Hi, love," he mumbled, his voice thick with sleep. "Did you have fun?"

"We did," she whispered so quietly she could hardly hear herself.

"What time is it?"

Clare looked at her watch. It was almost midnight. She paused before answering. "It's eleven eleven," she said. "Make a wish."

"I already have everything I want," Jed murmured, throwing a warm, heavy arm across her body. Clare didn't reply. He'd already gone back to sleep.

She lay in bed stiffly for hours, trapped under Jed's weight. Every time she closed her eyes, Gabriel's horrific final expression gaped back at her. Around four, she couldn't take it anymore and finally eased herself out from under Jed's arm.

She put on a pot of coffee and sat in the kitchen waiting for it to brew. She stared at nothing with wide, terror-stricken eyes. It was only then that her shock started to be supplanted by grief. She'd never see him again. She'd never touch his warm, golden skin. He was gone. Not hidden from view behind a Yayoi Kusama sculpture—really and truly gone. And she had nothing of his to remember him by. She'd erased all his text messages. There were no photos of them together. Their whole relationship had been like a chimera.

She covered her face with her hands as tears started to stream from her eyes. She stayed like that for the next two hours, crying silently, until Sadie came out of her room.

"Morning, Mama."

Clare looked up. "Hi, love," she said, pulling Sadie into her chest so her daughter wouldn't see how red and puffy her eyes were.

"Mama, that's too tight," Sadie said, laughing, but Clare couldn't loosen her grip.

"Oh, my love," she said over and over.

Jed came out a few minutes later. When he looked at Clare, he laughed.

"What?" she asked, panic rising in her voice.

"You look like you had quite a night, that's all."

"What do you mean?"

"I mean, you look hungover. Beautiful, but a little worse for wear."

Clare looked in the mirror in the hallway. Jed was right: She looked awful. Her whole face was red, and her lips were so dry and chapped they were practically flaking. A manic, darting look gleamed in her eyes.

"How wild did the night get?" Jed asked.

"Not wild at all. I was home by eleven."

"I remember," Jed said, wrapping his arms around her. "My wish came true."

CLARE'S ANXIETY HAD felt manageable in the quiet familiarity of her apartment, but outside in the bright, clamorous world, it curdled into panic. Her mouth was dry, and her lungs felt like they weren't expanding enough. She stopped at every corner, even when the walk sign was on, because she didn't trust herself to understand when it was safe to go. She kept picturing herself walking into traffic, the stroller flying into the air and landing in a clatter. She would only cross when she saw other people doing the same. The commonplace world seemed rife with danger.

"Mama!" Sadie suddenly yelled, turning around to peer at her.

"What?"

"You're not answering me!"

"Sorry, sweetheart, Mama can't talk right now. I have to concentrate."

"Why?"

"To keep us safe."

"From what?"

"Honey, I can't talk right now."

"Why?"

Clare pinched her nose.

"Why?"

"I need two minutes, sweet pea. I need two minutes of quiet."

"Safe from who?"

From there on, Clare just ignored her. Every so often she would say in a falsely bright tone, "Two minutes, sweetheart."

Flashbacks were bombarding her hard and fast. Her memories of Gabriel were all jumbled. His hand on her waist, pulling her toward him. Then his wide, unseeing eyes. Clare straddling him, gasping for air. The blood seeping out of his chest. She'd feel a sort of sensual stirring and then it would be immediately replaced by nausea and revulsion. She worried she was going to pass out.

Clare made it to school with Sadie intact, then raced home with her eyes fixed on the pavement to keep from making eye contact with anyone she might know. Tears were streaming down her face beneath her sunglasses. She crawled back into bed with all of her clothes on and set the alarm for eleven a.m. As she lay there, desperate for sleep, she scrounged around in her mind for some small measure of comfort and—to her relief—found one: At the very least, it was over.

The affair was definitively over.

## CHAPTER 16

THE IMAGE OF GABRIEL'S DEAD body bombarded Clare insistently for the rest of the day. She physically recoiled whenever it popped into her mind. She didn't want to think about that night. Her memory of it had already gone fuzzy around the edges. She couldn't recall a word of her conversation with Lev and Cassandra. All she saw, over and over, was Gabriel's lifeless body soaking in a puddle of blood.

Had someone found him yet? Were the police there right now, photographing his body from every angle? Had the press caught wind of it? Had his family been notified?

She had no idea, and she didn't want to google his name. She hadn't fully considered the reason why she shouldn't, but it stemmed from the same inchoate impulse that prompted her to lie to Jed about what time she'd gotten home. She knew, deep within her bones, that it was imperative to act like she'd gone straight home from the party, like she'd told Lev and Cassandra. She hadn't gone to Gabriel's. She'd seen nothing. She knew nothing. There was nothing to search for. She did her best to erase the entire visit to Gabriel's from her mind.

But with every hour that passed, she wondered why nobody—Lev or Cassandra or even Tasha or Lauren or, god forbid, Dorothy—had called to see if she'd heard the terrible news.

By the following morning, Clare had started to suspect that she'd made the whole thing up: not just Gabriel's death, but their entire relationship. When she was younger, her mother used to accuse her of letting her imagination run away with her—Clare had always pictured a hairy orange beast galloping off into the distance, with her small slumped form heaved across his shoulders. Now she felt confused and off-kilter, as if the wall between reality and fantasy were nothing but a flimsy curtain blowing in the wind.

And then, over breakfast on Saturday, it all thudded back into reality. Jed was scrolling through his phone while absentmindedly eating a piece of buttered toast.

"Oh, Jesus," he said suddenly.

"What?" Clare asked, even as she knew.

"Gabriel Prévost was killed." He looked up at Clare in shock.

"*What?*" she asked, feeling like a character in a soap opera. "What happened?"

Jed shook his head and looked back at his phone.

"He was shot. At his house."

"By whom?"

"They don't know. It says his assistant called the police yesterday after he missed several meetings and didn't pick up his phone."

Clare was still holding her coffee mug in midair. She hadn't moved since he'd told her. "I'm so sorry," Jed said. "Are you okay?"

"Me?" She forced herself to take a sip of coffee. "Yes, of course. Why?"

"You were working together. You'd become friends."

"I wouldn't call us friends. We were colleagues. That's all."

Jed frowned at her. She realized she'd hadn't calibrated her tone exactly right. She was so intent on not betraying the depth of her grief that she had veered into callousness. "I mean, it's a shock. Of course I'm upset. But I didn't know him that well."

"I wonder if Alec has heard," Jed said, staring off into the distance blankly.

"Are *you* okay?" Clare asked after a moment.

"Hmm? Oh. Yes. I'm okay. You're right—it's a shock. It makes you grateful for what you have." Jed's eyes glistened wetly. He stood up and wrapped his arms around her. "I don't know what I'd do if anything happened to you."

"Wait, if he missed work yesterday, then he was killed the night before last?" she said. "Thursday?"

"Yes, that's what it says."

"I saw him."

Jed pulled away from her. "What?"

"Cassandra, Lev, and I stopped by his gallery after drinks; they were having a party. I just saw him for a second. It was packed."

Jed stared at her for a moment. "Jesus," he finally said. Then he wrapped himself around her again. "Thank god you're okay."

## CHAPTER 17

AN INSISTENT VOICE KEPT PIERCING Clare's horror and grief: *This isn't over,* it said. *It couldn't possibly be over.* Even as she hoped she might, by some miracle, escape from this mess unscathed, deep down she knew she couldn't. Her relationship with Gabriel—particularly its final, violent denouement—couldn't just fade into the past without even a ripple of a repercussion. That would be too absurd. Life wasn't an existentialist novel. Actions had consequences.

On Sunday afternoon, her small, desperate plea for a reprieve was officially denied. Clare was making Play-Doh snowmen at the kitchen table with Sadie when the phone connecting the apartment to the lobby buzzed. Gino was on the line, cheerfully informing her that two police officers were there to see her. "They wanna chat with you about something."

"Me?" Clare said numbly. "Okay. Send them up." She stood frozen for a moment, her hand still resting on the phone. She watched her daughter mash a mound of Play-Doh into a flat pancake and wished she could leave her there, in that bubble of innocence. But she couldn't.

"Honey, do you want to watch *PAW Patrol* in Mommy and Daddy's bed?"

Sadie eyed her suspiciously. "You said no TV today."

"I changed my mind. Come on—'Let's take to the sky!'" Clare sang the catchphrase of Sadie's favorite character in a manic, high-pitched warble.

"Okay," Sadie said unsurely, still suspecting a trap.

Clare ushered Sadie into her bedroom, appreciating for once how slow their building's elevator was. The doorbell rang just after she'd pressed Play. On the way to answer it, Clare stuck her head into the spare bedroom, where Jed was working, and told him that the police were there. She didn't wait for his reaction.

When Clare opened the front door, she found two plainclothes officers staring at her impassively. On the left, an Asian man who looked to be in his early thirties bounced lightly on his toes. Next to him, a woman who had twenty years, eight inches, and sixty pounds on him, stood stolidly with legs spread and arms crossed. They both wore button-downs, slacks, and bulky black sneakers that were trying to pass themselves off as dress shoes.

"Mrs. Bast?" the woman asked.

"Yes?"

"I'm Detective Pam Breznick of the NYPD. This is my partner Greg Nguyen." Nguyen nodded at her. "We're investigating the death of Gabriel Prévost. May we come in?"

She stepped aside to let them into the apartment. "Of course."

The officers stood in the foyer for a moment and looked around, taking in the floral wallpaper, the antique English console table, the hand-painted umbrella stand that devoured all of her cheap foldables into its unseen depths. It was all Dorothy's doing, and Clare wished for the umpteenth time that she had pushed back against some of it. Or all of it.

"Nice place," Nguyen said.

"Thanks. Can I get either of you something to drink? There's a reasonably fresh pot of coffee."

Nguyen opened his mouth to answer, but his partner cut him off: "We're fine."

As Clare led them into the living room, Jed appeared and introduced himself. "Mind if I sit in?" he asked.

"By all means," the senior detective said with a palpable lack of enthusiasm.

Once they were settled in Dorothy Bast's chintz hellscape, Breznick took out a small notebook from her leather satchel and clicked open a pen. "Mrs. Bast, could you please start by explaining the nature of your relationship with the deceased?" she asked.

Clare glanced briefly at Jed before answering.

"We had recently started working together."

"In what capacity?"

"I was advising—"

Jed cut her off before she could say another word: "I don't think there's any need to go into detail."

The two detectives and Clare all turned to look at Jed in unison.

"With all due respect," Breznick said, "we'll decide how much detail we need."

"Naturally, we're happy to help as much as we can," Jed replied, "but we're not going to be questioned in any detail without a lawyer present."

"I thought you were a lawyer, Mr. Bast."

"Not hers."

"You think she needs one?"

"I think everyone needs a lawyer, Detective Breznick, but maybe I'm biased."

"Would you prefer to do this down at the station then?" she asked. "*With* a lawyer?"

"I'm sure that won't be necessary," Jed said. "We're happy to answer in broad strokes. That should be sufficient."

"How about my partner and I decide what's sufficient, and your wife gets to speak for herself. Shall we try that?"

Jed spread his hands as if to say *Be my guest.*

Clare had watched this entire exchange with mounting alarm. Why was Jed getting confrontational?

Breznick took a breath, clearly trying to contain her annoyance. "Mrs. Bast, while working for Mr. Prévost, had you become aware of any business problems? Personal problems? Any enemies? Recent fights?"

Clare glanced at Jed, who nodded.

"He never mentioned any problems at work. And I never met any of his clients. As for his personal life, I knew very little."

Breznick turned to Jed. "Had you met him, Mr. Bast?"

"Yes, I met him at a party at the Museum of Contemporary Art around two weeks ago."

"And that's the only time you met him?"

"That's right."

"Is that where you met him, too, Mrs. Bast?"

"I met him in September at a party at Jed's boss's house. Alec Wolfe.

He and his wife had bought art through Gabriel and become friendly with him."

"So you *had* met some of his clients?"

Jed was about to interject again when the other detective, Nguyen, yelled, "What the hell!," and pulled his feet up off the floor.

All three turned to stare at him. "What's the matter, Greg?" his partner asked.

He shook his head and unfurled himself. "Sorry—I just—that startled me." He pointed toward the floor where Noodle had poked his head and front paws out from under the couch.

"That's our daughter's rabbit," Clare said. "He likes to burrow."

They all stared at Noodle, who grew uncomfortable and pulled his head back into hiding.

"He should be in his hutch," Jed said sternly.

Nobody answered.

"Listen," Clare said, "I want you to catch whoever did this. But I'd only been working with him for about a month, and sporadically at that. Mostly what we did was discuss undervalued artists, interesting newcomers, overblown trends, things like that. I'm sorry I can't help you more—truly."

"When was the last time you saw him?" Breznick asked.

Clare and Jed spoke at the same time:

"Thursday night," Clare said as Jed barked out: "Don't answer that."

"The night he died?" Breznick asked.

"Along with about a hundred other people. At the party at his gallery."

"Clare, stop talking," Jed said. He stood up. "I'm going to have to end this interview now. Thank you for stopping by."

Breznick studied him.

"Do you have something to hide, Mr. Bast? Or does she?"

Jed shook his head and smiled.

"I'm sorry, Detective, that trick's not going to work here."

Clare looked at her husband in surprise. She'd never seen this side of him before: cocky and imposing.

"I could charge you both with obstruction of justice," the detective said.

"And I could wish you the best of luck in that endeavor," Jed replied smoothly.

Breznick stared at him for a second with undisguised dislike, then stood up and said, "C'mon, Greg. I think we wore out our welcome."

As they were leaving, Breznick handed her card to Clare. "Call me if you'd like to help us find who did this."

Clare reached out to take it and noticed with horror that her hand was trembling. She took the card and shoved her hand into the back pocket of her jeans.

She and Jed stood in awkward silence until they heard the thud of the elevator door opening and closing. Then she turned to Jed, wide-eyed. "What was that? Were you *trying* to make it look like we had something to hide? You practically goaded her into charging us with obstruction of justice."

"Clare, that will never happen. You're peripheral to this whole thing. They're not going to waste their time on you."

"But why shouldn't we help?"

"You just don't want to get more involved than you have to in something like this. Trust me."

Clare sighed but said nothing.

"It's over now," he assured her. "I promise."

She hoped that Jed's confidence wasn't unfounded. But that voice inside her—the one that didn't believe in miracles—knew it probably was. And when she took her hand out of her pocket to start Sadie's dinner, it was still shaking.

## CHAPTER 18

SADIE HAD THE NEXT DAY off school for Veterans Day. Clare broached the idea of taking her up to the Bronx Zoo—she wanted a distraction—but Jed said he needed the car to bring home some boxes from work. He was old-school, like his father. He took notes longhand and preferred the phone to email. His desk was always stacked with paperwork, and he carted so many files back and forth from the office that she often could barely lift his bag.

"You're working today?" she asked.

"According to Alec, Veterans Day is a fake holiday."

"Does Alec actually know any veterans?"

"I didn't ask."

Clare took Sadie to the Central Park children's zoo instead, but the day was cold and wet and she couldn't shake off her grief. Their visit was cut short when a goat bit Sadie's finger.

The next morning, Clare was so eager for three hours alone that she and Sadie got to Saint Mary's fifteen minutes early. By the time Sadie was safely in her classroom, Clare was practically itching for solitude, but Mina caught up with her outside the school and suggested they get coffee: "It's been so long since we caught up." She smiled at Clare hopefully. She was visibly pregnant now, which made her face rounder and almost childlike, and Clare was beset with a deep sense of shame. She'd treated Mina terribly. She'd taken advantage of her countless offers to keep Sadie after school way too many times without ever reciprocating. All she'd cared about for weeks was fitting in her visits to Gabriel.

"That sounds great," Clare replied, even though it was quite possibly the last thing in the world she wanted to do.

They started walking together toward their usual coffee spot, but Clare suddenly stopped in her tracks. Detective Breznick was leaning against the mailbox on the corner with her gaze fixed on Clare. Next to her, Greg Nguyen fiddled with the plastic lid of a coffee cup. Breznick pushed herself off the mailbox and started walking toward them.

"Oh, wait," Clare said. "I'm so sorry. I totally forgot—I have a meeting today."

Mina looked confused. "What?"

"I can't do coffee today. I'm so sorry. Can we do it tomorrow instead?"

Clare walked away before Mina could answer. She had to halt the detectives' progress before they got any closer to the school. She didn't want anyone from St. Mary's overhearing their conversation.

Clare reached them at the corner. She stopped, as if waiting for the light, and hissed, "What are you doing at my child's school?"

She could feel Mina's eyes on her back.

"We thought you might be more motivated to help if your husband weren't around," Breznick said.

"I'm sorry, but like Jed said, I can't speak to you without a lawyer."

"But he doesn't know that you were sleeping with Gabriel Prévost, does he?"

"What are you talking about?" Clare asked with unconvincing indignation.

"Before you commit yourself to the denial track, Mrs. Bast, ask yourself this: Can you be sure that Mr. Prévost's phone doesn't have any compromising messages on it? That he didn't tell anyone about your relationship? That no one ever saw you?"

Clare didn't answer. Of course Gabriel's phone would still have their messages on it. She had always erased them immediately, but he'd had no reason to do the same.

"We've been very discreet in our line of questioning so far," the detective went on. "If you're going to stonewall us, we'll have no choice but to get a little more direct."

"Just to be clear," Clare said, "you're threatening to tell my husband about the affair if I don't talk to you?"

"Like you said—you want us to catch the killer. So why won't you help us if you have nothing to hide? We can easily go through other, less-pleasant means of compelling you to answer."

She didn't seem to have a choice. "There's a diner a few blocks away," she said reluctantly. "We can get a coffee there."

While they walked, Clare mentally shuffled through her options. She could stonewall them again, hoping that they were bluffing about telling Jed. Alternatively, she could explain exactly what had happened, right down to finding Gabriel in a puddle of blood. Or she could take some middle course.

By the time they turned the corner onto Madison, she had settled on a strategy: She would be as open and honest as possible about the relationship with one exception—the night of Gabriel's death. She couldn't tell them that she had been at his house while he was murdered. They'd immediately barrage her with questions she had no answers to: Why hadn't she called the police? Or at the very least an ambulance? Why had she just run? She couldn't even really explain to herself why she'd done what she'd done. Her behavior had been bizarre at best, and deeply suspicious at worst. She was pretty sure that it was illegal to find a dead body and not report it.

No, she had to pretend that she'd gone straight home from the gallery. She would bury the truth deep in her mind, behind enough locked doors that even she would begin to doubt that it had happened.

A stick-thin woman in black leggings waved at Clare as she passed by.

"Hi," Clare said vaguely, with no clue who the woman was.

Clare led the two police officers into Three Guys, where she hoped the clamor would drown out their conversation. They settled into a booth at the back and ordered three coffees.

The investigator leaned back in her seat and looked around. The place was mostly filled with elderly patrons reading the paper. Two well-dressed women conferred over fabric samples laid out on the table between them. The air buzzed with the familiar sounds of diners everywhere: the low murmur of conversation punctuated by clanging silverware, rattling plates, and periodic shouts from fast-moving waiters.

"So," Breznick said after they'd ordered, "let's talk about your affair with Gabriel Prévost."

"I'll tell you whatever you want to know," Clare said, "but *please* keep

Jed out of this. The truth would kill him." She realized her poor choice of words as soon as they were out of her mouth.

Breznick looked at her for a moment before answering. "Mrs. Bast, I'm investigating a homicide. My priority right now is finding the culprit, not saving your marriage." She paused to shake and rip open a packet of Splenda. "But who knows? Maybe I'll be feeling more generous later on, depending on how cooperative you are."

Clare spread her hands. "I'm here. I'm cooperating."

"So how long had the relationship been going on?"

"Just a few weeks."

"Can you be more specific?"

"It started in early September, and we ended it toward the end of October. Two months or so, start to finish. A little less."

"It was over by the time of his death?"

"It had been over for nearly two weeks by then."

"Who ended it?"

"He did."

"Why?"

"I can't really speak for him. He didn't have a great explanation. He felt guilty. He said he was worried about how our relationship was impacting me and my marriage."

"How thoughtful of him," Breznick said dryly.

Clare didn't respond.

"Were you angry when he dumped you?"

"No."

"Hurt?"

"No," Clare lied. "We weren't in love. It was just— I don't know what it was. It was a mistake. I'd been planning to end it myself." That part, at least, was true. "I love my family."

"Where did you meet up?" Breznick asked. "Hotels? His place? Your place?"

"His."

"Do you have a key?"

"He had a keypad."

"Do you know the code?"

Clare hesitated. Her first instinct was to say no, but she stuck to her plan. "Four-seven-nine-two."

Nguyen took over the questioning while Breznick scribbled in her notepad. "Can you tell us about the last time you saw Mr. Prévost?" he asked. "You said it was at his gallery the night he died. Why did you go there, if you'd broken up?"

"I hadn't planned on it. I was having drinks with two old friends nearby, and they wanted to stop by."

"Can you give us the name of your friends?"

Clare did, spelling each one out.

"And how long did you stay at the party?"

"Less than an hour."

"And then what?"

"Then I went home."

"At what time?"

"I think it was around eleven."

"Anyone who can verify that?"

"I said goodbye to Lev and Cassandra, and my husband woke up when I came in."

Breznick jumped back in. "That alibi won't count for much if your husband won't even speak to us long enough to corroborate it."

Clare looked up sharply when she heard the word alibi. *Suspects* needed alibis, not witnesses.

"So you were working together and sleeping together?" Breznick pressed on. "Did that get complicated?"

"We weren't working together."

"You told us yesterday you were working with him. And you're not the only one to have mentioned it."

"That's just what we told people. Including Jed."

"So you did no business with Gabriel Prévost?"

"No."

"None at all?"

"None at all."

"Do you work?"

"I'm getting my doctorate in art history at Columbia."

"What are you studying?" Nguyen asked.

"I'm focusing on the painter Blake Webley as the bridge between the Abstract Expressionist and Minimalist movements."

"Sounds interesting," Nguyen said.

"It is, and I'm happy to tell you all about the 1950s American art scene, but I don't see how this is going to be helpful. I don't know anything about what got Gabriel killed. I'm as shocked as anyone. We'd only known each other for a short time, and I wouldn't be surprised if he was sleeping with other women. It was a fling, and now I'm just praying that it doesn't ruin my marriage. Can't you understand that?"

The two detectives appeared utterly unmoved. "Do you have any evidence he was sleeping with other women?" Breznick asked.

Clare sighed. "No. But since you ask, how did you know about me? His phone?"

Breznick and her partner exchanged a look.

"We're still working on getting access."

"How then?"

The detective raised an eyebrow as if to say, *What makes you think I would ever share that information with you?*

"Well, look, as I said, I don't have anything helpful to tell you. If I did, I would. I want the killer caught as much as anyone. But I'd also like to protect my marriage, so I'd rather this be our last conversation."

Breznick took her time extracting a piece of Trident gum from its wrapper and putting it into her mouth.

"Mrs. Bast, every piece of evidence we've found so far suggests that this crime was personal, not a burglary gone wrong. There were no signs of a forced entry. According to the security company's logs, either the intruder or Gabriel himself punched in the correct door code. And all of his valuables were left in plain sight. All of which indicates that this was a crime committed by somebody Gabriel knew."

Clare felt dizzy for a moment. A brief vision of an empty white wall flashed in front of her. But her attention was redirected to Breznick, who was now leaning closer and speaking forcefully.

"Now, you've taken great pains to assure us over and over again that you don't have any helpful information for us, Mrs. Bast, but let me be frank: We don't have very many leads. As far as Mr. Prévost's personal life goes, *you're* the juicy story. You're the married woman he was sleeping with. It makes me wonder—could you be the reason Gabriel left his own party early, as several people have mentioned?"

Clare said nothing.

"If I were you, I would think long and hard about whether you remember anything that might point us in another direction. Because I don't think you realize how badly you need there to be another storyline."

"I had nothing to do with Gabriel's death," Clare sputtered.

Breznick chewed her gum in silence.

Clare told herself not to say another word, but she was too unnerved to listen to common sense. How could they think she'd killed Gabriel? It was completely outlandish.

"Women don't *shoot* people," she said.

"It's actually the number one way they do kill people," Nguyen said, nodding thoughtfully.

"I've never even held a gun in my life."

"There's nothing else you want to add?" Breznick asked after a moment.

Clare shook her head.

"Well, I hope you'll call if you think of something. And you should probably let us know if you have plans to travel out of town anytime soon."

Nguyen put a ten-dollar bill on the table, and they both scooted out of the booth. Clare stared blankly at the seats they'd just abandoned. She could still see the imprints of their bodies pressed into the red vinyl.

Over the weekend, as she'd contemplated the possibility of the police seeking her out, she'd assumed that she would be just one name on a long list that they had to get through: Gabriel had countless friends, acquaintances, clients, and, as she'd said, probably lovers. But now she realized how naive she'd been. How couldn't she have seen this coming?

She was a suspect. An actual suspect.

Why do people kill? Love, lust, money, power, revenge. She was knee-deep in the first two, which still shocked her. But it had just never occurred to Clare that anyone could think of her as a murderer. She couldn't even send back a bad glass of wine at a restaurant.

But these cops didn't know anything about her. They didn't know what type of person she was. Just because she couldn't fathom killing someone didn't mean other people couldn't think it about her. If studying art had taught her anything, it was that people can see the same thing—a landscape, a face, a situation—in wildly different ways. So much so that you might suspect that they weren't looking at the same thing at all.

## CHAPTER 19

I DON'T THINK YOU REALIZE *how badly you need there to be another storyline.*

The detective's words echoed in Clare's mind as she walked out of Three Guys. She turned toward the park instead of her apartment. She needed air.

Of course there was another storyline, she thought bitterly—*the truth!*—and the NYPD had two crackerjack detectives, along with the latest forensic equipment, at their disposal to figure it out. But how hard would they look? She thought back to all the times Jed had complained about the cops while working on pro bono matters: how they ran roughshod over the facts, how all they cared about was clearing cases.

She climbed the steps up to the reservoir path and leaned against the cold metal railing. The day was gray and overcast. The water shone dully like tarnished silver. A lone seagull dipped into it and came up empty. The cold air stung Clare's face and brought tears to her eyes. She pinched the top of her nose to stop them.

How had she gotten herself into this situation? How had such a banal bad decision turned into *this*? She took out her phone and did what she should have done much earlier: She called Maggie.

"Is everything okay?" Maggie immediately asked. It wasn't even seven in the morning in Denver.

"No," Clare replied.

"What happened?"

"I had an affair, and the man I was sleeping with got killed. The police just questioned me about it."

"*What?* What are you talking about? Start over. Start from the beginning."

Clare took a deep breath. "Around two months ago, I met this guy at a party. An art dealer. And then, I don't even know how it happened. There was this painting—"

Clare stopped.

*Longfin.*

She'd completely forgotten about *Longfin*. That whole night had blurred into a hazy, horrific memory that she jerked her attention away from whenever it tried to pierce her consciousness. But now the image of *Longfin* emerged clearly from the veil of darkness. When she'd crawled out from under Gabriel's bed, the first thing she'd noticed was that *Longfin* was gone.

"Clare? Are you there?"

"I gotta go. I'm sorry. I'll call you back. I love you."

"*Clare—*"

She hung up the phone and started walking briskly along the dirt path surrounding the reservoir. She'd always found it easier to think when she was in motion.

Maggie immediately called back, but Clare silenced the call.

How had she forgotten about *Longfin*? They'd taken *Longfin*. They'd even taken the goddamn nail it was hanging on.

No, not they. *He*. The man in the black Reeboks. The person who killed Gabriel. It was all coming back to her now. *There* was her other storyline! It had been a break-in gone wrong: plain-and-simple theft.

"*Theft!*" she said out loud, banging her fist into her palm. A woman in a green Dartmouth sweatshirt swerved to give her a wide berth.

She needed to call Breznick and Nguyen. As soon as they learned that *Longfin* had been stolen that night, they'd shift their focus away from the harmless affair Gabriel had been having.

Except . . .

Clare felt her exultation deflate like a pinpricked balloon. She was too close to *Longfin*. Way too close.

The sale had been kept quiet: Not many people even knew that *Longfin* had been sold to Gabriel in the first place, much less that it was still hanging on his wall three months later. Once the police realized it had been stolen, those people would now comprise the list of suspects, because the killer had clearly known *Longfin* was there; he'd gone right for it and left everything else behind. Whittle that list down to the people who also had access to his home? Clare could think of only one person on it: herself.

And, last but certainly not least, she was a Blake Webley scholar. She was writing her fucking dissertation on *Longfin*.

She had found another storyline, but she was *still* the main character.

She was at the northwest side of the reservoir now, up near Ninety-Fourth Street, and she could hear the steady *plock-plock* of tennis balls rebounding on the courts behind her. She stopped walking and leaned against the railing to consider her predicament.

She was the only person—besides the thief—who knew that *Longfin* had been stolen the night that Gabriel was murdered. The police were working with incomplete information. Of course they'd focus on the married woman Gabriel was sleeping with; it was all they had to go on.

But she couldn't tell them that it had been stolen, because she was equally implicated by *that* fact. Not to mention that she knew it was missing only because she'd been there at the time. Whatever she did, wherever she went, the glare of suspicion found her. She was like a woman on stage being chased by a spotlight.

What was she supposed to do?

She needed the police to know that *Longfin* had been stolen—without their finding out that she'd witnessed the theft and only if she could prove that she hadn't had anything to do with it, despite all appearances to the contrary. How could she manage that? Especially since she herself had no idea what had happened.

She pressed her forehead against the cold metal railing. She couldn't do nothing. They were coming for her one way or another. Her only hope was to figure out what had happened that night.

She was highly unequipped to investigate a murder but couldn't escape the inevitable conclusion that she was the only one who *could* do it: She was the only person working with a complete set of facts. The only one who had the missing piece of the puzzle: *Longfin*.

Or was she?

As her hands gripped the fence and she stared into the slate-gray water, she urged her brain to do the work that it used to excel at: analyzing and categorizing information, drawing conclusions, proceeding logically. *Think*, she told herself. *Just think*.

Who else had known that Gabriel was keeping *Longfin* at his house?

Maybe his ex-wife Beatriz; he'd said they were still close. Maybe his partner, Michael Kline. These were just possibilities, though. The only person who *had* to know that the painting was still there—other than herself—was the buyer. He obviously knew that he hadn't taken possession of it yet.

And Gabriel knew the buyer. He'd implied that he'd go a long way to keep this particular client happy. If they'd met in New York, perhaps the buyer even had Gabriel's door code.

So who was he? Who was the buyer?

Clare racked her brain to try to remember anything Gabriel had said about him. He'd definitely referred to him as a "he." Gabriel had also implied that he was someone important—someone he'd wanted to retain as a client in the future. So presumably he was a wealthy and active collector. What else?

All of a sudden, she heard Gabriel saying, clear as day: "Who turns down the chance to own a Webley for a couple of months?"

Own.

Gabriel had owned *Longfin*. He'd bought it outright, so that his client wouldn't miss the opportunity, and he was going to sell it to him in January, for tax reasons. *Maybe*, Clare thought, *the buyer was trying to save himself a couple of million dollars*. He could have convinced Gabriel to put up the cash for *Longfin*, while keeping his own name out of it, and then simply taken what he wanted. For free. All he had to do was come up with some bogus story about tax savings.

She chewed on her cuticle. It was pure conjecture, she realized that. But it was all she had to go on at this point. If she did nothing, her life would be destroyed. Her only options were going down without a fight, or trying, as best she could, to fix things. She had to figure out what happened that night.

In that moment, the poet Ashbery's words came back to her all of a sudden: He'd called Webley's work "exquisitely brutal." It seemed to Clare that the power of Webley's work had been externalized somehow, made a real force in the world. It had brought Gabriel and Clare together, but perhaps it had led to his death, too.

## CHAPTER 20

THE FIRST STEP OF HER plan came to her in the shadow of the grand double-towered El Dorado building on the Upper West Side. The place to start was with the buyer, and Gabriel's business partner, Michael Kline, was the person most likely to know his identity. She couldn't ask Michael straight out—he'd never break a client's confidentiality just because a stranger asked. She'd have to find a more roundabout way—she'd take a page from Tasha's book and use nuance instead of force.

Back at her apartment, she dialed the number for the Prévost-Kline gallery right away. If she stopped to think about what she was doing, she'd lose her nerve. This wave of adrenaline and resolve was a welcome relief from the panic and helplessness she'd been feeling for the previous few days, so she would ride it as long as it lasted.

A harried-sounding female voice picked up: "Prévost-Kline, this is Rachel speaking."

"Hi, Rachel, I was hoping to speak with Michael Kline about a Blake Webley work?"

Rachel didn't even bother to respond; Clare just heard a click and then a lower-pitched ringing sound.

"Michael Kline speaking."

Clare dove right in. "Hi, Michael, I'm an art historian at Columbia, and Gabriel Prévost had kindly offered to let me come study a Blake Webley painting in his possession: *Longfin*, from 1958. I don't want to be insensitive, given recent events, but would it be possible for you to facilitate a viewing in his absence? It may be my last chance—anyone's last chance—to study it before it disappears from public view forever."

"*Longfin*," Kline repeated in a drawn-out surfer's drawl. "Gabriel bought that back in August, so it'd be long gone at this point."

"He actually showed it to me at his house quite recently."

Kline's tone became slightly less laconic. "How recently?"

"About two weeks ago." There was no way she was going to tell him she'd seen it the night he died.

"Huh. That's weird."

Clare felt some vindication: It *was* weird. She may not know all the ins and outs of the art market, but she knew enough to recognize that something about that situation was unusual. Why would Gabriel have a painting he bought for a client in August on his wall in late October?

"It was at his house, you said?"

"That's right. He said he was holding on to it for a while before delivering it to the buyer in January."

"Why would he do that?" Michael mused aloud, almost to himself.

"I think he mentioned a tax issue," Clare said. "Couldn't you check the contract?"

"No, the gallery wasn't involved in the purchase of *Longfin* at all. Gabriel had a consulting business on the side."

"Do you know who his client was, in this case?"

"Like I said, I wasn't involved. But I heard that he'd recently hired someone to work with him on it. Someone from Columbia, too, now that I think of it. Maybe you know her?"

The fiction that she had been working with Gabriel had spread further than she'd realized.

"That's probably me," Clare said. "We'd been discussing ways I could be of use to him."

Michael didn't respond. Perhaps he was wondering why someone who worked for Gabriel didn't know that he had his own consulting business.

"Can you tell me who's handling his estate?" Clare asked.

"I am. He made me the executor."

"So how will you find out who the buyer is?"

"At some point, I'll go through all his paperwork and inventory, but the police haven't let me into his house yet. It's still technically a crime scene."

"So you don't actually know if *Longfin* is there or not."

"I'd never imagined it would have been there at all, but after talking to you, I'm not so sure."

"When you do find out, would you mind letting me know who the buyer is? I know it's inappropriate to even ask, but you can't imagine how desperate I am to see *Longfin* again. It would be a real shame if this work disappeared from critical dialogue forever."

"I can't make any promises, but I'll see what I can do. What did you say your name was?"

"I didn't. It's Clare Regan." She used her maiden name because she wanted to keep Jed—and every other Bast—as removed from her investigation as possible. She rattled off her number and thanked him again.

As soon as Clare hung up, her phone started ringing again. It was Maggie, trying for the eighth time since Clare had abruptly ended their call. She picked up.

"Hi," she said. "I'm sorry."

"Jesus, Clare, you can't just drop a bomb like that and then disappear!"

"I know. I'm sorry. I'm so sorry."

"Tell me what is going on."

Clare lowered her voice, even though she was alone in her apartment.

"I started sleeping with this man named Gabriel a while back. We broke up two weeks ago, but he was killed in his house this weekend, and the police don't know who did it. They came to question me yesterday and again today, and they are being surprisingly aggressive about it. Like they think I'm involved somehow."

"Does Jed know?"

"About the police? Yes. About the affair? No."

"Are you going to tell him?"

"No."

Maggie was quiet for a moment. "I think you should—"

Clare answered before Maggie had even gotten the sentence out: "I can't."

"Lots of people have affairs, Clare. It's a shitty thing to do, yes, but relationships recover. And Jed adores you. I really think he'll forgive you."

"His mother threatened to take away Sadie."

"What? She can't do that. This isn't the nineteenth century."

"No, but she is close, personal friends with the top custody judge in the state. She also has proof that the affair negatively affected Sadie, not to mention millions of dollars to throw at lawyers."

"Clare—"

"Besides, I don't want a divorce. I love Jed."

"Do you?" Maggie asked gently.

"Of course I do. It was just a lapse in judgment."

"I still think you should tell him."

"Maggie, you don't understand, I *cannot* risk losing Sadie. If Jed finds out the truth, I promise you his mother will find a way to manipulate the situation to punish me. She probably already has a divorce lawyer on retainer.

"And even if I did somehow end up with joint custody, I'd still lose her, you know? She'd get entirely sucked into that Bast world. She'd summer in East Hampton and ski in Vail along with all her Harwick friends. What would I have to offer that could possibly compare? Some shitty studio apartment? Vacations in beautiful Binghamton? No—if we got a divorce, Sadie and all the other Basts would go on living their charmed life, while I stood on the outside, peering in."

"Clare, I think you're getting ahead of yourself. Divorces are not fun, I'll grant you that, but people get through them. You'd get through it. And Sadie's affections are not contingent on your finances."

"I can't. I just can't. Anyway, I think there may be a way out of this so that Jed never has to find out."

"What do you mean?"

"I know something."

"What do you know?"

"I don't know yet."

"Clare, do you hear yourself?"

"Everything will be cleared up in the next few days. I'm sure of it."

"I can come to New York. I can get on a plane right now. Just say the word."

"No. I have a plan."

"This sounds like a terrible idea."

"It's not," Clare said, hanging up on her yet again.

## CHAPTER 21

A FEW DAYS LATER, CLARE sat next to Jed in an Uber, winding through the quasi-industrial neighborhood of Red Hook, Brooklyn. She hadn't wanted to attend Gabriel's memorial service, but she thought her absence would be more conspicuous than her presence. She only hoped she could keep her emotions in check.

"Where exactly is this place?" Jed asked for the second time, peering out uneasily at the dilapidated garages and empty lots.

"We're close. Look"—Clare pointed out the window—"there's the Tesla showroom. You're fine." She hadn't wanted Jed to join her, but he'd insisted, and she couldn't think of an acceptable reason why he shouldn't come.

The Prévost-Kline gallery wasn't big enough to hold everyone who had wanted to come pay their respects, so Michael and Beatriz—the hosts—had chosen Pioneer Works, a contemporary arts organization in Red Hook. Clare had been there once before: It was a sprawling space that housed galleries, studios, classrooms, technology labs, a darkroom, and, off to one side, a big, beautiful garden.

As Clare and Jed stepped into the building, the space opened up before them like a church. It had polished cement floors, towering ceilings, and faded brick walls. Large white pillar candles flickered everywhere. Björk's *Biophilia* played softly from hidden speakers. The gallery near the front was filled with dozens of knitted tentlike structures that swung from the ceiling. Inside them, video screens glowed. *Beatriz and Michael had made a good choice,* she thought.

The mood was more subdued than a cocktail party, but not by much. There must have been nearly a hundred guests already milling around, but she and Jed were among only a handful of them actually wearing black. David Byrne was chatting in a corner with Lawrence Dunn, a high-profile dealer who specialized in contemporary installation pieces. Nearby, Rand Ashland, one of the first artists that Gabriel and Michael had represented, was signing the guest book.

Folding chairs had been set up in front of a small raised stage. Clare and Jed took their seats toward the back, not wanting to displace people who knew Gabriel better than they did. A man who looked so much like Gabriel that it took Clare's breath away walked up the aisle to the front row. He was the only man Clare had seen, other than Jed, wearing a tie. It must have been one of Gabriel's brothers. The lawyer, she guessed. Once seated, he kept his back to the scene behind him.

Clare, on the other hand, angled herself in her chair so she could see the crowd trickling in. She was here with an ulterior motive. She was determined to figure out the real story behind Gabriel's death, and the memorial service was where she would have access to almost everyone who might know anything.

She'd spent the last few days thinking almost nonstop about *Longfin*, and her questions had compounded exponentially. Why hadn't the museum sold *Longfin* at auction, which was the usual practice for deaccessioning a work of art? Instead, they'd sold it directly to Gabriel and asked him to keep things quiet. Why had they even deaccessioned a Webley in the first place, given how scarce they were? And why had Gabriel kept the painting in his house for nearly three months?

As she came up with a series of vague suspicions and unformed theories, she became convinced of one thing: The mystery of *Longfin* hadn't started with its disappearance, but rather with its sale.

The art market may as well have been custom designed for unscrupulous behavior. It was sometimes called the largest legal, unregulated business in the United States. Globally, it was worth somewhere around $65 billion. Work by the top hundred artists had an annual growth rate almost triple that of the S&P index.

What's more, as Gabriel himself admitted, value was determined by a hazy, esoteric process steered—if not outright controlled—by just a handful of select dealers. That made art an ideal vehicle for laundering money: An object's monetary value could be increased or decreased at convenient times. Besides, it was a lot easier to transport a painting worth fifty million dollars than the same amount in cash. When Mexico passed a law in 2012 limiting cash deals and making it impossible for buyers to remain anonymous, its local art market cratered: Sales fell by seventy percent in a single year. To many, this suggested that most of the biggest art buyers had previously been drug cartels.

Clare had heard countless other salacious stories: The Salvador Dalí bought with cash that reeked of marijuana. The Botero sculptures filled with cocaine. Was it possible that the *Longfin* deal had attracted someone who would think nothing of killing the middleman to get what he wanted? Clare didn't think Gabriel was the type to break any laws, but he definitely swam in that swamp of dark money and secret deals. He'd said himself that he thrived in it.

WHEN ALL THE guests were seated, Michael Kline climbed onto the dais. In black wide-legged pants and a matching Nehru-collar shirt, he resembled nothing so much as a therapist from Esalen.

"Thank you all for coming," he said, pressing his palms together. "I know Gabriel would have been deeply moved to see everyone he loved in one room together."

He unfolded a piece of paper and recited the poem "Sunday Morning" by Wallace Stevens. When he reached the fifth stanza—"Death is the mother of beauty; hence from her, / Alone, shall come fulfilment to our dreams / And our desires"—a woman toward the front let out a strangled sob. Clare craned her neck to try to see who had made the sound, but her view was blocked.

Michael shared a few of his own memories of Gabriel, which stretched back nearly thirty years. He recalled how even during their desperate efforts to keep their gallery afloat in the beginning, Gabriel could always find the humor, or the beauty, in any situation.

"Art was so much more than his business," he said. "It was his mode of living, a way of weaving beauty into every moment and every action. I have no doubt that he is now surrounded by such radiant splendor it could go by no other name than heaven. Let's try to take comfort in that thought, rather than mourn his loss. Gabriel wouldn't want us to dwell in our grief. Instead, let's vow to live as he lived. Let's all go out in pursuit of beauty, in its many varied forms. That is where we'll find Gabriel now."

Clare felt tears welling up and squeezed her eyes shut to try to stop them. She took a few deep breaths and managed to prevent an outburst. But when she opened her eyes again, she saw that almost everyone in the room was crying, including Jed.

Clement Rosier, the MoCA curator, spoke next. He said that when he'd first moved to New York from France, Gabriel had made such an effort to welcome him that he'd thought he'd been hitting on him. "You can't imagine how disappointed I was to discover that Gabriel was just that exceedingly rare thing: A warm and open man, who, unfortunately, was very, *very* straight." That got a laugh.

Tony Fang, the old It kid of the early-aughts art scene, got up and spoke next. He had been an early addition to the Prévost-Kline roster: a Chinese American painter who made meticulous copies of old masters with tongue-in-cheek additions like a Casio watch on a cardinal's wrist or a tiny Hello Kitty barrette in some duchess's hair. He'd abruptly fallen out of favor after Jerry Saltz wrote a scathing review that dismissed him as a "Xerox machine rather than an artist," but Clare knew Gabriel still took him out to dinner every few months.

A woman behind Clare whispered loudly to her partner, "He looks terrible." Clare couldn't help but agree. Tony hadn't been in the public eye for twenty years, so his gray hair and stooped posture seemed to have sprouted overnight.

"I first met Gabriel when he visited a student exhibition at Cooper Union. Of all the dealers passing through, he was the only one who took any interest in my work. He saw the humor in it when no one else did. Over the subsequent years, he became a mentor, a colleague, and a friend. He was the most loyal man I know."

Tony then trained a cold stare on his audience.

"Everyone in this room abandoned me in one way or another, but he never did. He was a good man. It shouldn't have been *him* this happened to."

He stepped away from the microphone, and the audience sat in stunned silence. Some, like Gabriel's brother, glanced around in confusion. Who was this lunatic?

Beatriz Barros, Gabriel's ex-wife, stood up and made her way to the lectern. She was every inch as glamorous as Clare had imagined, in an oxblood-red pantsuit, gold stilettos, and impeccable eyeliner.

"Thank you, Tony," Beatriz said in a husky, accented voice and moved on quickly. "Gabriel and I met in Venice fifteen years ago. We married after three weeks and divorced after eight years. Aside from those first three weeks, I think the last seven years were our happiest. Outside of marriage, we allowed each other more freedom and more grace. As you all know, Gabriel was kind, vivacious, talented, and passionate, but these words sound too hollow, too insubstantial to describe the man he was. That is one of the few things we always agreed on: the need for art to express emotions and ideas that words alone cannot. And so I will give up trying to explain who Gabriel was or what his loss means. His life was a work of art, and all of you are a testament to that. Thank you for coming."

Beatriz went back to her seat, and the music came back on shortly after. When Michael Kline stood up, the rest of the crowd followed suit. The ceremony was over.

CLARE AND JED joined the flow of people heading outside. It had grown darker, but flames from a large firepit threw flickers of light on the people gathered around it. Jed spotted Tasha at the far side of the garden, wearing a black pillbox hat with a netted veil, like a newly widowed fourth wife.

"Should we go say hi?" Clare asked.

"I think I need a drink in order to face that hat. Do you want something from the bar?"

"Just a Pellegrino, thanks."

Clare wended her way across the garden, gravel crunching underneath her feet. Tasha greeted her, as usual, with a kiss on each cheek.

"Is Alec here?" Clare asked.

Tasha gestured toward a long table laid with food, where Alec was talking to someone Clare didn't know while trying to stuff an enormous wedge of Brie into his mouth.

Clare spotted Greg Nguyen and Pam Breznick, the two police officers who had visited her earlier in the week, standing directly behind Alec. They were both wearing black suits with white shirts and talking to Gabriel's brother.

"What are they doing here?" Clare asked.

Tasha followed her gaze. "I have no idea. Are they caterers?"

"They're the police. Didn't they question you? They were asking about Gabriel's clients."

"No—at least not that Alec mentioned. When did they interview you?"

"Earlier this week—since I'd been working with Gabriel."

"Did they say what they think happened?"

"No, but speaking of Gabriel's work, any chance you could tell me who he bought *Longfin* for?"

Tasha looked startled by the sudden change of topic. "*Longfin?*"

"The Blake Webley painting he bought from MoCA. I thought you might know, since you're on the board."

"I remember when we deaccessioned it, but I haven't a clue what Gabriel did with it. Why?"

"For my dissertation. I was only halfway through my chapter on *Longfin* when the museum sold it, and I don't think I can finish it without seeing it again. I was hoping to reach out to the owner directly and beg for a last glimpse."

"If I remember correctly, Gabriel said his client wanted to stay anonymous."

"I know, I know. I just thought you might be able to pull some strings . . ."

"As much as I love throwing my weight around, I can't help you on this one. From the museum's perspective, Gabriel was the buyer."

"The board didn't press him on who his client was?"

"What Gabriel did with the painting after he bought it was none of our concern."

Tasha had hit on one of the dirty little secrets of the art world.

Institutions selling art were supposed to perform due diligence to confirm that their buyers were using legal cash. But the whole process was usually undertaken more for appearances' sake rather than with any real stridency. If Christie's, for instance, were to turn away a buyer over suspicions about his finances, that person could simply take his hundreds of millions of dollars to Sotheby's. Often the seller performed due diligence on the person acting as the buyer's agent—the dealer—instead, even though everyone involved knew that wasn't the real purchaser.

Clare could recall one story where Christie's—uncharacteristically—pushed a dealer to name his client, because there'd been rumors it was a Russian oligarch on the sanctions list. The dealer simply made up a fake name, which the auction house ran through an international database, obviously encountering no issues. By the time Christie's realized the name was fake, the painting had already been sold and collected. What did they care? They'd made their multimillion-dollar commission and could still claim to have acted in good faith. Private transactions were even more rife with secrecy: The buyer and the seller were each represented by other parties, and all the players signed confidentiality agreements.

"So no one at the museum knows who the buyer is?"

"I don't think so. The board certainly doesn't. It's possible Angelica does, but she's pretty checked out." Angelica Hines, the museum's current director, was nearing seventy-five and not exactly at the top of her game.

Clare felt her hopes deflating. She tried another angle.

"Out of curiosity, why did MoCA decide to sell *Longfin*?"

"That would have been Clement's decision—he's the head of that department. If I'm remembering correctly, he said that the work was duplicative—MoCA has something like a dozen other Webleys—and that the time was ripe to sell. He thought we could get an all-time high, which would translate into exciting new acquisitions. He didn't say as much, but I'm guessing he knew that Gabriel was interested; they were close friends after all."

"Clement knew about Gabriel's offer before he decided to deaccession *Longfin*?"

"Maybe." Tasha waved at someone across the room. She seemed unbothered by the question's implications.

"But Tasha, that's terrible," Clare said. "That sets the precedent that anyone with enough money can just stroll through the museum saying 'I want that one, and that one, and that one.' It turns one of the country's top public art institutions into . . . Bloomingdale's."

Tasha laughed. "Bergdorf's at the very least, I hope."

Clare didn't smile.

Tasha put her hand on Clare's arm. "Clare, you're just like Jed, you take everything so seriously. Listen, it wasn't like Gabriel slid Clement a slip of paper with a number written on it. I'm sure he communicated his client's interest, that's all. This kind of thing is a dance—a type of seduction. Clement is very good at reading the signals. And I don't think you realize how badly the museum needs cash right now. The pandemic nearly destroyed us. You'd be shocked at how many museums are deaccessioning these days."

"And Clement could make that decision all on his own?"

"Of course not. The proposal always comes from the relevant curator—they know the collection best—but the decision must then be approved by the director and the board."

"How often do the director or the board reject a petition to deaccession."

"I'm not sure I've ever heard of that. Presumably, it's rare."

"Aren't deaccessioned works usually sold at auction?"

"Usually, yes, but in this case, why give a commission to Sotheby's when there was already a deal?"

"I don't know, Tasha. Something seems off here . . ."

"Clare, what exactly are you implying?"

Tasha's air of distracted nonchalance had evaporated. Truthfully, Clare didn't know what she was implying—not yet. She decided it was best to backtrack before Tasha got offended. She was on the MoCA board. She'd okayed the sale. If Clare suggested that there was something off about it, she was ultimately accusing Tasha herself of malfeasance.

"I'm just eager to see the painting again, that's all. I think it would help me get my writing back on track. Would you mind asking around the museum to see if anyone knows where it ended up?"

"I told you I don't do favors."

"Don't think of it as a favor. Think of it as an opportunity to throw your weight around."

Tasha allowed herself a small smile.

"I'll see what I can do. But don't get your hopes up."

JED HAD NEVER returned with Clare's Pellegrino, so she went to get one herself. She found her husband still at the bar, chatting with, of all people, Clement Rosier. Clement was as dapper as ever in a gray suit and a green silk scarf knotted effortlessly around his neck. But his eyes were bloodshot, and his glasses were smudged.

When Clare approached, Jed turned and handed her one of the two drinks he was holding. "Sorry, honey, I got waylaid. You remember Clement Rosier from MoCA?"

"It's good to see you again. I was actually just talking about you."

"All good things, I hope," Clement said.

"Of course," Clare said. "Tasha and I were discussing *Longfin* because I'm writing my dissertation on Blake Webley."

"Right, I think you mentioned that when we met."

"I was hoping Tasha might be able to tell me who bought it so I could see it one last time, but she couldn't help. Any chance you know who Gabriel bought it for?"

"Not a clue," Clement said. "One thing Gabriel was very good at was keeping secrets."

Was that true? He'd told her about *Longfin* right off the bat.

"If you hear of it surfacing again, would you let me know?"

"Sure. But I'm not really on that side of things, you know . . ."

Out of the corner of her eye Clare noticed Beatriz moving through the crowd, back into the building. Clare excused herself from Jed and Clement and followed at a short distance. She stepped inside the building just as Beatriz disappeared into the bathroom. Clare waited a beat and then went in, immediately spotting Beatriz's gold pumps under the door to one of the stalls. The others were empty. Clare turned on the water and began washing her hands. When Beatriz came out, Clare caught her eye in the mirror and smiled.

"Beatriz?"

"Yes?"

"I just wanted to tell you what a fan I am of your work."

Beatriz turned on the tap at the sink next to Clare. "Thank you, that's kind of you to say."

"I also wanted to tell you how sorry I am for your loss. I'd become friendly with Gabriel only recently, but he spoke about you often. And with great fondness."

Clare could feel Beatriz examining her in the mirror. "You're Clare," she finally said.

Clare lowered her voice. "He told you about me?"

"Of course. We told each other everything. He told me when it ended, too. He was devastated."

*Well* he's *the one who ended it*, Clare thought but didn't say. Despite herself, she was annoyed at him for telling his ex-wife about her. Clement had clearly overstated Gabriel's talent for discretion.

"Have the police told you anything about what they think happened?"

"Not really. They asked who his enemies were, and I told them that he wasn't the kind of person to *have* enemies. I know it's a ridiculous thing to say, but I keep thinking how this is all so out of character. It's just not *like* him to get murdered. You knew him, you know what I mean. He wasn't the type of guy to leave vitriol in his wake. He liked parties, good music, communion, you know? I mean, look at us, exes are supposed to hate each other, right? But we still spoke several times a week; we still spent every Christmas together."

"Maybe there were things about his business you didn't know . . ."

"Gabriel wasn't a crook, and he wasn't involved with crooks either."

"There was no one from his past? No angry exes, old business partners, disappointed clients, dropped artists? I mean, everyone has *some* conflict in their life."

"Conflict, yes. But murderous rage? Never."

Beatriz yanked a paper towel form the dispenser and began drying her hands vigorously.

"Did he by any chance tell you who he bought *Longfin* for? The Blake Webley painting?"

"No. Why?"

"I'm writing my dissertation on Webley. That's how we met."

"Ah—Gabriel said you were smart. But no, I don't know anything about that." She tossed the paper towel in the trash. "I should really be getting back out there. His poor brother is such a fish out of water."

"Of course. I'm sorry to hold you up. It was nice to meet you, even under these circumstances."

"You, too. And I'm sorry, also—for *your* loss. I should have said that before."

Clare was touched by the gesture. She didn't doubt that Beatriz's grief was larger than her own. "Thank you."

"You know—" Beatriz said and then paused.

"What?"

"I told the police about you. I had to. Not your last name—I don't know it—but it was probably enough for them to figure it out. I'm sorry if that makes things harder for you."

"That's okay. They would have found out eventually."

Beatriz nodded, then turned and left the room.

As Clare replayed their conversation in her mind, she realized that Beatriz had contradicted herself: Either she was wrong, and Gabriel *didn't* tell her everything, or she was lying, and she knew more about *Longfin* than she'd admitted. It wasn't much to go on, but it was all she had—the silver bullet she'd come here looking for was nowhere to be found.

When Clare opened the door to the bathroom, she saw Breznick and Nguyen, the detectives, strolling back into the building from the garden.

She immediately popped back into the bathroom and enclosed herself in a stall for a full two minutes. When she emerged again, they were gone.

Clare had hit her limit. She found Jed and told him she was ready to go home. He took out his phone to order an Uber.

They rode back to Manhattan in silence. Jed seemed as relieved as she was to be leaving Red Hook and returning to their safe uptown bubble. He still didn't know how fragile it really was.

## CHAPTER 22

THE NEXT MORNING, JED TOOK Sadie to see his parents, and Clare used the time to call Lev. He knew all the art-world gossip, and Clare wanted to know what people were saying about Gabriel's death. They'd exchanged shocked text messages the day the news broke—Clare had used the opportunity to reinforce her version of the events, asking how long they'd stayed after her early exit—but she hadn't actually spoken to him or Cassandra since the night that Gabriel was killed.

On the phone, Lev had a hard time covering up the thrill he obviously felt at having been at Gabriel's party that night. Apparently, it was something of a badge of honor now.

"Can you imagine if we'd been five blocks away and *not* gone?" he asked, as if that would have been the real tragedy.

Clare could imagine it. She imagined it daily. She longed for it. If she hadn't gone to that stupid party, Gabriel would probably still be alive. She was the reason he'd left the gallery and gone home in the first place.

"What have people been saying about the murder?" Clare asked. "Does anyone know what happened?"

"People definitely have theories, but most of them are bananas. Someone told me he was involved with the mob or some nonsense like that. And then he obviously had a reputation for sleeping around, so maybe he bedded down with some psycho killer. Or it could have been a disgruntled artist he'd refused to represent. Oh, the wildest one I've heard is that the whole thing was a performance piece."

"What? Like Gabriel faked the whole thing?"

"No, like his actual death was a work of art by some deranged performance artist. It would actually be kind of legendary, if you think about it . . ."

"It really wouldn't."

"Well, anyway, that's what I've heard."

"He had a consulting business on the side, did you know that?"

"I knew he had some private clients."

"Does anyone think his death might have had something to do with that?"

"Not that I've heard. That's a good angle, though."

"I heard he recently bought a Blake Webley painting from MoCA for some mystery client—maybe you could find out who he bought it for?"

"Did he? When?"

"This past summer, I think."

"Oh, well, that's too long ago to matter."

"Speaking of MoCA," Clare said, "do you have any intel on Clement Rosier?"

"Everyone thinks he's going to be the next director. Some people find him difficult, but who isn't in this business?"

They wrapped up their conversation—Lev had heard about Tony Fang's eulogy and wanted a blow-by-blow before they hung up—and then Clare tried the same approach with Cassandra. She had even less information than Lev, but at least showed slightly more reserve about her brush with scandal.

THAT AFTERNOON, JED headed into his office and Clare took Sadie to the park. It was mid-November, and the temperature had abruptly dropped the night before. For the first time, it felt like winter was near. While Sadie played, Clare sat on a bench in the playground with her hands tucked underneath her to keep them warm.

Clare's panic had abated slightly since her conversation with the police at Three Guys. They hadn't tried to contact her again, and at Gabriel's memorial service, they'd ignored her altogether. Clare told herself that their insinuations over coffee had been nothing more than a scare tactic. They would say anything to get someone to talk. It was one of the oldest tricks in the book. It hadn't worked on her, and now—she hoped—they would move on.

Her own improvised investigation at the memorial service hadn't yielded much either, but what Tasha told her about the sale of *Longfin* had left a bad taste in her mouth. She couldn't pinpoint the problem—or how it might have led to Gabriel's death—but she was starting to suspect that it all might have something to do with Clement Rosier. He clearly had a conflict of interest if Gabriel was an old friend of his.

Clare watched Sadie go down the slide on her stomach, face-plant in the sand, and start laughing hysterically for the ninth time in a row.

"Don't you want your mittens, honey?" Clare called to her.

Sadie glared at her, incensed that her mother would make such an unreasonable suggestion.

A tall woman materialized out of nowhere next to Clare. "I guess that's a no," she said.

"Apparently," Clare replied, marveling at the woman's playground getup: four-inch heels, brown leather pants, and a long, crimson, cashmere coat. She was at least six feet tall, with curly black-and-gray hair straining for release from a tortoiseshell barrette.

The woman sat down next to her. "She's adorable."

"Thanks," Clare replied. "Which one is yours?"

"No children for me—too sticky."

Clare eyed her companion more closely. "What brings you to the playground then?"

The woman plucked a long hair from her coat and flicked it to the ground. Then she rotated her body so that they were facing each other on the bench.

"I came to see you, Clare."

## CHAPTER 23

CLARE FELT HER INSIDES GO cold. Her eyes darted back to Sadie, who was burying her hat in the sand, wholly unconcerned with the conversation Clare was having a few feet away.

"Why would you be here to see *me*?" she asked.

"I'm looking into the whereabouts of Blake Webley's 1958 painting *Longfin*, and someone suggested that you might be a good person to talk to."

"Who suggested that?"

"I'm not at liberty to say."

"Are you with the police?"

The woman laughed throatily and gestured to her outfit.

"This is a Brunello Cucinelli coat that cost ten thousand dollars."

"That's not an answer."

"No, I'm not with the police."

"Who are you then?"

The woman pulled a card out of her wallet and handed it to Clare. Raised serif type on heavy ivory-colored cardstock spelled out: Elise Vargas, Art & Antiquities Intelligence. A single 212 phone number. No website. No email.

Clare handed it back to her.

"Keep it," Elise said, waving it away.

"I don't want it," Clare replied, placing it on the bench between them.

Elise didn't react. She was still watching Sadie with a vague smile on her face.

"I started my career not too far from here," she said. "At Sotheby's." She inclined her head east, to where the auction house's headquarters were. "I didn't find the work very interesting. And the salary was a joke. I could have lived on it, I *did* live on it, but it bothered me that I seemed to be the only one who actually did. The other women I worked with—and they were almost all women—wore Cartier watches and lived in doorman buildings. It took me an embarrassingly long time to figure out that they were being subsidized by parents or trust funds or partners. It didn't seem possible to form any real camaraderie with people like that." She turned to Clare. "Did you feel like that when you started out at the Met?"

"No," Clare replied, though she had often felt exactly like that.

"I worked with a client there, a Swiss man, who told me about some of the difficulties he encountered as a collector. As you know, value can be somewhat arbitrary in the art market. It's based on an always-shifting set of criteria—public opinion, less-than-public opinion, public sales data, less-than-public sales data. You can't make a good deal without good information, but good information isn't easy to come by. Information that isn't googleable. Information that sometimes takes the form of a rumor or a gut feeling. What's knowable is nebulous, shifting. And I decided that that is where I would make my living—in that gray area. I would chase down the information that was hardest to find and was therefore the most valuable. I started working freelance for my Swiss client, then a friend of his, and eventually I started my own firm. And that is what I've done for the past twenty-odd years. I work with galleries, collectors, banks, insurers, auction houses, you name it. It's fascinating work."

Clare was reminded of Rene Russo's character in *The Thomas Crown Affair*, whose job—and wardrobe—she'd always envied.

Elise recrossed her legs. "Well, most of the time it is. There are plenty of duds in the mix, too. That's actually what I thought this *Longfin* job was at first: just a simple matter of sorting through paperwork that nobody else wanted to deal with. Not the sexiest work, but hey, I've got expensive tastes." She flicked an invisible speck off her coat.

"Then a funny thing happened: The more I looked into this case, the more interesting it got. And it just keeps getting stranger and stranger at every turn."

"Who hired you?"

"Again, I'm not at liberty to say."

"What makes you think I'm going to answer your questions if you won't answer mine?"

Clare had been asking rhetorically, but Elise nodded thoughtfully.

"Well, a few reasons. One, I believe you actually care what happens to this painting. Two, it may have something to do with Gabriel Prévost's death, and I believe you'd like to find the person responsible for that. But mostly it boils down to the fact that you're treading water in fifteen-foot waves, and I'm the only lifeboat in sight."

As Clare took this all in, Sadie ran over and hugged her knees. "Mama, will you push me on the swings?"

"Play on the slide for a few more minutes, then I will."

"Who's that?" Sadie asked, pointing at Elise.

"Hi, Sadie," Elise replied. "I'm a friend."

"Honey, give me five minutes, then we'll do the swings. Okay?"

"Okay, Mama." Sadie skipped cheerfully back to the slide.

Clare took a breath and turned to Elise. "Thank you for your concern, but I assure you, I'm just fine."

Elise leaned in and spoke quietly: "Clare, you are so far from fine, I don't even know where to begin. Every time I turn a corner in this investigation, *there you are*. Let's start with the obvious: You were sleeping with the murder victim. You were working with him, too, and both of those things started right after he procured a painting that you have an avid—not to mention documented—interest in. What's more, you've told at least one person how distressed you were at the idea of this painting going into private hands—which it was about to do. Oh"—Elise snapped her fingers, as if the thought had just occurred to her—"and he got killed just days after he dumped you. Plus, you are one of the few people who had access to his home."

"How do you know all that?" Clare asked in a low voice.

"I'm very good at my job."

"I didn't kill Gabriel."

"I don't care."

Clare frowned at her, and Elise clarified: "I care about the painting. That's it."

"I didn't take the painting either."

"I agree. Why would you question Michael Kline and Beatriz Barros about it if you'd taken it? Why make a fuss?"

"Exactly. I'm sure the police will come to that conclusion, too."

Elise laughed. "You have that much faith in the NYPD? You're their primary suspect, and they haven't even made the *Longfin* connection yet. What do you think will happen when they do?"

Clare felt like she'd been punched in the gut.

"How do you know I'm their primary suspect?"

"Like I said, I'm very good at my job."

Clare glared at her in frustration. She wanted to wipe that glib smile right off her face.

Elise seemed to recognize that she was at her breaking point. "I have a source in the department," she conceded.

"Well, why *haven't* the police made the *Longfin* connection?" Clare asked. "Don't you have a duty to tell them something that could help their investigation?"

Elise raised an eyebrow. "Don't you?"

Clare didn't answer.

"Listen, my clients hire me to make problems go away, not to complicate the ones they already have. Over the years I've found that the police have a real talent for making things worse. And frankly, I don't have any reason to go to them. At least not yet. I've come across exactly zero evidence connecting Gabriel's murder to *Longfin*."

"What have you come across then? Why are you here?"

"Let's call them . . . a series of irregularities."

"What kind of irregularities?"

"Tit for tat, Clare. I've now answered quite a few of your questions. You've gotta give me something. That's how this works."

Clare pressed her fingers against her temples. She could feel a headache forming.

"I'm not your enemy here," Elise said. "Our interests are aligned. I want the painting. You want to prove that someone other than you killed Gabriel. I'm convinced that we each have a part of the puzzle; we just need to put them together. We can figure this out, Clare, you and I. Why don't you start by telling me about the last time you saw *Longfin*?"

Tell a complete stranger that she'd been at Gabriel's house, mere feet away, while he was murdered? That she might even have done something to stop it and didn't? That it was her fault he hadn't been laughing and drinking at his gallery's party at that very moment?

Clare looked over and studied Elise Vargas. She didn't have the stooped shoulders that very tall women sometimes develop in an effort to make themselves smaller. Hers were thrown back, head held high. Clare wanted to trust her. She wanted to put herself in this woman's hands. But she had already lost so much control; she was desperate to hold tight to whatever crumbs she had left.

She couldn't trust a complete stranger. She just couldn't do it.

"I can't help you," Clare said. "I'm sorry."

Elise looked at her for a moment, and then nodded. "Well, you have my number if you change your mind." She stood up and strode out of the playground, her high heels seeming to give her no trouble at all in the sand. When she was about to open the gate, she turned back to Clare.

"Call me if you need a lifeboat," she called out.

Clare ignored her and stared fixedly ahead. Elise's card still lay on the bench next to her. After a few moments, Clare picked it up off the green, peeling paint and tucked it into her coat pocket.

"Come on, Sadie!" she yelled. "Let's do the swings."

## CHAPTER 24

LIKE A NASTY INFECTION, THE panic returned. It was inescapable. Whatever Clare was doing—stirring DayGlo orange cheese into pasta, washing her face, folding laundry—she did it with an ever-present understanding that time was running out.

What Elise had said about the police had horrified her. *Clare* was their primary suspect? She knew that Breznick hadn't liked her, but for her to actually think that Clare had murdered Gabriel was something else entirely. Clare had been operating under the naive assumption that innocent people don't go to prison for murder. Or rather, not innocent people like her. There were all sorts of uncomfortable assumptions hiding behind those three words—*people like her*—but she'd never thought to question them until now.

Whenever Clare had struggled with anxiety before—in what she now thought of as her past life, pre-Gabriel—she'd always been able to summon up a quiet, rational voice that knew that she was overreacting: That other mother hadn't *really* been judging her for not working; Sadie's cough wasn't *really* pneumonia. But now, that voice was silent. She was in the kind of trouble that she couldn't rationalize away.

The police would be back. She was sure of it. And this time, they'd probably bring handcuffs.

Was it only a matter of days? Hours? Minutes? Her heart pounded against her ribs like a metronome, counting down the seconds until her life was torn apart.

The only thing her investigation had yielded was a vague suspicion of Clement Rosier. She'd come up with plenty of theories about how he might have manipulated the deaccessioning process, but none that connected him to Gabriel's death. She needed more information.

ON MONDAY AFTERNOON, Clare called Tasha to ask if she'd been able to find out who Gabriel had bought *Longfin* for.

"I did ask around," Tasha replied, "but nobody knew a thing. I even took a look at the contract. There's no mention of a third party. It's entirely standard in every respect. MoCA sold the painting to a well-known and well-regarded art dealer, and payment was received promptly. Case closed."

"Thank you for looking into it," Clare said, trying to hide the depth of her disappointment.

"Aren't there other Webleys you can write about for your dissertation? I can get you in to see one in the storage facility."

"Sure, that would be great," Clare said hollowly.

The panic rose up again. The less she understood about this crime, the more in danger she was of having it pinned on her.

Was it worth sharing her theories about Clement? Tasha might be offended, but she might also have some helpful information. At this point, Tasha was her only source into the deal.

"Tasha, I've been wondering whether Clement might have had ulterior motives for deaccessioning *Longfin*," she said, carefully measuring her tone.

"What are you talking about?"

"Just hear me out. He makes, what, a couple hundred thousand dollars a year? That's peanuts in the circles he travels in. His friends buy villas and van Goghs while he has to scrimp and save for a Thom Browne suit. That is a frustrating position to be in. He's so close to so much wealth, but he doesn't quite have access to it. What he *does* have access to is thousands of works of art worth hundreds of millions of dollars. And he has an enormous amount of leeway to determine the terms of a sale. If he could loop in a dealer—and we already know he was old friends with Gabriel—he could sell a work for, say, ten million—the museum gets that—and then Gabriel could flip it for twelve, even fifteen, and the two of them could split the proceeds. It's easy money, ripe for the picking."

Tasha didn't reply right away. When she did, her tone was cooler. "Just to be clear, Clare, you're accusing Clement *and* Gabriel of defrauding MoCA?"

"It's just a theory."

"Well, it doesn't make any sense. For that plan to work, Gabriel would have had to have gotten a sweetheart deal on the painting, and he didn't. Gabriel's offer was astronomical. We were all amazed when we heard. There's no way anyone could have flipped it for much more—if anything. It's more likely that they would have taken a loss."

"How much did MoCA sell *Longfin* for?"

"Eighteen million dollars."

Tasha was right: There was little chance Gabriel could have found a buyer who'd pay more than that for a relatively small Webley.

"Clare, I'm only going to say this once: It is not a good idea to go around accusing Clement of wrongdoing. As you know, the art world is a small place, and when you finish your degree, you're going to find it very difficult to get a job if you're on his blacklist. You cannot make unfounded accusations about him. Not only is it unwise from a professional standpoint, it's also irresponsible. You could do serious damage to the museum's reputation, and I've given a lot to that place. I don't take a threat against it lightly."

"I'm sorry," Clare said. "I really am. I think Gabriel's death has knocked me a little off-kilter."

"We're all upset about Gabriel, Clare."

"Of course. I appreciate all your help, Tasha, I really do. I promise I won't cause any trouble for the museum."

"Or for yourself," Tasha said in a gentler tone.

"Or for myself," Clare agreed.

## CHAPTER 25

CLARE WANTED TO KEEP HER promise not to cause any more trouble. But trouble had arrived of its own volition before it took up permanent residence. She was just trying to deflect it somewhere else.

She'd had no luck finding out who Gabriel had bought *Longfin* for, but in the course of her investigation she'd stumbled on, perhaps, a more important question: Why had MoCA decided to sell it?

According to Tasha, it had been Clement's idea. Clare had checked with Britt, her old friend who worked at MoCA, and she'd confirmed that the top departmental curator always started the deaccessioning process. So what prompted him to propose that particular painting?

Was it possible that Clement and the mystery buyer had been working together to con *Gabriel*? Clare played out the scenario in her mind: Clement would instigate the sale of *Longfin*, and the buyer would ask Gabriel to put in a large offer on his behalf. Then, once the painting was outside the museum's security system, they could hire someone to simply take it from Gabriel, who'd put up the cash.

Of course it was *possible*. She could come up with any number of potential scenarios. The problem was the lack of certainty. How would she ever find out the real reason that Clement had decided to deaccession *Longfin*?

Then in a sudden moment of clarity, it came to her: She could just ask him. Tasha had told her to keep her nose out of it, but the sale of *Longfin* actually *was* her business. She was a Blake Webley scholar. She should know if Webley's reputation was undergoing a shift, one way or another. The eighteen-million-dollar price tag had shocked her. What if Webleys were surging in value—or they were about to—for some reason the public didn't yet know? It was like the Warhols all over again: Someone could be manipulating the market.

So Clare simply called up Clement Rosier and asked to take him out for coffee. When he suggested a date two weeks into the future, Clare dropped Tasha's name, and they set a plan for the following morning.

CLARE WAS SEATED at a prime table at Intaglio, the Michelin-starred restaurant next to MoCA, at ten o'clock on the dot. Her eyes were fixed on the revolving door at the entrance, as her foot tapped nervously against the table leg.

When Clement did arrive, ten minutes late, he looked better than he had at the memorial service. The color was back in his face, and his walk was jaunty. He kissed Clare on both cheeks, greeted their waiter by name, and ordered a green tea.

They exchanged small talk until his drink came, at which point Clement fell silent. He looked at her expectantly.

Clare cleared her throat. "So, as you know, I'm studying Blake Webley's work, and I was wondering if you could share some of your decision-making process behind the recent deaccessioning of *Longfin*."

A wariness settled behind Clement's eyes.

"Look, I know deaccessioning is a dirty word right now, but the fact is, museums have to do it, and I don't think it's fair for outsiders to criticize the decisions we make to keep the doors open to the public."

"Clement, please don't misunderstand me, I'm not criticizing your decision. I simply want to understand. It would help me get a sense of how Webley's reputation has evolved. I need to get my finger on the pulse. I just want to know what your opinion is on Webley. As a scholar. That's it. I'm not publishing this anywhere. It's just for my own edification."

Clement took a lighter out of his pocket and started playing with it. "Well, to start with, it wasn't like I unilaterally decided to deaccession *Longfin* myself. The decision was made in concert with the staff and the board of trustees."

"Correct me if I'm wrong, but doesn't the process usually start with the curator? Since you're the expert in the field and therefore best suited to make the judgment?"

"Yes, I put it on the list, but everyone from the director to the CFO signed off on it. I mean, Webley is great, of course, but we're the Museum of *Contemporary* Art. We need more works by contemporary artists. I wish we could acquire them while also holding on to our entire collection, but that's not the reality of the situation. The pandemic nearly wiped out half the museums in this country. No one is swimming in cash right now. But we have to fund these acquisitions somehow if we want to stay relevant."

"You sound like Tasha."

"She and I share this perspective. MoCA has a single, unified directive right now: diversify, diversify, diversify. The board and the staff are all on the same page."

"Why not sell an Agnes Martin? You have plenty of those."

Clement rolled his eyes. "We can't deaccession a *woman*."

"Why Webley, though, whose works are so scarce to begin with?"

"I don't believe Webley is as groundbreaking as you do. Frankly, I find his work derivative. De Kooning and Martin changed the entire course of art history. I don't think you can say the same about Blake Webley."

Clare felt unaccountably offended on behalf of her chosen subject. She wanted to launch a multipronged defense of his lasting significance, but that was not why she was here.

"Did your decision have anything to do with Gabriel's offer?" she asked as mildly as she could.

Clement abruptly stopped fiddling with his lighter. "What do you mean?"

"Did Gabriel make his offer—a quite substantial one, as I understand—before or after you decided to deaccession *Longfin*?"

"*After*, and I don't appreciate the insinuation. It wasn't even my idea to sell to Gabriel."

"Whose was it?"

"I don't remember. But certainly not mine."

"Who would usually decide that?"

"I don't know. The CFO maybe? The board? Usually it just goes to auction."

"But not this time. Why?"

"Someone knew a buyer who was offering several million over market."

"Who did? What buyer?"

"Why are you pressing me on this, Clare? Not to put too fine a point on it, but what business is *Longfin* of yours?"

"As a Webley scholar . . ."

Clement rapped the table with his lighter. "Clare, enough. You already told me you haven't touched your dissertation in years. So what is this sudden surge of interest? If it has anything to do with Gabriel, you aren't doing him—or his legacy—any favors. You're just some dilettante he was guilted into hiring."

Clare felt like she'd been slapped. "What do you mean?"

"You are not a part of this world, Clare. You don't know how it works. So stop throwing around half-baked conspiracy theories. I don't care how powerful your friends on the board are."

Clement stood up, pocketed his lighter, and strode out of the restaurant without another word. Clare stayed in her seat, trying to figure out how their conversation had gone so wrong.

When the waiter approached, she gestured for the check.

She'd been too aggressive, obviously. But even as she thought it, a small voice in her head pushed back at this assessment. Had she really? Her questions had been perfectly logical. Why did you sell *Longfin*? Where is it now? One day, someone organizing Webley's catalogue raisonné—maybe it would even be her—would seek him out to ask those very same questions.

So why had he reacted by storming out of the restaurant?

TEN MINUTES LATER, Clare was on the Madison Avenue bus heading back uptown, watching tourists and early Christmas shoppers with large bags navigate the crowded sidewalks. She tried to imagine what her life would look like at Christmastime. Even if she wasn't in jail—god forbid—she doubted that she, Jed, and Sadie would be stringing up lights and singing carols together. She knew she would need to tell Jed what had been going on soon. At any moment, she might lose the opportunity to tell him herself; instead, he would hear it from someone else: the cops, most likely, and that would be much worse. The guillotine was hovering right above her neck. Despite all her efforts to unravel Gabriel's murder herself, she'd discovered nothing. She had exhausted all her options. She had no place left to turn.

Where would she even go when it all fell apart? Their apartment was in Jed's name—at Dorothy's insistence. They hadn't yet been married when they closed on it, and she never thought to revisit the paperwork afterward. Not surprisingly, Dorothy had also pressed Clare to sign a prenup. But even without it, Clare would feel too guilty asking Jed for a dime after cheating on him.

How had she gotten to this point? How had she become a kept woman, without any resources of her own? She'd always made her own money. And how had she become an adulterer when she'd never even cheated on a high school boyfriend? She had let her attention wander and somehow become an entirely different person without even noticing.

She took out her phone to check what her bank balance actually was. She remembered it being somewhere around two thousand dollars—not even enough to cover one month's rent and a security deposit. But when her banking app opened, it showed an entirely different number.

Her account had more than fifty thousand dollars in it.

Clare refreshed the page in case it was a mistake, but the same balance came up.

How was that possible? She hadn't made any deposits since her Columbia stipend ended four years earlier. She paid for all their household expenses from her joint account with Jed.

She tapped to view the recent transactions. A wire transfer of fifty thousand dollars had landed in her account a week earlier from a company called Kallsten Holdings Ltd.

What the hell was Kallsten Holdings? And why had it wired her fifty thousand dollars?

WHEN CLARE GOT home, she immediately called her bank and told them that there had been a mistake. The agent she spoke to took her name and account number and then confirmed that the deposit had been intended for her.

"But I don't know anyone at Kallsten Holdings. I haven't done any business with them."

"I'm not sure what to tell you, ma'am. They've made no effort to recall the funds. It might just be your lucky day."

"But who are they? Do you have any contact information you can give me?"

"No, ma'am."

"But . . . I don't understand."

And then, all of a sudden, she did.

## CHAPTER 26

CLARE HAD BEEN ASKING HERSELF for days why the glare of suspicion kept reflecting back on her. Elise Vargas had said as much, too: "Everywhere I turn, *there you are*." The only explanation she could come up with was that whoever had killed Gabriel was setting her up to take the fall for it.

It sounded ludicrous in its grandiosity. After all, who was she? A nobody. As Clement had said: just some dilettante. But now that fifty thousand dollars had mysteriously appeared in her bank account, the thought wasn't as easy to dismiss. The deposit gave the impression that she'd been paid off for *something*. Someone was trying to make her look guilty.

But why? Because the affair made her a convenient target?

And who? She'd never heard of Kallsten in her life. She tried googling it, but nothing came up.

What was she supposed to do now? She'd always held on to the idea that at some point, if things got too bad, she could solve everything by coming clean: to Jed, to the police, to everyone. It would most certainly make things worse before it made them better, but ultimately, she'd thought, the truth would prevail. Now she wasn't so sure. Not if someone was manipulating things by planting arrows that pointed only to her. And she had no way to figure out who was doing it.

A thought occurred to her. *She* was useless at this sort of thing, but there were plenty of people who weren't. She just had to ask the right person for help.

"HI," MAGGIE SAID, unable to keep the anxiety out of her voice even for that one syllable. Clare knew that Maggie was worried about her. This request wouldn't help her cause.

"I was wondering if you could do a favor for me."

"Anything."

"Know any financial reporters by any chance?"

"There's one woman I know fairly well, Lisa Gutiérrez."

"Can you ask her to look up a company called Kallsten Holdings Ltd.?"

"Hang on—let me write that down. What is it?"

"It's a company that just wired me fifty thousand dollars."

"For what?"

"I think to set me up."

Maggie was silent for a moment. "To set you up for what?"

"The theft of *Longfin*? Gabriel's death? Take your pick."

"Clare . . ."

"I know it sounds crazy, Maggie. I know that."

"So why am I asking a colleague to look into it?"

"Because however crazy it sounds, someone I don't know wired me a massive amount of money for no reason and without telling me."

"Have you asked Jed? Maybe he had something to do with it."

"It's not our *joint* account. It's my own personal bank account. He's not a signatory."

"He could still wire money into it. Anyone can. All they need is your account number and your bank's routing number."

"Is that true? Shouldn't there be more security?"

"Most criminals aren't trying to *give* people money; they're trying to take it. The rules are there to protect transfers going in the other direction."

"Even if it sounds crazy, I'm convinced that someone is setting me up. Four days after Gabriel died, fifty thousand dollars landed in my bank account for no reason whatsoever. Plus, there's the fact that I'm a Webley scholar. And that I was sleeping with Gabriel. It all fits. I'm the fall guy."

"Clare, don't take this the wrong way, but nobody forced you to study Blake Webley or sleep with Gabriel. That's not a conspiracy; those are just your choices."

"Maggie, I am asking you to trust my instinct. I know you think I'm losing my mind, but please suspend your doubt for one moment and help me. Be on my side. Let me have this trash doll. *Please.*"

Maggie sighed. "I'm always on your side. You know that. Email me what you have, and I'll pass it along. But I just want to put in my two cents that I really think you should tell Jed everything. And the police. You're not a detective, Clare."

"I know I'll probably have to come clean at some point. But the more information I have when I do, the better it will go."

"I'll let you know what Lisa says."

"Thank you, Maggie."

"Just be careful, Clare."

"I'm being careful. I promise."

Clare hung up, and half a second later, someone knocked on her front door. Who could that be? The doormen hadn't called up to announce anyone.

Whoever it was pounded on the door again.

Clare shut her laptop, which still had her Kallsten search on the screen, and went to the front hall to peer through the peephole.

It was the detectives.

"Mrs. Bast?" Breznick called out. "It's the police. Please open up."

This was it. This was the moment she'd been dreading.

"Mrs. Bast? Your doorman told us you were home. Please open the door."

Clare did as she was told. Her face was ashen, and she couldn't even muster a greeting.

"We've got a few more questions for you, Mrs. Bast," Breznick said. "Can we come in?"

Questions. That was a small measure of relief. At least they weren't whipping out the handcuffs straight off the bat. Clare led them back into the living room. Her mouth felt like it was filled with sand.

When they'd sat down, Breznick said, "Greg, can you hand me that printout?"

Her partner rummaged in his bag and pulled out a slip of paper. Breznick took it but kept her eyes on Clare.

"Mrs. Bast, was Mr. Prévost threatening you?"

"Threatening me? No, of course not."

"But he wanted you to leave your husband."

"What?"

Breznick took a pair of reading glasses out of her jacket pocket, unfolded them, and put them on. She widened her eyes slightly and then rattled off Clare's phone number. "That's your number, correct?"

"Yes."

She looked back down at the sheet of paper and began to read. "On September nineteenth he sent you a text message at nine eighteen p.m.: 'Leave your husband.' Three days later, eleven fourteen a.m.: 'Leave him.' The following day: "'Did you leave him yet?'"

"That's not— No. That was just a joke we had."

"A joke?"

"He didn't actually want me to leave Jed. He wanted—he knew I was unhappy, and he wanted me to do something about it."

"Seems like he wanted you to do something pretty specific about it. *Leave your husband.*"

"I can see how it looks like that. But it wasn't—"

"Remind me what time you got home on the night of Mr. Prévost's death?"

"Around eleven."

"And your husband was here?"

"Yes, he woke up when I came home."

"And you claim he didn't know about you and Mr. Prévost."

*Claim?*

All of a sudden Clare saw where the detective was going with this. The police didn't suspect *her.* They suspected Jed—the wronged husband, out for revenge.

That was infinitely worse than getting hauled off in handcuffs. She'd cheated on the poor man; she'd lied to him; and now she'd unwittingly turned him into a murder suspect. Some combination of guilt, horror, and fear welled up from her stomach, and she thought for a moment she might throw up.

"Absolutely not," she said. "I would have known if he'd found out."

"So you're saying you could keep your affair hidden from him, but he couldn't have kept his knowledge of it a secret from you?"

"Jed doesn't have a devious bone in his body."

"I can't tell whether you're overestimating him or underestimating him."

"I'm just telling the truth."

"I thought you were the devious one?"

Clare started to object, but Breznick cut her off. "So both of you stayed home for the rest of the night?"

"Yes."

"But there's no one who can verify that."

Clare exhaled loudly. "I can verify it."

"So he's your alibi and you're his. That's convenient."

"They're not alibis. It's just where we were. We're normal people. We're *parents*."

Breznick stared back at Clare impassively. She was like a boulder, impossible to budge even an inch. How could Clare get through to her?

"My husband is a lawyer. He has the utmost respect for the law. He doesn't even jaywalk." She wished she could embed these two police officers in her home for a month so they could see what Jed was like. How he pretended to eat his daughter's toes until she couldn't breathe she was laughing so hard. How he always cried during *Finding Nemo*, when Marlin is chasing after the boat with his son on it. Every single time. He was a nerdy dad who wore pleated khakis, not some psychotic murderer. "I swear to you, Jed had nothing to do with this. The idea is just absurd."

Clare felt her eyes well with tears. An accusation would wreak total and utter destruction on Jed's life, and it would be all her fault. She couldn't allow that to happen to him. She felt a sudden burst of love and pity for him, almost as if he were her child.

She had to tell the police about *Longfin*. Maggie and Tasha were right. She couldn't figure this out. It had been absurd for her to ever think she could. She couldn't let the police keep working with incomplete information. Telling them about *Longfin* might further implicate her, but it would go a long way to exonerating Jed. She owed him that much, at the very least.

"You've got this all wrong," Clare said. "You're looking at the wrong person."

"Oh really?" Breznick scoffed, glancing at her partner in amusement. "Then please, point us in the right direction."

"This past August, MoCA—the Museum of Contemporary Art—sold a painting to Gabriel: *Longfin* by the artist Blake Webley. I am almost positive that that painting got Gabriel killed. Someone stole it that night."

Breznick and Nguyen exchanged another look. It was less amused this time.

"Gabriel's murder had nothing to do with our relationship," Clare went on. "It had to do with *Longfin*. Someone knew that *Longfin* was hanging on Gabriel's wall—that's a short list—and they took it. They killed Gabriel and stole an eighteen-million-dollar painting. And they're going to get away with it. Don't you see? If you keep chasing after Jed and me, they're going to get away with it."

"How do you know it was stolen the night Gabriel died?"

Clare felt paralyzed. She knew she had to tell the police the truth, but she found that she couldn't. She just couldn't do it. They'd eviscerate her. They'd charge her with obstruction of justice, at the very least. They'd take Sadie away from her.

As she sat there with her mouth agape, Breznick pressed: "Think about how this sounds to us for a moment, Mrs. Bast. You are obviously desperate to clear your and your husband's names, so you've concocted this story about a painting that nobody else has mentioned once in the course of our investigation. You're the only, single person to bring it up. You're the only, single person to claim it was at Gabriel's house. And you're the only, single person to claim that it was stolen the night he was killed, despite the fact that our investigation has found no evidence of theft at all. It's your word against everyone else's. And you're hardly a disinterested witness."

"It's *not* just my word," Clare said suddenly. She jumped up and went into the hall closet. Elise Vargas's card was still in her coat pocket. She fished it out and handed it to Breznick.

"She knows about *Longfin*. Call her. She'll tell you."

The detective took the card and stood up to leave, much to Clare's relief. At the door, Clare begged her to at least give her some advance warning if she was going to question Jed.

Breznick looked at her like she was insane. "Absolutely not."

AFTER THE DETECTIVES left, Clare attempted to exorcise her anxiety by cleaning the apartment from top to bottom. She scrubbed and vacuumed and Cloroxed every surface in sight. She emptied out the fridge. She dry Swiffered and wet Swiffered. She cleaned Noodle's cage while he cowered under the couch. But when she was done, she felt no calmer.

Two scenarios kept playing on a loop in her mind. In the first, the police arrested her for Gabriel's murder. They peeled a sobbing Sadie off of her, limb by limb, finger by finger, and Clare never got to hold her sweet girl again.

In the second, they came for Jed. Clare watched his face register everything: confusion, panic, comprehension, betrayal. His only crime had been choosing her, loving her. How had it gotten to this point? How could she have put Jed in this position? This was so far beyond any worst-case scenario that Clare had ever imagined. She hadn't been inventive enough to come up with this: Gabriel dead and Jed a suspect.

The only thing she'd worried about was having to watch Jed's face crumple in sadness and pain. That was the worst thing she thought was going to happen. She had been planning for the chance of a rain shower when a monsoon was cresting just over the horizon.

And she did desperately need a lifeboat after all.

# CHAPTER 27

JED SEEMED TOTALLY AT EASE when he got home from work, so Clare knew that Breznick hadn't confronted him yet. At least there was that. He had just turned on *PBS NewsHour* when Maggie called back.

"It took Lisa all of ten minutes," she said.

Clare went to take the call in their bedroom, shutting the door behind her.

"Tell me."

"Kallsten is a holding company registered in Cyprus and owned by a man named Peter DeGroot."

Clare combed her memory for some recognition of that name. She found nothing. She'd never heard of Peter DeGroot in her life.

"I don't know that person. Why would he give me fifty thousand dollars?"

"Do you know what a nominee director is?"

"No."

"According to Lisa, it's someone hired to be the face of a shell corporation. Legally, Peter DeGroot owns Kallsten Holdings, but most likely he's a front to hide the identity of the real owner. When a company is incorporated, the documents are made public. If someone doesn't want their ownership to be known, they hire a nominee director, and *that* person's name is listed on the public documents instead.

"Later, in a separate transaction, the nominee director gives power of attorney to the real owner, who's called the UBO, the ultimate beneficial owner. The nominee director signs a nondisclosure agreement, so the contract is confidential. That's why it's very, very difficult to find out who really owns these companies.

"Peter DeGroot acts as the nominee director for more than a dozen holding companies. That's his job. He's a lawyer who lives in Cyprus and helps people set up shell corporations. He doesn't have any actual managerial powers at any of them. His entire purpose is to be a blank mask. A cipher."

"So how do we find out who really owns Kallsten?"

"We don't."

"What do you mean 'we don't'?"

"According to Lisa, it's practically impossible to find out the UBO of a well-protected shell company. She can't do it. The police can't do it. Barring another breach like the Panama Papers, no one can."

Clare let that verdict sink in for a moment. Her search had led her to a shadowy shell company in Cyprus from which she could extract no information, no confession, no proof of her innocence, nothing at all. As Maggie had said, Kallsten was a cipher. The person setting her up was a ghost. How do you catch someone like that?

The answer came to her with a sinking sense of defeat: You don't.

## CHAPTER 28

THE NEXT MORNING, CLARE CALLED Detective Breznick right after she dropped off Sadie at school.

"Did you talk to Elise Vargas?" she asked.

She'd been up half the night wondering if the police would know about *Longfin* in the morning.

"I did." Breznick sounded like she had half a bagel in her mouth.

"And?"

"She said she *is* looking into the sale of *Longfin*, but she hasn't found any evidence of wrongdoing, financial or otherwise. She described it as a forensic accounting job. She also said she had no reason to believe that *Longfin* was stolen from Gabriel's house, either on the night he was killed or any other night."

Clare felt a strong urge to push Elise Vargas off a building. She drew in a deep breath and exhaled slowly. "May I ask, have you interviewed Clement Rosier yet?"

Clare heard some typing in the background, as if the detective were looking up the name.

"The MoCA curator?"

"He's an old friend of Gabriel's. He spoke at the memorial service. He's also the person who sold *Longfin* to Gabriel back in August."

"*Longfin* again, Mrs. Bast?"

"Something was wrong with that sale. I'm sure of it."

Clare's distrust of Clement had never cohered into a proper allegation. The MoCA transaction *sounded* fishy to her, but that's as far as she'd gotten. And she still had no idea how it might have led to Gabriel's murder.

But she needed the police to look into *Longfin*, because it was the only other storyline she had. More than that: It was the truth. The painting *was* stolen the night Gabriel was killed. The motive was greed, not revenge. It had nothing to do with a jealous husband.

But if Clare admitted that she'd lied to the police—that, in fact, she'd been present for both crimes—she had no doubt they'd view that as a mark of her own complicity.

Breznick swallowed another mouthful of her breakfast.

"My partner has spoken with Mr. Rosier."

"And?"

"You met with him, too, right?"

"Yesterday? I know I didn't handle it the right way, but—"

"Not yesterday. Back in August. Right before the museum decided to sell *Longfin*."

"What?"

"You two met in his office for about an hour, and four days later, he emailed the director of the museum with a proposal to sell *Longfin*."

"That meeting had nothing to do with *Longfin*. It was about my career."

"Isn't your career devoted to studying Blake Webley's work?"

"Yes, but—"

"And *Longfin* in particular?"

"You've got this all wrong."

"You were the one who told us to look into *Longfin*. Now you don't want us to do that anymore?"

"I do, but—"

"I heard you were upset it was going into a private collection. Because you wouldn't have access to it anymore."

Clare felt a heaviness settle in her chest. Who had told her that? Michael Kline?

"I'm an art historian," she said. "I believe great art should be accessible to everyone. That's a pretty common attitude in my profession."

"So you *were* upset?"

"'Upset' is too strong a word. I thought it was a shame, that's all."

"Was *Longfin* integral to your work?"

"No."

"Don't you devote a whole chapter of your dissertation to it?"

"Yes, but my argument is about his grid paintings in general. I could have chosen any one of them."

"But you didn't."

"No."

"Did you start sleeping with Gabriel Prévost to gain access to *Longfin?*"

"Of course not."

"Do you realize that you are the only person who has ever suggested that *Longfin* had something to do with Gabriel Prévost's death. *You*. The woman who met with Clement Rosier days before he began the process of deaccessioning *Longfin*. The woman who started sleeping with the very person who bought it from the museum shortly after the deal went through."

"Why would I tell you about *Longfin* if I had something to do with it? You weren't even looking at *Longfin* before I mentioned it."

"Mrs. Bast, you have no idea what we are or are not looking at during our investigation. Make no mistake: You are a suspect, not an ally. What I know for certain is that you were deeply entangled in this situation from the beginning. Maybe you're right: Maybe something went wrong with the deal somewhere along the way and that's what led to Mr. Prévost's death. If that's what happened, we'll find out. And if you were involved in Mr. Prévost's murder, we'll find out. You seem to think you can manipulate us into looking only at what you want us to see, but I assure you, you cannot."

Clare didn't respond. At least she'd never told them about being at Gabriel's the night he was killed. It would have been the final nail in the coffin. She'd be in jail already.

At this point, it was probably only a matter of time.

CLARE NEEDED TO talk to Elise Vargas, but she'd given her business card to the detectives without writing down the number first. Instead she called Lev, who, predictably, knew the woman and had her number.

Elise picked up on the first ring: "I thought I might be hearing from you."

"Why did you lie to the police?"

"I didn't lie to the police. I *don't* have any evidence that *Longfin* was stolen from Gabriel's house."

"They're going to arrest an innocent person. Doesn't that matter to you at all?"

"Of course. And clearly it matters to you. So it sounds like now you've got nothing to lose by telling me what you know."

Clare stopped in her tracks as the penny dropped.

"Did you purposely make me look like a liar to the police so that I'd be desperate enough to trade information with you?"

"Of course not. As a rule, I say as little as possible to the police. Your desperation is just . . . an unexpected bonus."

"Fuck you."

Clare rarely cursed. It felt fantastic. She said it again, louder.

A mother pushing a stroller glowered at her. "This is a *family* neighborhood," she hissed.

"Well, I have a family, and I hate this fucking neighborhood!" Clare shot back.

The woman looked over her shoulder and picked up her pace, clearly unnerved. Clare wondered if she was losing her grip. She had certainly misplaced her impulse control.

"Clare, are you all right?" Elise asked.

"I'm fine. Sorry."

"Let me be clear about something: I am not your friend. I am not your lawyer. I've been hired to track down *Longfin*, and that is what I am doing. You have information that I need. Give it to me, and I will do my best to help you. Like I said: tit for tat."

"Fine," Clare finally said. Elise had been right at the playground: She was drowning and Elise was the only one dangling a life preserver even remotely close to her.

"You'll tell me what you know?"

"Yes."

"Wonderful," Elise said. "I'm just leaving a meeting now. Can you meet for coffee in about half an hour at the Mark?"

## CHAPTER 29

CLARE ARRIVED AT THE RESTAURANT a few minutes early, but when the host led her to a banquette in the back, Elise was already there, tapping at her phone. She looked up when Clare approached.

"Thanks for meeting me on such short notice."

Clare took off her coat and hung it on the back of her chair.

"What would you like?" Elise gestured for the waiter. "I already ordered a pastry basket."

Clare asked for an Earl Grey tea and began unwinding her long scarf from her neck. When she was settled in her chair, she said to Elise without preamble: "Who hired you?"

"Clare, I've already told you, I'm not at liberty—"

"Tit for tat. That's the deal."

"Clare, even if I tell you, it won't do you any good."

"I'll take my chances."

Elise leaned back in her seat. "I was hired by the executor of Gabriel Prévost's estate."

"Michael Kline? Why?"

"Shortly after someone dies, the executor of the will is required to file an inventory of the estate's assets with the state probate court. When Michael inventoried Gabriel's assets, he kept coming up with an eighteen-million-dollar margin of error."

"*Longfin.*"

"It's unclear whether Gabriel still owned it at the time of his death."

"How is that possible?"

"At first, Michael assumed that the deal had closed long ago: that Gabriel purchased *Longfin* in August, sold it on to his buyer, and it was no longer in his possession at the time of his death. It's not Gabriel's MO—it's not really any dealer's MO, as I'm sure you know—to hang on to a painting for any length of time before passing it on. But then Michael heard from *you*. You told him on the phone that you'd seen *Longfin* at

Gabriel's house a mere two weeks before his death, so Michael started to look into the situation a little more closely. He subsequently stumbled upon a few irregularities that prompted his call to me."

"What irregularities?"

Elise began counting on her long, elegant fingers. "One, Gabriel's cleaner remembered seeing it on the bedroom wall as recently as October twenty-seventh, so clearly he didn't resell the painting right away, for whatever reason. Two, Gabriel took out a line of credit to finance the sale, and he hadn't paid it back at the time of his death. Why would he keep paying interest on money he didn't need anymore? And three, he hadn't canceled his quite-substantial insurance policy on it yet either.

"For all intents and purposes, Gabriel was behaving very much like a man who had *not* actually resold the painting. And I haven't even gotten to the strangest part." She paused dramatically.

Clare prodded her to go on: "What's the strangest part?"

"Sorry, Clare, that's where the free ride ends." She took a miniature baguette from the pastry basket and tore it violently in two. "Your turn. Tell me about the last time you saw *Longfin*."

Clare waited for the server to set down her tea. When he was out of earshot, she said, "The last time I saw *Longfin* was about five minutes before Gabriel was killed."

Elise abruptly stopped chewing. "What do you mean?"

"I was at his house when it happened."

"You haven't told the police that?"

"I haven't told anyone."

She put the bread down. "Walk me through that night. From the beginning."

Clare described her drinks with Lev and Cassandra, the party at Prévost-Kline, going home with Gabriel, the noises from downstairs, the Jean Arp sculpture. The black Reeboks. The horrific aftermath.

Clare had hoped to feel relief when the truth finally poured out, but she felt only apprehension. It was out of her hands now.

Elise was all business. "How long was the intruder in the house before going upstairs?"

"Not more than five minutes, if that."

"So it's safe to say they went there for *Longfin*, right? They knew where it was, and it was all they took."

"Right," Clare agreed.

"And they picked a night when Gabriel was supposed to be out of the house, at his gallery's big anniversary party. So whoever did this presumably went in to steal the painting, not to kill Gabriel."

"You think Gabriel's death was an accident?"

"I can't say for sure, but it seems like a fair assumption."

Clare's guilt compounded. Gabriel really would still be alive if they hadn't left the party at Prévost-Kline early. Whoever broke into his house had been banking on its being empty. She thought of that brief moment at the Hotel Chelsea when she'd tossed back the dregs of her martini and decided to accompany Lev and Cassandra to the party. Or when she'd spotted Gabriel across the crowded room and gone to him like a magnet. When she'd pressed her body against his in the crowd. And when she'd agreed to leave the gallery with him. In each moment, she'd held his life in her hands without even realizing it. If only she'd decided to go home at any of them—like any decent person would have—Gabriel would still be alive.

"So who knew *Longfin* was there?" Elise asked. "Not only in the house, but on his bedroom wall? Other than you and the housekeeper."

"I've been asking myself the same question, and the only answer I can come up with is the buyer. He knew Gabriel still had *Longfin* because he *didn't* have it yet."

"True, though he wouldn't necessarily know that the painting was in his bedroom or even at his house. Did Gabriel tell you anything about the buyer?"

Clare shook her head. "And neither will anyone else. Or they don't know."

"That doesn't give us much to go on," Elise said.

Clare felt a surge of encouragement at that "us." She leaned closer to Elise.

"I can't stop thinking about the seller," she said quietly. "Clement

Rosier. He's the one who decided that MoCA should sell *Longfin* in the first place, and then he chose the dealer, who just happened to be a good friend of his. That's obviously a conflict of interest."

"I suppose it's possible that there was some sort of fraud going on," Elise conceded. "But even if the sale *did* skirt the rules, I don't see Clement breaking into Gabriel's house to steal the painting. It's nearly impossible to fence a well-known work of art, and why would he take that risk when he's so close to his dream job? He'd probably *rather* that position than a few million dollars in cash. After all, you can't buy the directorship of the Museum of Contemporary Art."

Elise's logic was hard to refute. Had Clare fixated on Clement too soon? Had she been too eager to find another storyline?

"Let's table Clement for a moment," Elise said. "I want to return to the buyer for a second, because we happen to have just stumbled upon the very strange discovery that I mentioned before. And now you've earned the right to hear it. Thanks to you, I now know for certain that Gabriel never sent the painting to the buyer, which makes things much more interesting." She paused.

"There is nothing in any of Gabriel's records to indicate who the buyer actually was. I mean, *nothing*. No contract. No invoice. Not so much as an email or a text message. And Gabriel kept meticulous records. His contract with MoCA is there in triplicate."

"What does that mean?"

"Haven't you wondered why the buyer hasn't reached out to the executor of Gabriel's estate to ask about *Longfin*?"

"I'm not exactly privy to Michael Kline's personal correspondence."

"Well, I am, which is how I know that nobody has called him to ask about it. Isn't that odd? If an art dealer bought you an eighteen-million-dollar painting and then ended up dead, wouldn't you follow up with *someone* about it?"

"I don't buy a lot of eighteen-million-dollar paintings, but I see your point."

"The simplest explanation would be that there *was* no buyer. There never was."

Clare frowned. "You mean Gabriel bought the painting for himself? I don't think he had that kind of money—you said yourself that he had to take out a line of credit. Plus, he *told* me he bought it for a client."

"He could have been lying to you."

"Why would he lie to me about that?"

"Clare, think about how much information the thief had prior to the break-in: He knew Gabriel's schedule; he had the door code; he knew *Longfin* was there; he knew *Longfin* had been moved to the bedroom, or at least he knew to look there once he didn't find it downstairs. All of that information would most easily have come from Gabriel himself."

"What do you mean?" Clare asked. "Are you talking about insurance fraud?"

Elise raised an eyebrow. "You'd be surprised at how many of my cases boil down to just that."

"He wouldn't."

"You never know people as well as you think you do. That's the one constant in this business."

Clare considered this. She couldn't imagine Gabriel committing insurance fraud. It seemed beyond the pale. But then again, she'd always thought the same thing about having an affair. Elise was right: For most people, morality got much more flexible in desperate times.

"But why would the intruder kill him if they were in on it together?"

"I don't know. Maybe Gabriel startled the guy. The house was supposed to be empty, right? Then all of a sudden there was Gabriel, brandishing a weapon in the dark. Maybe the thief panicked and shot without thinking. Tensions are always running high at moments like that."

"I guess it's possible," Clare said, racking her brain to think of an alternative explanation that wouldn't implicate Gabriel in an insurance scheme.

"What about this?" she asked. "What if there *was* a buyer, and it was his plan all along to get Gabriel to put up the cash and then take the painting from him without paying up. To do that, he would need to remain completely unknown. He would have to deliberately erase all evidence of his identity from Gabriel's files. And he wouldn't have to reach out to Michael to ask about *Longfin* because he already had it. *He's* the guilty party."

Elise brushed some breadcrumbs off the table. "It's not a bad theory."

"So those are our two options then? There was no buyer because it was insurance fraud or there *was* a buyer and that's who killed Gabriel and stole *Longfin*?"

"Yes, I think so."

"Are you sure there's nothing recoverable on Gabriel's computer?"

"If there ever was something to begin with, it's gone now."

"What about Gabriel's assistant at Prévost-Kline? Maybe she would know some of his private clients?"

Elise looked at Clare approvingly.

"You'd be good at this job," she said. "But I already questioned her. Gabriel didn't use her on any of his private deals. She did take phone messages for him every now and then from clients who weren't gallery clients, but she couldn't remember any names."

Another dead end. It was Kallsten all over again.

Then it clicked.

"Call her back. Ask her if she recognizes the name Kallsten Holdings."

"What's that?"

Clare didn't want to tell Elise about the money in her bank account if she didn't have to.

"I'll tell you if she knows it," she said.

Elise took out her phone and scrolled through it for a moment before dialing.

"Rachel? It's Elise Vargas again—I'm the investigator helping Michael Kline sort out Gabriel Prévost's estate?"

Clare heard a tinny, indecipherable voice coming out of Elise's speaker.

"I just wanted to check one more thing with you," Elise said. "Do you remember ever hearing from someone at a company called Kallsten Holdings?"

Clare bit her cuticle.

"Are you sure? Take your time."

As the tinny voice answered, Elise shook her head at Clare; Rachel hadn't heard of it.

Clare's hopes deflated. Yet another dead end.

Then she remembered something: Maggie had given her the name of that lawyer. Kallsten's nominee director.

"Wait!" she cried. "Ask about Peter DeGroot."

Elise gave Clare an annoyed glance. "Sorry, Rachel, one more thing. Does the name Peter DeGroot ring a bell?"

There was a pause.

"When was that?"

Another pause.

"Can you spell that for me?"

"Got it. Thanks so much for your help."

Elise hung up and nodded at Clare. "She remembers the name Peter DeGroot. He was one of Gabriel's private clients, and they spoke often. But she said he worked for a company called Axion, not Kallsten."

Clare banged her fist on the table. Finally, *finally* she was getting somewhere. She'd managed to extract one small thread from the Gordian knot confronting her.

"So Axion was Gabriel's client," she said. "That's who he bought *Longfin* for."

"But who is Peter DeGroot?" Elise asked.

"He's a lawyer who acts as a front for a whole bunch of shell companies in Cyprus, including one called Kallsten and, apparently, another called Axion."

She told Elise about the deposit in her bank account and recounted her conversation with Maggie.

"Don't you see? Peter DeGroot instructed Gabriel to buy *Longfin*. Then he had Gabriel killed and used a different shell company try to frame *me* for the murder."

It felt like a victory—*finally*, after all her digging, she'd figured out who the buyer was—but the exhilaration faded quickly.

Peter DeGroot was just some suit who signed paperwork. Axion, like Kallsten, was probably just an empty shell company with a hidden owner. As Maggie had said, no one—not even the police—would be able to uncover the UBO.

All she had was another dead end. And a sore hand.

"What are you doing?" Clare asked Elise, who was tapping on her phone.

"I'm asking my tech to do another search of Gabriel's hard drives, this time targeting the names Peter DeGroot and Axion."

"Do you think she'll find anything?"

"Well, she did a pretty thorough sweep the first time."

Elise checked her watch. "I have another meeting to get to." She gestured to the waiter for the check. "Clare," she said, "I don't usually give unsolicited advice, but I'm going to make an exception in this case. You need a lawyer. And my guess is that they'll tell you the same thing I'm going to tell you now: It's time to go to the police."

"You mean tell them about everything? The night of the murder? The money from Kallsten?"

Elise nodded.

"They'll arrest me."

Elise reached out for the bill and scanned it. "They may. But if you're lucky, they'll only charge you with obstruction of justice, rather than murder and grand theft. And if they find out about any of this on their own—which they almost certainly will—then I don't think you'll be so lucky."

"What's the penalty for obstruction of justice?"

"It varies."

"Jail time?"

"Don't jump to the worst-case scenario. You just need to take this one step at a time."

Clare noticed she said "you" this time, not "we."

"What if I *do* tell the police everything? How will it help if they can't figure out who owns Axion?"

"Honestly, I doubt the NYPD will be able to do anything. It's not like some lawyer in Cyprus is going to break privilege just because a local city cop without jurisdiction—or power of extradition—demands it."

"So what, *Longfin* will just disappear forever? They'll get away with it?"

Elise placed the pen neatly on top of the signed check. "They very well could."

"So what is the point of even going to the police in the first place, if they're totally useless?"

"To protect *yourself*," Elise said. "That should be your priority now. Forget about *Longfin*. The police are going to find out about that money from Kallsten eventually. It'll be much better if you tell them."

"I need to talk to Jed before I do anything. He needs to hear the truth from me."

"Let's see if my tech finds anything," Elise said. "I'll call you as soon as I know. But if she doesn't, my advice is to tell Jed the truth and then immediately call the police."

Clare put her head in her hands.

"Coming clean might even feel like a relief," Elise said. "Truly."

Clare took no comfort in that possibility; she was feeling crushed by the physical weight of dread. Her life as she knew it was about to end. And the only thing she could do about it was count down the hours.

## CHAPTER 30

THAT NIGHT, CLARE AND JED were expected at his parents' apartment for dinner. When the babysitter arrived, Clare almost told her to go home. She was clutching Sadie in her lap, and she couldn't bear to give up the weight and warmth of her.

"Let's go, hon," Jed said, standing at the door tapping his umbrella.

"Good night, sweetheart," she whispered to Sadie, giving her one last hug. "I love you."

Jed and Clare walked up to Eighty-Eighth Street in silence, under gray clouds threatening rain. They were in the elevator in his parents' building when a text came through from Elise: "Nothing on Axion or DeGroot in Gabriel's files."

Clare lowered herself slowly onto the bench and pulled off her coat, which suddenly felt like a straitjacket.

"Are you all right?" Jed asked.

She nodded. She couldn't speak. Her last whiff of hope had just been extinguished. She'd have to tell him everything. Tonight.

"What's the matter?" Jed asked. "Do you feel sick?"

"No," she said hoarsely. "I just got lightheaded for a second."

"We'll get you some water upstairs."

She said it all in a rush so that she wouldn't lose courage later.

"I need to talk to you about something when we get home."

Jed didn't answer. When she forced herself to look up at him, he was staring down at her with a beatific smile on his face. He reached down to take her hand.

"I'm looking forward to it."

Clare realized with a sinking sensation that he had misread her in the worst possible way and was thinking about their sole sexual encounter in months. She could not have played that worse. His hopes were up, and he'd be even more crushed by the real news.

"I'm not pregnant."

His smiled abruptly disappeared. "Oh."

"Sorry."

"No need to apologize."

The elevator continued to climb slowly. Just before it reached the penthouse, Jed said, "Maybe we can work on that later." His coy smile—an attempt at charm—broke her heart.

She couldn't bring herself to play along with it. She just shook her head sadly. "I don't think so."

"What do you mean? Not tonight or not ever?"

"I don't want another child, Jed."

His face darkened. "Since when?"

This was a disaster. Why were they having this conversation now, of all times?

"Since I had Sadie. I don't want to do it all over again."

"And you just get to decide that unilaterally?"

"Well, yeah, kinda . . ." Clare said. Didn't she? She was the one who would have to carry a baby and deliver it and care for it. "At least for myself."

"Good to know," Jed snapped, just as the elevator doors opened.

Dorothy was standing in the doorway, her spindly arms already outstretched for an embrace. "*Darling*," she said as she reached for Jed, accidentally scraping Clare's arm with her ring. "Come in, come in, come in."

CLARE TURNED DOWN her usual glass of Sancerre, not because she didn't want it but because she didn't trust herself to have it. Jed, on the other hand, was already on his second martini ten minutes later.

The Basts' usual rat-a-tat exchange of news and gossip was especially irritating to Clare, since so much of it centered on Gabriel's murder. The case had become the topic du jour on the cocktail-party circuit, and hearing her in-laws volley the details of his death back and forth like a competitive sport sickened Clare.

"Don't you have any intel?" Lauren asked her.

"No," Clare said dully. "I don't know anything."

In twenty-four hours, it would be abundantly clear to everyone in the room that this had been a blatant lie.

"Do you think it was a robbery?" Grant asked. "I'm not gonna lie: It made me glad that we don't live in a town house. Remember, hon, we almost put in a bid on that place on Seventy-Fourth?"

Lauren put a hand to her heart as if they'd narrowly escaped catastrophe.

"Oh my god, you're right. I'd totally forgotten about that. Thank god we didn't. It's just so horrible." She turned back to press Clare. "Didn't the police tell you anything when they interviewed you?"

"No," Jed said, "and please don't go around telling people that the police interviewed us about it."

"Why not? You happened to know the guy. Who cares? So did half of New York."

"Because I'm an attorney, Lauren. It's not a good look to be tied up in any of this."

"Well *you're* not tied up with it. Clare's the one who was working with him."

"What are you implying?" Jed snapped.

Lauren held up her palms defensively. "Nothing, I'm just saying."

"Children, children," Dorothy murmured.

"Clare hardly knew the guy." Jed said. "She just gave him advice a few times. Right, Clare?"

"It was very informal," Clare agreed.

"Were you working with him when he bought that painting from MoCA?" Lauren asked.

Clare turned to her sharply. "What? No. And how'd you hear about that?"

"Well," Lauren said, leaning forward and smiling. This was clearly the moment she'd been waiting for. "Don't say anything, but I'm on the Harwick fundraising committee with this mother in Chloe's class, Freya Michelson, and Freya's father-in-law, Dick Michelson, is on the board at MoCA. *He* said that the police interviewed the top curator at the museum. And apparently Gabriel bought a painting from the museum a little while ago. And I guess they think it's related."

"How do you buy a painting from a museum?" Grant wondered aloud.

No one answered him.

"That was months ago," Jed muttered. "Clare didn't even know the guy then."

"But wasn't it a Blake Webley?" Lauren asked Clare. She knew very well that Webley was the topic of Clare's dissertation.

"Apparently," Clare said.

"So what's the deal?"

"I don't know," Clare repeated. "It doesn't make sense to me either."

"It's all just ghastly," Dorothy said, pursing her lips sourly. She gave Clare a pointed look.

"Terrible," echoed Grant.

"'Indescribably brutal,'" Jed mumbled with a strange, off-kilter laugh.

"Um, what?" Lauren asked, scoffing at her brother.

"That's what some poet said about Webley's paintings. Right, Clare? Who was it again? He called them 'indescribably brutal.'" He sneered. "Certainly seems prescient now."

Clare felt like she'd been slapped. "What did you just say?" she asked Jed in a low voice.

"I said those words seem prescient. It means prophetic."

"I know what prescient means," Clare said. "Where did you hear that?"

"Um, probably from the Webley scholar I'm married to?" He always became sarcastic when he drank.

Clare shook her head. "Not from me. The phrase is 'exquisitely brutal.' That's what Ashbery said. Not 'indescribably brutal.'"

Jed pantomimed a face of exaggerated contrition. "Yikes, sorry."

Clare felt like some unseen presence had gripped her throat with ice-cold fingers.

*Indescribably brutal.*

That was precisely how Gabriel had misquoted the line, minutes before he'd kissed her for the first time.

Why would Gabriel and Jed both be mistaken about the same quote in the exact same way? It was too specific to be coincidence. Wasn't it?

She stared at Jed. His facial muscles were loose and slack from the alcohol. He didn't look well.

"Aaanyway," Dorothy said in a singsong voice. This was how she typically pivoted whenever the conversation turned antagonistic. Unfortunately, she had nothing to follow it up with, and the word hung in the silence awkwardly.

"Oh," Dorothy said, finally grasping on a topic. She turned to Jed: "Eduardo asked me to tell you that he fixed the sink that was giving you trouble."

"Eduardo our caretaker?" Lauren asked.

"That's the only Eduardo I know," Dorothy said with a tinkling laugh. "He said he ran into you at the house the other day."

"Why were you out in East Hampton?" Lauren asked Jed.

"I had to get something."

"When was this?" Clare asked.

"A few weeks ago, I think. It doesn't matter. I realized I'd left a file out there I needed."

The dinner bell rang, and they all shuffled into the dining room to eat. Jed stayed sunk in inebriated gloom throughout the meal, speaking up only to spar with Lauren. Clare spent the meal lost in her own mind, trying to interpret Jed's various slips. How did he know that *Longfin* was bought "months ago"? How did he know anything about it at all, in fact, when she'd deliberately avoided discussing the topic with him? Why had he gone out to East Hampton without mentioning it to her? And why had he used the exact phrase Gabriel had to butcher John Ashbery's quote?

In the cab ride home, she asked Jed as casually as she could, "You only met Gabriel that one time at the MoCA party, right?"

"Yeah. Why?"

"No reason."

He leaned his head back and closed his eyes, unaware that Clare was churning with anxiety and suspicion next to him.

When they got home, he fell into bed, too drunk to remember that he and Clare were supposed to have a conversation that night, which was probably for the best. Clare wasn't so sure she was ready to open up to him after all.

## CHAPTER 31

THREE HOURS LATER, WHILE JED snored on, Clare crept out of bed and tiptoed over to his bedside table. She eased his phone off its charger and pressed the screen against her body to block the light.

She brought it to the living room and sat on the couch. Noodle lifted up his head to look at her before settling back down in his cage. Clare tapped in Jed's password—0617, their anniversary—and the display opened onto a picture of Sadie and her in the pool in East Hampton.

She swiped down and searched his phone for the word "Gabriel." Dozens of hits surfaced. Emails with a colleague named Gabriel Santos. More songs by Peter Gabriel than she would have imagined.

She amended her search to "Prévost." This time, nothing came up. She put the phone back down in her lap. She should have felt relief, but she didn't. She picked it up again and typed in "Kallsten."

Nothing.

Finally, she searched for "Axion."

Clare froze as Jed's device indicated that it had found fifty-two relevant files. Then the number began to climb. She watched the figure grow with a sinking sense of doom. Finally, it stopped. One hundred and thirty-three results. Mostly emails. She recognized the name Peter DeGroot on one of them and opened it. All it said was: "See signed documents attached. -Peter." She opened the attachment; it was a six-page PDF in barely legible legalese. Something about a wire transfer. She went to another email. This one was from Alec: "Axion redeeming $12.5M. Pls start paperwork."

"What are you doing?" Jed asked from the doorway.

Clare gasped and dropped the phone in her lap. She hadn't heard him come out of the bedroom. He was standing in the hallway, looking rumpled and confused. His eyes were glazed over.

"Nothing. I couldn't sleep. What are you doing?"

"Water," he mumbled, hobbling stiffly into the kitchen. Clare tucked his phone under the couch cushion and listened to the sink run. Jed stumbled back to bed without saying another word to her.

Clare's heart continued to pound for several minutes. When she heard his snoring start up again, she retrieved his phone and kept searching.

An hour later, she'd been through dozens of emails, reminders, and calendar events, and she still wasn't clear on what Axion *was*. It had to be one of Gatepost's investors, but that's all she was able to glean. Every message was brief and imprecise. That's how lawyers—and probably bankers, too—deliberately did business: Keep everything vague. Don't put anything in writing if you don't have to. Preserve deniability.

It was true that Jed resorted to email only when necessary. A few years back, when David Beckham's account had been hacked, Jed had crowed about the athlete's foolishness, the implication being that he—Jed—had more foresight. That's why he was always laden down by paperwork; he never put anything online.

So what, if anything, was Jed hiding? She had to know, and the phone wasn't going to tell her. The answers, if they existed at all, would be written in his lovely prep-school script on some yellow legal pad shoved into a stack of dozens just like them.

Clare heard another scuffling in the room and quickly pushed the phone under the cushion again. But it was just Noodle, shifting in his hay. She remembered the first time she'd heard that rustling, hiding in the spare closet out in East Hampton. The one that no one used—or so she'd thought.

It now occurred to her that in the car on the way to East Hampton that weekend, the day before Sadie's birthday, Jed had thanked her effusively for getting all the presents. But he must have already bought Noodle. He was a good liar, she realized for the first time. That must be the mark of a very good liar: You don't even suspect they're capable of it.

She'd been shocked at his parents' apartment earlier that evening when, tipsy and sloppy, he'd made reference to several things he wasn't supposed to know about, like MoCA's sale of *Longfin* and Ashbery's quote. Not to mention his recent visit to East Hampton that he'd neglected to mention to her.

Was *that* where he stashed documents he didn't want anyone to stumble across—at his parents' house? And if so, could one of them explain the connection between Axion, Gabriel, Gatepost, and her?

She wasn't willing to let that what-if go unanswered. Her whole future rested on the answer. And she already knew Jed's favorite hiding spot.

## CHAPTER 32

JED OVERSLEPT, AND CLARE USHERED Sadie out of the apartment quickly and quietly so she wouldn't have to face him. It was too early to go to school, so they went to the park and watched the morning joggers expel great puffs of white air in the cold. The edges of the reservoir had frozen over, and dirty paw prints marked the surface. Sadie threw rocks into it, watching the birds scatter in alarm.

After Clare dropped Sadie at school, and arranged an afternoon playdate for her with Mina, she walked east, past her apartment, toward the garage on Second Avenue, where she and Jed kept their car.

Their car?

*His* car. He'd both picked it out and paid for it.

More and more she was coming to realize how little was truly hers. She'd thought that Jed was incapable of making a choice without her; now she realized that he'd made every choice that mattered. She just got to choose what milk they drank.

Soon she was crossing the Triborough Bridge and merging onto the Long Island Expressway. Waze estimated that it would take her less than three hours to get to East Hampton.

And then what?

She didn't know. In three hours, while Mina picked up Sadie from school yet again, her own future forked. Either nothing would change, or her life would veer into wild, uncharted territory: a place where everything she thought she knew was wrong, where all her assumptions turned out to have been built on fault lines.

CLARE PULLED INTO Dorothy and Abe's driveway, turned off the car, and sat for a moment, listening to the engine click. When it stopped, the world around her was silent, except for the lonesome, insistent cawing of a crow. She climbed out of the car and slammed the door shut behind her. Every sound she made echoed in the cold, still air.

The Basts' beautiful manicured hedges were now wrapped in burlap shrouds, and the trees were barren. She shivered. She was wearing only a light trench coat. She hadn't remembered that it was always colder out here than it was in the city.

She retrieved the spare key from under the flowerpot on the back porch—Jed kept their copy on his key chain—and stepped inside the house. They never spent time here in the winter. Every October, the furniture was covered, and the water was shut off. Dust motes drifted slowly through a shaft of sunlight. A floorboard creaked beneath her.

"Hello?" she called out.

No one answered. She hadn't expected anyone to, but she was still relieved that this, at least, was going according to plan.

She climbed the stairs without taking off her coat, and walked straight to the closet at the end of the hallway. She opened the door to find the same dark recess where she and Sadie had hidden from monsters. She reached into her coat pocket and pulled out the light bulb she'd put there that morning. After removing the old bulb from the ceiling fixture, she screwed in the new one and pulled the cord. With a loud click, light flooded into a place that hadn't been illuminated in years.

What a sad, dingy hideout this spot had been. The floor was scattered with mouse droppings, just as Jed had warned. It smelled like mildew and mothballs. She felt a pang of pity for Noodle, who had been locked in there for a full twenty-four hours.

Nothing looked amiss, as far as she could tell. The shelves were still crammed with ragged towels in various eighties hues: teal, pink, faded yellow. A wicker basket rested on a poorly folded picnic blanket, overflowing with broken swim goggles, expired sunscreen, and dented Ping-Pong balls: the detritus generated by a wealthy family at leisure.

She felt beneath a stack of towels and then began going up, sliding her hands in between each layer.

Nothing.

She stood on her tiptoes and peered into a shelf stuffed with baseball hats, umbrellas, and bags of birdseed. She put her hand in and felt along the back wall.

Nothing.

With every shelf she searched without success, her hopes mounted. She wasn't going to find any files here—incriminatory or otherwise. It had been ridiculous to think she would. A brief lapse in logic. A passing bout of paranoia.

And then her fingers brushed against something rough and hard behind a pile of moth-eaten sweaters. She pulled her hand back as if she'd been burned. Then she started pulling sweaters off the shelf.

She quickly uncovered a flat wooden crate, slightly bigger than a pizza box. It was made of cheap, pale plywood, the kind that could give you a splinter if you so much as looked at it the wrong way. There were no markings on it, except for a few cragged and misshapen metal staples that had already been pried open. It was now held closed with one cobalt-blue bungee cord pulled taut across the width of it and another orange one stretching from top to bottom. She unhooked them and let them fall to the floor.

This was it. This was where her future forked.

She pulled off the top of the box.

It was not the files she'd come searching for.

There, nestled in gray foam, was *Longfin*.

## CHAPTER 33

CLARE SAT IN THE DRIVER'S seat of the Volvo squeezing her hands into fists to try to stop them from shaking. She needed to leave now if she was going to pick up Sadie from Mina's apartment on time, but she could barely grip the steering wheel. She banged her palms against the dashboard, hard, and then started the car. She wouldn't—couldn't—let panic dictate her actions anymore.

As she backed out of the driveway she glanced at the wooden crate, buckled into the backseat like a child. She couldn't leave it there in that dank closet, surrounded by junk and vermin. She felt responsible for it; she wanted to keep it safe. But mostly she wanted to thwart Jed's plans for the painting, whatever they were. *He* could be the one left scrounging for answers this time.

Her heart was still pounding erratically as she pulled onto Main Street. And she couldn't get her thoughts to settle down; each one arrived like a gunshot and disappeared just as quickly. The image of Gabriel's face as she'd last seen it; the ragged hole in his chest, seeping blood. Jed scooping up Sadie and giving her a raspberry on her bare belly. Jed smiling at her for months and talking about having another child while all along he'd known about the affair. Jed calmly driving their car—this car—out to East Hampton after he'd killed Gabriel.

Because he *had* killed Gabriel, hadn't he? Wasn't that what this meant?

Clare couldn't think of any other explanation that made sense. How else would Jed have ended up in possession of the painting that was stolen the night Gabriel was killed? Could he have been the one wearing the black Reeboks standing inches from her face while she lay cowering, naked, under Gabriel's bed? Was it possible that those feet had belonged to the father of her child all along? And had he left Sadie *alone* that night while he went downtown? Left her sleeping in an empty apartment so that he could go kill his wife's lover? Somehow the idea of Sadie helpless and alone in her little bed was the most horrifying part to Clare.

No, Jed would never have done that. He would have hired someone to break into Gabriel's house for him—that's what Basts do. They pay other people to do the jobs they consider beneath them. She thought of Mimi and Eduardo and the countless nannies, cooks, housekeepers, landscapers, doormen, travel agents, personal assistants, and drivers in their collective employ.

Why not killers, too?

The question she couldn't answer was: Why take *Longfin*? Jed had no interest in art. He certainly wasn't an art smuggler; the only thing he could think to do with it was stuff it in the closet of his parents' summer home. Maybe Clare had been too quick to discount jealousy as a possible motive. Look at Helen of Troy. It was the oldest story in the book. Perhaps Breznick had been on the right track after all; maybe Jed really had killed Gabriel for revenge, and taking *Longfin* had just been an attempt to point the police in a different direction.

But how had he found out about the relationship? She'd been so careful. Could something he'd seen at the MoCA party have made him suspicious enough to hire a private detective to follow her? Fisk & Baum had a firm like that on retainer—not a seedy private dick, but a fleet of corporate investigators in a big shiny office building on Park Avenue. They didn't do cheating-spouse cases, but if Jed had a business relationship with someone there, he could have called in a favor. The investigator could easily have learned the door code by watching Gabriel punch it in.

But could Jed really have come home all those nights knowing the truth and smiled as if everything was fine? Clare tried to think back. Had he ever seemed off? She couldn't remember. He was always there, always Jed. He might have been more stressed than usual at work, but it never seemed like anything more than that. But then, she'd been undeniably distracted. Whenever she was at home, she lived in her head, in her fantasies, reliving moments with Gabriel. His hand running up the back of her leg, his crooked smile, his head thrown back, eyes closed, a hoarse gasp.

Clare thought of Gabriel's face again now, but this time it was cold and lifeless.

AS CLARE APPROACHED the city again, she felt no surer of what to do. The monotony of the drive had at least regulated her heart rate, but her mind was still a seething tangle.

She knew she should call the police. That was the most prudent course of action. But she dreaded the consequences that phone call would unleash: The hours of being interrogated. Sadie's questions about where her father was. The guilt of turning Jed in. The public shame that would reverberate through the rest of Sadie's life: her wanton mother and homicidal father. As soon as Clare made that phone call, everything would spiral, quickly and painfully. She dreaded setting off that chain reaction. She wanted to put it off as long as she possibly could.

But the longer she held on to *Longfin*, the more of a liability it became. What if she was caught red-handed with it? There'd be no way she could talk her way out of that, not with Breznick already convinced of her guilt. It would take nothing more than a fender bender on the LIE.

She instinctively slowed the car down to the speed limit.

Plus, how long would it take Jed to notice that it was missing?

Clare took a deep breath. She told herself to focus only on the next task at hand. Like Elise said: Take it step-by-step. Put on the left blinker. Get in the E-ZPass lane. Turn on the FDR. Take the Ninety-Sixth Street exit. Go get Sadie.

Protect Sadie.

But protect her from what? Not from Jed. He would never hurt her. For all his faults, he was a wonderful father.

And protect her how? By leaving him? To go where, exactly? She had no money, and she certainly wasn't going to touch the Axion funds. The people she saw most regularly were Jed's friends. She'd let many of her own friendships founder in recent years. There were people she could call in an emergency, and they would certainly let her stay with them. But for how long? And what did that look like? Lev and Cassandra didn't have extra bedrooms. Sadie couldn't couch surf.

She could go stay with Maggie for a while, but she'd eventually have to come back to New York. Her life was here. Sadie's life was here.

TWENTY MINUTES LATER, Clare dropped the Volvo in the garage and started walking to Mina's house with the crate cradled awkwardly in both hands. She still didn't know what to do with it, but she knew she couldn't leave it in the car. Part of her wanted to just shove it in the nearest trash can and forget she'd ever found it. She wished she could pretend this entire day had never happened and put all thoughts of Gabriel and *Longfin* behind her. She could move forward with Jed and pretend that he hadn't done what he'd done. She could remind herself over and over that he was a good father and that was enough. Boring looked pretty good at the moment. That could be enough.

But she couldn't let it go. Maybe it was the art lover in her that wouldn't let her toss a Blake Webley painting into a reeking mound of city trash. Or maybe it was just the fact that for the first time since Gabriel had died, she felt like she wasn't a pawn in someone else's game anymore. She had the upper hand now, because she was the only person in the world who knew where *Longfin* was. Even the thought gave her a small thrill. She was holding Blake Webley's *Longfin* in her arms. She could just disappear into the sunset with it. Clare and *Longfin*, happily ever after.

Except not. Because any life without Sadie would be unbearable. When she had a child, she'd effectively outsourced her own happiness. And the Basts would never let her take Sadie away from them.

She readjusted the box in her arms. It was big and unwieldy. She wouldn't even be able to hold Sadie's hand when they crossed the street. She reached Mina's building, and as the doorman opened the door for her, he said, "Hoo-boy, you want a hand with that?"

"That's okay," Clare said. "It's not heavy."

Upstairs, she rang Mina's doorbell and got a similar reaction.

"Oh wow, what do you have there?" Mina asked.

"It's Jed's birthday present. I picked it up on the way here." The lie came to her easily. She'd gotten better at it over the past two months. As soon as she said it, a temporary solution to her problem occurred to her. "I didn't realize the box was going to be so big," she added. "I have no idea how I'm going to get it home with Sadie, much less hide it from him."

"Do you want to leave it here?" Mina asked, as Clare knew she would. "Come get it another day?"

"Are you sure that wouldn't be an inconvenience?"

"Of course not. We can put it in the hall closet. No one will even notice it. Follow me."

"That would be great. Thank you so much."

Clare shoved the painting in the back of the closet Mina opened for her and swept the hem of a long black coat around the front of it. Just as Mina shut the door, Sadie came running out and hugged Clare around the knees. "Mama!"

"Hi, sweets," Clare said, kissing the top of her head. She found the normalcy of the moment mildly bracing. "Ready to go?"

CLARE WALKED OUT of the building feeling surprisingly unburdened. Without the crate in her hands, it was easier to pretend that it didn't exist. She and Sadie held hands and swung them lightly back and forth. It was just past five p.m., and the sun was already setting.

"It's so dark," Sadie marveled.

"The sun sets earlier and earlier this time of year. The days get shorter and the nights get longer."

"And the cold gets colder."

Clare laughed. "That's right."

"Can we go sledding tomorrow?"

"There's no snow yet, honey. We probably have a few more weeks to wait for that."

Clare tried to envision their lives when the snow came. Would they still be living with Jed? The idea didn't seem as crazy to her as it had on the drive back into the city. Her horror had slowly faded and been replaced by something else: fear. Not fear of Jed, but fear of the unknown. Fear of a life without him, without all the foundations she'd built up beneath her.

She stopped walking suddenly, struck by that thought. Did she really fear solitude and uncertainty more than living with the person who had potentially killed Gabriel? If he had, then she had no idea what else he was capable of. What had happened to her? Clare had once yearned for the unknown. She remembered once suggesting to Jed that they go live in Rome for a few years. He had looked at her like she was crazy.

"I can't practice law in Rome," he said. "I can't even practice in Connecticut."

When she was researching the years Blake Webley spent in downtown Manhattan, she'd come across a passage from *Moby-Dick*: "Go from Corlears Hook to Coenties Slip, and from thence, by Whitehall, northward. What do you see?—Posted like silent sentinels all around the town, stand thousands upon thousands of mortal men fixed in ocean reveries."

That line described how she used to feel all the time: like a mortal man fixed in an ocean reverie. She'd wanted the great expanse. She'd wanted whatever was out there, over there. The unknown. But once she'd had Sadie, everything had changed. That old restlessness began to feel dangerous. She became protective, careful, closed-off. She shut all her open doors lest something unwanted come in to harm Sadie.

Until she'd met Gabriel, that is.

Gabriel had been her year in Rome. Her ocean reverie. And look where it had led.

"Mama, come *on*," Sadie said, pulling on her arm.

She let herself be yanked along by her daughter. They were a few blocks from their apartment, and she still had no plan. Maybe that *was* her plan: Do nothing. Proceed as normal. Wait and see. But when they reached their corner, Sadie stopped abruptly. "Look," she said, pointing.

The facade of their building was lit up with a red and blue glow emanating from the lights of two police cars idling outside. The sight of them sucked the air from Clare's lungs. It was happening. The moment she'd tried so hard to fight off had finally come.

But who were they here for? Her or Jed?

"Hey, I have a fun idea," Clare said to Sadie. "Should we go out for pizza instead of eating dinner at home?"

"Yes!" Sadie yelped.

Clare picked her up—something she rarely did anymore—and held her tightly against her chest so that her daughter was facing over her shoulder, away from the building.

Before she could back away, Detective Nguyen emerged from the lobby, followed by Jed and Detective Breznick. Jed's hands were handcuffed behind his back, and Breznick was steering him by his shoulders toward the first waiting police car. Nguyen rushed ahead of them to open the back door.

Halfway between the building and the curb, Jed abruptly stopped and turned to look directly at Clare, almost as if he'd sensed she was there. They locked eyes. Neither of them showed any expression. They just stared at each other. Clare tried to glean something from his expression—guilt, fear, anger—but he just looked tired. Then Breznick pushed him lightly from behind and he started walking again.

Clare backed away quickly in the other direction so that Sadie wouldn't witness her handcuffed father being stuffed into the back of a police car.

## CHAPTER 34

WHILE SADIE WOLFED DOWN HER slice of pepperoni, Clare tried to figure out her next move. She needed to talk to Jed so that she could figure out what was going on. To do that, she needed to get him out of jail. She called Dorothy to ask if she could leave Sadie with her while Clare went down to the precinct. She didn't pick up, so Clare sent a text: "Please call me when you get this."

Then: "Jed's been arrested."

Three gray dots pulsated as Dorothy composed a response. Then they disappeared. No message came through.

CLARE TOOK SADIE out for ice cream after pizza, trying to delay the moment when they had to return to their apartment. She didn't know what they'd find there.

When they did finally get back, it was mercifully empty. The police had clearly searched the place, but they'd at least been courteous. It wasn't ransacked. A few drawers had been left open, and the corner of the living room rug was folded back. That was all. Sadie didn't even notice.

While she ran Sadie's bath, Clare called Dorothy. This time, she answered.

"Hello?" she queried politely. Dorothy liked to pretend that caller ID didn't exist.

"Dorothy, it's Clare. Are you around to watch Sadie for a couple of hours? I have to go down to the police station to figure out what's going on."

"Don't worry about a thing, dear. I've got it handled."

"I really appreciate that. How soon do you think you can get here?"

"No, dear. You stay with Sadie. We'll take care of Jed. An old colleague of Abe's is already with him at the precinct—he's the best criminal defense lawyer in the city."

"I can meet him there. I'd like to see Jed when he gets released."

"The most important thing you can do right now is take care of Sadie. Jed wouldn't want you at a police station at this hour anyway."

It was seven p.m.

"Dorothy, I should be with Jed right now. I'm his wife."

"And I'm his mother. Which is why I'm taking care of him."

"So that's a no then?" Clare asked with more testiness than she usually allowed herself with her in-laws. "You're refusing to watch Sadie?"

"Let's each stick to our strengths, shall we?"

"Fine," Clare snapped. "I'll hire a babysitter."

Dorothy's voice lost its own veneer of politeness. "You'll do no such thing. I warned you about that man. You got Jed into this. *We'll* get him out of it. Jed will come home to our house tonight, and we will let you know when you are invited to see him."

"Dorothy—" Clare started to say, but she'd already hung up.

Clare set her phone on the sloped edge of the porcelain sink, and it slipped into the basin with a clatter. She sat heavily on the floor, her back against the tub.

She shouldn't have been so surprised. Of course Dorothy was taking care of things. But what was her angle? After seven years, Clare knew that Dorothy *always* had an angle, whether it was inviting a ringer to the member-guest tennis championship or orchestrating socially advantageous friendships for her children.

Was she going to try to convince him to initiate divorce proceedings? Was she already hatching a plan to pin everything—including Gabriel's death—on Clare? She wouldn't put it past Dorothy. She'd use any advantage she had to protect her children. Dorothy was a far more frightening adversary than Jed had threatened to be. It occurred to her that it wasn't out of the question that Dorothy had put *Longfin* in that closet herself. And she certainly had a spare fifty thousand dollars to wire into Clare's account.

Sadie appeared in the doorway completely naked except for a pair of hot-pink goggles twisted around her head. Clare couldn't even bring herself to smile.

AFTER CLARE PUT Sadie to bed, she tried calling Jed, Dorothy, Lauren, Grant, and even Abe. No one picked up. The Basts were closing ranks.

Clare pictured the flurry of activity at the apartment on Eighty-Eighth Street, with her mother-in-law manning the phone like a wartime general. As Dorothy had once told Clare, the Basts had two things going for them: a keen understanding of the law and many, many friends to help them use it to their advantage. This was the moment when favors were called in. Clare tried not to think about the family court judge.

Clare decided to work off her nervous energy by searching the apartment. Maybe the police had missed something. She started with Jed's briefcase and the desk in the office, but, as far as she could tell, none of the papers looked incriminating. She searched every hiding spot she could think of: the medicine cabinets, the toilet tanks, behind the books on the bookshelves, the underside of the furniture. She even checked his closet for a pair of black Reeboks. She didn't expect to find them—if Jed had actually broken into Gabriel's house himself, he wouldn't have been stupid enough to hang on to the clothes he'd been wearing. But she was still relieved they weren't there.

Finally, Clare collapsed onto the couch. She'd found nothing. She reluctantly decided that it was time to call Detective Breznick. She didn't want to, but she couldn't think of any other way to find out what, exactly, Jed had been arrested for. Nothing was online yet, and the Basts had left her out in the cold.

If Breznick was surprised to hear that Clare hadn't been in contact with her husband, she didn't show it. She answered Clare's question tonelessly: "First-degree manslaughter."

"Oh my god," Clare whispered. Even after finding *Longfin*, she'd never actually believed that Jed had killed Gabriel. But clearly Breznick did.

"Based on what evidence?"

"You can direct your questions to the Manhattan DA's office going forward," Breznick said. "But I wouldn't expect them to share the details of their case with the defendant's wife."

Clare hung up and looked around the apartment. The silence was oppressive. She picked up her phone again and called Maggie.

"Hey," Maggie said, sounding distracted. She was probably still at work.

"Hi," Clare said in what she thought was a normal voice, but Maggie immediately snapped to attention.

"What's wrong?" she demanded.

"Jed's been arrested."

"*What?*"

"For killing Gabriel."

"Wait, slow down. The cops think Jed killed Gabriel?"

"Yes."

"Is he okay?"

"I don't know. He won't pick up my calls."

"Are *you* okay?"

"It still feels very surreal."

"This has to be a misunderstanding."

"I'm not so sure about that."

"Clare, there is no way Jed killed someone."

"That's what I assumed at first, too."

"What do you mean, at first?"

"I found something."

"What did you find?"

"I don't think I should say over the phone."

"I can leave for the airport right now. I could be at your place by morning."

"Don't do that. You've got work. Besides, I'm sure you're right: This will all get sorted out soon."

CLARE WAS JUST climbing into bed when her phone rang for the first time since Jed's arrest. She reached for it eagerly, but it wasn't a Bast. It was Elise. Clare swiped to answer it.

"I just heard the news," Elise said. "I'm sorry."

"Thanks."

That was the limit of Elise's social niceties. "You can probably guess why I'm calling," she said.

"You want to know whether Jed has *Longfin*," Clare said flatly.

"It would certainly help my investigation if he did."

Clare wasn't sure how to answer. Elise had come through on her end: She'd told Clare what she knew; more, even, then she needed to. And maybe Elise would be able to quietly get the painting back to its rightful owner: Gabriel's estate.

Still.

Telling Elise the truth would implicate Jed more than he already was. Clare wasn't ready to do that before she'd talked to him. Plus, it was the only leverage she had. Without *Longfin*, she'd have nothing to bargain with.

"The police didn't find anything here, as far as I know," she said. "And I haven't spoken to him."

"I'll have to try to question him sooner rather than later," Elise said. "But you might have better luck than me getting answers out of him."

"Elise," Clare said, surprised she even had to spell it out. "I can't interrogate my husband on your behalf."

"Don't we both want *Longfin* back where it belongs?"

Where did it even belong after all this? Clare had no clue.

"I couldn't help even if I wanted to," she said. "He's not picking up my calls." She did not add: Besides, he doesn't know where *Longfin* is; only I know that. It's in Mina Gellman's front-hall closet.

"Can you at least give me his number?"

"Elise, I really can't. He's my husband. I need to step back."

"I understand."

Suddenly, something occurred to Clare. Hadn't Elise said she had a source at the NYPD? "Actually, wait. I'll give you Jed's number if you do me a favor. Can you ask your police contact what evidence they have against Jed?"

"I wouldn't call that an even trade, but yes, I'm happy to help."

"Thank you."

"One more thing," Elise said. "It's probably meaningless, but I did want to mention it, just in case."

"What's that?"

"My tech found something, or rather, a lack of something. Apparently, Gabriel deleted a significant amount of data from his computer on October nineteenth."

October nineteenth? The date sounded familiar, but she couldn't immediately pinpoint it.

"What data?"

"No clue. All she knows is that a user signed in as Gabriel erased approximately two gigabytes from the hard drive."

"But what does that mean?"

"That's the extent of what I know. The information could very well be meaningless. Maybe he was just doing regular data maintenance."

Gabriel hadn't seemed like the type of man who did regular data maintenance.

After she hung up, Clare checked the calendar on her phone. October nineteenth was Dorothy's birthday. That couldn't possibly be related, could it?

The night before, she noted, had been the MoCA party, when Jed and Gabriel met.

## CHAPTER 35

THE NEXT MORNING, A LOUD, persistent buzzing penetrated Clare's dream. She immediately sat up and looked around the bedroom, half panicked. Where was that sound coming from?

It took her another couple of seconds to recognize it as the phone connecting their apartment to the lobby.

Clare stumbled out of bed and ran to the kitchen.

"Hello?" she answered, out of breath.

"Morning, Mrs. Bast, I've got a visitor here to see you," Gino said in his usual upbeat voice, betraying no indication that he knew about Jed's arrest the night before. Clare was sure he did; he was just very good at his job.

"Who?" she asked. Jed? No, he owned the apartment. Gino wouldn't need permission to let him up. Dorothy?

"Maggie Wheeler."

"Oh!" Clare shouted louder than she'd meant. "Send her up. Thank you."

Clare ran to the front door, opened it, and drummed her fingers against the doorframe as she waited for the elevator to climb up to their floor. When it finally lurched open and she saw Maggie inside, she burst into tears.

"You're here."

"Of course I'm here, you loon," Maggie said, stepping out of the elevator and pulling Clare into a hug.

"Thank you for coming," Clare whispered.

"Don't worry. We'll get this all sorted out."

Sadie appeared in the doorway, rubbing her eyes. "Hi, Aunt Maggie," she said.

"Sadie!" Maggie exclaimed, kneeling to give her a hug while Clare turned away and tried to dry her eyes. "I'm so happy to see you."

"What are you doing here?"

"I came to meet Noodle, of course! Will you introduce me?"

Sadie nodded. "Daddy's at work, so it's my job to fill his water bottle. I'll show you how to do it." Sadie had accepted Clare's explanation of Jed's absence without question the night before. For once, Jed's long work hours had come in handy.

THE THREE OF them ate breakfast together, then Maggie took Sadie to school. Alone in the apartment at last, Clare took a long, scalding hot shower. When she was done, she got dressed and opened her laptop. She googled her husband's name. Nothing about the arrest came up. She allowed herself to savor the relief but wondered how long the grace period would last.

When Maggie returned, she handed Clare an iced coffee and flopped onto the couch.

"That place is a *scene*. Why do all the girls wear party dresses to school?"

"I don't know. It's just what's done, apparently."

Clare took the top off her coffee and poured in a splash of milk. "Were people staring at you? I wonder if any of them know about Jed yet."

"It was hard to tell. They definitely sensed that I didn't belong. Maybe because I smell like I've been on a plane all night."

"God, I'm sorry, I haven't even offered you a shower yet. Do you want one now?"

"In a bit. Come talk to me."

Clare settled next to Maggie on the couch and caught her up on the events of the past few weeks: her scattershot investigation, her meetings with Elise, the link between Gatepost and Axion. By the time she finished, with the discovery of *Longfin* the day before, Maggie looked shellshocked.

"Are you a hundred percent sure it was the painting stolen from Gabriel's house?"

"Yes."

"Could anyone else have put it there?"

"I guess any of the Basts could have, but *why*? Besides, that closet was Jed's own personal hidey-hole."

"You need to talk to him," Maggie said. "My editor always says that just because you can't think of an alternative explanation doesn't mean one doesn't exist."

Clare let out a long, frustrated groan. "How did this happen? How is this my life now? I mean, I know what I did was shitty, but it was normal shitty. Like you said: People have affairs. I made mistakes. But none of them ever seemed fatal. I never thought they would lead *here*. How could I?"

"This isn't your fault, Clare."

"I appreciate the sentiment, Mags, but yes, it is."

"You didn't kill Gabriel."

"I fucked him. I kept fucking him. None of this would have happened if I hadn't."

"You don't know that."

Clare gave Maggie a look like *C'mon*.

"You don't honestly think that Jed killed Gabriel, do you?" Maggie asked. "No offense, but your husband doesn't seem like the type to kill his wife's lover in a jealous rage. The man can't even change a flat tire, and I've never seen him get worked up about anything."

"I don't know what to think. It doesn't *feel* true, but the facts remain: Jed lied about knowing Gabriel. Jed worked with the client Gabriel bought *Longfin* for. And the one I really can't wrap my head around: The painting that went missing the night Gabriel was killed showed up at *Jed's parents' house*, of all places. How on earth do you explain that? Besides, the police obviously had to have a reason for arresting him, right?"

"You need to talk to him," Maggie said again.

"I've tried. He won't pick up my calls. None of them will."

"Try harder. Sadie is going to need to see him at some point."

"I don't know how to talk to him. I don't know what combination of contrition and anger is appropriate in this situation. I know I destroyed his life. But if he killed Gabriel, if he killed Gabriel while I was fifteen feet away, then I don't want to apologize to him. I want to run far, far away from him."

Clare's phone starting ringing, and she patted around the sofa for it. When she found it, she saw that it was Lev calling, and she let it go to voicemail.

A minute later, Tasha called.

She looked at Maggie. "I guess it's starting."

Clare took out her laptop and googled Jed's name again. This time, a news item on the *New York Post*'s website was the top result: "White Shoe Lawyer Arrested in Slaying of Chelsea Art Dealer."

Clare shut her eyes. She'd been wrong. This, right now, was the moment her future forked. Now was the dividing line between her old life and her new one. The whole world knew that Jed had been charged with manslaughter.

She quickly scanned the article. The one silver lining was that her relationship with Gabriel had not been mentioned.

Yet.

She was sure the reporters would find out about it eventually. But at this point, they had little information beyond what was in the headline. The motive was said to be "personal." There was no mention of what she most wanted to know: the evidence the police had found.

Her phone rang again. This time it was Alec. He was probably calling for details about the charges against Jed. Gatepost's employees and investors must be in a panic over the arrest of its general counsel.

Clare blocked the call. She couldn't talk to him or anyone else at Gatepost until she understood what role Axion had played in the mess that led to Gabriel's death.

While Maggie showered, Clare grabbed a piece of paper and tried to draw a diagram connecting Jed, Kallsten, Axion, Gabriel, Gatepost, *Longfin*, and herself, but she'd never been any good at math, or drawing, for that matter, and she soon crumpled it up and tossed it across the room.

Maggie was right. Her best source for untangling the mystery was obvious. She just had to force him to talk to her.

## CHAPTER 36

AN HOUR LATER, CLARE WALKED up to the Basts' apartment building on Eighty-Eighth and Fifth. Their doorman, Luka, greeted Clare by name as he held the door for her. But when she proceeded to the elevator bank, he asked her to stop.

"Sorry, Mrs. Bast. Mrs. Bast—the other Mrs. Bast—asked us to call up if you came to visit."

Clare stepped away from the elevator and tried not to look cowed. Luka spoke quietly into the phone at his desk while keeping his eyes trained on her. He hung up and smiled.

"She'll be right down."

Clare had assumed that she would at least be permitted upstairs, but apparently not. The arrow above the elevator slowly completed its semicircle from Lobby to Penthouse, paused, and then retraced its path. As Clare watched it, her anxiety mounted.

The door opened to reveal Dorothy in a light-blue boucle-knit skirt suit, kitten heels, and sapphire earrings. She spread both her hands wide. "Clare, darling, so good to see you."

She enveloped Clare in a sticklike embrace and brushed a papery cheek against hers. The show was presumably for Luka.

"I came to speak to Jed," Clare said.

"This isn't a good time. He's meeting with his lawyers right now."

"Does he know I'm here?"

"As I said, he's in a meeting."

Clare walked over to the lobby's small seating area. "I'll wait," she said, settling into a green wingback chair.

Dorothy and Luka exchanged a glance. The doorman looked uncomfortable.

"I don't know how long he'll be," Dorothy said.

"That's all right. I'm sure Luka will let me use the building's restroom if the need arises."

"As you wish, dear."

She pushed the elevator's call button with a shiny, lacquered nail and disappeared.

Clare sat at her post for the next forty-five minutes. She stopped turning her head every time the elevator door opened, because it was never Jed.

Until finally, it was.

When he appeared in front of her, slumped and unshaven, his eyes flashed with some emotion that she couldn't quite pinpoint, a mixture of anger and defeat. He was wearing a baggy yellow Lacoste sweater that looked like it probably belonged to Abe. An indeterminate brown splotch stained the front of it. Clare felt a surge of pity for him, but the thought of Gabriel's blood-soaked body quickly extinguished it.

"What?" he asked sullenly.

Clare stood up. "We need to talk."

"Oh, you mean about how you were fucking some art dealer while I was at work, supporting our family?"

Clare tried to keep her tone measured. "Yes, among other things."

Jed sighed dramatically in a way that reminded Clare of their daughter. "*Fine*," he said turning around to call the elevator back.

"How about we take a walk instead," Clare suggested.

"The lawyer said there might be reporters outside."

"I'd rather not go up to your parents'."

"We can go down to the gym then," he said. "No one ever uses it."

Clare had never been to the building's basement before. She followed Jed through a dark corridor with low ceilings and bare light bulbs, getting more and more nervous. She'd wanted to speak to him without his family present, but she hadn't guessed that she'd be entirely alone with him in a dank, isolated basement.

Jed held a door open for her. A motion-activated light flickered on, illuminating a small, dusty room with a treadmill, a stationary bike, and a rack of hand weights. It looked like it hadn't been touched—let alone used—in a decade.

Clare took up a position against the wall by the rack of weights. She figured they were the closest thing to a weapon available. But she had to admit that Jed didn't look capable of violence. He hadn't even mustered the energy to wipe a glob of toothpaste from the corner of his mouth.

Jed leaned against the opposite wall. They faced each other like prize-fighters in a ring, the machines on one side of them, a dusty mirror on the other. Clare noted, with a small measure of relief, that there was a camera mounted on the ceiling.

"So," Jed said, "you were sleeping with Gabriel Prévost."

Clare nodded.

"For how long?"

Clare swallowed audibly. "About six weeks."

Jed raised his eyebrows in surprise.

"I'm sorry," Clare said. "I really am."

"Oh, you're sorry?" Jed asked, his tone slick with sarcasm. "Well, that fixes everything. Let's call the cops who arrested me and tell them you're *sorry*."

"I had no idea it would turn out like this. Obviously. I kept meaning to stop it, but . . ." She trailed off. She had no explanation.

Jed continued to stare at her stonily.

She tried again: "It meant nothing." This was a lie, but she couldn't tell him the truth: that meeting Gabriel had felt like a shot of adrenaline straight to her heart. There was no point wounding Jed any further.

"What it meant or whether you're sorry is irrelevant," Jed snapped, sounding like the lawyer he was. "It doesn't matter how either of us *feels* about it. It won't change the fact that I'm facing murder charges because you fucked some sleazy art dealer."

"Jed, I know I betrayed you and hurt you deeply. I'll feel remorse about that for the rest of my life. But you can't stand there and claim that the charges against you are entirely my fault."

Jed's lips parted in shock; he'd clearly expected more contrition from her. "*Excuse me?*"

"There are other things implicating you in Gabriel's death."

"Like what?"

"Like the fact that you have *Longfin*," Clare said calmly.

Jed's nostrils flared. Clare hoped for a second that he'd have no idea what she was talking about. Then his eyes narrowed. "You found it?"

"Yes."

"Is it still there?"

"No."

Jed pushed back a lock of hair that had flopped forward into his eyes. "*Goddamn it.*"

"Jed, did you—" She stopped herself.

Jed smiled for the first time since she'd seen him. "Did I what? Did I kill Gabriel? Is that what you want to ask?"

Clare nodded.

"No, I did not kill Gabriel, but thanks for the show of good faith. I didn't even know you were fucking him. The detective who arrested me was kind enough to share that information."

He didn't appear to be lying, but Clare had obviously lost the ability to read her husband—if she'd ever truly had it in the first place. The air between them bristled with distrust.

Clare started spinning the lightest barbell around in its slot, just for something to do with her hands. The sound of metal grating on metal was unpleasant, but she preferred it to silence.

"This is all somehow about Gatepost, isn't it?"

Jed looked surprised by the question, then he let out a long, slow sigh. "Yes."

"And Axion?"

"How do you know about Axion?"

"From Gabriel's assistant. Please tell me what's going on."

Jed climbed onto the exercise bike and began to pedal at a snail's pace.

"Remember how I told you that most of the assets under Gatepost's management belong to a single investor? That's Axion."

"Okay. But who—or what—is Axion?"

"That's what I've spent the past few months trying to figure out. When I started at Gatepost, I was troubled right off the bat by its overwhelming reliance on a single client. What's more, that client was based in Cyprus. That was a serious red flag to me.

"I asked around internally, and no one knew much. It seemed crazy that none of the portfolio managers knew where their money came from. But it was a black box. I mean, it could have been a front for the Ayatollah of Iran for all we knew."

"I thought banks had to know who their clients were."

"Banks do. Hedge funds don't. There are huge loopholes in financial regulations: Unlike banks or mutual funds, hedge funds don't actually have to report where the funds they invest come from. They have very little obligation to even determine for themselves who their clients actually are."

"What they don't know can't hurt them?"

"More like, what they don't know, they can't be prosecuted for. All they have to do is prove that they made the most minimal effort to determine that the funds were clean."

"But you didn't think that was enough?"

"It's not like I thought Gatepost had to conduct a full-blown investigation, but for its own good, I thought we should at least know who we were in bed with. Especially since Cyprus is a magnet for dirty money. That's what I told Alec, shortly after I started. He told me in no uncertain terms to leave it alone. He said he'd gotten Axion on board by promising total discretion. That was my first inkling that something was amiss."

"And let me guess: You didn't leave it alone."

"How could I? I'm general counsel. If Gatepost was doing something illegal, I was implicated, too. We all were. I couldn't take that chance. I either needed reassurance that Axion was legit—or more certainty that it wasn't. So I started digging. I searched every drive on the network. I went through Mark's"—his predecessor's—"old emails. I even went down to the company's storage facility in New Jersey and looked through old paperwork. That's why I was working all the time. I was doing that on top of my regular job.

"It took me months, but I finally found what I was looking for: a 2009 email to Mark from Peter DeGroot—he's our designated point of contact at Axion. It said, 'I'll need to run this by Viktor.' One minute later he followed up: 'Please disregard. That message was sent in error.'"

Jed stopped pedaling and looked at Clare, waiting for her to react.

She shook her head in bewilderment. "Who's Viktor?"

"Don't you know? You're the reason I figured it out."

Clare racked her memory but came up with nothing. "I don't know any Viktors sitting on hundreds of millions of dollars," she said. "I don't think I know any Viktors period."

"Don't you remember speaking with Tasha's godfather, Viktor Semenov, back at the beginning of last summer? It was about Blake Webley."

"*That* Viktor?"

"When I saw that email, I realized it had to be the same Viktor. Plenty of hedge funds start with family money. Plus, Cyprus attracts a lot of business from Russians who want to funnel money out of the country, so Putin can't get his hands on it. It makes total sense that Alec and Tasha founded Gatepost with the help of her godfather. They made a lot of money, and they helped get his money out of Putin's reach."

"That's not illegal, is it?"

"It wasn't then. It is now."

"What do you mean?"

"The United States imposed economic sanctions on Viktor Semenov in 2022, after Russia invaded Ukraine. It's illegal for any American to do business with him."

"Oh." The news landed with a thud in Clare's gut. She remembered hearing someone say that Tasha's family members were oligarchs close to Putin, but she'd dismissed it as mere rumor.

"Which means that Gatepost is actively committing fraud," Jed said, "day in, day out."

"But why would they do that? Family loyalty?"

"Believe me, they're not doing Viktor any favors by keeping his money. The Justice Department has an entire task force devoted to sniffing out funds that belong to sanctioned oligarchs. If they find out who really owns Axion, they'll freeze all three quarters of a billion dollars, and Viktor will probably never see a dime of it again. Most Russian oligarchs have moved their investments from the West to the Middle East by now. If I were Viktor, that's what I would do. It's probably his plan: he's already started pulling Axion's money out of Gatepost, but he has to go slowly. That's how hedge funds work: They make it very difficult for investors to redeem their investments."

"But why would Gatepost *want* to keep Viktor's money if it's so risky?"

"Because without his money, Gatepost is done. They never went out of their way to do any marketing or pitch new clients. Or maybe they did, and they didn't succeed. Alec's returns are fine, but nothing extraordinary. And investing in hedge funds has gone out of favor over the past few years. Besides, from Gatepost's point of view, the risk of staying the course is minimal: Viktor's ownership of Axion is, in fact, very well hidden. Without a whistleblower, I doubt the feds would ever make the connection."

"So did you report it? Are *you* the whistleblower?"

"I couldn't. Under client confidentiality rules, I had to go to Alec first. I told him I knew Axion belonged to Viktor Semenov, and I advised him to do what any lawyer would: freeze Axion's account and report it to OFAC immediately."

"OFAC?"

"The Office of Foreign Assets Control. It's the arm of the Treasury Department that enforces sanctions."

"And what did Alec say?"

"To my surprise, he agreed. He said I was right: Gatepost had made a mistake in trying to continue the relationship with Axion after the sanctions went through. He said he'd talk to Tasha over the weekend, and then we'd report it to OFAC first thing on Monday morning."

"Did you?"

"No. We didn't."

"Why not?"

Jed stared at her for a moment, as if trying to gauge whether she already knew the answer to that question. When he seemed to determine that she didn't, he said, "Because of you, Clare."

## CHAPTER 37

*"ME?"* CLARE ASKED. "HOW DOES this have anything to do with me?"

"We had this conversation on Friday, October eighteenth. Does that date ring a bell?"

"Vaguely."

"It was the night of the party at MoCA."

Clare had a vision of Gabriel pushing his weight into her in the bathroom hallway, his hands fumbling at her dress. That couldn't be what Jed was referring to, could it?

It wasn't. Jed proceeded to tell Clare *his* version of that night: "I was ordering another drink at the bar when Tasha sidled up to me and struck up a conversation. Your work with Gabriel came up, and she suggested that our professional paths might cross one day."

"Yours and mine?" Clare asked.

"Yes, and I told her I didn't see how they possibly would. That's when Tasha informed me that Gabriel handled all of Axion's art acquisitions. In other words, she wanted me to know that Gabriel was doing business with a Russian oligarch on the US sanctions list, and you were helping him."

"But that doesn't make sense. Tasha would never have admitted that her godfather owned Axion."

"She didn't have to. She knew I'd already found out on my own. All she had to do was reference Axion, and I'd know what that meant: Viktor Semenov. Then she said that Axion's last purchase was a Blake Webley painting, and so of course you must have been involved in the sale. 'Let's hope that nothing unpleasant comes to light about Axion,' were her exact words."

"She threatened you?"

"She was careful with how much she said, but she was very clear that if I exposed the true owner of Axion, *you* would pay the price."

Clare picked up a dumbbell and gripped it tightly. She wanted to remind herself of the weight and heft of the real world. So much of what she'd assumed about other people—and herself—over the past few months had been wrong. The reality she'd built up had been nothing but a puff of smoke. She'd considered Tasha something akin to a friend.

"But her threat was totally toothless," Clare said. "I *wasn't* working with Axion. Or with Gabriel, for that matter. Why didn't you just tell me about the conversation?"

As soon as the words were out of her mouth, she wished she could take them back. She'd done nothing but hide the truth from him for weeks on end.

Jed's eyes flashed with anger. "Well, I didn't know that then, did I? You told me you'd taken a job with Gabriel Prévost. It made sense that you'd work on a Webley transaction. How was I supposed to know that that was a lie? I never imagined you were fucking the guy."

"Okay," Clare said, shame flooding her body from head to toe. She thought back to the night of the party. Jed *had* seemed unnaturally quiet when she returned from the bathroom. "So that's why you told me to stop working with him in the taxi home?"

"Yes."

"And what did you do about Axion?"

Jed stepped off the bike and walked over to the mirror. He examined himself for a moment before turning away.

"I did nothing," he said. "Tasha's threat worked. On Monday morning, I told Alec that I'd been mistaken about Axion, and that there was no need to get the authorities involved after all."

Clare replaced the weight on its rack with a loud clank. Jed had turned a blind eye to Gatepost's misdeeds in order to protect her. Jed, who had always prided himself on his ethics. He'd even dreamed of being a judge one day. But he'd scarified his integrity for *her.* It was almost the worst thing Clare could have done to him.

"I'm so sorry," she said quietly. "I wish I'd known. I had nothing to do with Axion, I swear."

"It wouldn't have made a difference, Clare. Everyone *thought* you were working with Gabriel. That's all that mattered. Even if you were never legally connected to the Axion deals, your reputation would have been ruined. Don't you see that? If it came out that you were working with some sleazy dealer who sold art to sanctioned Russians, no university or museum would ever hire you. It would be a black mark on your name you'd never get rid of."

Clare considered this and had to admit that he was right. The cover story she'd made up to hide an affair would have cost her her entire career. It still might.

"And if I'm being honest," Jed said begrudgingly, "I had my own reputation to consider, too. Nobody would be lining up to hire a general counsel who just tanked his own hedge fund. And we were finally making good money. I didn't want to give it up. I honestly don't know how much of it was to protect you and how much of it was to protect me. We're a family. I was protecting *us*."

"You still could have told me what was going on," she said. "There was clearly something weighing on you."

"I was ashamed, Clare. I didn't want you to know that every day I went in to work and broke the law. My hope was that Axion would keep taking out their money, slowly enough for Alec to find new clients—or maybe for me to find a new job—and eventually, Axion wouldn't be a risk to us anymore."

Clare ran her finger through a layer of dust on the weights and tried to get a handle on this new information. She wanted to throttle Tasha, but she was at least reassured that Jed had an explanation that made sense.

Well, not for everything. She realized they hadn't even gotten to the heart of the matter yet.

"But Jed, none of this explains how you got *Longfin*."

Jed threw up his hands. "I don't know. I'm as confused as you are. It just showed up at our building."

That was not an explanation she'd seen coming. "What are you talking about?"

"A few days before Gabriel was killed, a messenger delivered it to our building. Gino handed me that big wooden crate when I came home from work. It was the night you went out with Mina."

Clare shook her head, unable to make sense of this. "Why would Gabriel send *Longfin* to you, of all people?"

"Who knows?" Jed said bitterly. "To set me up? That'd be a pretty good strategy for stealing my wife."

"That doesn't make any sense, Jed. Gabriel is the one who got *murdered*. He certainly didn't set that up."

"I realize that, Clare. I have no idea why he sent it to me, or if it was even him at all. There was no note, no message, nothing."

"Didn't you consider that his murder might have had something to do with all this? You didn't think to tell the police?"

Jed glared at her.

"Don't you understand? Whatever 'this' is, I'm a part of it. My hands are dirty. And you're part of it, too. It's my job to protect you. The best-case scenario right now is me *only* getting disbarred. So no, I was not about to tell the police that you and I were both doing business with a sanctioned Russian. I didn't think that would help our case. They were obviously already suspicious. And I had *Longfin* sitting ten feet away in our guest bedroom the entire time the cops were there. I was panicked. All I could do was try to get them out as quickly as I could. The next day, I drove it out to East Hampton. I didn't know what to do with it."

"Wait, *Longfin* was in our apartment when the police showed up?" A sense of disorientation suddenly washed over her. Something wasn't clicking into place. There was a problem with Jed's timeline. How could Jed have been sent *Longfin before* Gabriel died? Clare had seen it on his wall mere minutes before he was killed.

"No," she murmured, more to herself than Jed.

"What?"

Clare stared at her husband with wide eyes. His rumpled clothing and five-o'clock shadow were just an act. It was like he'd put on a sad-husband costume. "You're lying," she said in amazement. "You're still lying to me."

Jed clenched his jaw. "I'm not lying to you."

"You are," Clare said. "You couldn't have been sent *Longfin* before Gabriel died, because I saw it at his house the night he was killed."

Jed began to protest then stopped himself and didn't speak for a moment. "You were in Gabriel's house the night he was killed?"

Clare nodded, feeling ashamed.

An expression flitted across Jed's face, but she couldn't quite tell what it signified. Guilt? Fear? Anger? She didn't wait to find out. She leaped for the door, yanked it open, and started running down the dark corridor.

Where was the elevator? Had it been on the left or right?

"Clare, *stop*," Jed called. He was right behind her.

By some miracle, the elevator was still waiting. She got on and started furiously pounding the buttons marked Lobby and Door Close at the same time.

Jed threw himself against the door just as it was shutting and edged it back open with his body.

"I want to see Sadie," he said, with a desperate edge to his voice.

"Jed, please let me go," Clare pleaded, her voice sounding small and frightened.

Jed seemed to realize all at once that she was terrified of him. He jolted back, as if he'd already hurt her.

"I'm not keeping you here against your will," he said, stepping clear of the elevator door.

They stared at each other in silence as the door slid shut between them. Clare had a sudden memory of watching him watch her walk down the aisle on their wedding day, his eyes filled with tears. How had they ended up *here*?

Clare exited the lobby quickly, not bothering to say goodbye to Luka.

Once outside, she started to run.

## CHAPTER 38

CLARE SLOWED DOWN A BLOCK from her apartment to catch her breath. Every time she thought she had a grip on the facts, the story changed. Was Jed guilty or innocent? The answer seemed to change hour by hour. She no longer knew what was true and what was a lie.

When Clare got up to her apartment, she plastered a smile on her face. Maggie and Sadie were playing Candy Land on the living room floor.

"Hi, lovebug," she said, leaning down to kiss the top of her daughter's head. "How was school?"

"Good," Sadie said without looking up from the game.

"Sadie, I'm just going to chat with your mom for a minute," Maggie said, unfolding herself from the floor. "You can play for me."

Clare went to hang up her coat in the hall closet and met Maggie in the kitchen.

"How'd it go?" Maggie's forehead was creased with worry lines, and she had dark bags under her eyes. She'd probably slept only a couple hours the night before, if that.

Clare recounted her entire conversation with Jed in the Basts' basement. Maggie's eyes kept widening in shock.

"I don't even know where to begin," she said when Clare was done. "Remind me who Tasha is? Does she work at Gatepost, too?"

"She's Alec's wife. They own it together, but she makes a point of saying she doesn't work there. Alec runs it."

"It sounds like she's got a pretty firm hand on the tiller either way."

"She's not really the type to watch from the sidelines."

Maggie took two mugs out of the cabinet and filled them with coffee. Clare opened the fridge to grab the milk.

"So you think Jed is lying about how he got *Longfin*?" Maggie asked.

"He has to be. I saw it on Gabriel's wall the night he died."

Clare handed the milk to Maggie, who held it aloft without making any move to use it. "It seems like an odd story to make up," she said. "It's so easily disprovable. Have you asked the doormen if they remember receiving a large wooden box?"

"Not yet," Clare said. "They'd probably say anything Jed asked if he slipped them a big enough tip. Besides, a package could mean anything: an Amazon delivery, a prescription refill. A new pair of black Reebok sneakers."

"Is there anyone else you can corroborate his story with?"

"Well, Tasha."

"You *could* just go ask her," Maggie said, finally pouring a splash of milk in her coffee. "Deal with it head-on."

"Not until I have more information. She holds all the cards right now." Clare leaned against the counter and took a sip of coffee. "The thing I don't understand—well, *one* of the things—is how Tasha had this threat or blackmail or whatever you want to call it all ready to go, just hours after Jed told Alec that he'd figured out who owned Axion. It doesn't seem possible for—" She abruptly stopped talking and put down her mug. "Oh my god."

"What?" Maggie asked.

"Oh my god." Clare brought her hand up to her mouth. "I'm such an idiot."

"What do you mean?"

"She set us up. It wasn't a *coincidence* that I started working with Gabriel. Tasha orchestrated the whole thing. She dragged me down to his gallery after their party, after encouraging me to start working again. And the last time I saw Clement, the MoCA curator, he told me that Gabriel had hired me as a favor to someone. It must have been Tasha."

"I don't understand."

"Gabriel was already working for Axion, so all she had to do was loop me into the scheme. Actually, she went even further than that. She set up a phone call between her godfather and me over the summer, and she arranged a meeting between Clement and me just days before he decided to deaccession *Longfin*. She covered every angle to make it look like I was involved in MoCA's sale of *Longfin* from the get-go—and at every step along the way: with Viktor, with Clement, and with Gabriel. That's why I kept turning up at every phase of the investigation—Tasha *put* me there."

"But why would she do that?"

"So she would have that threat in her back pocket. She *manufactured* the threat. Jed said he started pestering Alec about uncovering Axion's true owner soon after he started working at Gatepost. Alec must have mentioned it to Tasha, and they must have decided to put a safeguard in place. If Jed *did* find out about Viktor, they'd have their next move all lined up and ready to play. And if he didn't, well, who cares: All she'd done was set up a few meetings."

"*Aunt Maggie!*" Sadie yelled from the living room. "Come *on*!"

"Let me finish my game with Sadie," Maggie said. "Then we'll continue this conversation."

Clare nodded absentmindedly. She brought her coffee over to the kitchen table and sat down to try to untangle everything she'd learned over the past forty-five minutes. She ran a quick search on her phone of Viktor Semenov. Apparently, he'd bought art openly and under his own name for years before the sanctions were put in place. He wasn't a huge player in the market, but he was noteworthy enough to have garnered a mention in *ARTnews* when the sanctions went into effect.

She'd been such an idiot. Why hadn't she googled Viktor before they spoke on the phone? She'd assumed it was just a courtesy chat with a friend's doddering, older relative. That's how Tasha had presented it, at any rate.

Clare couldn't help but marvel at Tasha's machinations. She was like a chess master who could see sixteen moves ahead. She'd obviously been putting together this plan for months, and it had worked; she'd created clear and consistent evidence connecting Clare to the sale of *Longfin* while hiding all the underlying connections that implicated Tasha herself. She'd made the truth the most unbelievable scenario of all.

Of course, all this was predicated on Jed's account being true. But then he'd lied about how he got *Longfin*. Why not about his interaction with Tasha, too?

Clare got up to pour herself another cup of coffee. She needed a firmer grasp of the facts. Jed's story had spawned as much new uncertainty as she'd had before. The questions were breeding like rabbits. What Clare needed were answers. And some sort of proof. She wished she could just ask Gabriel, but that obviously wasn't possible.

Unless—

Clare remembered the conversation she'd had at the Mark just two days earlier.

Unless there *was* a way to hear his version of things.

ELISE PICKED UP on the first ring: "Any news?"

"You have access to Gabriel's emails, right?"

"The ones he *didn't* erase."

"Can you send me all the messages he exchanged with Tasha Wolfe?"

"The socialite?" Elise asked.

"She's more than that."

"Remember, if you want a favor—"

Clare finished the sentence for her: "Tit for tat. I know."

"You're a quick study."

"I found out who owns Axion. It's Tasha's godfather. That's who Gabriel bought *Longfin* for."

"Who's Tasha's godfather?"

"I don't know his name yet," Clare said after a momentary pause. "That's what I'm hoping to find in the emails."

She wasn't ready to out both Gatepost and Gabriel for doing business with a Russian oligarch on the US sanctions list. Even Clare herself had, if unknowingly, received money from an account connected to him. Could she be implicated, too? She needed to start thinking like Tasha: sixteen steps ahead. She couldn't keep following her whims wherever they took her. She would not blab everything she knew to Elise without considering the repercussions first.

"I'll have my tech pull the emails," Elise said.

"Thank you. Any word from your NYPD contact?"

"Not yet. I have a call in to him."

"Keep me posted."

Clare took another sip of coffee, though she did not need it anymore—she was suddenly buzzing with adrenaline—and went to join Maggie and Sadie in their next round of Candy Land.

## CHAPTER 39

CLARE MOVED THROUGH THE LIVING room, turning on lamps. It was only seven o'clock, but it was already dark outside. Crews of workmen were putting up Christmas trees all along Park Avenue. In a few more weeks, they would all be lit up at once while the whole neighborhood sang carols. It was one of Clare's favorite nights of the year.

Both Sadie and Maggie were sleeping. Clare had managed to hold it together during dinner and bedtime, but now she felt her self-discipline wavering. She poured herself a glass of wine and settled on the sofa.

Could her suspicions about Tasha be right? Could she have misread the woman that badly? Clare recalled with mortification how much she'd admired Tasha when she first met her. She'd envied her shamelessness: the very quality necessary for pulling off a scheme like this. Shame was a guardrail. Shame stopped people from having affairs and plotting elaborate traps for their so-called friends to fall into. Without shame, there was no telling what people might do.

Clare's phone pinged, releasing her momentarily from her self-recriminations. It was a text from Elise: "Check your email."

A FEW MINUTES later, Clare stared, transfixed, at her computer screen. Elise had forwarded a file from her tech that contained all the emails exchanged between Tasha and Gabriel since 2020. It felt like magic, like Clare had summoned Gabriel from the dead. She heard his voice, thanking Tasha for inviting him to a dinner party at her apartment. Here he was again, weighing in on a Diebenkorn painting that Alec and Tasha wanted to buy. Clare touched the screen, half expecting to feel the warmth of his skin under her fingertips.

Ridiculous.

Clare reminded herself why she was doing this. She forced herself to scroll slowly through the early messages, which were straightforward and mundane, until she found an exchange from September 2022 that piqued her interest:

Hello, darling. One of Gatepost's VIP clients wants to diversify into art and asked me to recommend an advisor. Naturally I thought of you. Let me know if you're interested. (A word to the wise: You'll literally be lighting piles of money on fire if you don't take me up on this.) xx T

Tasha, how did you know I have a fondness for piles of money? I'm happy to meet your client, as long you vouch for him. Gabriel.

I'm so glad to hear it. His name is Peter DeGroot and he's one of Gatepost's oldest clients. He's based in Cyprus, and he conducts business through his holding company there. I'll fill you in further at coffee tomorrow. Via Quadronno at 11am? xx T

Their next exchange came two months later.

Gabriel, thank you so much for the beautiful peonies. They were entirely unnecessary, but much appreciated. xx T

I'm glad you enjoyed them, Tasha. I think I probably owe you a couple dozen more. Peter is on a serious buying jag. Thank you again for introducing us. Gabriel.

A large gap in communication followed. Then some more benign exchanges. The next email of note had come from Tasha, just that past June:

Gabriel, I just heard that Clement is thinking of deaccessioning a Blake Webley painting—*Longfin* from 1958. I know Peter has been dying to get his hands on one for years. Thought you might appreciate the heads up. xx T
P.S. Did you get your invitation to our anniversary party? I hope you can make it. I want to introduce you to someone there.

Tasha, thanks for the tip. I just left a message for Peter, and I'm actually due to have lunch with Clement later this week. As for the invitation, I will gladly attend. I did very well by the last person you introduced me to, so I'm looking forward to meeting another. Happy early anniversary to you both. Gabriel.

Gabriel, I shouldn't have gotten your hopes up. This meeting will not be quite as fruitful for you as Peter has been. Consider it the favor you owe me in return. It's about my friend Clare.

Clare physically recoiled at the sight of her own name but kept reading.

She's getting her doctorate in art history at Columbia, but she's totally stalled. She's stopped working on her dissertation and isn't even sure she wants to continue with her degree. I can tell she's depressed and at loose ends. I hate seeing her this way. Is there some consulting work you could throw her way? She's honestly quite talented; you might even want to hire her full-time. I just want to get her out of her rut. Please? x T

Clare's face was on fire by the time she finished reading the email, her anger at Tasha competing with a sense of total humiliation. Gabriel's response was exceedingly gracious, and it broke Clare's heart:

Tasha, I'd be glad to meet your friend. I'm sure I
can find some use for her. Best, Gabriel.

The day after the party, Tasha wrote again:

I'm so glad you and Clare hit it off last night. I'm coming
down to the gallery tomorrow at 10am. I'll see if I
can convince her to join. See you soon. xx T
P.S. Don't you dare tell Clare I asked you
to hire her. She'd be mortified!

On that point, Tasha was correct. Clare was deeply mortified.

The next flurry of emails concerned the seating arrangements for the MoCA party. Clare noted grimly that Tasha had, in fact, been setting Gabriel up with that blond editor. Another gap in communication followed. Finally, Clare came to the very last email they exchanged, sent by Tasha on November 4.

Gabriel, just confirming our plans. Everything is all set from my end, so just let me know you're on board, and I'll start making arrangements. This is the best solution for everyone.

Gabriel wrote back:

I don't want to know the details.

Two days later, he was dead.

## CHAPTER 40

WHEN CLARE LOOKED UP FROM her computer screen, a new and unfamiliar feeling was coursing through her veins: rage. She was teeming with fury at Tasha, who had treated both her and Gabriel like puppets in a pantomime.

She remembered the feeling of Gabriel's fingers brushing against hers as they passed the cigarette back and forth on the Wolfes' balcony the night they met. His eyes reflecting the lights of the city. The thrum of blood in her body as she got close to him. It had felt so natural at the time, but now she realized that the whole encounter had been manufactured. Gabriel had just been doing a favor for a well-connected client. Their entire relationship had been nothing more than a plot point in Tasha's plan.

At least, she told herself, he hadn't been in on the rest of it from the start. He wasn't a criminal, and she wasn't his mark. He would have had no reason to suspect that Peter DeGroot was a proxy for Viktor Semenov. And he hadn't *seduced* her as a favor to Tasha. He was only supposed to hire her. There had been something real between them. She had to believe that.

Clare took a deep breath. At least now she had evidence that Tasha had orchestrated her professional relationship with Gabriel, *and* Gabriel's relationship with Axion. It wasn't just speculation anymore.

Tasha had needed ammunition against Jed, so she'd used Gabriel to entrap Clare in sanctions fraud. But that was only one piece of it. How had everything else fallen into place for her so perfectly? Why had Clement decided to deaccession *Longfin* from MoCA's collection at the exact moment that Tasha needed to incriminate a Webley scholar? It was too convenient and neat.

Clare shut her laptop.

She was sure of two things: Life was rarely neat; and Tasha Wolfe was not a woman who relied on coincidence.

## CHAPTER 41

EARLY THE NEXT MORNING, CLARE stood outside the Museum of Contemporary Art, shivering in the cold and wishing she'd worn gloves. She held a takeaway coffee in one hand and a green tea in the other.

The museum didn't open for another fifteen minutes, but a crowd had already formed outside the entrance. A security guard was trying and failing to organize the mass into some semblance of order. Clare craned her neck and scanned their faces.

Finally, Clare spotted the sun glinting off Clement's thick glasses. He had a scowl on his face as he tried to push his way through the horde of tourists. *Good*, Clare thought; she needed them to slow his progress. Her only hope was to convince him to stop and talk to her before he shoved past her, which would obviously be his first instinct, given the tenor of their last encounter. She approached him from behind, and started speaking before he'd even caught a glimpse of her.

"Clement, it's Clare Bast. I'm so sorry for suggesting that you had somehow manipulated the sale of *Longfin*. I was wrong. I know now you had nothing to do with it."

Clement glanced at her but kept walking.

"Please listen for a moment, Clement. Was Tasha the one who suggested deaccessioning *Longfin*? Did she also suggest using Gabriel for the sale? I'm pretty sure she had something to do with Gabriel's death. If you'll just give me a moment, I can explain."

Clement stopped walking, but he stared stonily ahead rather than at her.

"She told me that deaccessioning *Longfin* was *your* idea," Clare said, "and that *you* chose Gabriel. At the time, I assumed she was telling the truth and you were lying to cover your tracks, but I had it backward, didn't I?"

Clement glanced around him, as if nervous who might be overhearing their conversation.

"I brought you a green tea," Clare said, thrusting the cup in his direction. "Can we just take a walk around the block? Five minutes. That's it."

He still hesitated. He stared at the cup in her hand without making a move to take it.

"You have no reason to trust me, but please listen while I tell you what's been going on. Then decide whether or not you want to help catch Gabriel's killer. Because you and I have both been pawns in a scheme that started long before Gabriel was killed. We've both been played."

Clement took the cup.

"Thank you," Clare said.

"It's not for you," Clement replied testily. "It's for Gabriel."

They walked toward Fifth Avenue, where a string of horse-drawn carriages lined the southern edge of Central Park. The horses were stamping their feet and blowing out plumes of steam from their noses.

"Go ahead," Clement said. "Explain."

"My theory is that Tasha came up with a scheme months ago to get the museum to sell *Longfin* to Viktor Semenov, her godfather. The point of it was to implicate me in the deal in order to blackmail my husband."

"Viktor Semenov, the Russian collector? He's on the sanctions list."

"That's why Tasha had to go through a middleman—Gabriel—and that's why my purported involvement in the deal allowed her to blackmail Jed."

"Gabriel wouldn't sell to someone on the sanctions list."

"I don't think he knew that that's what he was doing. Viktor and Tasha were using a shell company based in Cyprus."

"I asked him who his client was," Clement said. "It occurred to me at the time that it could be Tasha herself, or her husband, which obviously would have been against museum regulations. He said it was . . . some Dutch guy."

"Peter DeGroot."

"Yes, that's the name."

"Peter DeGroot is a cover for Viktor Semenov. Think, Clement—whose idea was it to deaccession *Longfin*? Really?"

Clement pushed up his glasses to squeeze the top of his nose. "*Merde*," he said under his breath.

He expelled a long, weary sigh. Clare could see it hang suspended in the cold air in front of him.

"Tasha took me out to lunch in May or maybe early June," Clement began. "We usually catch up every few months or so. She always wants to hear the museum gossip. As soon as we sat down, she started complaining about Angelica. Tasha can't stand her."

Angelica Hines, a longtime curator at the museum, had been appointed interim director of MoCA in late 2019 when her predecessor had died suddenly of a stroke. Then, when the pandemic hit, she'd scored points for stability and jettisoned the "interim" from her title.

Clare knew the complaints about Angelica's leadership. She hadn't made any big, splashy acquisitions. She paid too little mind to contemporary artists, bogged down instead by a plodding fidelity to old ideas and old movements. She'd made no plans for expansion or renovation, and fundraising had flagged. Donors all wanted their name on a wing, or at the very least, a gallery. Nobody was keen to part with a million dollars just to keep paying salaries and heating bills. But the board couldn't muster up the votes to fire her—she was the museum's first female director, and she was already nearing seventy-five. The hope was that she'd retire soon on her own.

Tasha would have known that Angelica's endurance was a sore spot for Clement; he'd been waiting for the directorship for years. His patience was undoubtedly starting to wear thin.

"Tasha suggested that I introduce Angelica to some up-and-comers, since I knew that world better than she did," Clement said. "She asked me which artists I thought MoCA should be looking at, and I think I said Kenzo Nomura, Kathy Orr, and Simon Weeks.

"Tasha replied that Nomura and Orr were already selling in the low seven figures. We both knew that the museum was not swimming in cash. The pandemic ran through most of our reserves. But Tasha said that there was a greater openness than ever before to deaccessioning, so maybe that was a possible solution. She named a few paintings she'd be happy to let go of, by Warhol and de Kooning and some of the minimalists. Then she mentioned Webley. She said that the market was hungry for Webleys, and she actually knew a *very* motivated buyer who had had his eye on *Longfin* for years.

"Later, over coffee, she told me not to get discouraged. She said the board had its eye on me; it was just wary of seeming to push Angelica out, since she'd given her life to the museum. She suggested I organize a splashy new show that would draw attention to the difference between Angelica and me. I mentioned that I'd been kicking around an idea highlighting Nomura's climate activism. She got really excited about that. She said a show like that would generate some real buzz. She made some joke about how she would gladly sacrifice a Webley for a couple Nomuras, and she was sure the rest of the board would, too. I told her that I'd always found Webley overrated. Then she said, 'It's really not a bad idea at all, Clement. You should do it.' And just like that, the idea was mine."

Now, standing on Fifth Avenue with Clare, Clement shook his head at the memory. "Until this moment, I really thought it was my idea, too; that's the worst part. A couple weeks later, like the rube she took me for, I asked Tasha if she might pass along the name of her 'very motivated' Webley collector. Of course, she was happy to share the name of his dealer, who I was delighted to find was my old friend Gabriel." He rolled his eyes.

"Then Tasha asked you to meet with me?"

He nodded. "Probably a few days after our lunch. Of course I agreed. What was thirty minutes of my time after she'd just dangled the directorship right in front of me?"

*What was thirty minutes of his time?* Clare thought. *Incontrovertible evidence that she and Clement took a meeting just days before the sale of Longfin was set into motion.*

"So then you started the deaccessioning process, and Tasha helped usher it through the approvals?"

"As you can imagine, she's a very influential presence on the board."

"Clement, would you be willing to tell the police all this?"

"I could lose my job," he said warily.

"I realize that, but Gabriel lost his life."

"What's the connection? How did deaccessioning *Longfin* lead to Gabriel's death?"

Clement had just articulated her exact problem. Clare had no idea what the link was. Why would Tasha have had Gabriel murdered? It didn't make any sense. It was too drastic, too risky. His death had invited so much scrutiny, and her whole plan had been to *avoid* scrutiny.

"I don't know," she admitted. "But I'm sure it did."

A yellow taxi roared past them blaring its horn, visibly startling Clement.

"Listen," he finally said, "if you find evidence that the sale of *Longfin* led directly to Gabriel's death, then I'll agree to testify."

"Even if you lose your job?"

"Even if I lose my job. If Tasha had a hand in Gabriel's murder, I want her to pay for it."

"Thank you, Clement."

"Don't thank me yet," Clement said, turning to walk back to the museum. "You still don't have any proof."

## CHAPTER 42

CLARE DECIDED TO WALK HOME, despite the distance and the cold. She spent the time deliberating whether she truly believed Tasha had actually had a hand in Gabriel's murder. It didn't make sense to her, but she knew there were parts of the picture she wasn't seeing.

Plodding up Fifth Avenue along the park, she was suddenly startled to hear the tinkling melody of an ice-cream truck. She watched it drive past her, admiring the owner's doggedness: It was barely forty degrees out.

When she was growing up, her mother had told her that the truck played that song to indicate that it was all out of ice cream. Clare always felt sorry for the kids running after it; they clearly didn't understand that there was nothing left. It took a long time for her to realize that she'd been the dupe, not them.

WHEN CLARE GOT back to her building, she was glad to see that Gino was behind the desk in the lobby. She'd been waiting for him to come back on duty so she could ask him about the package that Jed claimed to have received from Gabriel.

"Hi, Gino," she said. "I have an odd question for you. Do you remember a large crate arriving for Jed around three weeks ago?"

"Unfortunately, my memory's not what it used to be," he said with a wink, "but that's why we keep this." He pulled out a large logbook and slapped it on the desktop.

"What date are you looking for?" he asked.

"It would have been the first week of November, I think." Jed had said it had arrived a few days before Gabriel's death; he'd died on Thursday, November 6.

Gino rifled through the pages until he found the one he was looking for.

"You guys got a lot of packages that week," he said. "Mostly UPS and FedEx, but one from a private courier on Tuesday, November fourth."

"Do you remember what that last one looked like?" Clare asked.

"Sorry, Mrs. Bast, I don't. We get a lot of deliveries."

"Did you by any chance note the name of the messenger service?"

"I didn't." Gino turned the book around so she could see herself. His index finger picked out a single line: "Nov. 4, 3:59pm, delivery via messenger, Apt PH, Jed Bast."

The entire page was stacked with cramped, handwritten entries. It would be hard for anyone—Jed, for instance, or someone he bribed—to slot in a fake delivery after the fact.

As Gino pulled the book back toward him, Clare's phone chirped. She took it out to silence it—Jed had been calling all day, and she still wasn't ready to talk to him—but instead saw that it was a text from Elise.

"According to my contact," it read, "NYPD found Jed's prints at the scene."

Clare put a hand on the desk to steady herself. "No," she murmured.

"You all right, Mrs. Bast?" Gino asked.

She blinked at him. Was she all right? No. She was miles from all right. Her husband had murdered her lover and lied about it to her face.

"I'm fine," she said with a smile. "Everything's fine."

Apparently, she'd absorbed more of Dorothy Bast's affectations than she'd thought.

UPSTAIRS, SHE DIALED Elise before even taking off her coat.

"Tell me everything," she said, fumbling with her buttons with her free hand.

"Here's what I know," Elise said. "The forensics team that was sent into Gabriel's house after his death found very little physical evidence. Apparently, someone had cleaned up."

With her hand frozen on a button, Clare realized that *she* was the one who had cleaned up. She'd wanted to get rid of her own fingerprints, but of course she'd erased any evidence left by the real killer, too. She wondered for the umpteenth time if all of this could have been avoided if she'd only called the police from Gabriel's house. But life wasn't a canvas; you couldn't simply paint over your mistakes.

Elise continued: "Forensics did find half a bloody footprint and a few smudged fingerprints, but those didn't lead anywhere . . . until they arrested Jed. Yesterday they were able to confirm with ninety-eight percent certainty that at least one of the fingerprints matched his."

"I don't understand," Clare said, slumping down on the sofa with her coat still on. "How is that possible?"

"Jed was in Gabriel's house. There is no other explanation."

*My god*, Clare thought, letting the words sink in. *Who did I marry?*

Jed was probably asking himself the exact same thing, she had to remind herself. They'd apparently both married strangers.

"What about the footprint?"

"Those are all the details I was given."

Clare thanked Elise and gave her Jed's cell number in return for the information. She was done protecting him. If Jed's fingerprints were at the crime scene *and* he had *Longfin*, Clare could no longer tell herself that he'd had nothing to do with Gabriel's death.

Clare shrugged off her coat and took it to the closet to hang up. The sight of Jed's lime-green bike shoes lined up neatly inside it immediately filled her with overwhelming fury. Dropping the coat, she carried the sneakers into the kitchen and hurled them into the trash can. Using both palms, she shoved them down into a congealed mass of Sadie's leftover oatmeal.

"Are you okay?" Maggie asked from the doorway. She'd dropped Sadie at school and been working from the spare bedroom since then.

Clare let the lid of the trash can close with a sigh. "The police found Jed's fingerprints at the crime scene."

"*What?* How?"

"He did it, Mags. There is no other explanation. I married a murderer." She slumped down onto the floor and leaned against the wall. "Actually, it's worse than that: I married a nice man and turned him into a murderer."

"Clare, if Jed killed Gabriel—and that's still a big *if*—it is not your fault."

"You're a good friend for saying that, but you know it's not true. I started all of this. I'm the one who went to Gabriel's house to see a painting. I'm the one who took off all my clothes in his living room. I'm the one who went back to do both of those things over and over and over again. Of course Jed was livid when he found out. Wouldn't you be?"

"Naturally. But I wouldn't kill someone over it. And neither would you."

Clare shrugged. "Jed probably thought the same thing about himself. But when rage takes over, you're not in control anymore."

"Jed doesn't seem like the type of guy who lets rage take over. I've never even seen him angry."

"Exactly—maybe he squashed it all down too far, and it finally erupted."

Maggie sat down on the floor next to Clare. "I'm sorry this is happening," she said.

Clare leaned her head on her friend's shoulder. "What am I going to tell Sadie?" she asked.

Maggie had no answer.

## CHAPTER 43

CLARE JOGGED THE LAST TWO blocks to Saint Mary's so she wouldn't be late for pickup. She didn't know whether divorce was imminent, and Dorothy's threat to fight for full custody of Sadie filled her with terror.

As Clare knelt down to hug her daughter, she realized how much Sadie had grown in the past few months. She was taller than almost all of her classmates, including the boys. Clare suspected she'd inherited her own mother's long, lean build. She felt unreasonably gratified to recognize a Regan trait in her daughter, since her face and hair were practically carbon copies of Jed's. She wondered what else she'd inherit from her father, whether through nature or nurture.

Clare wasn't foolish enough to believe that there was such a thing as a gene for murder, but she couldn't pretend that Sadie would escape unscathed from her father's conviction. At the very least, she'd have to grow a thick skin; at worst, she'd turn into a guarded, angry person. It could define her entire life. She might someday blame Clare for all of it. Even without Dorothy's interference, she realized, she could lose her daughter.

Clare clutched Sadie's hand tightly during the entire walk home. In the elevator, when she finally let go, both their palms were hot and clammy.

WHEN CLARE SWUNG open the front door, she spotted Jed immediately. He was sitting on the sofa in the living room, calmly scrolling through his phone, as if he'd never left.

"Daddy!" Sadie yelled, running to him.

He put down his phone and pulled her up onto his lap. "Hi, my pet. Daddy's missed you so much."

"What are you doing here?" Clare asked. Her heart thudded in her chest. The last time she'd seen her husband she'd been running away from him. Since then, she'd only grown more convinced that he was a killer.

"What am I doing in my own home? I'm here to see my daughter."

"You should have called first."

"I tried. You didn't answer. But anyway, I don't believe I have to ask permission."

"Where's Maggie?" Clare asked, glancing around the empty apartment.

"For some reason she seemed uncomfortable being here all alone with me," Jed said dryly.

"Where is she?" she repeated, her panic building.

Jed rolled his eyes. "She went to get a sandwich."

Clare stood frozen in the doorway, unwilling to venture any farther into the apartment. Jed whispered something in Sadie's ear, and she immediately scampered off to her bedroom.

"I brought her that Peppa Pig Playhouse she wanted," Jed said. "I thought it might buy us some time."

Clare stepped inside and closed the door behind her. Whatever happened, she wasn't going to flee the apartment without Sadie.

"The police found your fingerprints at the crime scene," she said without preamble.

Jed rubbed his face roughly. "I know."

"Why?"

"Because I went to Gabriel's house. *Before* it was a crime scene. If I'd known he was going to get killed, believe me, I would have wiped the place down."

"Why were you at his house?"

"I was going to tell you all of this yesterday, before you stormed out. For god's sake, will you sit down, you're making me nervous."

Clare perched cautiously on a chair across from him. Her phone buzzed with a text from Maggie: "I'm close. Call if you need me." She noticed that Maggie had also texted five minutes earlier to say that Jed was home, but she hadn't seen it.

"Why were you at his house?" she asked him again.

Jed sighed. "The day after Tasha threatened me at the MoCA party, I called Gabriel at his gallery and told him we needed to meet. He suggested his house, probably because he didn't want his coworkers to overhear me screaming at him about sleeping with my wife.

"Of course, I still had no idea about the affair at that point. I just wanted to tell him that he needed to cut all ties with you. And that he never should have roped you into his sleazy little Axion scheme to begin with. I was trying to protect you."

"What did he say?"

"First he was confused and then he was furious. He had no idea that Axion was owned by Tasha's godfather. Like me, he always spoke with Peter DeGroot. Tasha had introduced them a few years earlier, and Gabriel clearly hadn't asked too many questions because he was making million-dollar commissions. He was as livid at Tasha as I was that she'd gotten him mixed up in sanctions violations. He'd already done several deals with Axion at that point. If that came to light, he'd be ruined, too."

That's why Gabriel had ended things with her, Clare realized. He'd been trying to protect her. Could it also explain the data he'd erased? After Jed left, Gabriel had presumably wanted to get rid of anything connecting him to Axion because it was evidence of fraud. That would explain the large gaps in communication between him and Tasha—and the lack of any emails between him and Peter DeGroot.

"What happened next?"

"Nothing. I never spoke to Gabriel again. After *Longfin* showed up at our building, I tried calling him, but he didn't pick up. And then he was . . . gone."

Clare sat down on a chair facing her husband and studied him. He looked the same as he had in the gym: angry, exhausted, scared. Was he lying? She just didn't know. She wanted to believe him . . . but how could they both be telling the truth about the last time they saw *Longfin* when the stories so obviously contradicted each other?

She wondered for the first time whether she could have been mistaken about seeing *Longfin* on Gabriel's wall the night he died. Maybe it hadn't been there at all. Hadn't there been studies showing how trauma can alter one's memories?

Besides, if he was lying, wouldn't he have come up with a better story for how he got the painting? The more she'd come to appreciate the complexity of Tasha's plan, the less likely Jed's involvement seemed. She didn't believe he had that kind of shrewdness in him. Tasha's emails with Gabriel also went a long way toward corroborating his version of events. Then there was the handwritten logbook in the lobby.

Clare studied her husband. He was perched on the couch wearing the same sad and weary expression he'd worn when his grandmother died. His pants were hitched up to reveal that he was wearing the pink polka-dotted socks that Sadie had picked out for his birthday the year before. Clare *knew* this man.

She made a decision to trust him. Gabriel's death could possibly have been averted entirely if she or Jed had kept fewer secrets in the preceding weeks.

Clare settled into her chair more comfortably and set her phone on the table next to her.

"Tasha orchestrated this entire thing," she said. "She convinced the museum to sell *Longfin* to Gabriel, then asked Gabriel to hire me so I'd be implicated, too. She *created* the threat to blackmail you with."

Jed frowned. "What?"

The moment you went to Alec with your first worry about Axion, she set this whole thing in motion: my conversation with Viktor, my introduction to Gabriel, everything.

"How do you know?"

"Have you met Elise Vargas, the private art investigator?"

"She keeps leaving me voicemails. I haven't called her back."

"We've sort of been working together. Michael Kline hired her to find *Longfin*."

Clare proceeded to recount everything Elise had told her. Then she explained what she'd learned from Gabriel's email records and her conversation with Clement.

When she was done, Jed looked dumbfounded.

"Tasha convinced MoCA to sell a priceless work of art in order to blackmail me?"

"Compared to the seven hundred and fifty million dollars she stood to lose if Viktor's connection to Axion came to light, *Longfin* was small potatoes."

"She's insane," Jed whispered.

"She's *not* insane," Clare replied. "That's the problem. She's incredibly intelligent and calculating, which is why I just don't understand why she would have had Gabriel killed. It doesn't make sense. According to her, everything was going swimmingly. You'd capitulated. No one knew about Axion. Gatepost's secret was safe."

"Well," Jed said, "Gabriel knew once I told him, and he was furious. Maybe he confronted Tasha and threatened to go to the cops."

Clare shook her head.

"He couldn't go to the police, because he'd already sold other paintings to Axion. If the truth came out, he'd be liable for violating sanctions, too. At the very least, his reputation would be irrevocably tarnished.

"But," Clare added, realizing it as she spoke, "he still had *Longfin*. That gave him the upper hand. He could have refused to sell it to Axion, Viktor, or anyone else associated with Tasha Wolfe—even if he had to take a haircut on the resale price."

"Would she even care, though?" Jed asked. "As you said, her plan had already accomplished its goal: I'd capitulated."

"Maybe Tasha had had more than one objective. You said Viktor was taking his money out of Gatepost, right? And that without him, Gatepost would collapse. So she must have been desperate to keep him. Maybe she was trying to appease him by sourcing him a Webley.

"Think about it: After the sanctions were put into place, she'd immediately connected him to Gabriel so Viktor could keep collecting art. It seems like she was doing everything she could to keep him happy.

"When I spoke with Viktor on the phone, it was clear that his enthusiasm for Webley was real. He said he'd always wanted to own one, but they were difficult to come by. As an influential MoCA trustee, Tasha was in the rare position to force one onto the market. Not a bad thing to dangle in front of him, in exchange for keeping his money at Gatepost. Or at least stopping the withdrawals. Tasha was killing two birds with one stone: placating Viktor and stopping you from exposing Axion. She came up with a plan that could do both."

"Axion *did* stop the withdrawals," Jed said. "There wasn't a peep from them during the last redemption period."

"Well, there you go," Clare said. "He was staying put for *Longfin*. If Gabriel refused to sell it to him, Tasha would have had to tell her godfather that she'd failed to deliver on her promise, and he'd start withdrawing his funds again immediately. Gatepost—and, by extension, the Wolfes themselves—would be ruined."

"But murder is a far cry from blackmail," Jed said. "Do you really think Tasha had Gabriel *killed*?"

"I don't think Gabriel was supposed to die. That was never part of anyone's plan. The person who broke into his house that night had one objective: to steal *Longfin*. Gabriel was supposed to be at a party at his gallery."

"So you're saying you think Tasha stole *Longfin* in order to keep her promise to her godfather?"

Clare shook her head, getting lost in the minutiae of their conjectures. "I don't know. Tasha's plan was malicious, but it was always low risk—at least to her. All she'd had to do was set up a couple of meetings. The hardest part would have been convincing Clement to deaccession *Longfin*—or rather, convincing Clement to suggest that the museum consider deaccessioning *Longfin*—and that had turned out to be a cinch.

"But committing grand theft would take it to a whole new level. And Gabriel would obviously have known who stole it and gone straight to the authorities, even if he got in trouble for sanctions violations. He couldn't just take an eighteen-million-dollar loss lying down."

"So what happened?" Jed pressed. "Who stole *Longfin*—and why?"

"It must involve Tasha, but I don't see how."

"So we've got nothing? I'm going to prison and she's going to get away with it?"

Clare just stared at him.

"I don't know," she said finally. "I've hit a dead end. Tasha is the only person who knows what really happened, and she's obviously not telling."

Tears suddenly filled Jed's eyes. "I can't go to prison, Clare," he said, his voice growing high and panicked. "I can't."

"You won't."

"I was just trying to protect you," he said so quietly she could hardly hear him.

"I'll come clean to the police," she said. "I'll tell them I was there the night Gabriel was killed."

Jed's face went rigid. "Don't do that, Clare. It won't help, and we can't risk us both being sentenced to prison time. Sadie needs at least one parent around."

"I can't let you take the fall for my mistake."

"You *cannot* tell the police that you lied to them. Take it from me as both your husband and your lawyer. We need to be pragmatic here. Promise me."

"Okay," Clare relented. "I won't."

Jed's jaw relaxed. "Good."

## CHAPTER 44

CLARE WAS FILLING A POT with water in preparation for yet another sad dinner of spaghetti and jar sauce when Maggie returned.

"Is everything okay?" she asked. "What happened with Jed?"

"The good news is I no longer think he killed Gabriel," Clare said.

"What's the bad news?"

"I have no idea how to convince the police of that."

"I don't think that's your job, Clare."

"But no one else is even trying! The investigators have shut the case. If I don't do something, Jed will end up in prison."

Maggie dropped her bag on the floor and sat down on a tall stool.

"God, what a mess," she said, seeming to have abruptly run out of reassurances.

Clare inspected her friend more closely. She had dark purple circles under her eyes and her shoulders were slumped forward in defeat.

"Are *you* okay?" Clare asked, walking over to her.

Maggie put her head in her hands. "I just talked to Dave. His mom's cancer is back."

"Oh no," Clare said, rubbing Maggie's back. "I'm so sorry."

"I've got to go back to Denver."

"Of course. I completely understand. You've already gone above and beyond."

"I'm sorry, Chach. I love you."

"I love you, too."

MAGGIE LEFT FOR the airport half an hour later, and Clare and Sadie spent a quiet night together. Once Sadie was asleep, Clare climbed directly into her own bed fully clothed. She was exhausted. Her conversation with Clement—just that morning—already seemed like a lifetime ago.

As she waited for sleep to come, Jed's last words to her—"I was just trying to protect you"—replayed on an endless loop in her mind. That's exactly what Tasha had counted on, she thought sadly: his loyalty to Clare.

As the words continued to echo, something odd happened: the tone started to change. Jed's voice became deeper and slower—with just the hint of an accent.

"I was just trying to protect you."

It was Gabriel speaking the words now: "I was just trying to protect you."

He'd said that to her the night he died, Clare suddenly remembered. It had seemed condescending at the time, but Gabriel was never patronizing to her. So what had he meant?

Clare sat up in bed.

She was onto something. She was sure of it.

She had so many pieces of the puzzle; she just couldn't figure out how they fit together. Everyone's overlapping versions of events—her own, Jed's, Elise's, even Tasha's and Gabriel's—merged into a cacophonous clamor.

Clare suddenly threw off the covers and jumped out of bed.

The emails.

Clare brought her laptop back to her bedroom and opened the file that Elise had sent her the night before. She read through the emails between Tasha and Gabriel again. There was something there that she hadn't caught the first time. She knew it. An odd tone shift, or something.

And then she found it.

Two days before Gabriel's death, Tasha had written:

Just confirming our plans. Everything is all set from my end, so just let me know you're on board, and I'll start making arrangements. This is the best solution for everyone.

And Gabriel had written back: "Go ahead. I don't want to know the details."

As soon as Clare reread the words, she saw it all in stunning clarity.

She jumped out of bed yet again, but then she just stood in her darkened room, frozen. There was nothing for her to do. She was alone in the apartment with Sadie. She couldn't go anywhere.

So she got back into bed once again to try to wrangle sleep into submission—but not before sending off a quick email of her own to Michael Kline.

## CHAPTER 45

THE NEXT MORNING, AFTER A few hours of fitful sleep, Clare dragged herself into the kitchen to make coffee. As it slowly dripped into the pot, she checked her phone.

She had one new email, from Michael Kline: "I've been instructed by my lawyer not to speak to you or your husband."

"Oh, come *on*," Clare groaned, slamming the phone down on the kitchen counter. It slipped out of her hand and skittered across the slick granite onto the floor.

"Mama?" Sadie said from the doorway. Her face was wrinkled with anxiety.

Clare rearranged her face into a smile. "Hi, sweetheart. Sorry about that loud noise. I dropped my phone."

Sadie eyed her skeptically.

Her daughter, Clare realized, had been quietly absorbing all the fear, anger, and deceit in the air for weeks. Maybe longer. She looked like she'd aged ten years overnight; her expression had a weariness to it that broke Clare's heart. She pulled her into a hug.

"I'm sorry, sweetheart. I know things have been confusing recently. Everything will get sorted out soon."

"Daddy will come back home?" Sadie asked hopefully.

What was Clare supposed to say? She didn't want to lie.

"I don't know," she said finally. "But we both love you with our whole hearts, and that will never change."

It was a well-worn platitude, but at the moment, it was all she had to offer.

A FEW HOURS later, Clare dropped Sadie at the Basts' apartment to spend a few hours with her father. Soon, Clare knew, she and Jed would have to talk about their current living situation. Did he want to move back home? Did she want him to? She didn't know the answer to either of those questions, but they would have to force some sort of decision for Sadie's sake.

As she walked out of the Basts' lobby, she called Elise to ask the same question she'd put to Michael Kline.

"What's up?" she answered.

"Do you have the address of Tony Fang's studio?"

"That artist everyone loved like twenty years ago?"

"Yes."

Elise didn't miss a beat.

"I can get it. Give me fifteen minutes."

THIRTY MINUTES LATER, Clare stood in front of a shuttered car-repair shop in East Bushwick. The run-down building above it had huge swaths of casement windows with missing panes. Clare buzzed the bell for 5A. Nothing happened. She pressed the button again. As she waited, an older woman dragging a rolling grocery cart came out of the building, and Clare held the door for her. She got no thanks, but she did gain entry.

She trudged up five flights of stairs and paused to catch her breath before knocking on the dented metal door marked A. Loud electronic music blared from behind it. Nobody answered her first knock. She banged as hard as she could with her fist and was about to turn around, defeated, when she heard the music turn off. The silence pounded in her ears.

She heard the unlocking of several heavy bolts and then the door opened a crack. A sliver of a face appeared in it.

"Tony Fang?"

His eyes darted down the hallway. "Yeah?"

"My name is Clare Regan." She went with her maiden name in case he'd read the news about Jed's arrest. "I'm working with Michael Kline on Gabriel Prévost's estate. May I come in for a moment?"

"What's this about?"

"It concerns Mr. Prévost's will; I'd prefer to discuss it in private, if you don't mind."

The man waited a beat before opening the door to let Clare in. She stepped into a huge, sundrenched studio and found herself surrounded by old master paintings at every stage of completion: Titian's *Flora* propped against an easel; Tintoretto's *Tarquin and Lucretia* leaning against a wall. Even though this was exactly why she'd come here—because he was known for his meticulous copies of recognizable masterpieces—they were still astonishing.

"This is . . ." Clare stepped closer to examine one of the paintings. "This is incredible. How do you do it?"

Tony shrugged, but he was obviously pleased by the question.

Clare spotted a small plastic jar of bright red powder on a table. She moved closer and squinted to read the label. "Is this Venetian red?" she asked.

He nodded.

She picked up another bottle. "And rabbit-skin glue?" Artists had been using that for centuries to prime canvases for oil. "Do people still use this?"

"I do."

Clare couldn't help but think of Noodle. She put the bottle back down.

"Is there somewhere we can talk?" she asked.

Tony led her over to two ratty armchairs in a dusty corner. A paint-splattered CD player sat on a metal filing cabinet next to a Mr. Coffee machine. Clare noticed a film of mold on top of the inch of oily brown liquid still in the pot.

"Coffee?" he asked.

"No," Clare said too quickly. "Thanks."

Tony smirked. He'd been messing with her. "So, did Gabriel leave me a million dollars or something?" he asked, sinking into the slightly less-filthy seat.

Clare took the other one.

"You're not too far off. I'm here regarding a job you did for Gabriel Prévost in late October."

"I haven't shown at the gallery for years."

"No, if I've been informed correctly, Gabriel personally commissioned a painting from you around then. It had nothing to do with the gallery."

Tony crossed his arms over his chest and shook his head. "Nope."

"Are you sure? Because Gabriel put a provision in his will that provides a small mark of appreciation to the person who helped him out on this project."

"Can't help you. Wasn't me."

Clare recrossed her legs. "Look, I understand the sensitive nature of this job. Let me just assure you right off the bat that you're not in any trouble here. All I'm trying to do is carry out Gabriel's final wishes."

"I suppose I'm glad to hear I'm not in trouble, but still, you've got the wrong guy."

Tony stared at her aggressively. He didn't blink. He wasn't going to break, Clare realized. Either that, or she was on the wrong track entirely.

She smiled. "I'm sorry for the intrusion then. I must have been misinformed." She stood up. "Would you mind if I used your restroom before I go?"

He nodded to a hallway at the back of the room.

"Thanks," she said. She started walking toward the back of the studio as slowly as possible. As she did, her eyes roved around the room hungrily. She saw a Raphael, a Caravaggio, and two Manets. She had to hand it to him—the man had breadth.

When she reached the entrance to the hallway, she spotted a few small canvases that appeared to be just the right size. They were stacked against the wall, facing inward. She walked past them and found the bathroom. It was about as appalling as she'd expected. She stood in the center of the room and counted to twenty. When she came out, she moved quickly. She walked directly to the small stack of small canvases and knelt down, hearing her knee crack as she did.

She kept up a constant patter: "Your work is beautiful; do you mind if I take a look at some of it? Do you do mostly old masters or—"

"Hey," Tony said, standing up. "Leave those alone."

She ignored him and tipped the canvases backward one by one so she could see the front of them.

And there they were.

Four studies of *Longfin*, all incomplete. The impasto on the first was wrong. The red on the second was too dark. The incisions on the third were too thick. The fourth looked like it had been smeared in frustration. These were Tony's practice runs—his early, failed efforts to copy *Longfin*.

"Put those back," he said in a low voice, walking toward her.

Clare had seen enough. She leaned the canvases back against the wall and stood up. "I'm sorry, I didn't mean to pry." She glanced at the door, hoping he hadn't relocked the deadbolts. "I'll get out of your hair now. Thanks for your time."

"Who the fuck are you?" Tony asked. He was closer to the door than she was, and he stepped in front of it.

"I'm no one," she said. "And I'm going."

He reached out and put his palm against the door. Clare wondered how far he would go to stop her from leaving. He seemed to be wondering the same thing. His face rippled with uncertainty. He didn't know how to get himself out of this situation either.

"I'm not trying to cause you any problems," Clare said slowly and quietly. "I just want to get home to my daughter."

"I didn't do anything wrong," Tony said, looking for a moment like a panicked little boy.

"I know that."

"He told me he wasn't going to sell it. I don't mess with that shit. And I had nothing to do with . . . anything that came after."

"I know. I believe you. Please, just let me go. You'll never hear from me again. I promise. You will not hear from me, or the police, or anyone. I swear."

Tony stared at her. She held his gaze.

After what felt like ages, he lifted his hand gently off the door, and Clare took her chance.

"Thank you," she whispered, as she opened the door and slipped out. She ran down the stairs and out of the building without pausing. She was three blocks away before she stopped to catch her breath.

## CHAPTER 46

CLARE CLOSED HER EYES AND leaned her head back against the jostling subway car carrying her back to Manhattan.

At the very least, she had proof that Jed was telling the truth.

Gabriel had sent *Longfin* to Jed two days before he died, and he'd *also* had it hanging on his wall the night he was killed. There were two *Longfins*.

But why?

She thought she knew the answer. But at the moment, she was preoccupied by a more important question. Listening to the dull *ka-thunk ka-thunk* of wheels on the track, she wondered: Which painting was the forgery? The one that was stolen by the man in the Reeboks or the one currently stashed in Mina Gellman's hall closet?

She didn't know. At the same time, she saw the rare position she was in. She was the only one who *could* know. She was a Webley scholar, and she was probably the only person, other than Tony, who had seen both paintings close-up. Her Webley expertise might finally be an advantage rather than a liability.

She tried to envision both paintings.

On the night of the murder, Gabriel's room had been dark. She'd only seen it over his shoulder while he was on top of her. She couldn't say whether it was real or not. She would have had to get up close in a much brighter environment. She would have had to have spent some time on it.

On the other hand, she'd seen the painting she found in East Hampton up close. She'd touched it. She tried to remember that sensation. Was it the same as the one she'd felt when she'd brushed her hand over *Longfin* at Gabriel's apartment that first day she'd gone there? She remembered feeling the power of the painting that day, feeling the heat of Gabriel's body next to hers. Just moments before she kissed him and brought down this whole catastrophe on their heads.

She envisioned herself in the closet. When she'd pulled out that canvas, the sight of it had hit her like a punch in the gut. But was that just because of what it implied—Jed's lies? Jed's presumed guilt?

No. She didn't think so.

When she opened her eyes, she knew which one was the forgery.

The question was: Would Tasha?

## CHAPTER 47

JED BROUGHT SADIE DOWN TO the lobby so Clare wouldn't have to interact with his mother. And vice versa.

"Do you want to walk us home?" Clare asked him. "I have an update."

Jed agreed, and the three of them set off down Fifth Avenue, looking by all appearances like a normal, happy family.

Clare told Sadie she had a *very* important job to do: She needed to count all the red cars they passed on the way back to their apartment.

"I can do it," Sadie answered solemnly.

With their daughter distracted, Clare turned to Jed. "I figured out that we were both telling the truth about *Longfin*," she said. "Gabriel sent it to you before he died, and I also saw it on his wall the night he was killed."

"How is that possible?"

"There were two *Longfin*s. Gabriel had it copied."

"Why would he do that?"

"Listen to the email Tasha sent Gabriel two days before he died." She took out her phone and read from the screen: "'Just confirming our plans. Everything is all set from my end, so just let me know you're on board, and I'll start making arrangements. This is the best solution for everyone.' Gabriel wrote back: 'Go ahead. I don't want to know the details.' What does that suggest to you?"

Jed shook his head. "Nothing."

"Don't you see? It was insurance fraud. They were both in on it." Elise had been right: all the markers were there. Whoever took *Longfin* knew the door code, the painting's location, and Gabriel's schedule.

"We're assuming that Gabriel refused to sell *Longfin* to Axion once he found out that it was Viktor's company. So Tasha needed to pivot if she wanted to keep Viktor happy. She couldn't just take *Longfin*; Gabriel would immediately point the finger at her. So she came up with a better plan, one that would keep everyone happy. She'd arrange for the painting to be 'stolen' from Gabriel's house and make its way to Viktor in Russia. Gabriel could then file an insurance claim and recoup his eighteen million. Viktor would get *Longfin*—for free, no less—and Gabriel would be able to pay back the money he owed to the bank without implicating himself in another sale to Axion. Tasha was basically buying his silence. Gabriel agreed but told her that he didn't want to know any of the details. He needed plausible deniability later."

"But you said that Gabriel copied the painting," Jed said. "Why would he do that?"

"I'm guessing it was his final *fuck you* to Tasha. He had to agree to her plan—he needed to pay back that eighteen million dollars to the bank after all—but he didn't have to let her win. He came up with a plot of his own. He copied *Longfin* and hung the forgery on his wall, so *that's* the one Viktor would end up with. He probably thought Viktor wouldn't even know the difference. And even if he did notice, there would be nothing he could do about it. He couldn't sue Gabriel—the painting would have been reported stolen. He'd have no recourse.

"Of course, Gabriel knew there would be an insurance investigation, so he planned ahead. He sent the real painting to you, because (a) you were the only other person who knew what was going on with Tasha and Axion; (b) you couldn't report it to the police without implicating yourself—and me; and (c) the husband of the woman he was sleeping with is the last person anyone would suspect of hiding it for him."

"And maybe," Jed added, "because he knew *you'd* take care of *Longfin* if anything went wrong."

This hadn't occurred to Clare, but it made sense. She and Gabriel both cared deeply about *Longfin*. He'd trusted her to make sure that it never fell into the wrong hands. She felt a sudden pang of guilt for stashing it in Mina's hall closet. She needed a better plan for it than that.

"So you think *Tasha* stole *Longfin* and killed Gabriel?" Jed asked. "That's a pretty big risk for someone in her position to take."

"Not Tasha herself. She probably hired someone, someone who was given the entry code and thought he was going into an empty apartment to take a painting off a wall, with the owner's full knowledge and agreement. Then someone appeared downstairs unexpectedly, brandishing a weapon. The intruder panicked. He probably shot without thinking—or in self-defense—and then took the painting and ran." Clare paused. "Or rather, he took *a* painting."

"Does Tasha know she has a forgery yet?"

"That's the eighteen-million-dollar question."

They'd reached their building. The windows in the buildings around them glowed in the gathering dusk.

"Seven red cars!" Sadie announced. "Seven!"

"Great work," Clare said.

"Is Daddy coming home with us now?"

Clare and Jed exchanged a glance.

Jed squatted down to give Sadie a hug. "Not yet, sweetheart," he said. "I'm going to spend a few more nights with Grammy and Gramps."

"Will you run inside and tell Gino how many red cars you saw?" Clare said to Sadie.

When they were alone, Clare turned to Jed and said, "We need to discuss our plans for the future at some point."

"How can I make any plans when I don't even know whether I'll be in prison in six months?" he asked peevishly.

"I'm going to fix this. I promise."

"You're *not*, Clare. You might think you figured out what happened, but you have no proof. That email from Tasha is hardly a smoking gun. She knew what she was doing; she kept it vague."

"Clement said he'll testify that Tasha pressured him to deaccession."

"It's not enough. You know that. There's nothing connecting Tasha to Gabriel's death."

Clare sighed. He was right. She and Jed were implicated in so many plausible versions of the story, and the *truth* was the one that strained credibility. Tasha had made sure of that.

"My offer still stands," she said. "I'll tell the police everything."

Jed shook his head. "Implicating yourself won't prove my innocence, and we can't risk losing Sadie. You promised."

Clare felt mired in powerlessness.

"What should we do about Thanksgiving?" she finally asked, switching to a topic of conversation over which they actually had some control.

"I thought we were spending it with my parents."

"I'm not sure I'm still invited. Your mother pretty much kicked me out of the family."

"I'll speak to her."

"Maybe you, Sadie, and I could just do something low-key at our apartment."

A look of discomfort crossed Jed's expression. "My mom's taken care of everything for me since the arrest. I don't think I can ditch her on Thanksgiving."

"Well, she's been pretty terrible to me. I don't think I can *face* her on Thanksgiving."

They stood locked in a standoff for several silent seconds.

"Clare," Jed finally said, "if we're ever going to be able to move past all this, then you're going to have to find a way to make peace with my mother."

"I can work on that," Clare replied carefully, "but it's not going to happen in the next few days."

"What are you saying?"

"I'm saying that maybe we should spend Thanksgiving apart this year."

"What about Sadie?"

"She and I can do something small at home."

"Well, I'd like to spend the holiday with her, too. And I know my mother wants all her grandchildren there."

"You want to take Sadie to your parents' without me?"

"Well, I want you there, too. You're the one who's refusing to come. Don't make her pay for that decision. She loves spending the holidays with her cousins. How much fun is she going to have all alone with you?"

The question lingered in the air between them. This was the fear Clare had been trying to communicate to Maggie: What if she had nothing to offer Sadie in comparison to the Basts' abundance of wealth, travel, excitement, and sheer numbers? What if Sadie chose them?

When Clare didn't answer, Jed's frustration bubbled over. "*Goddamn it,* Clare. I'm facing the very real possibility of life in prison. All I'm asking is for one more holiday with my family."

"You're right," Clare said. "I'm sorry. Of course Sadie can spend Thanksgiving with you."

Jed expelled a long, slow breath through his nostrils. He seemed unnerved by his own outburst. "Thank you."

"But you're *not* going to prison."

Jed shrugged in resignation. "I don't know how many times I have to say it: It's not up to you."

"But all the evidence is circumstantial. No one can prove you killed him because you *didn't.*"

"Clare, nearly all criminal convictions are based on circumstantial evidence. Just the fingerprints and the motive could be enough." Jed leaned in closer and continued in a quieter, firmer voice: "And if anyone were to connect Gabriel's missing painting to me, I would be toast. Do you understand?"

"*Longfin?*" Clare asked. She still hadn't picked it up from Mina's apartment.

"It needs to disappear," Jed said so softly she could barely hear him.

Clare was about to argue that she couldn't just toss a Blake Webley painting in the trash, but she stopped herself. Of course she would sacrifice some old pigment on canvas to save Jed.

"Consider it done."

## CHAPTER 48

EARLY THE NEXT MORNING, CLARE texted Mina to invite her and Lisbet out to lunch. They agreed to meet at Serafina, an overpriced Italian restaurant on Madison Avenue, at noon.

"If it's convenient," Clare added, "I can grab Jed's birthday present from your apartment afterward."

Mina gave her a thumbs-up.

Once they were seated, and the girls were occupied with crayons, Mina inclined her head toward Clare and said quietly: "I heard about Jed. I'm so sorry. Let me know if there's anything I can do."

Tears unexpectedly filled Clare's eyes. Mina's kindness was a shock to her system—and, she knew, entirely undeserved.

"Thank you," she said. "He's innocent, of course. But it's been a rough couple of days."

"Does Sadie know what's going on yet?"

Clare shook her head. "I'm hoping the charges will be dropped before we have to tell her."

Mina looked at her with poorly disguised pity, as if she knew Clare was being delusional.

"WHAT *IS* THAT?" Sadie asked when Clare picked up the crate with *Longfin* in it from Mina's closet.

"It's a birthday present for Daddy," she replied, shifting the weight in her arms.

"But Daddy's birthday isn't until July."

"We'll have to keep it a secret until then. From everyone."

"I'm good at that," Sadie said.

"I know you are, sweets."

As they walked down Park Avenue, Clare felt like she was carrying a ticking time bomb. If *Longfin* were to be discovered in her possession, she and Jed would both be screwed. Jed would be convicted, and they'd charge her as an accessory. What would happen to Sadie then? Her daughter would grow up with Dorothy as a surrogate mother. Clare couldn't help but picture a teenage Sadie in diamond earrings, pursing her lips in disgust at someone's lack of prowess on the tennis court.

No, she wouldn't let that happen. She had to get rid of *Longfin* immediately. But what was she supposed to do with it? If she threw it in a public trash can, there was still a small but real risk of someone finding it and tracing it back to her, either through DNA or video footage. She couldn't burn it; she'd set off her building's smoke alarm within thirty seconds. Clare's panic mounted with every step closer to home they got. Jed had told her in no uncertain terms that *Longfin* had to disappear, and instead she was bringing it directly into their house. It seemed like the closer they veered toward catastrophe, the more reckless she got.

Clare wondered vaguely if that was what happened to Tasha: Every time her plan hit a roadblock, she'd reacted by taking bigger and bigger risks to preserve it, until eventually she found herself crossing lines she never dreamed she'd even come to.

Small mistakes compound quickly—Clare had learned that lesson, too.

# CHAPTER 49

CLARE GOT TO WORK AS soon as Sadie was asleep.

She carefully removed *Longfin* from the crate and set it face down on a blanket on the floor. Then she painstakingly removed each rusty staple—presumably put into place by Webley himself—to separate the canvas from the stretcher. All the while, she issued a silent prayer of thanks to the professor at Columbia who'd urged her to take a painting conservation and restoration course.

Once the canvas was loose, she encased it in five layers of Saranwrap. Then she added a sixth for good measure.

The next step involved letting Noodle out of his cage, removing his food and water containers, then carrying his cage into the kitchen to shake out all the woodchips that lined the bottom of it. She replaced the absorbent pee pad at the bottom with a fresh one, and then carefully laid *Longfin* on top of it. She winced as she covered it with another pee pad and then refilled the cage with woodchips.

After replacing the food and water, she let Noodle back in and admired her handiwork. The cage looked like it always had. There was absolutely nothing suggesting that an eighteen-million-dollar painting now lined the bottom of it.

Clare spent the next hour breaking apart the stretcher and the crate and putting the pieces in large contractor bags. She was just getting out of the shower when Sadie woke up and asked for pancakes.

AFTER DROPPING SADIE at school, Clare went home to collect Noodle—cage and all—and bring him to the home of the bunny-sitter she'd booked the night before. By the time she stumbled out of the woman's Yorkville apartment, she was giddy with exhaustion. She bought a bathtub-sized iced coffee at Dunkin' and started walking back downtown.

There, it was done. She'd fulfilled her promise to Jed: *Longfin* was out of the apartment, and she'd be shocked if anyone was able to track it down. Probably not as surprised as the bunny-sitter, though.

Her plan was deranged. She knew that. Even before she'd found herself covered in sweat, paint, and fur at four in the morning, she'd known that.

But Clare had spent too long doing what was expected of her. That was partly why she'd married Jed, she knew now: When a rich, dashing, kind man proposes marriage to a poor nobody from Binghamton, she's supposed to say yes. Only a fool would say no.

But look at how that had turned out.

*Maybe*, she thought, *a touch of recklessness was just what the doctor ordered.* After all, that was the genius behind Tasha's plan: No one had suspected her of misdoing because the scheme was so out of left field.

Perhaps fortune really does favor the bold.

Just as that thought occurred to her, she looked up and noticed that she was about to pass the Wolfes' apartment building.

## CHAPTER 50

TASHA GREETED HER AT THE door with an easy smile and her customary double kisses. "Darling, come in," she cooed.

*If it was a facade*, Clare thought, *it was a very good one.*

"I'm sorry to barge in on you so close to the holiday," Clare said. She'd texted Tasha to ask if she could come up to chat five minutes before. "Are you heading out of town for Thanksgiving?"

"We'll be here," Tasha replied. "The girls are flying in from Boston on Wednesday." Both Wolfe children went to boarding school in Massachusetts.

"How nice," Clare said, feeling lightheaded and wishing she hadn't drunk so much caffeine.

Tasha led her into the living room and gestured for her to sit on the peacock-blue velvet couch.

"So tell me," she said, settling on a chair close by, "how are you doing? What do you know about Jed's situation so far? We want to help, but Alec hasn't been able to find out much."

"It's not good."

"But it doesn't make any sense," Tasha said, sounding genuinely confused. "Why do the police think Jed killed Gabriel?"

Clare realized that Tasha had never known she was sleeping with Gabriel. She still thought they'd only been working together. Clare took some satisfaction from knowing that at least part of her relationship with Gabriel had unfolded outside of Tasha's interference or knowledge.

"I was sleeping with Gabriel," she said. There was no point hiding it now. The affair would come out sooner or later, and maybe Clare's disclosure would encourage Tasha to lay her cards on the table, too.

The surprise showed on Tasha's face immediately; her features went slack, making her look both older and oddly vulnerable—but it lasted for less than a second before she regained her composure.

"So *that's* why the police think Jed killed him?" Tasha asked with barely concealed delight. Clare could practically see the thoughts running through her mind: If the police were convinced that the motive was jealousy, they wouldn't look into the *Longfin* deal at all. This was a better outcome than Tasha could have even hoped for.

Clare nodded.

"And what does Jed say?" Tasha asked.

"That's what I wanted to see you about."

Tasha leaned back in her seat and crossed one leg over the other. A slingback heel dangled from one foot. She examined Clare's face, trying to glean something from her expression. Clare held her gaze.

"Let me guess," Tasha said finally. "He told you some wild tale about how everything is all my fault?"

"He did, actually."

"Desperate men will say anything, Clare."

"That may be true, but frankly, I'm not sure Jed is clever enough to concoct a story that would explain all the strange, conveniently connected events of the last few months: my phone call with your godfather, my meeting with Clement, Gabriel's death, the money in my bank account. Jed is a lawyer of good intentions but average abilities, Tasha, not Keyser Söze."

Tasha laughed, as if amused that Clare was finally seeing the light. "Do you know, I never understood what you saw in him in the first place. I know Alec hasn't been impressed by his work at Gatepost."

"Well, of course he hasn't," Clare said. "But that's because Jed uncovered the fraud that you and Alec were trying to hide."

Tasha's face didn't change expression. "I don't know what you're talking about."

"I'm referring to the fact that your primary investor is on the US sanctions list."

"You've gotten bad information, Clare."

"Right, it's not Viktor directly. It's the shell company he hides behind: Axion."

"I must cite client confidentiality there. I take our legal obligations very seriously, even if your husband does not."

Tasha's housekeeper entered the room carrying a tray with a French press, two coffee cups, and a small pitcher of cream. She placed it on the table and started pouring out the coffee. Tasha and Clare both fell silent and watched her do this. When she was done, she walked out of the room as silently as she'd arrived.

Tasha poured milk in her coffee, then leaned back in her seat, bringing the cup with her.

"Do you know how I knew that Jed was doing a shit job?" Tasha asked Clare. "Alec started gaining weight. Whenever he gets stressed, he overeats in this manic, deranged way. Last May I found him in the kitchen shoving slices of plain white Pepperidge Farm sandwich bread into his mouth at three in the morning. He jumped a foot in the air when he saw me. His face looked like I'd caught him masturbating, which honestly would have been less upsetting. That's when he filled me in on the mess Jed had made." Tasha scoffed and shook her head. "Jed, of all people. Do you know how ridiculous it is to have to waste your time and energy worrying about the threat posed by someone like Jed Bast? The whole raison d'être of a man like that is that he does *not* pose a threat. He's the human equivalent of Pepperidge Farm sandwich bread: soft, tasteless, and inoffensive—but slightly revolting if you have too much."

"Jed is not sandwich bread. He's just kind and good. I don't know why that should be so disgusting to you."

Tasha wrinkled her nose in distaste.

"Why did you even hire him, then?"

"He *begged* Alec for the job after Mark died. He was practically on his knees: 'My firm doesn't value me. I can do so much more.' That usual bullshit. So Alec did him a favor. After all, he had the right credentials, and he was an old family friend. He had to know that a general counsel's *one* job is to protect the company, right? Any idiot knows that. Well, any idiot other than Jed, it turns out."

Tasha delicately placed her coffee cup on the table and recrossed her legs.

"Let me tell you what *actually* happened," she continued. "Alec discovered very early on that Jed was not up to snuff. Even after a very long grace period, Jed continued to miss deadlines and make careless mistakes. Alec gave him a number of second chances, but finally he ran out of patience. He made the decision to let Jed go, but when he tried to actually go through with it, your husband went nuts. He made up some wild story about Axion being owned by my godfather and threatened to report us to the feds. We didn't need that kind of trouble, so Alec let him stay."

"You're telling me that *Jed* was blackmailing *Alec*?" Clare asked doubtfully. "And Alec just relented? That hardly seems in character for him."

"Alec capitulated in order to protect *me*. Jed's story—though false—would have spawned vicious rumors about us, no matter how vigorously we disputed it. In this business, even the illusion of misconduct is enough to send investors packing. Trust is everything. And unfortunately, Jed's fiction contained a kernel of truth. My godfather has, in fact, been sanctioned by the United States—which I've never denied. But contrary to Jed's lies, Viktor has no relationship with Gatepost whatsoever. Why would we be that stupid?"

"Jed said you kept Viktor's money because Gatepost would collapse without it."

Tasha rolled her eyes. "Oh, *Jed said* that. Honestly, Clare, I thought more highly of you than this. Did you really fall for his lies so easily?"

Clare didn't know how to answer that question. All her theories about Tasha's malfeasance had suddenly abandoned her. She couldn't access any of her previous indignation. Was Tasha right? Could Jed be the one making everything up? She tried to remember what had so convinced her of Tasha's guilt before.

"What about *Longfin* then? Why did you pressure Clement to deaccession it?"

"What does *Longfin* have to do with any of this? MoCA sold it months ago because we were trying to diversify our holdings. There's no conspiracy there. Check the minutes from our board meetings if you want."

Clare felt herself losing traction. Who was she supposed to believe? In the absence of proof, she had only her instincts—and how could she trust them? They'd led her to embark on the affair that got her into this mess.

"Why did you send that email to Gabriel two days before he died?" she asked. She could recite it from memory by now: "'Just confirming our plans. Everything is all set from my end, so just let me know you're on board, and I'll start making arrangements. This is the best solution for everyone.'"

Tasha started laughing. "*That's* your smoking gun? Seriously? Gabriel helped me buy Alec an Anselm Kiefer painting for Christmas. We were trying to figure out how to deliver it to the apartment without tipping him off."

"But *you* connected Gabriel to Axion," she said.

"Do I sometimes connect our investors with helpful resources? Or course. We're a boutique firm. We pride ourselves on our client service."

"And then you encouraged *me* to start working with Gabriel."

"I was worried about you, Clare. I thought a job would help get you out of your rut."

"You don't do favors."

Tasha threw up her hands. "Clare, I don't know what to tell you. I was trying to help you out without embarrassing you. This is not the thanks I thought I'd get. I mean, honestly, how dare you come over and accuse me of all kinds of wrongdoing without a shred of proof.

"If you were really sleeping with Gabriel, then it's obvious that Jed killed him. It's always the husband. What you're doing now—blaming me so you don't have to face up to his guilt, and your own—will never work. Sooner or later you will have to face the fact that there are only two people responsible for Gabriel's death: you and Jed. It's the oldest story in the book. This nonsense about Viktor is a complete fiction."

Clare tried to get her thoughts straight. *Did* she have any proof that Viktor owned Axion? No. All she had was Jed's word. He said he'd found an email from Peter DeGroot that referenced Viktor. But she'd never seen it herself. If it had existed, chances were it wouldn't any longer five minutes after she walked out Tasha's door.

Emil slipped into the room silently, perhaps alerted to trouble by the rising volume of Tasha's voice. "Is everything okay, Mrs. Wolfe?"

"It's fine, Emil," Tasha said. "We're just wrapping up here."

As usual, Clare's attention was hijacked by the gun-shaped bulge under Emil's jacket. Then her gaze traveled downward and landed on an all-too-familiar pair of black Reebok sneakers.

Clare's mouth went dry as she registered the significance of those shoes.

Tasha hadn't hired "someone" to steal *Longfin*. She'd simply asked Emil to do it. Why hadn't he occurred to her before? It was his role to handle threats against the Wolfes, and there was no doubt that Tasha had felt threatened.

*He was* the one whom Gabriel had surprised downstairs. *He was* the one who'd reached for his ever-present gun and fired without thinking. *He was* the one who had stood an arm's length away from where Clare was hiding, frightened for her life, and taken *Longfin* off the wall.

Clare abruptly stood up. What was she doing here? What had she been thinking? These were dangerous people.

"You're right, Tasha," she said hurriedly, pulling on her coat. "I shouldn't have come here. I'm sorry."

Tasha stood up, too, alarmed by Clare's sudden change in demeanor. She exchanged a look with Emil.

"Why the sudden hurry?" Tasha demanded.

"I have to make Sadie's dinner," Clare said, already walking out of the room. She reached the front door and tried to turn the knob. It didn't budge. She twisted the deadbolt—one of two—and tried again. Nothing happened.

"Clare," Tasha said, directly behind her now.

Clare turned around and pushed her back against the door. Emil was standing next to Tasha, his hand hovering just inside his jacket.

"Please open it," Clare said, trying not to betray her growing alarm.

"Before you go," Tasha said, "I want to impress upon you what a bad idea it would be for you to go spreading falsehoods about me or Alec or Gatepost. I am very, *very* protective of my family."

"I won't," Clare assured her.

"They're just lies made up by your husband in desperation."

"Of course," Clare said. "I see that now."

Tasha and Emil exchanged a long, unreadable glance. Tasha gave a small nod, and Emil started moving toward Clare.

"Wait!" Clare yelled, unable to hide her panic now.

Emil reached for her shoulders and maneuvered her to one side. Then he unlocked the door and held it open for her.

Clare took her chance. She slipped into the foyer and immediately rang for the elevator. Her heart pounded against her ribs as she waited for it to arrive. Nobody spoke a word.

Then the godforsaken alligator arrived and the doors slid open.

Clare threw her body into the elevator car and pressed it against the back wall. Tasha and Emil stayed in the open doorframe, watching her. The last thing she heard as the doors closed was Tasha's singsong voice trilling, "Thank you so much for stopping by, darling."

## CHAPTER 51

WHEN CLARE WAS A BLOCK from Tasha's building, she dialed Breznick's number with shaking hands.

"It's Clare Bast," she said. "I know who killed Gabriel."

"The case is out of my hands," the detective intoned wearily.

"It was Emil, the Wolfes' bodyguard."

"I'm not interested in any more conspiracy theories."

"It's not a theory. Check his black Reebok sneakers: I swear they will match the footprint found at the crime scene."

"Mrs. Bast, do you honestly think a judge is going to issue a search warrant based on a claim *by the defendant's wife* that someone else did it?"

"What would you need for a search warrant?"

"Let it go, Mrs. Bast."

Clare was tempted to finally come clean, to tell Breznick right then and there that she had been hiding under the bed while Gabriel was killed. That she'd seen the killer's shoes. But there was no guarantee that the detective would believe her—she was the definition of an unreliable witness—and she remembered the promise she'd made to Jed outside his parents' building. She couldn't risk it.

"What if it was *your* husband?" Clare asked. "Would *you* let it go?"

"I'm not married," Breznick snapped back. "But if I were, I'd take a good long look at the facts and ask myself whether I was being taken for a ride."

"I *have* looked at the facts," Clare retorted, her exasperation rising. "I feel like I'm the only one who has."

Breznick didn't answer. She'd already hung up.

Clare resisted the urge to hurl her phone against the pavement and watch it shatter into a million pieces. She could admit that Breznick had a point. She *had* been deluded. She'd been in the dark for months about Tasha's machinations, Gabriel's ulterior motive and Jed's cover-up of Gatepost's misdeeds. But her vision had finally cleared. She could see with startling clarity what had happened. The problem was that no one would believe her. She had no proof.

She'd recorded her conversation upstairs on her cell phone, but Tasha had been too smart for such a clumsy ruse: She'd admitted nothing outright.

Clare realized then that if she wanted to clear Jed's name, the path toward justice would require a rather drastic detour. The law couldn't help her anymore.

## CHAPTER 52

ON THANKSGIVING DAY, CLARE DELIVERED Sadie to the Basts' apartment as agreed. Her daughter would spend the night there, and Clare would pick her up on Friday afternoon.

Clare said a brief hello to Jed—Dorothy, thankfully, was nowhere to be seen—and hugged Sadie goodbye. When she left, Mimi held the door open for her and handed Clare a set of car keys.

"Mr. Jed said you needed them."

"Thank you, Mimi," Clare said. "I'll return them tomorrow."

"If it helps Mr. Jed, keep them as long as you want. My cousin doesn't mind."

Clare made eye contact with Jed, who nodded briefly at her. He hadn't wanted to go along with her plan, but he hadn't been able to figure another way out of this mess either.

CLARE FOUND THE rusty 2004 Honda Accord parked where she'd been told it would be. The back bumper was dented, and when Clare got in, she noticed that all of the seats were ripped and the foam padding was spilling out. She didn't care. She quickly confirmed its most important attribute—the lack of a GPS navigation system—and stuck the key into the ignition.

She drove first to the bunny-sitter's apartment on East Eighty-Ninth Street. Then, with Noodle safely ensconced in the backseat, she headed toward the FDR Drive. The rabbit wedged his nose through the bars of his cage to sniff at the upholstery.

"Don't worry, Noodle," Clare said, glancing in the rearview mirror. "This is our last adventure."

THREE HOURS LATER, just as dusk was falling, she pulled onto the Wolfes' street in Southampton. She slowed the car to a crawl but did not stop. She studied the area around her and noted with relief that all the houses except two were dark. There was no sign of life at the Wolfes'. They were probably sitting down to Thanksgiving dinner in Manhattan just about now.

Clare kept driving and took a right onto Ox Pasture Road. When she reached the lake, she turned again and pulled into the parking lot of Agawam Park. She maneuvered the car into a spot in the back corner and turned off the engine. It clicked quietly as Clare climbed into the backseat. She pulled Noodle gently out of his cage and placed him in her lap. Then she carefully extracted the Saran-wrapped canvas.

"I'll be right back," she whispered as she replaced the rabbit.

She hoped that was true.

CLARE RETRACED HER route on foot. She wore all black and smelled faintly of rabbit droppings from the rolled-up canvas tucked under her jacket.

Thirty minutes later, she was back on Halsey Neck Lane.

She found an opening in the hedge of the property next to the Wolfes'—easy enough in late November, when all the leaves were gone. After another glance around, she got down on all fours and crawled through it.

She made her way along the border of the neighbors' property until she was roughly parallel with the guesthouse where she and Jed had stayed that past summer. Then she cut through another desiccated hedge and emerged in the Wolfes' backyard.

She paused there, listening. Nothing happened. There was no alarm. No flashing lights. Still, she waited for another five minutes before proceeding. She got down on her stomach and started to army crawl inch by inch across the lawn. She didn't know if the Wolfes had cameras on their property, but she knew that if she moved slowly enough in her all-black outfit, she would be virtually invisible against the night's darkness. Her progress was painstakingly slow, and she had to muffle a cry when a hidden sprinkler nozzle dug a long scrape into her stomach. Halfway to the guesthouse, she stopped. She had planned to use the door code she still remembered to gain entry, but it was risky: She didn't know if the code had changed or if a security system would be activated. Now she noticed a small structure along the back hedge that hadn't been visible from her previous position. It was too small to be anything other than a storage shed. That would be perfect. Nobody protected their hoses and trowels with an alarm system, did they? She hoped not. She altered her course and continued her slow trek across the lawn, finally reaching the shed several minutes later. Staying low, she reached up with one arm to test the latch. It didn't budge. She sat up on her knees to look at it. There was a rusted combination padlock holding the door closed.

A groan of exasperation escaped her lips.

There were four dials. She made a silent plea in her mind as she rotated them to match the guesthouse code: eight-nine-eight-nine. She pulled gently on the lock, and the shackle gave way. She was left holding only the padlock's body in her hand. It had worked.

She eased the shackle out of the latch and put it on the ground. She waited another minute before opening the door as slowly as possible. When the gap was a foot wide, she shimmied her body through it and closed herself inside.

The shed was pitch-black. She knew from the outside that it was around six feet by four feet. If it was anything like the Basts' shed in East Hampton, a single wrong move would send a pile of rusted rakes and old bikes clattering to the ground. She waited for her eyes to adjust to the darkness, hoping the moonlight shining through the sole window would provide enough illumination. When she was finally able to make out the broad shapes around her, she got to work.

Wasting no time at all, she took *Longfin* out from under her jacket and slipped it behind a bag of what she guessed was potting soil in a corner. She covered it with a tarp she found folded on the floor. She wondered if this was the last time she'd see this painting.

If all went according to plan, it wouldn't be.

BY THE TIME Clare got back to her apartment, it was two in the morning, but she was still too revved up from the adrenaline to sleep. As Noodle dozed fitfully, she made herself a cup of green tea and watched the Christmas trees sway listlessly in the wind from her old familiar perch on the couch. Then, at six, she left the building. She walked to a bodega ten blocks away, bought a breakfast sandwich and a coffee, and asked to borrow their phone.

Elise sounded annoyed when she picked up. "Hello?"

"It's Clare. I'm sorry to call you so early."

"What's up?"

"I know where the painting is."

Clare heard a rustling sound as Elise presumably pushed off her covers and sat up in bed.

"Where?"

"Before I tell you, I need your word that you'll call the police and report what you found and where you found it right away."

"Of course. I'd do that anyway."

"And you can't tell them that I tipped you off."

"Deal. Just tell me where it is."

"Get a pen."

OUT ON THE street, Clare tossed her coffee and sandwich in the trash. She was still too jittery for either. She walked over to Central Park, which was emptier than usual for a Friday morning. A few joggers passed by, but most people were probably either sleeping off their holiday hangover or away visiting family. Clare sat down on a bench and closed her eyes. The dull hum of a leaf blower competed with a pair of chattering birds.

Jed had been right: They hadn't had enough evidence on their own. Tasha's plan had been too neat. She'd considered and reconsidered nearly all its permutations. The one thing she hadn't taken into account was the possibility that Gabriel would copy *Longfin*. Without it, Tasha probably would have gotten away with everything. But now, the police would find the painting in the Wolfes' shed and have no choice but to reopen the investigation. Breznick would finally get that search warrant, and they'd pick apart the Park Avenue triplex. She'd find Emil's black Reeboks—he lived there, too—and, with any luck, even more incriminating evidence.

His phone, showing his location the night Gabriel was killed? The clothes he'd been wearing? By this point, it would be obvious that Breznick had blundered by zeroing in on Jed too hastily, but she could salvage her reputation by building a new, airtight case against the Wolfes.

There was no reason for the police to find out about Viktor Semenov's involvement or Tony Fang's forgery. All they needed was a simple story: Tasha wanted *Longfin* for herself, but she couldn't buy it since she was on MoCA's board. She'd pressured Clement to sell it to Gabriel—Clement would testify to that—and then sent Emil to take it.

At least this is what Clare hoped would happen. She'd done her best to lay the groundwork for this chain of events. The rest was out of her hands.

Tony Fang's forgery had provided the linchpin of Clare's plan, but the real credit for the idea belonged to Tasha herself. Clare had taken inspiration from her very first dinner with the Wolfes, when Tasha had laid out her strategy for achieving her goals: "No matter how hard I pushed or how loudly I yelled, nobody was ever going to feel threatened by *me*," she'd said. "I had to use more roundabout methods."

## CHAPTER 53

AFTER A SHORT NAP AND a long shower, Clare left the apartment to pick up Sadie. Over the past twenty-four hours, she'd felt her daughter's absence like a physical ache. She'd never been apart from her long enough to miss her with such intensity before. She couldn't wait to scoop her warm little body up in her arms.

She was so occupied with closing the distance between herself and Sadie that she didn't notice the window of an idling black Mercedes-Benz slide open as she left her building.

"Clare!"

She turned in the direction of the voice and spotted Tasha, wrapped up in a fur coat, peering from the backseat of the car.

"What are you doing here?" Clare asked, alarmed. She'd hoped that Tasha would be in police custody by now. Or, at the very least, sequestered with a team of high-powered lawyers, plotting her strategy.

"Get in the car and I'll tell you everything."

Clare took a step back. "I'm not getting in a car with you."

"We need to talk."

"About what?"

Tasha lowered her voice. "About *Longfin*."

"We can talk out here."

Tasha rolled her eyes and opened the door. She put on a pair of oversized black Celine sunglasses and stepped onto the curb.

"The point was *not* to be seen in public together," she muttered.

"Why not?"

Tasha fingers latched on to Clare's elbow with a viselike grip. "The police found *Longfin* at our house in Southampton this morning," she whispered.

Clare maintained a straight face. "How did it get there?"

"Alec, obviously," Tasha snapped. "How else?"

Clare couldn't tell if Tasha actually believed this. She certainly must have been baffled when the police found *Longfin* at her house; as far as she knew, it was with Viktor in Russia. Did she really think that Alec had intercepted it somehow?

"I don't understand," Clare said. "How did Alec get his hands on *Longfin*?"

"Apparently, he stole it. *He's* the one who's responsible for Gabriel's death."

"What do you mean?" Clare asked. "Why would Alec steal *Longfin* and kill Gabriel?"

"Listen, Jed was right." Tasha leaned in closer and lowered her voice. "My godfather *does* own Axion. When the sanctions went into effect, Alec assured me that he would cut ties with him. Instead, he tried to convince Viktor to *keep* his money at Gatepost, despite the risk. That's where *Longfin* came in: I had mentioned that MoCA was thinking of selling it, and Alec offered it to Viktor as an enticement."

Clare wondered for a moment whether this was true. Could it really have been Alec all along? No, she decided. Tasha was the one who'd sent that email to Gabriel—"this is the best solution for everyone"—and threatened Jed. Tasha was simply editing herself out of the story, and making Alec the protagonist instead.

"What do you want from me, Tasha?"

"You and I need to get our stories straight."

"Why do I need a story?"

"Because Jed helped Alec do it."

"What? Why would he do that?"

"When Jed found out that Viktor owned Axion, he threatened to go to the feds. Alec convinced him to stay by offering him equity in Gatepost worth millions. Jed suggested using Gabriel as the dupe—he must have already known about the affair. If Gabriel were to be 'accidentally' killed during the theft, it would be the perfect cover for revenge. It was just bad luck for him that the NYPD didn't notice that *Longfin* had been stolen."

Clare was amazed: Tasha always had another pivot up her sleeve.

"I don't believe it."

"Suit yourself. I'll be fine either way. I'll just tell the police that I had no idea what was going on. After all, I have no role in the operation of Gatepost. I'm trying to look out for you."

"We both know that isn't true. Why would you think I'd throw Jed under the bus?"

"Clare, don't be a fool. You told me yourself that Dorothy made you sign a prenup. You'll be left with nothing when he leaves you. The *only* way you'll have access to the Bast money is if Jed winds up in prison. You think he'll be able to sue for a contested divorce from behind bars? Just tell them that Jed found out about your affair weeks ago and was livid. He threatened to kill Gabriel, and you were too scared to tell the police the truth."

"And what makes you think the police will believe us?"

Tasha rolled her eyes.

"Clare, we're just two stay-at-home mothers. What do we know about theft and murder?"

Clare couldn't help but shake her head in amazement. "You're unbelievable," she murmured.

Tasha took it as a compliment. "I learned early on that you always need a plan. Fate is punishment for the ill prepared."

"I know you don't really believe that Jed had anything to do with this, so what actually happened? How did *Longfin* end up at your house?"

"I told you: Alec and Jed must have stolen it from Gabriel's—"

"No, Tasha. Not the story for the police. The truth."

Tasha licked the top row of her teeth. She was annoyed. "I don't know," she admitted.

"Didn't Viktor have it?"

Tasha took off her sunglasses, as if to see Clare more clearly. "Yes," she said carefully. "I thought he did. Alec must have cut a separate deal with him."

"Have you asked Viktor what happened?"

"It's late there."

"Not that late," Clare said. "He was wide awake when *I* called."

Tasha narrowed her eyes, as if reappraising Clare. "You what?"

"I thought he might be inclined to step in and help you out. So I made sure he knew that *Longfin* was found on your property. He was understandably disappointed to learn that you'd sent him a forgery and tried to pass it off as the real thing."

Tasha's eyes darted from side to side, like a deer caught in the crosshairs. She wasn't used to being the one in the dark.

"What are you talking about? What forgery?"

"The one you stole. You stole a fake *Longfin* and didn't even realize it." Despite herself, Clare was enjoying this. "Whoops."

A look of hatred settled behind Tasha's eyes.

"What have you done?"

"Me? Nothing." Clare smiled innocently. "I'm just a stay-at-home mother. What do I know about theft and murder?"

"You will regret this."

Clare was already walking away. "Goodbye, Tasha," she said over her shoulder.

CLARE WAS STILL shaking when she arrived at the Basts' apartment. When Jed opened the front door, she pulled him out into the elevator hall to tell him what had happened.

"Are you sure you should have told her about the forgery?" he asked.

"She'd find out about it eventually. But what can she do? What would she tell the police—that she accidentally stole a fake painting? I don't think so. Her best bet is to play dumb and try to pin everything on Alec, which she's obviously already figured out."

"That could work."

"It could, but I imagine Emil will turn on her. Either way, the most important thing is that the charges against you are dropped."

"Let's hope."

"I'm so sorry about all of this, Jed. Truly."

"I know you are. And I want you to know that I've given it a lot of thought and I've decided we should just put all this behind us and move on with our lives. I've forgiven you."

"You've forgiven me?" she asked.

"I just want to be a family again."

"Jed, we'll always be a family."

She wanted to stop there, but she didn't. She forced herself to keep going. She'd put off this moment for too long. "But I don't think we should necessarily stay married."

Jed looked like he'd been slapped. "*You* don't want to be married to *me* anymore?"

Clare shook her head.

"But I gave you *everything*," he said, sounding more baffled than anything else.

"I know. And I'm grateful for all of it—most of all Sadie. I'll never regret having married you, and I still want you in my life . . . just not as my husband."

"Why not? We were so happy."

"Jed, if you were happy, it was probably because I'd molded myself into someone who would make you happy."

"What are you talking about? No, you didn't."

"I did. From the moment I met you, I couldn't believe how kind and confident and charming you were. I thought you must know something I didn't, so I let you make all our decisions for us. Every single one. It was *your* idea for me to quit my job and go back to school. It was *your* idea for me to move in with you and then for us to get married quickly. It was even your idea to have Sadie. I don't blame you for any of it. I know you didn't force these things on me. You just knew how you wanted your life to look and I didn't. So I went with it. I assumed your choices were the better choices. I mistook them for my own. So yes, of course you loved me. You made me just what you wanted."

Jed shook his head. "That's nonsense. Total nonsense." He expelled a long, frustrated sigh. "Listen, we've been through a lot in the past few days. Let's table this conversation and come back to it when we're better rested."

"I'm not going to change my mind, Jed."

The door to the Basts' apartment suddenly swung open to reveal Dorothy's emaciated frame hovering in the doorway.

"What's going on here?" she asked suspiciously.

"Nothing, Mom," Jed said dully. "Clare's here to pick up Sadie."

"So soon? But we're having so much fun together."

"This is the timing we agreed on, Dorothy," Clare said.

"I'll get her," Jed said, slipping past his mother into the apartment.

"Well, come inside," Dorothy said in an exasperated tone. "We don't want the neighbors to talk."

Dorothy shut the front door behind Clare, and they stood awkwardly facing each other in the foyer. Clare had never felt as much like an intruder in the Bast household as she did now.

"So I hear you and Jed have decided to work everything out," Dorothy said, pursing her lips.

Jed had obviously discussed his plan with his mother first.

"We'll see," Clare replied noncommittally.

Dorothy narrowed her eyes.

"What does that mean?"

"It means 'we'll see.'"

Dorothy scoffed. "I hope you realize how lucky you are, Clare."

"I do," she said, meaning it.

"Then why aren't you down on your goddamn knees thanking your lucky stars that we're taking you back?" Dorothy spat. A thread of spittle quivered on her pink-shellacked lip, and one eye twitched with rage.

Even Clare, who had grown accustomed to her mother-in-law's hostility, was surprised by this sudden burst of vitriol. Then, in a flash, everything became clear to her.

"Dorothy," she said, "I finally understand why you hate me. I always assumed it was because you thought I was a social climber, but now I see that it's the opposite. I didn't care about the Bast pedigree *enough*. Your only consolation for Jed marrying a peon like me would have been the opportunity to savor my awestruck wonder at your charmed existence. To revel in my perpetual, fawning gratitude.

"Oh, I'll admit, I was dazzled by the lifestyle at first. And I hoped you would like me. But you needed something I couldn't give you. You wanted me to envy you and fear you and desperately try to be like you, and instead, I had the temerity to find you ridiculous. Which I do, by the way. I think you're petty and arrogant and small-minded, and I find your world stifling and dull. So honestly, feel free to cast me out of it. Go right ahead. I'm done caring what you think. Just remember this: I will never, *ever* let you do to Sadie what you did to Jed, who just wanted to work in legal aid but got stuffed into an ill-fitting version of his father's life, and now doesn't know what he wants at all. Our daughter's last name may be Bast, but I would sooner die than let her become another *Dorothy* Bast."

Clare's voice had slowly risen in volume as she spoke, and when she finished, the air between them seemed to tremble in the sudden silence.

Dorothy's lips parted in shock, but no sound came out.

"Mama!" Sadie suddenly cried, rounding the corner and careening into Clare's arms. "I missed you so much."

"I missed you too, lovebug," Clare said, squeezing her tightly. "Now say thank you to Grammy, and let's go home."

*One year later*

## EPILOGUE

CLARE CHECKED HER WATCH FOR the fourth time.

"Sadie, come on, we're going to be late." She tapped her fingers impatiently against the doorframe.

"I'm *coming*," Sadie said, skipping out of the apartment in mismatched sneakers. Clare said nothing. She was just glad that Sadie could put on her own shoes now.

The elevator arrived within thirty seconds of Sadie pressing the button. Clare lived in a big, modern building on 110th Street and Fifth Avenue, in a two-bedroom apartment overlooking the northern boundary of Central Park. Clare liked to needle Dorothy by constantly referring to the fact they lived on the same street, even though her address placed her squarely in South Harlem instead of a block away from the Guggenheim.

The charges against Jed had been dropped, but he had, as predicted, been disbarred for helping cover up the sanctions fraud at Gatepost. He was living with his parents while he tried to figure out his next move. Even though he'd landed there due to the twin indignities of unemployment and divorce, Dorothy and Mimi couldn't have been happier to have him under their roof again. They doted on him to such an extent that Clare doubted he was in any hurry to leave.

One of the best parts about Clare's new building was that if they budgeted five or ten extra minutes in the morning, their commute to Saint Mary's could wind through Central Park. Today, however, there was no time.

That was fine by Clare. She still loved the walk south on Madison or Fifth Avenue. In a mere ten blocks, they passed the Museum of the City of New York, the hospital where Sadie was born, the lush Conservatory

Garden, and the Metropolitan Museum, which now owned *Longfin*. As Gabriel's heir, Beatriz had donated it on the condition that it be put on permanent display. The museum had readily agreed. The scandal had done wonders for the painting's popularity.

"Sadie, slow down!" Clare yelled. Sadie had gotten a scooter for her fourth birthday and promptly discovered her inner motocross racer. Clare picked up her pace to try to catch up with her daughter. They were almost at Ninety-Sixth Street, and the crosstown traffic there made her nervous. As they waited at the corner for the light to change, Clare texted Elise: "Running a few minutes late."

She'd taken a job at Elise Vargas's firm earlier that year. The decision had been financially motivated—she was the family's sole breadwinner now—but when she'd packed up her dissertation materials and officially withdrawn from Columbia, she'd felt only relief. She'd never wanted to dissect critical theory; she just loved art.

"Remember," Clare said, taking Sadie's hand to cross the street, "Daddy's picking you up from school today."

"I know. He and Grammy are taking me to the Boat Pond."

"That'll be fun."

"Except Grammy doesn't let me ride my scooter. She says it's not safe."

"And what does Daddy say?"

Sadie shrugged.

When they reached the corner, Clare knelt down to face her daughter. "Honey, you can ride your scooter if you want to. As long as you look where you're going and stop at every corner, you'll be fine."

"Can you tell Grammy that?"

A small smile formed on Clare's lips. "I'd be happy to."

Clare's phone buzzed with a response from Elise: "Have you seen the news yet?"

Clare texted back three question marks, and Elise sent a link.

It was an article in the *Post* with the headline "Socialite Found Guilty of Theft and Manslaughter."

Tasha had been arrested the past December after Emil struck a plea deal with the DA's office. He'd testified that Tasha had sent him to pick up *Longfin* from the brownstone and make it look like a robbery. Since she'd assured him the house would be empty, he'd been startled when a man attacked him; he'd fired by instinct. The trial had been going on for weeks, and now, it appeared, the verdict was in: Tasha was guilty of all charges. She faced up to twenty-five years in prison.

Clare took a moment to let the news sink in. It was hard for her to picture Tasha in jail. What would she wear?

The article included a photograph taken the moment the verdict was read. The defendant, in a silk blouse and cashmere blazer, had looked neither cowed nor frightened. Her expression had been one of sheer defiance. Outside the courtroom, her lawyers had assured a huddle of reporters that they were already preparing their appeal.

Of course they were. Tasha always had another pivot up her sleeve.

Clare wasn't concerned about an appeal. Her new job had given her both the resources and the expertise to start building a dossier on Tasha's misdeeds, which, unsurprisingly, were not limited to the *Longfin* affair. If she ever got close to slithering off that particular hook, Clare was well prepared to hold her accountable. She had also started quietly building smaller files on Alec Wolfe and Viktor Semenov. If she discovered that either of them had had anything to do with Gabriel's death, then they, too, would pay.

Clare was done waiting for fate to take its course. *Things can't go on like this*, she used to think to herself. Why had she ever thought that they would stop on their own? It was up to her to change her circumstances. Ultimately, her affair had done just that, but it had also cost Jed his career and Gabriel his life. Next time, she would be more careful. She'd go in with her eyes open and a plan in hand. Tasha had been right about that, at least: Fate was what happened to the ill prepared.

# ACKNOWLEDGMENTS

This book would not exist without the support, encouragement, and brilliance of my agent, Jenn Joel—along with her assistant, Sindhu Vegesena—at CAA. My gratitude extends to Jonathan Burnham and Andrea Walker, who created such a welcoming, fruitful home for me at Harper. Many thanks also to Ezra Kupor, Lydia Weaver, and Nora Reichard for helping usher this book into existence.

Thank you to the friends who helped shape all my ideas about motherhood, work, sex, relationships, and, of course, grisly murder: Halsey Anderson; Abigail Ericson; Liz Campbell; Kat Clements; Leah MacDonald; Natalie Pica; Elizabeth Rhodes; Haven Thompson; Nell Van Amerongen; Julia Vaughn; and especially Molly Tranbaugh. Martha Campbell—cofounder of the beautiful Berry Campbell gallery in Chelsea—deserves special thanks for walking me through the ins and outs of the art industry. Any errors (and gross exaggerations) are my own.

Thank you to my family: Lindsey and Charlie Schilling; Palmer Ducommun; Bob Ducommun; Jim and Nancy Beha; Jim and Alyson Beha; Len and Alice Teti. But above all, thank you to my mother, Lynn Ducommun, who raised me with superhuman stores of love, encouragement, and laughter while making it look effortless.

There are not enough words in the world to express my gratitude to Chris Beha for many reasons, but especially for reading countless drafts of his wife's book about adultery and offering only encouragement and brilliant advice in return. I love you.

And finally, thank you to Olive and Henry, the lights of my life.

## ABOUT THE AUTHOR

ALEXANDRA ANDREWS is the author of *Who is Maud Dixon?*, which was published in twenty-eight languages around the world and named a Best Book of the Year by *The New York Times*, NPR, *TIME*, *The New York Post*, and *Entertainment Weekly*. She lives in Brooklyn with her husband and children.